Echo
Heron

Mercy

SIMON & SCHUSTER

NEW YORK   LONDON   TORONTO   SYDNEY   TOKYO   SINGAPORE

SIMON & SCHUSTER
Simon & Schuster Building
Rockefeller Center
1230 Avenue of the Americas
New York, New York 10020

This book is a work of fiction. Names, characters, places
and incidents are either products of the author's
imagination or are used fictitiously. Any resemblance
to actual events or locales or persons, living or dead,
is entirely coincidental.

DESIGNED BY MARC STRANG

Manufactured in the United States of America

1   3   5   7   9   10   8   6   4   2

Library of Congress Cataloging in Publication Data

Heron, Echo.
Mercy/Echo Heron.
p.   cm.
I. Title.
PS3558.E698M47   1992
813'.54—dc20   91-40815
CIP

ISBN: 0-671-68438-8

"A Cloud in Trousers" from *The Bedbug and Other Selected Poetry* by
Vladimir Mayakovsky. Copyright © 1960 by Harper & Row, Publishers,
Inc. Reprinted with permission of HarperCollins Publishers.

Dedication

For Michael A. Salato, Sr., my father, who told me the best stories and taught me all the old songs.
  and
For David Joseph Neseralla, a fortunate resident of the state of normalcy and kindness, who gently guided me into the right way of loving.

Acknowledgments

My thanks are due, first and foremost, to Dominick Abel, my agent, for his continued faith in me and for patiently and competently nursing me through bouts of the dreaded writer's sickness.

Special acknowledgment also goes to the countless number of incredible women and men I have had the honor of meeting over the years who have dedicated themselves to caring for others—yours, dear nurses, are the very best of hearts.

I also want to give warmest appreciation to: my best friends and allies, Jane O'Hara Justice and Mary C. Bianchi, for sharing with me their wisdom, humor, and love; Daniel, Kathleen, and Matthew Heron, my family, for their unflagging, down-to-earth love; Nancy Schuepbach, for enriching my life with her many awesome talents and her gentleness; Trish Lande, my editor, for taking me with her and for making me think twice before I leap; Janis Mahan Butefish, for taking me into her life and allowing me to hang out for all those years, waiting for the cornbread and clabber; my friend and advisor on matters of the mind and heart, Margie Dingfelder, MFCC; my little sister Mari Salato, for her unconditional love; Lucy and Arthur Bianchi for taking me in as daughter number 6; and to my son, Simon Heron, for the gray hairs, hugs, and laughter.

Also special thanks to: Joan Frasson for her humorous mumblings and emergency runs to the hospital; Paul Joseph Hamilton for his assistance with matters of logic. And thanks to Aaron Angel, M.D., for his advice and his refreshing attitude toward nurses; and once again to Thomas M. Meadoff, M.D., for sharing with me a few tidbits from his incredible wealth of knowledge.

And, thank you to a group of the steadfast and special-spirited: Colette Coutant Trembly; Michael J. McClure; Loy Carson; Catherine Murray Barnes; Diana D. Parnell, M.D.; Linda Stone and Jake; Nancy J. Evans; Norman L. Smith; Mary Dale and James Scheller, M.D.; Sylvia Lang; Tagore, Fay, and Roger Somers; Kathy Sinnett; and Karilee Shames.

Monday

1 Her extraordinary feet, encased in badly worn, size 12-EEE running shoes, carried her slowly toward the white building she had come to regard as the enemy.

On impulse, she stepped over the soggy lawn to a wind-sculptured manzanita partially obscured by the morning fog. She checked her watch. Six forty-five: fifteen minutes before she had to report for duty.

Leaning against the smooth red bark of the shrub, she closed her eyes and let her mind wander off its leash to a warmer moment, seeing herself stretched out on a grassy slope overlooking a blue and tepid sea. She strained to hear the waves, but the noise of early-morning San Francisco traffic drowned out the auditory illusion as exhaust fumes drove the vision from her mind altogether.

Catalina Richardson shook a few strands of red hair away from her eyes and heaved an irritated sigh. She'd been secretly practicing Gage's visualization techniques, but still she could not relax. Two or three times a night, she awakened to the racket of her own teeth grinding. Not that that was considered unusual. In her whole career she was yet to meet the nurse who did not suffer from some stress-related disorder, the most common being chronic fatigue, ulcers, faulty memory, skin problems, and aching joints. If Gage was, in fact, the Merlinesque marvel he hinted he was, she didn't know why he couldn't will her at least one good night's sleep.

Disgusted, she pulled the ribbed cuffs of her parka over her freezing hands and headed toward the entrance of Mercy Hospital. Of the entire sixth grade, she was the only girl who had not wanted to be a nurse; thirty years later, she was the only one who gave enemas professionally and waited to measure the results.

Each week for twenty years it had been the same—taking in a new group of the helpless or hopeless, watching over them, tending to their needs. Every disease, ailment, or trauma that had ever made the human body its target had passed her way at least once. And each week she would roll up the sleeves of her scrub dress and attack those bodily insults much in the same manner a fastidious house-keeper might go after a moldy shower stall.

Usually she found more than just an ailing body. No matter what the patient's age or acquired illusion of status or ruin he or she lived under, she inevitably uncovered the deeply injured spirit lost in the darker recesses of the soul. From the beginning, it was her awareness that this abandoned inner child could never be made entirely whole that bound her to her role as caregiver.

But lately Cat's interior landscape had been slowly rearranging itself in an imperceptible mud slide. The absence of the deep-seated excitement that at one time had roused in her the need to care now left room for a growing bitterness. The sounds and smells of human infirmity no longer inspired her compassion, but only suffused her with an oppressive reluctance, which rubbed salt into the I'm-wasting-my-life-there-must-be-something-more wound. When asked what she did for a living, Cat often replied she was a licensed mem-ber of the Sisters of Masochism, signed up for a full-time abuse po-sition.

For Cat, nursing was now like penetration without foreplay. Con-vinced there had been a terrible mistake, and that someone else, someone like Cher, or even Betty Ford, was living the exciting life meant for her, she longed to move into other avenues of employ-ment. Since meeting Gage, she had actually begun to explore the possibilities of taking a job in the ludicrous, but presently lucrative, business of metaphysics, even though she considered it her most disgraceful secret that after having read *Out on a Limb*, she'd sat in a hot bath staring at a candle flame, waiting to leave her body and alight in some distant and exotic land. Two and a half hours later, she'd hoisted her prune-wrinkled body out of the cold, soap-scummed water, making slanderous and profane remarks concerning the character and sexual activities of Shirley MacLaine.

God knew she could use a few metaphysical miracles to spice up her professional life—let alone her private one—although she wasn't altogether sure she hadn't been tapping into a kind of weird psychic hot line all along. Most times, all she had to do was look into a patient's eyes to know exactly what the diagnosis and prognosis would be.

As Cat crossed the doctors' parking lot, a fantasy flashed through her mind: She slowly approaches the bedside of a young liver cancer victim who is laboring through his last few hours. With cool assurance, she places her hand on his anguished but quite good-looking forehead, while her co-workers—including the asshole of medical deities, Dr. Gillespie—stare, transfixed by the soft white luminescence radiating from her stately body.

"Be healed," she whispers gravely as the patient miraculously pulls himself out of bed smiling, a rosy glow replacing the mustardy jaundice of his skin. "His tests," she says quietly, her enormous gray eyes tenderly forgiving her colleagues' doubts, "will no longer show even a trace of disease." The patient, she notices, is gazing into her eyes with admiration (or is it desire?) as he lifts his now robust hand to caress her face—

The shrill sound of a car horn tore through her brain. With the reflex of a true transplanted New Englander, Cat glared at the source of the blast and flipped it the finger. Had the red Bugatti been closer, she would have smashed its hood with her fist.

Dr. Nachmann, chief of surgery, rolled down the window and, with an unintelligible snarl, flipped a finger right back.

At first she was indignant (Goddamned superiority-complexed, overpaid doctors think it's just themselves and a world full of third-class citizens. Pricks, pricks—every goddamned one of them, pricks!)

. . . then embarrassed (Jesus, what a high school move. I'm forty-two years old—a professional. I've got to work with this guy. Maybe he didn't recognize me? Nah, no way he could have missed the flaming red hair, like a goddamned flag in the wind. Suppose I could lie—say it was my twin sister, the visiting nurse.)

. . . and finally pleased. (The old fart has some fire left in him somewhere.) It was nice to know she could reduce one of the false golden gods to adolescent rage without really trying.

Well, at least she'd have a good story for the nurses at change-of-shift report: the only time there was any kind of meaningful communication between the outgoing close-to-dead and incoming soon-to-be-tortured.

Cat sighed. Show-and-tell at Mercy Hospital Ward Two. God, how pitiful—having to stretch that far for a little fun.

13

Inside, she was enveloped by the smell of disinfectant and dirty socks; it was the Lysol-and-popcorn-odor combo so familiar to hospitals. The crowded admissions waiting area was already a scene of confusion and mounting impatience. Four or five Chinese women, each holding a fussing baby, added to the cacophony by yelling unheeded commands at a large assortment of children scattered throughout the lobby. A cluster of childless strollers, cluttered with shopping bags and hastily shed coats, blocked the entrance to the ladies' room.

In the very center of the lobby, three look-alike blond children played loudly, roughly swinging each other to and fro in a game of How Much Can You Take? She noted the sharp corners of the magazine tables, and calculated the number of seconds before the inevitable head bump would send searing screams through the air.

As if guided by Cat's thoughts, the smallest child, a girl, careened headfirst into the edge of one of the tables. There was a dull thud, a short pause, and then the earsplitting wail. The two boys listened for a moment and, unimpressed, perhaps for lack of a bloody show, loudly resumed their game without her.

Until a couple of years ago, she would have run to the child to give comfort, but now . . . well, now she was different. Live and let live. Pretend you didn't see. Save your energy for the big, unavoidable problems.

In front of the newsstand, Gage, looking much like a small and wiry elf, sat on a low stool next to Tom Mix, his head rhythmically nodding to that silent music only the blind can hear.

She made a quick study of the black man who, when standing straight, came to the top of her shoulder. Set back on his unusually high forehead was a semicircle of thick gray hair, which gave him a cerebral yet kind appearance. His face was full but not heavy, and unlike most people, who kept their thoughts hidden behind facial masks, Gage made his plainly visible through constantly changing expressions.

Gage's age was a mystery to her. It was ironic, she thought, that his polished-satin brown skin, that source of senseless hatred and persecution, had the property of being perfectly ageless. He might easily have been forty, maybe seventy.

He and his stand had first appeared in the lobby on Christmas Day the year before. Cat thought it appropriate timing, since she vowed the guy was straight out of a Dickens novel; small and blind, complete with a guide dog named Tom Mix.

14

But there was something mysterious and perplexing about the man that made him anything but a classic character—like the way he seemed to look *into* her when he spoke, and the way he always dressed in an oversized, hooded black sweatshirt and black sweatpants, as if he were a member of some secret order of sprite wizards. Most of the people on the planet with whom she associated were considered offbeat, but Gage was definitely just visiting.

It was odd the way the eccentric little man took to her alone, for no one but Cat had been able to pull him beyond a few testy words. At the sound of her voice, he came alive, tirelessly talking her ear off about peculiar things: other worlds, spirits, and the moving forces of the galaxies.

Unable to explain it even to herself, Cat knew there were times when she found Gage's presence deeply familiar and comforting—although his explanation that he had been her mother in a previous life, and that he was assigned to be her "guide" in this one, caused the logical and scientific portions of her mind to balk.

And as if that weren't enough, he claimed to have second sight.

She'd laughed at him for taking that nonsense seriously, and explained his "fits" away as part ingrained African theatrics and part lucky guessing, with some Mississippi backwoods storytelling mixed in for good measure. But of course, that was before he began invading her life with it.

At first she hadn't paid much attention to his cryptic ramblings about dark and light forces, assuming that whatever disease had robbed him of his sight had spread to his brain and destroyed all four aces. Later, he began the singsong riddles that predicted certain events in her life, which, without fail, took place—accurate to the letter. When he commenced warning her about the people or situations she needed to avoid, she began to listen in spite of herself.

Then he started showing up in her dreams. Though she tried to forget the vaguely disturbing nocturnal visions, weird phrases from his dream lectures on how to open herself to oracular powers came up during her waking hours. That she found Gage in her away-from-work thoughts at all irked her.

Enough was enough of his prognostication drivel. He already knew too much about her. Worse yet, he *told* her what he knew, forcing her to actually think about those things she'd worked for years to repress. She made up her mind; she absolutely would not greet the man today.

And then she walked directly toward Gage and his dog.

. . .

15

Kneeling to stroke the shepherd's heavy coat, she caught the strong scent of woodsmoke that had always been their smell. She had often imagined them sitting by a cozy fire having one-sided conversations befitting a blind man and his dog.

She spoke stiffly, keeping herself at a protective distance. "Good morning, Gage. How're you and Tom Mix doing today?"

From under the perpetually half-closed lids, Gage's eyes wandered as if they had a life of their own. "We be doin' fine, Ms. Catalina," he said in a voice that despite its deep guttural sound was, to her, hypnotically gentle. "But I see you havin' some hard times comin' down out of them hills by the ocean this mornin'."

A nervous smile took over a corner of Cat's mouth. In spite of herself, the fact that he always distinguished her moods, if not actually read her thoughts, gave her a perverse thrill—rather like looking in a mirror and finding she'd grown a Siamese twin.

"It's always hard coming in here, Gage," she said dryly. Especially Monday mornings. Just as I start to get the idea that there is another kind of existence that hasn't got anything to do with blood and shit and disease, I have to come back to this hellhole."

"Aw c'mon, girl." Gage laughed. "It ain't *that* bad."

Cat flared, resentful that her misery was not being taken seriously. "Yes, it *is* that bad. After twenty years, I think I'm finally running out of codependency gas. I hate this job. I resent the goddamned hell out of this tuck-and-roll routine. I'm missing my chance at having a normal life, Gage. This job drains me, it makes me—"

Cat stopped the torrent and bit her lip. What the hell was wrong with her, and why was she telling these things to the newspaper man? Had she lost her grip? Was this the beginning of menopause?

"Then what'd we do without your fine self around here, Ms. Cat? And besides . . ." A sly quality crept into Gage's voice. "That ol' Doc Nachmann, he needs a ball of fire like you to get his blood up once in a while."

"Gage, I don't know how you do that, and I don't believe that crap about you being sent here as my guiding light, but someday I'm going to do something that embarrasses you so much you won't be able to face me for days."

"Honey child," Gage snorted, "nothin', I mean no thing, you ever done or ever is gonna do be new to this old man. I reckon I seen every bit of everythin' there be to see." He pointed a bony finger more or less in the direction of her crotch, which Cat thought particularly ironic.

16

Taking a *Chronicle* off the top of the stack, she pulled several coins from her jacket pocket. "I don't care anymore," she mumbled. "Sometimes I get so goddamned tired I don't care about anybody. Sometimes *I* want to be the only one who needs me."

The black man appeared to regard her for a moment. "You know, Ms. Cat, my sweet Delia always used to say, 'You can't play jazz till you done the blues.' Now, I know you ain't happy, but that's 'cause you on the edge of somethin' big. See, we been put here to do good, so when you go up there with them sick folk an' do what you do, you doin' the Lord's work. You been given honor by helpin' them folk. Try thinkin' 'bout *them*, not your own self. Now"—he raised his eyebrows—" 'specially now, ain't the time for bein' selfish."

A deep flush rose to the roots of her hair. "Selfish" was one of her trigger words; it was what her mother had called her every time she attempted to stand up for herself or improve her life in even the smallest of ways.

"Oh, I don't know, Gage, I don't feel so 'honored' when I'm elbow-deep into somebody's fecal impaction, or when I've just been stuck with an AIDS patient's needle and the hospital tells me it's not their problem, or when the idiots who run this place regard me as some kind of brainless peon—and I do mean pee-on—so I won't ever suspect that I might be worth more."

The man stood. "Aw girl, stop foolin' with them two-bit notions an' get to the nitty-gritty. A little bit of shit an' risk don't amount to a speck of fly dust when you workin' doin' the Lord's business."

As he forced open his drooping lids, the sightless ebony eyes came alive, giving the impression they were beholding wonders. "The way I see it in my mind, girl, you already saved a whole army of lives an' took the pain out of a million folks besides. You should be walkin' in tall cotton with that big payback account just waitin' for you to make a withdrawal. But do Ms. Cat take advantage of what she got comin' to her? Hell no, 'cause she be too busy feelin' sorry for herself."

Cat snorted, her anger dissipated by Gage's backhanded praise. "Oh for Christ's sake, Gage, you sound like a preacher."

The man's face went sad and earnest at the same time. "You be right on that, Ms. Cat, I *am* a preacher in my own way. That be what He did with this old blind man—He made me see things real clear for other folk what they can't see themselves. This sight be His. He only lets me borrow it time an' again."

Gage laid his fingers lightly on her arm. Her skin responded with goose bumps as five distinct lines of heat radiated into her flesh.

17

"I'll tell you one thing, sister. I'll tell you there be somethin' all around you . . . lots of commotion an' pieces of things I can't hardly see. More than ever before with you, girl."

The black man swayed a little from side to side humming an odd melody. The heat from his body enveloped her.

She had seen him do this before. It was the signal that the sight was about ready to take over. She observed him closely, hoping for some trip-up, wanting to prove once and for all he was a fraud.

"Soon be some serious changin' of lives near you," he sang in a low voice. "Secrets an' lies, a wish to die. Silence an' chains to break, peace to make. A love to last, dark roads to glass. Dancin' flame an' silver light . . . sil . . . silver light."

A heavy, depressed feeling went through her, making her blanch. Her arm burned where his fingers lay, but she was unable to pull it away.

"Search out color in the night . . . find the way . . ." Gage shook with violent tremors. "Dear Jesus!" he cried. "The silver light seeks . . . it seeks . . ."

Tom Mix whined and nudged his master's leg with his nose. Gage blinked a few times and shook his head. Taking an uncertain step backward, he sat down heavily on the wooden milking stool behind him.

Shaken from his grip, Cat swiftly knelt next to him. "Hey, Gage, you okay?"

The man drew a tattered gray cloth from his pocket and wiped his face. "God Almighty! There be powerhouse stuff goin' on with you, sister. Could've knocked me to my knees." He bent his head closer to her in the attitude of one ready to disclose an important secret and took her hands in his. "Child, you gotta keep yourself closed an' open. You gotta be watchin' out for bad stuff comin' down your road."

The heavy feeling returned, sliding down Cat's throat and wrapping itself around her windpipe. "What bad stuff? What'd you see?"

"Nothin'," Gage said, frowning. Clearly, he wasn't going to tell her everything. "Can't see it no more, but I know for sure you gotta let the faith in." He rubbed her hands gently between his. "You got yourself a heap of healing an' serious work to do before it . . . before you . . . before then."

Whether it was his sincerity or the fear that still gripped her, Cat suddenly felt exposed and extremely vulnerable. She pulled her hands away from his. "Tell you what, Gage." She forced a spiteful Bette Davis laugh. "I'll start believing in your voodoo bullshit when you conjure me up a winning lottery ticket."

18

Gage flinched and stiffened as if he'd been struck. "I didn't ask to take you on, Ms. High an' Mighty Richardson." His voice was thick with injured feeling. "Your sass don't make me exactly flush with happiness neither. I wish I was helpin' somebody who appreciates the gift, not somebody who don't see nothin' except shit.

"You been sent as my job an' I don't ask questions, I just do what I been sent to do. You don't never have to hear nothin' I say, just like you don't never have to look an' see the sun shinin' neither."

Instant remorse punched her in the heart and made her crumble. The man meant her no harm. She supposed in his own way he genuinely believed he was taking care of her.

"Look, Gage, I didn't mean it like that. It's just that I was brought up believing in hard facts like lab results and mathematical logic and—"

"An' things like your mama comin' back to apologize for the pain, and you not gettin' through that mule nature you got on you so she can rest in peace?"

His words cut her. That awful dream about her mother. How the hell did he know about *that?*

Stroking salt-and-pepper stubble, Gage half smiled. "I tell you, Ms. Cat, a little of your sugar used to sweeten my coffee right now. My gramma used to say that when I was pushin' her patient nature around."

A group of retarded children burst noisily through the double doors of the rehab center and ran into the lobby. A Down's syndrome boy stopped to wave cheerfully at Gage and Tom Mix. Unable to comprehend why the man did not return his greeting, the child began waving with both hands, his movements growing more frantic.

"Wave," Cat said quietly. "There's a boy here who's waving at you."

With the bearing of innocence itself, Gage waved happily in all directions until, with his special sonar, he located the boy and made a low, sweeping bow. Delighted with Gage's response, the boy ran off giggling and flapping his hands.

"See?" said Gage. "We gotta help each other."

Cat glanced at the lobby clock, sucked in a breath, and groaned. "Got to go. If I don't get myself upstairs in the next three minutes, you'll be helping me find another job.

Cat turned to leave and, without thinking, waved goodbye.

On cue, Gage waved back.

. . .

Halfway up the first flight of stairs, Cat came upon Dr. Cramer leaning, immobile, against the handrail. Staring blankly at the flat pink paint of the stairwell, the chief of cardiology did not blink when she passed her hand in front of his eyes, but instead turned the glassy stare in her direction.

"You okay, Dr. Cramer? You look like you're in your seventy-second consecutive hour of duty."

The huge hulk of a man, famous for his tendency toward eccentricity, waggled his eyebrows. "Catechols," he said, and lapsed back into appraising the wall.

"Catechols?" Cat echoed.

Dr. Cramer nodded and returned to his statue-like state.

Momentarily concerned that the man might be in some sort of deep, motionless seizure, she waited until he blinked, and then she tiptoed to the next set of stairs.

On the fourth-floor landing, she passed an attractive man carrying a Coach briefcase and wearing a hand-tailored Italian three-piece suit. He gave her full breasts a furtive though appreciative sidelong glance, which then slid down to her belly, her hips, and inevitably landed on those giants of grotesquerie—her feet. Looking away quickly, he hurried on. He had been told somewhere along life's path not to stare at others' deformities.

His reaction did not bother her. Ever since her parents broke the news that foot binding was illegal, she had stopped thinking of her feet as a handicap and taken them in her stride.

At eighteen, she was told by a palm reader that her feet were a sign of higher evolution and distinguished her from all others. By twenty-five, she was noted for her collection of shoes, the most bizarre being a pair of wooden clogs carved in the shape of sailing ships, complete with sails on the tops and rudders at the heels.

By thirty-five, she was fond of saying no one could doubt that she had her feet firmly planted on the ground.

Cat guessed Chaps a millisecond before the pungent backdrift of the man's cologne hit her nostrils.

Through experience, she knew he was the type who drank Corona beer with a twist of lime, had an MBA, kept a 1959 Porsche Speedster in the garage but drove a BMW, wore a gold Rolex, played tennis at the club four times a week, had a standing weekly appointment for hair styling, manicure, and pedicure (*with* clear polish), and described his Burberry raincoat as "an essential, tasty piece of status." With a little coaxing, he would also say that when he wore his Burberry, it showed the world the man he really was.

20

Cat had him figured out years ago; with or without the Burberry, he was the type of man who, especially in bed, had nothing to say.

During the more self-destructive times in her life, she'd made a habit of picking men of his type when she wanted to feel used. She could always count on them to be cold, condescending, lazy, and immaculately clean, as in: *"Me?* You want *me* to put *my* mouth on *that?"*

With a soft backdrop of Earl Klugh or George Winston, he'd wear the same vacant stare she'd seen on men when they practiced the guitar. His type of man could be counted on to imagine June's or January's soft-focused, callipygous, prominently nippled, barely pubic-haired *Playboy* centerfold while pumping like a mad mechanical drummer until he brought himself to orgasm, totally blocking out the fact that another human being was present.

Twenty or so seconds after his small victory, he would rinse himself off, brush and floss, then devise some complicated though transparent excuse to dump her off at home and be back in time to watch "Saturday Night Live" unhampered.

Taking the rest of the stairs two at a time, she refused to stop and catch her breath until she reached the fifth floor. Not bad, she thought, ignoring the burning in her throat. Forty-two years old and still in shape. Not quite ready for menopausal therapy.

She slipped her arm free of her purse and covertly touched the flesh of her own well-shaped gluteus maximus; there was only the minimal amount of flab—only a little bit of extra space for deadly creeping cellulite.

Even with the bridge of freckles spanning her face high cheekbone to high cheekbone, Cat realized she was still able to elicit jealous glares from women and lustful, longing glances from men. Although, living in San Francisco, more often than not it was vice versa. If and when those looks stopped coming, she knew she could always count on the dozen or more times a year she would be mistaken for Mariette Hartley, whom she considered an all-time beauty.

She'd long since discarded the notion her mother had programmed into her that she was the ugliest example of human flesh ever to hit life. She'd also dropped the if-I-wasn't-born-with-it-I-won't-wear-it 1960s earth mother philosophy and decided that one day when she'd won the lottery, she would have her breasts bobbed and stuffed. And if the plastic surgeon asked her why she wanted them done, she would tell him that when she was naked, they drooped so badly her pubic hair tickled her nipples.

The thought made her laugh briefly, until the old sense of futility kicked back in.

All the vanity—for what?

As a matter of self-preservation, she'd sworn off the emotional vampires after a disastrous love affair four years before: the last of a series of equally destructive relationships that had stolen a quarter of a century from her life. Battle-weary and disillusioned, she was done indulging in the drama of passion and sex. The days of feverish back arching and hip thrusting were over, she was sure, leaving in their wake a torturous mixture of sorrow, vague longing, and hopelessness.

Even though she'd been through all the therapy one person could safely stomach, she still harbored bitterness about her lonely, celibate life. Somehow she was left feeling that she'd been cheated out of something really good.

In the beginning of that desolate period of self-imposed celibacy, Cat had turned away from offers of emotional support and made the deliberate choice to free herself of all attachments. As if to commit a kind of living suicide, she swept bare the clutter of her life.

She started small, using a garage sale as her vehicle. Her closets and hope chests were relieved of a small mountain of clothes, twelve pounds of costume jewelry, and some seventy-eight pairs of shoes. Every corner and cubby was searched out and despoiled of dust-collecting artifacts, each one holding some precious or woeful memory: an improperly dried sprig of lilacs from her first wedding night; a pair of snow boots from her second; a miniature bottle holding one drop of mercury from her father's drugstore; a champagne cork from her thirtieth birthday, celebrated under the Eiffel Tower; even a Utica Club beer cap and an empty condom packet commemorative of the humid night at summer camp during which she lost her virginity on a dare.

Gone was the mahogany sleigh bed where guests and rejected lovers had slept, goodbye to the antique oak stationery which had waited a hundred and fifty years for someone to write one good poem on its open leaf, good riddance to the rocking chair in which she'd hoped to rock the children no one was willing to have with her.

With the exception of her Persian cat, The Great Saphenous Vein, and the bare essentials of life, everything she owned was fostered out to new homes.

But that was only half the load. She celebrated her thirty-eighth birthday by silently dismissing, one by one, those she termed her

"California friends." Most of them were typical type-A, status-conscious yuppies who actually read *Town and Country* cover to cover and judged people's true character by what investments they'd made and which brand of espresso and pasta makers they owned. Half of what they earned they snorted in locked bathrooms, then flaunted the other half in expensive cars and any variety of trendy toys they couldn't really afford but refused to live without.

Only slightly taken in by their opaque charm, she'd gone along for the ride for lack of something better to do and because someone, usually one of the husbands she was currently bewitching, always paid her way. With them she sailed, golfed, faked it at doubles tennis, played Trivial Pursuit in the plush lounges of posh ski lodges, trekked in strange lands with unpronounceable names, attended formal balls, weekended in Carmel-by-the-Sea, played best friends with the pretty wives, and had intellectually sophisticated arguments in Jacuzzis at the very best hotels about the true meaning of politics, religion, sex, and life in the sixties. She even went so far as to join the hunt club despite her fear of horses.

But the society that had it all left her empty. On the verge of soul malnutrition, she installed an answering machine and disconnected the doorbell.

Of course, they wanted her back. Even though she wasn't truly of their class, Cat had been amusing and a good sport. They overlooked her disturbing directness and tactless honesty when she confronted them with unwanted truths about themselves; she was stable—solid as a rock. To her and her alone they'd divulged all their secrets and in her invested their time and money. They felt she belonged to them, and they would not let her go without fighting the negative forces that kept her from their protective circle.

As part of their last-ditch effort, the pebble-on-the-window visits came late in the evening, after the fifth glass of a solid but mellow California Chardonnay or the second line of really good cocaine.

They told her that living that way, apart from other human beings, was, well, really dear, not quite human.

In response, Cat explained calmly but with purpose that like Garbo, she *vanted* to be alone, darling. True, loneliness and boredom occasionally surfaced in panicky spurts, but she ignored these regressions by cramming her empty hours with the usual and not so usual things lonely single people did in a largely gay, largely conservative city.

She ignored the classes that prepared one for being lonely and single, and instead read libraries of books, surveyed all the back

23

alleys of San Francisco, listened to taped lectures by Rajneesh and Joseph Campbell, scanned the pink section of the paper for admission-free happenings, and taught The Great Saphenous to relieve himself in the toilet, then flush.

Once, she spent four months writing a short story about an invisible woman, entitled *Melinda Gets Vague,* but eventually grew bored and lined the wet garbage pail with the pages.

Still, no matter how hard she tried to suppress it, awareness of being alone was the pea under her mattress. There had to be more for her, but what it was and where it was to be found she couldn't say. She often likened her emotional state to feeling a little hungry and standing in front of an open refrigerator, staring undecidedly at the contents and hoping that the Frigidaire genie would come forth and tell her what she wanted.

Sometimes when she played the part of the tragic failed romantic, Cat felt herself to be what Colette called "a lady on her own," resigned to the idea that her mature years would be barren, with no one to love but her cat and no purpose except to attend Wednesday night bingo at the retirement home for aged nurses.

Yet when she honestly reviewed her life each morning, Cat found she was neither happy nor unhappy, but rather discontent and waiting—not for a lover, or at least it didn't have the usual high-pitched strain of *that* kind of waiting; it was the sort of waiting one does when on the brink of discovering something beyond immediate comprehension, as in the split second before a slightly suspicious Fay Wray opens the front door to King Kong.

2 Ward Two went by several names. The patients often referred to it as the Dump, while the physicians jokingly called it Turf Tundra. The nurses there said they worked in the Ward from Hell.

Because of its multifaceted nature, Ward Two was considered unique by the medical community. Divided in two sections, a thirty-two bed step-down ward and an eight-bed acute unit, the fifth floor ward had been designated as the catchall department for those patients the other units did not have room for, or simply did not want. For thirty-one years, Ward Two, the Ellis Island of Mercy Hospital, had received the huddled masses from oncology to obstetrics, proctology to psychiatry.

As Cat came on the floor, one nurse rushed to finish charting, while two others ran in and out of patient rooms, dispensing late six and early seven a.m. medications plus answering the call lights of those confused postsurgical patients who were just coming to consciousness and praying out loud that no more trucks would hit them.

After all this was completed, there was still the final and unpleasant, though seemingly crucial, task of rousing patients from a deep, restful sleep and hoisting them out of bed, into the ice-cold atmosphere and onto a rickety scale for the morning weight.

Pausing in the doorway of 516, Cat beheld the senior anchors of the night crew, Trish and Mathilde, standing transfixed in front of a sleeping patient's television, both of them absentmindedly chewing the dead skin of their cuticles.

She knew what they were watching. It was just three days before the second anniversary of the *Challenger* explosion. The morning news shows, always eager to exploit any tragedy old or new, were getting an early start at reminding the public of the disaster by re-playing pieces of film footage. She didn't particularly want to see it again, but overruled her own objections and stepped into the room.

On the screen was displayed a series of shots from the event, one playing after another in a constant staccato rhythm: the missile climbing into the clear, blue Florida sky, cut to the seven smiling astronauts boarding, another cut to the auditorium filled with stunned teenagers, and finally a replay of the expressions of disbelief and horror long since etched into every American memory.

Tears came to her eyes, and she wanted to cry for . . . whom? The wives? The husband? The children? The pictures changed again, and there was the major brass of NASA, wary and reluctant, cautiously answering the news media's questions, affirming the reporters' suspicions that someone had screwed up somewhere and someone was going to pay.

That was followed by the Howdy Doody look-alike from Pennsylvania Avenue, with his Brylcreemed pompadour and pathetic, watery eyes, sitting stock-still behind the seal of approval and sounding downright sincere for the gullible sector of Middle Americans who read *Reader's Digest* while sitting on the porcelain throne: one tear-jerking story guaranteed not to take longer than the average time needed for a morning bowel evacuation.

"The man never was much of an actor," Cat whispered, not taking her eyes from the TV. "He did much better at hiring himself out to the government as a professional moron."

Then came the endless succession of experts giving opinions and guesses while the video of seven people being blown to bits played over and over in a small inset in the upper right-hand corner of the screen. With disgust, she recalled that during the continuous live broadcast of the day's events, a ticker-tape listing of the regularly scheduled programs America was missing had run across the bottom of the screen with apologies for the inconvenience.

Cat glanced at her two co-workers and was repelled by how enthralled they were with the disaster. "Jesus you guys, how can you watch that crap all over again?"

Trish stopped watching long enough to toss her a poisonous glance. "Fuck you, Richardson. It's history on film, okay?" It was obvious from the way Trish's nostrils flared that she was in one of her more aggressive, bitter moods.

Cat ignored the remark but couldn't help noticing that Mathilde, the thickset Frenchwoman she'd worked with for six years, also wore an uncharacteristically sullen expression. They both stared her down defiantly, the way rotten kids gang up on an intruder. Her lower

26

level of contrariness reared its wrathful head and ordered her to push buttons. She targeted Trish.

"Don't you know what a mountain of political hype there was around that accident? We'll never know just how much the government had to do with it, just like we'll never know the real stories behind the deaths of JFK or Marilyn Monroe, or Bobby Kennedy or—"

Trish pushed by and gave her a curdling stare that would have maimed anything alive or dead less than fifty feet away. "Besides being full of shit most of the time, Big Foot, your negativity, not to mention your boring opinions, generally suck horse dick. However, I have great hopes that before you reach your next birthday, you might choke on your own tongue and succumb."

On another day, the woman's attack might have caused injury; today it fell into Cat's left-field sense of humor. She stuck out the tongue she was supposed to choke on and wagged her head after the fashion of the playground bully who's just unfairly scored the ball. "Say," she called out to the retreating figure, "was that a rock coming from the direction of a glass house that I just felt whiz past my head?"

In reply Trish gave Cat the second one-fingered salute she'd received in ten minutes.

"Hey, the same to you and the horse you rode in on," Cat called out, "except I think your horse would like me better for the obvious reasons."

In spite of herself, Mathilde twittered, sobered, then scolded. "Ooooh, you are too outrageous the way you speak to each other. Tsk! Horse dicks! You speak like bad children. I myself will put you both over my knees to spank! Why? Huh? Tell me why you make so many difficulties for the other women to like you all the time, huh?"

Cat pointed to herself in mock surprise and disappointment. "Me? You mean I'm *not* going to win The Most Popular Nurse of the Year award after all?"

Mathilde rolled her eyes and turned to leave. "In France they would say you are terrible like, ahm . . . ah, let me think. *Un mulet?* No. Ah *qui!* Like *un rouleau compresseur!*"

Without having any idea what *un rouleau compresseur* was, Cat nodded in agreement. She probably was just that.

So, what else was new? Even as a young girl she'd been looked on as difficult; a gangly anemic who preferred the company of cats to that of kids, and dissecting worms and toads in the cellar to playing dolls and two-court.

Somewhere along the line, the neighborhood kids got to calling

27

her "Red Spider Woman," and during her high school years it was generally believed that if one of her intense stares fell on a person for too long, it would hex the unfortunate soul forever.

She knew that most of the Ward Two nurses didn't like working with her because they thought her too unpredictable, too tactless, and too "East Coast"—whatever that meant. Gilly, Ward Two's head nurse, once told her several of the girls referred to her as "She Who Should Be Feared."

This news did not affect her. She looked on her fellow nurses as family and although she would never admit it, she cared for most of them unconditionally.

Their attitudes toward her stung only when she was feeling sorry for herself and dwelling on the fact that there had been only a few people in her life who had loved her enough to break through the outer crust and get to the marshmallow center.

The most important of those people gave her hair a yank as she flew by her, balancing an empty bedpan on her head. Cat noticed that Nora's five-foot frame was draped in an oversized, ankle-length scrub dress cinched by a wide red patent leather belt, the buckle of which was an extremely prominent cluster of rhinestone grapes.

Partial to flash and trash, Nora was by no means a slave to fashion. Cat guessed it was more than likely the two had never even met.

"It was quarter to two and I'd just walked in the door, when they called me and asked if I'd come in at three," Nora said, skillfully dodging an occupied wheelchair. "But I didn't forget to bring granola and yogurt for our breakfast. And wait till I tell you about what happened to me last night—you'll absolutely die!"

"Was it rape or love?" Cat called out after her.

The alluring hazel-eyed vamp let out a whinny of high-pitched laughter and disappeared into room 510.

As different as Laurel and Hardy in temperament, Nora and Cat had shared a thousand or more major lifetime events, including a total of two marriages, three abortions, two divorces, seven hard deaths, three nervous breakdowns, a dozen serious love affairs, and a couple of hundred fits of wheezy, weak-at-the-wrists, close-to-incontinent laughter.

Three thousand miles and thirty years away from their first meeting on the Boston Common, when Cat had lifted the small blonde girl up to the water fountain, their lives were still inextricably entwined.

She was startled by a man's voice behind her.

"Ah, excuse me, Red."

28

Cat winced and gritted her teeth. Why? Why in Christ's name did people do that to redheads? Nobody ever said, "Ah, excuse me, Chestnut," did they?

Swinging around, she glowered at the man, then sucked in a sharp breath. She had not bargained for his particular brand of smile.

Beyond the smile and the deep smile lines was a general framework that was, miracle of miracles, at least six inches taller than her own five-foot-eleven-inch stature. The rest of him followed an offbeat romance novel recipe: The thinning black hair was shot with white, and not just at the temples. Squinty dark blue eyes behind rimless glasses. High, slightly puffy cheekbones, an exquisite northern Italian nose, and a cleft chin with the beginning of another, fuller chin just behind it. His teeth were insignificantly crooked though badly capped, and under his oxford-blue shirt with the too tight starched collar was a growing spare tire that tugged at the buttons.

Overall, the odd combination of faults made him more than just another nice face in the crowd. In her world, men this pleasantly unique had long since ceased to exist.

"Yeah, Blackie?"

Dropping the smile, he adopted a look of mock seriousness. "Oops, sorry. I forgot how sensitive you redheads are about the color of your hair and everything else that comes into your paths. But if it means anything to you, I'd have to say yours is one of the most magnificent heads of hair I've run into in a very long time."

She frowned. Had his eyes actually *sparkled?* The act was pure corn, but God, that smile.

Except for licking at the sweat pumping out over her upper lip, she tried to appear unaffected. "Yeah, yeah, right. Whatcha need, big fella?"

Christ, did she really say that? Mentally she shrugged: So what? She was tough. His beer- and truck-commercial good looks weren't going to turn her into some self-deprecating bowl of lubrication, and besides, the odds were the guy was either married, a total misogynistic prick, or a screaming closet queen.

"I'm David Padcula," he continued, with that wonderfully easy masculine voice, "investigator with the Marin County Sheriff's Office, and I'm looking for Lucy Cross. Do you know where I might find her?"

Feigning deep thought for a moment, Cat did some quick on-the-spot research. The body said straight: no hip swishing or limp-wristed salutes, no perfectly trimmed, hedgelike mustache. He did not wear the tight, look-at-my-butt pants, but rather a dark blue wool suit with a summer-green linen tie and a wrinkled imitation–London Fog raincoat. The socks, one red, the other maroon, made her smile.

He was unmarried, she decided—not just because of the unmatched socks, but more, because there was no gold band on his ring finger, and nowadays no woman with any smarts at all let her man out of the house without clearly marking off her territory—especially acreage as attractive as this.

As for being a prick, well, what man wasn't? But there was something about his smile . . .

"Is there a girlfriend?"

Immediately catching her slip, Cat tried to recover. "What I meant was, ah, is she a friend or relative?"

Did the man mean to move that close to her? His nose couldn't be more than three inches from hers. She surprised herself and didn't move away, though she did bite her lip, aware of a severe disturbance in the region of her lower abdomen—a feeling rather like an unused motor turning over for the first time after a bad winter.

"She's the victim."

"The victim?" Cat repeated.

The man backed away, causing her a stinging split second of disappointment.

"Yes." He lowered his voice. "Assault with intent to commit murder."

"Whoa," Cat said in awe, then caught her breath. "Wait a minute—do you mean Lucy Cross as in Cross the famous artist?"

"That's the one. Any idea which room she might be in?"

Cat pointed to the nursing station. "See Blondie standing next to Mousy Brown? Ask them—they'll know what hair she's in . . . er, I mean what room."

She blushed, then felt a sudden uncontrollable desire to continue talking to him.

She let her shoulders relax and brushed back her hair. "Jeez, I'm sorry for seeming so scattered, but I'm just coming on duty. It's hard to get started at the crack of dawn, you know, and then, see, I have to deal with all these . . . *things,* like, oh, you know, like this place, and the other nurses . . ." She rolled her eyes. "And of course, there's this lousy weather we're having and then there's this blind guy in the lobby who keeps telling me about these weird psychic-type things that are supposed to happen to me and it freaks me out, but I can't—"

Without losing the smile (God, didn't his teeth get dry though?), he interrupted her monologue with a curt thank-you, saluted, and walked toward the nursing station. He hadn't stared at her breasts once, nor did he look back to sneak a full-body shot. He never even noticed her feet.

For a second she felt slighted, then embarrassed, afraid he might think she was an escapee from Ward Twelve. Considering the way she'd rambled on, who wouldn't wonder?

What did the guy say his name was? Padlock? Dreadlock? Dracula? Peculiar? Cat shrugged. What was the big deal anyway? The guy was probably just a chronic smiler and an alcoholic IV drug abuser, married to another guy whom he beat on a regular basis when he wasn't molesting unsupervised children in shopping malls.

Rationalization, no matter how outlandish, worked well for her.

In the small and airless space known as the report room, a registry nurse sat lacquering the nails of her right hand a pearlescent yellow. The nails of her left hand still bore old, chipped pink polish, looking for all the world like chewed-up wads of bubble gum stuck to the ends of her fingers. Using her newly painted fingertips, which now resembled tiny, pale yellow Easter eggs, the woman gingerly fished a makeup case out of her purse without disturbing anything else, after the fashion of a child playing pick-up-sticks.

Unable to watch the woman apply blue mascara over the already purple-caked lashes, Cat skimmed through the forty patient data cards, reading over the succinct summaries of illnesses, secret hang-ups, and social ineptitudes. Most of the information was useless, written to satisfy the sordid curiosity of the nurses rather than for any clinical purpose.

She pulled out a card:

"Ward Two, 515-B step-down. Congestive heart failure.

WALBINSKI, ANTHONY: Age: 56. Marital status: married. Occupation: retired electrician. Family: Six children living away from home. Personal: Cane dependent—shot in r. leg 15 yrs. ago in fight over woman. In prison 3 yrs. for murder. Married—to different woman. Has sex four times a week with girlfriend—wife uninformed of situation. DO NOT allow the two to visit simultaneously!"

She wondered what parts of her past would be chosen to be displayed—probably the wilder, less than normal, and downright kinky aspects. Sensationalism was, after all, the American way, even in the medical arena.

31

Because the nursing profession was a great lover of consistency, Cat chose three patients she knew from past admissions, one of whom would challenge and perhaps strengthen her patience or the lack thereof. The other four, including the famous and victimized Lucy Cross, were new tenants whose diagnoses caught her attention and held it.

Laurel, night shift's obese charge nurse, waddled in and dramatically collapsed in the chair next to her like a giant water balloon come to rest. "Fucking miserable," she said, laying her head on the bare table. "What else is there to say?"

Cat gave a one-handed massage to the exposed part of the young woman's neck. It was warm and moist. "What's up?"

"Well, it all started Friday exactly three and one half minutes after midnight, when Marin County nurses went on strike and we got eight of their patients dumped on us. So that meant that as of last night we started out with thirty in step-down, three in acute. Okay, fine. Tight, but what's to do?

"Then at half past the witching hour, ICU and recovery room begin receiving the surviving roadkill from last night's Highway 101 massacre and do a massive turf job directly to us. That translates to five acute admits and two step-downs, one right after the other with no time to breathe. I swear every patient on the ward has two or more IV's, is on loads of hourly meds, has pain in one end or the other, is confused and climbing over the side rails, or has terminal diarrhea. For this we are staffed with four nurses besides myself, two of whom are from the registry and have never worked the Ward from Hell before."

Laurel straightened the report notes, unclasped a pair of reading glasses from her breast pocket, rubbed her eyes, and continued. "The docs, even the normally tolerable ones, were all being total dorks. We figure it must have been a heavy sailing weekend because they all wanted everything done stat, but not one of them was willing to come in and check on their patients in person. As usual, we were the acting physicians, making the decisions to cover their butts.

"At one point the bed situation got so tight, we had to ask a few of the docs to let us bump some of their more stable patients down to Ward Seven. But no, they reminded us, that wasn't the subservients' decision to make.

"About the time we admitted a patient to the couch in the conference room, we started talking euthanasia and put all the patients' names into a hat. We threatened the doctors there would be one drawing per hour.

"And to top it all off, early Saturday morning our sick sinus syndrome in 515-D went into third-degree heart block with a rate of thirty-two, but Dr. Gillespie didn't want to disturb his weekend plans to put in a temporary pacemaker so he put the guy on an Isuprel drip instead. The lazy man's slow path to cardiology."

"Not quite," Cat interrupted. "More like the quick road to malpractice."

"Anyway, it just kept getting worse. Dr. Cramer was totally useless, skulking around, mumbling something about catechols and Inderal. There were no floats, no orderlies, no clerk, and out there fighting this chaos were the five of us. Only after I got on my knees and cried did the supervisor finally agree to call someone in from day shift. I suggested they call you, but the supervisor said the last time she called you to come in early, by the time she hung up she felt as though she'd been exorcised by phone.

"Finally, out of twenty-three calls, Nora was the only one kind or stupid enough to come in early."

The woman rubbed her temples and stared at Cat. "Can you believe this?"

"Why wouldn't I?" said Cat. "I ask what's new, and you give me a mild version of the same story I've heard every week for the last twenty years. Ah, our dear administration—how those bastards do love making megabucks off our hides. I mean, if they staffed us safely and gave us one or two more bodies to help out, their yearly salaries might drop a couple of thou, bringing them down to only a quarter of a million, and who the hell can live on *that?*"

Cat noticed Laurel looking at her curiously, as if she were surprised at the amount of venom in her voice. "Does that sound a touch bitter, my dear? You should hear me when I start in on how our director of nurses makes eighty thousand a year and doesn't do a lot of anything, unless you call sleeping with the director of finances hard work."

"You know," Laurel said thoughtfully, "for the life of me I'll never understand why you don't become one of our negotiators. You'd be so good at telling management what we want."

"Oh but I wouldn't. The first time an administrative lackey told me we weren't worth a cost-of-living wage increase, knowing that the only reason behind it is that we're women doing women's work, I'd lunge over the negotiating table and rip his goddamned throat out with my bare teeth."

That was when Cat noticed Alan sitting next to the copy machine, primly perched on the edge of his chair. He was fingering his mus-

33

tache, undoubtedly foraging for leftovers from breakfast. She groaned audibly and grimaced at the sight of the nervous, rat-faced man.

Drifting in for day report, Nora caught the look and gave Cat an affectionate hug. "It's all right, dear—it's only for eight or twelve or maybe even sixteen hours."

Cat groaned louder. She didn't like Alan, a marginal human being who she felt had been dry-cleaned of any personality whatsoever at birth. Alan was also the object of one of her two prejudices.

Her first intolerance stemmed from a minor problem she had with women drivers, although she had to admit that on occasion, they'd enabled her to expand her vocabulary of expletives. It was inexcusable the way women bought into the hypothesis that they were supposed to be weak-minded behind the wheel. (*Ahhhh, look at that, Roger. Isn't that cute? Just like a woman—the way she totaled all three of those cars trying to make a U-turn.*)

Her second prejudice was against working with Alan.

She'd never been able to figure out exactly what Alan's sexual leanings were, but she often told Nora she suspected he used Lee Press-On-Genitals to suit the occasion. Regardless of which way Alan swung, in her opinion this particular man had no business being in the nurturing field, except perhaps as muscles, and that was what orderlies were paid for.

In her career she had worked with only a handful of male nurses, the majority of whom she admired not only for their skill but for the courage it took to work in a predominantly female field. In the minority were the male nurses like Alan who paraded like peacocks in a woman's domain as frustrated, never-to-be doctors, pushing it so far as to don the physician's attitude of hyped-up superiority.

Curbing the desire to sneer at Alan, she went to the assignment board and wrote down the names of the patients she wanted. No one objected to her choices; no one ever did.

When all forty patients had been assigned, Laurel studied the list and glanced at Cat questioningly. "Did you really think through the assignment you gave yourself? Are you sure you want Cross *and* the kid that overdosed? They're both in acute, and the OD needs to be extubated and moved to step-down.

"Stella's on another planet half the time and on the commode the other half. Walker isn't going to make it out of here this time, so you'll have to go over all the grieving rigmarole with the wife and kids. Scaly Scanlin is his usual demanding, creepy self, Detlef still needs a lot of care, and the AIDS guy is stooling all over the place.

34

His *lover*"—Laurel fluttered her eyes and let her wrist go limp—"is flipped out.

"Why don't you at least switch the OD with somebody easy like Mrs. Johnson, or give your congestive heart failure to Alan and take the gallbladder? Even the posttrauma spine would be easier than this load."

Cat looked back at the board to make sure the names she chose matched the cards in her hand. "Why," she asked suspiciously, "after all these years, are you suddenly concerned about my case load?"

"It's the dark steamer trunks under your eyes," Laurel said. "After all, I don't think any of us could stand having you become one of those chemically impaired nurses who're constantly flying off the wall. You're already stranger than fiction as it is, dear."

Cat grinned and Nora laughed outright, both thinking of the joint Cat routinely kept taped to the top of her glove compartment, ready and waiting for the first toke the moment she pulled into her driveway.

"Guess I'd better double the dose of concealer cream," Cat said. "Either that or stop abusing myself until the wee small hours of the morning."

Laurel adjusted her reading glasses with an air of solemnity, and placed the patient cards carefully next to her notes. "Okay, all you bozos in the peanut gallery, report time is here, so listen nice to Uncle Bob. Starting with acute bed 500 . . . is everybody ready?"

Somebody groaned.

It could have been any one of them.

3 For him there were no more reprieves, and his hope had run out weeks before. Now he waited patiently for his life to choose its last moment.

Gowned, gloved, and masked, Cat approached the bed warily. Even with her intimate knowledge of death, she was still apprehensive about finding it staring back at her.

She stooped to check his IV and was caught by his soul gazing out, unblinking, from sunken eyes. Cat panicked a brief, mild panic. Was he gone? Had death beaten her to him?

Blink. Blink.

Nope, not yet.

"Hi."

"Oh, hi. I just wanted to see if you'd run dry." She indicated his IV bag.

"Oh." Yawn.

No more than a hint of the man's fetid breath passed her olfactory glands before she shut them down and surreptitiously held her breath. The red swelling of skin around his IV site caught her attention. "Bad news, sweet buns." (Was it okay to say that to a gay guy?)

"Uhn?"

"Your IV isn't working. The catheter has gone through the vein and it's letting all the fluid leak into your tissue." She looked away to avoid his eyes. "I've got to start a new one." Cat expected a groan of protest. Instead, the man gave a wonderfully huge smile.

"That all? Hey, no problem."

The smile, combined with the light from his eyes, opened him wide. It made her want to do everything for him.

36

"Yep, that's all, and I'm reeeealll good. I can slip in one of these needles in a second. No pain . . ."

He echoed her very thought: " . . . no brain."

They both laughed. On impulse, she slipped off her mask, removed her gloves, and laid a talc-covered hand against the center of his chest. His skin burned with fever.

I'm sorry, she thought, looking into the death-bright eyes. I'm sorry so many of you are dying.

With some effort, he took her hand, kissed it, and held it to his cheek. "I know," he said gently, as if reading her mind. "Thank you."

"Er . . . hi."

In the doorway stood a man who she supposed was her patient's lover. It was almost a mockery that he was so handsome and robust. For now anyway.

At the sight of him, the dying man's face glowed. "Hi, Doll." She's going to chase my veins around for a while, but she says she's reeeealll good." He coughed, out of breath.

Doll sat down on the other side of the bed and kissed him on the mouth. "I love you."

"Me too."

There were muffled giggles between them. Their eyes locked: life and death staring at each other through different windows of the same condemned building.

Doll caressed the man's skeletal shoulder, deftly avoiding an open bedsore. "Adrian sends his special love and says he'll bring some of his top-grade carrot cake tomorrow."

"Yum."

"And Billy said to give you one hundred kisses from him and Frankie."

"Only if you're the one to deliver them, Doll. You know how I loathe those scratchy whiskers."

There was more giggling, and Doll eased himself onto the bed, moving carefully so as not to cause any more pain. Sliding his arm under his lover, Doll cradled his balding head.

Unable to take her eyes off them, Cat watched boldly, fascinated by the tenderness that could exist between two men. An ache formed in the center of her chest and brought her to tears. When, in her whole life, had she ever received that quality of intimacy from any of the men she had loved?

Turning her back on the couple, she gathered equipment from the supply cabinet, while part of a poem by Mayakovsky ran, uninvited, through her mind.

37

. . . or, as the sky changes its hue,
if you wish,
I shall grow irreproachably tender:
not a man, but a cloud in trousers!

Without a word, she spread a thick towel under his arm and gently searched among the bruised, spidery veins for one large and strong enough to hold the intravenous cannula. Not much left. She could have kicked herself for telling him she was so good; now the extra pressure would make her nervous. She said a fervent, please-just-this-once prayer to get in on the first try, not to protect her pride, but because, for now, the small things meant so much to him.

After she had donned a set of gloves, she palpated a tiny thread of purple vein and tied him off several inches above the elbow.

"Here comes the poke." Unconsciously she held the tip of her tongue between her teeth, concentrating on the angle of entry through the papery flesh.

"Uhn." He squeezed his eyes shut and turned his head away.

Doll tightly gripped his lover's free hand. "I'm right here, love," he whispered. "Hold on."

It was not an easy IV. Without meeting the usual healthy resistance, she pushed the beveled tip of the needle through the thin wall of the vessel. She took painstaking care not to nick the other side of its fragile inner surface, advancing it in the direction of the flow of blood.

Like soft butter, she thought and pictured his veins as those strings of vessels found in an overcooked chicken, shredding at the slightest pressure.

She pulled gently on the syringe, and was rewarded with a slow trickle of dark red blood. She studied the syringe of scarlet fluid, fascinated by its harmless appearance. Most people would go weak at the knees knowing what it was. Pure poison. Certain death.

Cautiously she released the tourniquet, withdrew the needle from the hollow cannula, and immediately dropped it into the sharps box. The outside of the thick plastic container was clearly marked by a neon-orange sticker that read: PRECAUTION—AIDS."

"You can relax now," she said, pleased with herself. "I'm in."

He and Doll made her a present of grateful smiles.

Cat sniffed; there was another present under him, waiting to be cleaned away. Doll smelled it too and quickly slipped off the bed.

"Ah . . . perhaps you could step outside while I bathe him and change the bed." She wasn't sure just how much they shared. It wasn't unusual, even with long-married couples, for certain matters to be considered private.

38

Crestfallen, he hid his face. "Oh God, not *again?* I'm sorry, I can't feel it anymore. I can't even smell it anymore. I'm . . . It's so degrading. . . . I'm so sorry . . ." Sobs made his rib cage come alive.

Doll let his hand ride lightly over what was left of the man's hair and wiped away the tears with his fingers. "Shhhhh. So what's the big deal? What's a little diarrhea between lovers?"

Almost at once a muffled laugh replaced the sound of sniffles.

Doll turned to her. "You provide the soap and water, and I'll wash if you dry and powder."

When the soiled linen had been changed and the room smelled of baby powder, Doll scribbled something on a piece of paper and hung it at the end of the bed. It read: "Smile, my darling, shit happens."

4 The gray-haired radiologist stared at the black-and-white negative of death.

The second doctor, who was studying the unexciting X ray of an obese abdomen dotted with pockets of air, glanced over and executed a perfect double take. "Jeeeesus! Who's that?"

"That rather grim picture is of Mr. Peter Walker's lungs—interior decoration compliments of Le Cancer."

"How old?"

"Forty-three."

The second doctor, who was forty-five, took in a deep breath and mentally searched every millimeter of his lungs for something that felt like what showed on the film. "Holy Jesus shit."

Slipping the chest film back into the envelope marked "P. Walker: MLP/92543 Ward Two 511—Bed C," the radiologist sucked in his hollow cheeks and returned the envelope to the pile labeled for pickup. "Yes," he said, "I suppose even He did that."

Both doctors shook their heads. The radiologist reminded himself that life was imperfect and short; the second doctor was just glad they weren't his lungs. Without letting their thoughts go any farther, they dismissed the X ray from their minds.

Sandwiched between Tommy Johnson's fractured collarbone and Mrs. Bolman's gas-filled abdominal series, the ghost of Peter Walker's lungs awaited delivery.

From his bed, Walker stared out the window at the billboard plastered on the adjacent brick building. Enormous red letters, which appeared to be dripping blood from their bases, were boldly slashed across the flat black background

BLAZZIE'S SECRET . . .
For That Touch of Passion!

That was all. There was nothing else he could see that gave any clue as to who Blazzie was or what the significance of the bleeding red letters might be.

Blazzie did not sound passionate to Walker; Blazzie sounded too much like *bladder* or *ballsy* or *buggery* to be anything close to passionate. He envisioned Blazzie as a short, fat, balding man whose lardy buttocks could be found hanging over the sides of a barstool in some North Beach dump. His breath would reek of bourbon and he'd be holding a cheap cigar in one hand and a cheap broad in the other. What, wondered Walker, would a sap like that know about passion?

Yet something about the billboard, whether it was the funereal flat black background or the bleeding T's and S's, got under his skin. He found the whole idea of the billboard downright morbid and depressing, especially right outside Ward Two. He knew it was crazy, but sometimes he thought the damned thing had been put there on purpose to prey on his mind.

To shut out the sight, he moved his head slowly on the sweat-soaked pillow, careful not to disturb the green oxygen mask that had become a permanent fixture over his nose and mouth. This room was the end of the line all right, not like the last room he'd had on Ward Eight, all hotsy-totsy uptown with a park view. Besides the morbid billboard, most of Ward Two was shot. Its dirty yellow paint was cracked in road map designs and peeling away from the ceiling in strips that made him think of flesh falling away from bones.

It was only logical. He was through, and the Dump was where they put garbage to rest. The radiation and chemotherapy and puking had all been for nothing. This time they knew that the cancer, which had gradually been sneaking little pieces of his lungs, was now taking over, devouring what was left like hogs at feeding time.

Walker scratched his crotch and gave the other piece of human garbage in the room a moment of consideration; Mr. Detlef Meltzer, or "Det's Lips Melt 'Er,'" which was the way he liked to say it, had been placed in the pit to die too. The difference between them was that Detlef had already died once but managed to escape. Unfortunately, he'd made it back only halfway. Walker was praying for a one-way ticket.

He knew the morning they shaved Detlef's poor, aching head and rolled him away, it meant the end of the crusty old gomer. He'd tried to give the poor wretch the straight dope before they butchered him. He'd told him straight out, except Detlef had a major flaw: Detlef was a Jesus lover, and Jesus lovers, to his way of thinking, turned a deaf ear to anything that had to do with reality. Deeply rooted in mounds of self-righteous horseshit, Jesus lovers all believed they were going to sprout up and rub shoulders with God.

Not that he had anything against religion. His childhood had been virtually free of the religious drilling most of his friends were forced to endure. His parents believed that Easter and Christmas had been invented for the promotion and distribution of presents and rich food, and that Sundays were tagged onto the end of the week expressly for the purpose of sleeping in.

Divine power was introduced into the godless void of Walker's fifteen-year-old soul on the day Benny Newmann skated over a thin spot in the ice and drowned. Dazed, Walker had stood on the bank as they dragged his best pal's worm-white body from the frozen river. He'd tried to look away, but Benny's swollen and clouded eyes rested on his, silently bidding him to find a way to save himself.

The day of Benny's funeral, Walker began his blind search for a God who would give him faith to insure his soul. All in all, he found it very much like shopping for the perfect baseball glove. Each neighborhood offered a different God, claiming theirs was the True One, the Only One . . . the Very Best God on the market; all the others were Satan in disguise.

The Catholics lost him somewhere between the rich brocade robes and the rigid rules. He soured a little when he discovered that the cost of one priestly robe was more than one third of his father's yearly salary, and that to help pay for the garment, he would have to give up half of his newspaper money to the basket each Sunday. As if that weren't bad enough, this overfed God served up suffering as the poor's main meal, giving the subconscious message that a mysterious and wonderful heaven was available only to the magnificent of purse. Delivered with threats of hellfire and sadistic torture, the list of commandments was more than enough to keep the children of God in line, chaining them to a lifetime of guilt. Raising His holy eyebrows and pointing an accusatory finger, the opulent Catholic God would know instantly what blasphemies Walker had committed or even thought of committing at anytime of the day or night.

It was, however, the idiotic confessional exchange rate for these minor offenses that dealt Walker's potential salvation the final death blow. Giving the velvet-curtained confessional an unsanctioned try, he was fined three Hail Marys for two minor swear words, and six Our Fathers for peeking under Bethanne Rooney's skirt.

As for the rest of the deities, Walker found the Jewish God too complex and cloistered—divulging no secrets, standing apart from a world set against Him. The Presbyterians were thoroughly boring, the Episcopalians were without substance, and the Baptist crowd too hallelujah- and drama-bent.

The easygoing Eastern gurus were too abstruse; he simply was not able to grasp the ultimate message of "To know is not to know," although he did find the idea of free love without guilt appealing.

Despite the haunting memory of Benny's milky eyes, Walker remained godless and hungry for the easy fit of the perfect glove.

He was sure it was only because he couldn't claim membership in the Club of the Divine that Detlef wouldn't listen to his reasoning on why he should pack up and go home before the medical experts got to him with their scalpels. There had been no telling Detlef about how they'd saw off the top of his skull and cut out the rotten spots with a paring knife. Secure in the hands of God, Detlef simply waved away Walker's explanations about how the operation would leave him unable to talk, eat, laugh, shit or piss by himself.

Walker even took it upon himself to tell the man, although he wasn't exactly sure of his facts, that his pecker wouldn't ever be the same; he'd never part any woman's sweet flesh with the wad of soft pink dough they'd leave him with.

At that, Detlef came unhinged, flailing his arms, spitting and drooling out fiery, unintelligible words. Ashamed of himself, Walker shut up, for whatever else he'd been, Walker was not a cruel man. He held in his heart an all-encompassing fondness for his fellow human beings and a willingness to comply with others' needs. It was these two basic characteristics that won him a moderately contented, middle-of-the-road existence in an uncomplicated, comfortable marriage, raising three typical, "Brady Bunch"–like kids. Without even trying, Walker had earned a place in that rare collections of humans categorized as Pretty Darned Close to Normal. His youth, aside from the search for spiritual salvation, had been completely uneventful, grammar school accounting for nothing more than fleeting memories of graham crackers and milk, and high school passing in a blur of extracting football cleats from his face and shaking shop class sawdust from his socks.

After high school, Walker immediately took a job as a night watchman at a bank, but gave it up within two weeks. The work was too lonely: he wanted to be with people—be around them as much as possible—because more than anything in the world, Walker hated being alone.

His next job, as an orderly at San Miguel Hospital, fulfilled his need to be near people; the drawback was that most of them were sick, and Walker couldn't stand to see people suffering, especially the little ones in pediatrics. Every time they called him to empty the linen carts in the pastel pink and blue rooms, the tiny faces and miniature bodies hooked up to tubes and gray wires made him sick. Carrying the small wrapped bundles to the morgue ruined him for weeks.

He somehow managed to stay on for a couple of years, right up until his bosses added catheterizing male patients to his job description. Walker proved squeamish about that.

One full moon, the senior medical tech stood opposite Walker over an emergency room gurney for the express purpose of teaching him how to perform urethral catheterization on the bloodied man lying between them.

According to the medical tech, the patient had left a note explaining that after the death of his faithful poodle, Minnie, he just could not pull himself together. Thus, using a bullet as his scalpel, he'd scraped his memory clean by boring a hole through the right half of his brain.

An eyeball, rolling from side to side an inch below the man's splintered right cheekbone, watched Walker's trembling hands attempt to touch his flaccid penis.

"What do you think you're doing?" The man had addressed him through the burgundy pulp that was once his mouth.

Walker, the tech, and two emergency room nurses froze at the slurred but comprehensible words.

43

"I'm, ah, gonna put a tube up into your bladder to piss through," Walker answered, not sure which eye he should look at.

"Oh, okay . . . That's okay. Sorry to interrupt."

The thought that he was having a conversation with a man without a brain led to one about the Scarecrow in *The Wizard of Oz* having nothing on this guy. Walker couldn't help himself. He tried to pinch it back, but suddenly he was laughing, gripped by knee-slapping hysterics, until the man with half a head moaned and tried to sit up.

One of the nurses tied the man down and told Walker to hurry it up—they couldn't wait all day. Walker reached once again for the penis, but found he just could not bring himself to touch another man's.

Later, in the supervisor's office, he said he was sorry, told them he'd do a lot for humanity but poking rubber hoses down men's wangers was going too far.

They said they were sorry too; he'd been a good worker, and he was a great guy, well liked by all. Then they told him to get lost.

At the Getta Job Employment Agency, Walker decided to find out which job needed him. According to his scores on the Anderson Occupational Aptitude Test, the field of social work suited him one hundred percent. He pressed the occupational therapist to come up with a job that not only fit his talents, but also commanded prestige and respect.

After perusing his high school transcripts with a dubious eye, she suggested bartending.

Walker took the suggestion to heart.

For the next twenty-two years, he was the best bartender San Francisco's financial district had ever seen. One thing he knew— especially knew—was how to listen when people talked. He didn't just pay attention; Walker mainlined every word.

They came to him in droves: the unemployed corporate presidents; unscrupulous, ladder-climbing vice presidents; down-and-outers; high-society mistresses and dumped high-society wives. They were all so much alike he couldn't believe they didn't recognize each other.

After the third martini, most of them would start with the the-world-would-be-better-off-without-me rap. That was when he'd tell the story about the man with half a brain.

"So ya see," he'd conclude, lighting their cigarette and then his own, "sometimes suicide don't even work, and then think of all the problems you'd have."

Walker glanced over at Detlef again. The pitiful man was nothing more than a used-up body with a bald head that had been hollowed out and filled with stewed tomatoes.

The docs had offered to do the same for Walker. Cut him open, yank out a lung, and let him live hooked up to a breathing machine for his remaining weeks. He'd be a little better off than Detlef, of course. He'd have his brain, so that he could *think* about the tubes he was pissing and breathing through. Not to mention the one stuffed up his nose, which carried blue liquid food—food that six hours later, flowed out the other end onto a white plastic pad as puddles of blue liquid shit.

Walker told them to put their knives away. He would die the way his father and his grandfather had: in bed, in pain, tired, but tube-less.

Det's Jesus had deserted ship and left him swinging in the wind, or maybe when Detlef got to the edge of death, he'd discovered there really wasn't a God after all. Maybe that was the reason he turned back; he hadn't known where else to go.

Detlef farted as if in reply.

Walker smiled bitterly as his chin began to tremble. With difficulty, he sucked in a breath, coughed, and felt the pain explode, sending shrapnel to every part of his chest.

Blazzie, you son of a bitch, what a way to die.

5 The second doctor glanced over at the lighted X-ray screen, tilted his head back slightly, and adjusted his line of sight. "What's that you've got?" he asked.

The gray-haired radiologist continued staring at the film of a skull whose left parietal region was lined by a pattern of hair-fine cracks. It looked not unlike an egg that had fallen a short distance onto a padded surface.

"Ever heard of Cross the artist?"

45

The younger man moved closer to the screen, his chin almost touching the radiologist's shoulder. "You mean the pretty one on the cover of *Time* who did those pastel-colored oil paintings for the White House? The one whose eight-by-ten watercolors go for the upper limits of the six-figure price range?"

"That's the one."

"Auto accident?"

The older doctor released the film from the clips and slid Lucy Cross's skull back into its envelope. "Nope. Boyfriend."

The second doctor took the envelope and pulled the film back out, holding it in front of the single spotlight used for illuminating small bone fractures. He shook his head slowly. "Well, the son of a bitch did a good job. Was he arrested?"

"Nope. Disappeared without a trace."

"What's her neuro status?"

"Initially she had a couple of mild seizures, but those have stopped, and her EEG and CAT scan are normal. Her neuro man says even though she's neurologically intact, there's apparently a strong emotional component. She's completely withdrawn; lightens up every once in a while to say a few words, but then goes back to wandering around in the Valley of the Shadows and doesn't respond."

The second doctor adjusted his bifocals, making the gesture seem more of a mannerism than a necessity. "Maybe she's hiding—frightened into some other world."

The radiologist shrugged. "Yeah, maybe. Who knows what the old monkey brain does when it's agitated and locked up inside a cracked skull?"

An image instantly presented itself to the younger doctor. Once, while touring Barcelona, he'd witnessed a chained monkey being mercilessly tormented by a group of children.

"It retreats," he said, handing back the X ray. "It hides in the darkest corner it can find."

Cross fought to ignore the pain long enough to set her thoughts straight. She wanted to walk through and relive the whole thing, starting from the beginning and going all the way to the last, horrible day. But every time she stepped forward, she became entangled in the vision of the first time they made love.

It was the day he showed up unannounced at her cabin bearing a gift of fruit salad, a concoction even the sight of which made her gag. His physical beauty astounded her despite his attempt to disguise it under what she eventually came to call his California camouflage look: shaggy hair, gold chain, wrinkled baggy pants, Top-Siders, and a long-sleeved cotton shirt of lavender or some muted shade of pink.

She never knew how he found her secluded hideaway that first day, and never thought to ask until after the chaos, when the paramedics were moving her out. By then, the only person who could give her the answer had abandoned her. In those few moments before her consciousness faded to gray, her single agony came from the thought that there would never be another chance to find out.

Memories of her life before he came on the scene fought their way to the surface. Hers had been a story of luck—starting out as the struggling young artist fresh from art school, cut off from the family money and sick to death of eating discarded vegetables and fruits from grocery garbage bins. Starvation, pure and simple, forced her to use her wiles to charm a lecherous gallery owner into displaying one of her paintings. (Later, when it became public knowledge that his was the first gallery to exhibit the work of Lucy Cross, Monsieur de Vaudois was to say that he'd felt sorry for the peaked little waif with the overbite, and took the painting out of charity when she fainted dead away from hunger in his showroom. He also claimed credit for convincing the artist to drop "Lucy" from her signature and go only by the more dramatic, masculine-sounding "Cross.")

Then—like a somewhat altered script from *A Star Is Born*—there was the wealthy and famous art collector who, while slumming, "discovered" the pastel-colored oil hanging in an unlighted back corner of the gallery on his way to use the facilities. Within a year, her reputation as artist extraordinaire was soaring. Boarding school–innocent and indecently pretty, she was ideal prey for the celebrity crowd. It wasn't long before the gossip columns were speckled with her name, linking her romantically to certain rock stars and screen personalities. Later, there was a brief, poorly matched marriage followed by a widely publicized, unpleasant divorce.

When she wearied of the rounds of New York and L.A. parties and felt scorched rather than warmed by the limelight, she purchased five acres of coastal redwood forest, built her dream house, and settled in with her art and the garden.

Of the two it was, surprisingly, not her art but the garden that centered her. Each time she dug into its soil, she would bury her weariness and come away renewed. Afterwards, she would paint as if a master were working through her, making delicate shadings unfamiliar to her brush that gave her canvases the quality of being alive.

But the garden had not always affected her this way. Her love for

47

working the land was the legacy she received from her father the night they called to say his body had been found frozen in the earth of his beloved rose garden. Shaking with the news, she'd gone directly to the neglected garden outside her kitchen door.

All her life she'd watched her father toil over his flower beds, as resentful of his precious gardens as he had been of her gender and her art. Until the moment she stepped onto her own patch of earth, with its makeshift border of bricks and quake grass, she had not understood what the drudgery provided him that she could not. Until that night she had been certain the pale, fragile blooms he produced once a year had not deserved so much of him.

Heedlessly throwing rocks and clumps of weeds far from the boundaries of the garden, she worked the neglected soil until her hands bled in her final effort to please the man who could never be pleased.

In the early-morning light, she surveyed what she had done and, as if called to baptism by some higher power, lay in the rich brown dirt and burrowed into it until all but her face was covered. Her father had at last given her a sense of peace.

It was in order to work in the garden that Cross originally decided not to attend the popular Northern California spring gala for artists —that is, until Nathan called to do what an artist's agent did best: encourage, instill seeds of guilt, flatter, and finally, with a subtle iron hand, insist. All the best people would be there, he said, including some of her wealthier, more consistent buyers, not to mention all of the most important galleries and media people, the very ones who had helped put her at the top.

So at the last minute, urged by fears of possible missed opportunities, she'd wiped her hands free of dirt, brushed her luxuriant black hair back into a French clip, and applied a coat of deep red lipstick to set off the whiteness of her skin. Slipping into her most comfortable jeans, she threw on an emerald silk work shirt and was gone.

Forty minutes later, she arrived at the balloon-festooned, though apparently deserted, driveway in Sausalito and waited for the tram that would carry her to the gala at the top of the hill.

She'd heard nothing; in fact, she had been so unaware of his sudden appearance that he caught her in the act of doing a sniff check on the silky underarms of her blouse.

When the tidal wave of embarrassment subsided and she was finally able to lift her eyes, the man turned his back to her and studied his hands as if he did not trust them.

Uncomfortable with the silence, Cross waited a few minutes, then introduced herself to the back of his head. Scarcely glancing at her, he muttered a sullen "Hi" and promptly returned to keeping a close surveillance on his hands.

Shock made her skin go to goose bumps. It was *him*—the one Nathan had called her magical mirage.

She'd seen him once, two years before, sauntering down the main street of Bolinas with a springer spaniel bitch trailing behind him. It was his pink Top-siders and the tan baggy pants flecked with Naples yellow and alizarin crimson paint that caught her attention first. When she was parallel with him, she slowed the car enough to check him out, but not enough so he would notice her stare. His was, without a doubt, the most extraordinary man's face she had ever seen.

A few yards past him, she realized she'd forgotten to breathe. When she looked into the rearview mirror to confirm what she had seen, the man was no longer there.

After that, she began searching for him on side streets and in every restaurant and store. Even in her dreams, she was always on the verge of seeing him; then one of her recurring murky-swimming-pool-and-dark-house dreams would interrupt and he'd be gone.

For months she tried to sketch his face, but her memory failed to put the flawless pieces together; only the vague structure of a full, wide mouth and amazing eyes stayed with her.

She found herself falling into reveries where they would meet in Michelob commercial–type places reeking of New Wave sex and romance. Eventually they would live together in the country and have two, perhaps three superbly beautiful children. Till death did them part, they would never fall out of love.

Nathan had teased her, saying the man was only a mirage. "The French believe"—he sniffed the paint on one of her freshly done abstracts and smiled the contented smile of a successful agent— "there is for every man and woman one perfect lover who is the physical and spiritual ideal: soul mates if you please."

Cross absentmindedly added a smidgen of cobalt blue to the white smear of her palette. "Then I believe he is my perfect love. Something about him was different." She avoided her agent's gaze, turning so he could not see her blush. "I know it all sounds like it's straight out of a Harlequin romance, Nathan, but as soon as I saw him, I had this feeling that we were supposed to be together."

"Cross, my dear, naive child, despite what the French say, the perfect love is an illusion found only in dreams and romance novels. And even if you did find this lovely prince again, I'd be willing to bet

49

he won't be anything like your dreams. Men who are that handsome are used to having their way with women, though generally they don't like them much. I've seen these men operate, darling. You're much too vulnerable for a man like that."

Nathan raised his dramatically thick eyebrows and pressed down the back of his Andy Warhol–straw hair. "They're like cold fish with not an ounce of emotional stability or maturity about them. They're full of dramatic romantic gestures, but rarely do they know what the real loving of women is all about." He fingered the frayed end of an old piece of canvas. "You need someone who can speak in three languages—English, color, and love. These devils don't know that kind of rhetoric, Cross. They never play nice."

Cross stepped back from the large canvas and eyed the lavender and pink abstract. She shrugged. "Who knows? The only thing I know for sure is that I can't get this man's face out of my mind. I'd give anything to see him again. Even once from a distance would help me sleep at night."

Riding the tram toward the party, she forced herself not to gape. He resisted all her attempts to draw him into conversation, refusing to give up anything but noncommittal nods and one-word answers. The thought that he might be shy or self-conscious started her protective maternal juices flowing, until she observed him closely and instinctively pulled back.

Everything about the man was like barbed wire. Untouchable. Rigid. Her perfect lover was an attractive face without a heart, just as Nathan had predicted.

The disappointment over her lost fantasies stung for a moment and then dissolved. She would have to tell Nathan he was right—good thing they hadn't made any bets over it.

When they walked into the house, the divine face immediately headed for a group of men in the far corner. Halfway across the room, he developed a quasi-feminine sway she and Nathan had laughingly tagged the "Frisco Swish."

Her sense of who was and who was not gay was usually very good, even when the fact was carefully concealed; she wondered why she hadn't picked up his preference earlier. But swish or no swish, she noticed that all the women and several of the men in the vicinity stopped what they were doing and stared at him with longing. Two women—one wearing the L.A. Look, a face rendered expressionless by plastic surgery and a half-pound of makeup; the other with her

50

long hair in a single ponytail high off the side of her head, the universal sign of the bimbo—made a beeline for him and collided with each other midroom.

For a brief moment before dismissing him from her thoughts, she pitied him. The problems physical beauty could cause a man had never crossed her mind. It wasn't any wonder he was cold and self-protective, the way people gushed over him. With a tinge of embarrassed guilt, she recalled that she herself had almost stopped in the middle of the street to stare.

She made quick work of the obligatory false-smile-and-limp-hug rounds, submitted gracefully to the society page photographers, collected a plate of hors d'oeuvres, and found the ideal observation point halfway up a white marble staircase.

From her post, she watched the star-studded coupling crowd perform for one another, and eavesdropped with amusement on the bits and pieces of talk about what she referred to as the current rat race twaddle of art trends, money, politics, AIDS, condom commercials, and who was having whose illegitimate baby in Hollywood.

She had just bitten into a garlicky overstuffed mushroom, when he again seemed to materialize out of thin air. At once her tongue and teeth lost coordination and she dribbled half-chewed bread crumbs and finely chopped mushroom down the front of her blouse. Convinced that her breath screamed of garlic, she forgot her overbite and pulled her lips tightly together, causing them to blanch. He produced a pink handkerchief from his inside breast pocket and handed it to her.

"I hate crowds, especially parties," he said, moving his mouth in such a stiff manner that for a moment, she thought he might have been the victim of a stroke. "Would you go for a walk with me?"

Her initial irritation with him faded. Something did not ring true about his peculiar posturing and icy distancing. Instantly she decided he was vulnerable and in need of love although he worked hard to appear remote.

Ignoring her instinct to protect herself, she accepted his offer without hesitation. It would be all right; they would take a walk, and more than likely, he would turn out to be an artist just starting out who wanted a word of advice or an introduction to a gallery. She didn't have any problems with that. She was used to men coming on to her for whatever mileage they thought they could get out of her professionally. In the art world it was an accepted practice; even she had done her fair share of flirting in the beginning.

Making a bathroom excuse, she searched until she found the man-

51

ager of a gallery that routinely exhibited a large portion of her work. "Celia, I'm going for a walk with a mirage," she whispered, out of breath with excitement. "If I'm not back in thirty minutes . . . call the police."

She had to take deliberate, hard steps to keep her knees from turning to Jell-O. When that failed, she made herself relax, reasoning that this was not Jesus Christ walking at her side, but only a man after all. Laughing at what now seemed absurdly naive, she told him the story of how she had first seen him walking with the spaniel and what her reaction had been.

Her flattery seemed to touch off a spark in him; for as stiff and withdrawn as he had been, he was at once equally animated, speaking rapidly, jumping from one idea to another, yet never completing a thought. Parts of what he said seemed perfectly logical, though some of his rambling made no sense at all. For a second time that evening, she went against her better judgment and threw herself onto the roller-coaster ride of his disjointed monologue, convinced he was a genius and it was her own stupidity that kept her from understanding the depth of his complicated and brilliant nature.

His hands shook as he lighted a thin designer cigarette. "I started out modeling for J. C. Penney catalogs when I was sixteen. At the time, I was living in a condemned apartment house and washing cars to survive because neither one of the scum gave a damn."

"The scum?"

"My parents. Real pieces of work, those two. When I was little, my father would come home drunk, bragging about all the women he'd had. It was such a joke. There we were in this twenty-room penthouse with him in his custom-made Italian suit, and he'd be slapping me and my mother around like some pimp screaming about class and dignity." He kicked at a stone and sent it flying. "Man, I was dumb. I mean, the fucking *elevator* boy finally had to tell me the truth about my father and his low-life friends. I honestly thought he made all that money working behind a nice, clean desk in a respectable office somewhere. Instead, he's over on Battery Street doing jobs for the heavies."

Cross blinked. "I don't understand. What heavies? What jobs did your fa—"

"Forget it," he said harshly. "There was this one girl, used to come to the car wash and beg me to go with her so she could take care of me. She was older and trashy—not the type you were seen with in

52

public, but I wanted to show the scum that I didn't need them, so one day I went home with her. Her version of dinner was spreading peanut butter and mustard on bread with her fingers, but even that was more than my mother ever did for me.

"The girl didn't really care about me—all she wanted to do was screw. She never wanted to talk or listen to me. It made me sick, all that fucking. I had no intention of stooping to her level, so I finally cut her off. That was the first time I burned the bed sheets. It became a ritual whenever I ended with a woman. I burned the sheets we'd slept on. That way there wasn't any danger of them having any part of me . . . not even my smell."

Cross walked beside him in silence, not daring to comment or ask questions, not knowing whether to be afraid or fascinated. He was different from any man she'd ever known, and despite the gossip columnists' intimations that she was well versed in dealing with the male element, she didn't have a clue as to how to deal with him.

"My parents drove me crazy with all their fighting. I ran away a lot. Sometimes I'd be gone for two or three days before a cop would drag me home. Most of the time they never even knew I was missing."

He bowed his head and leaned against her briefly. The physical contact took her breath away, and she slipped an arm around him. At her touch, he drew back as if he'd been burned.

"Don't do that! I know it's probably hard for someone like you to understand, but I never . . . I'm damaged goods because of my mother. She made me . . ."

Cross held her breath and waited for the angry, sordid story of how he became a homosexual against his will. She was bewildered when he broke into sobs.

"I tried to make her love me, but it didn't matter how much I loved her. She was beautiful—petite like you, same black hair and brown eyes, even wore that same red lipstick. Everywhere I'd look, men's faces would be smeared with it."

Holding the cigarette between his lips, he squinted to avoid getting smoke in his eyes and threw a stick he'd found hard into the sky above them. "My father thought he was getting a good deal. He didn't know he was getting the town pump.

"The only times I felt safe were when she'd take me on these boat cruises. We'd lie on a deck chair for hours together and she'd hold me on her lap and sing old songs."

He softened and, for a brief moment, held a closed-mouth smile. "Sometimes the only way I can get to sleep is to make believe I'm in her lap on one of those deck chairs." He reached out and gently stroked Cross's throat with his fingers. At his touch, her body tightened.

"I imagine her throat the way it moved when she hummed; it was very soft."

He drew his hand away and suddenly flung his cigarette into the gutter, grinding it under his heel. "I was only six when she left me to run off with a door-to-door salesman. The slut actually left her only son to go off with some sleaze. Getting laid was more important to her than her own kid."

Torn between a longing to help him and wanting to run away, Cross shivered.

Taking off his jacket, he wrapped it gently about her shoulders and lighted another cigarette. In the flame, she saw that his tears and anger had disappeared as quickly as they had come.

"No one ever . . . I mean, nobody that I . . ." He inhaled deeply and held the smoke for a few seconds while he studied her intently. ". . . ever loved, I mean, really loved me back. I've never found a woman I could trust before.

"I couldn't trust her. She'd be all sweet and nice, suckering me in, and then, when I'd think everything was okay, she'd get drunk and say that she wished she never even had me. She pulled that on me a hundred times, and every time I'd hate her a little more until I started planning how I was going to kill her. I used to think I'd —"

"Wait," Cross said, frightened again by his escalating fury. "It's okay now. Really. All that is over. Why don't you tell me about your job. Tell me about what you do."

Without hesitation, he changed gears yet again. "Oh, you know, standing around while people photograph or film you is mindless work. 'Here boy, stand like this, sit like this, say it again and look into the camera like this.' It's like being a whore for the camera."

At the top of a steep hill lined with cars, he stepped over to a pickup truck and readjusted the side mirror so he could see himself. Making a ridiculous face, he pretended to get his finger stuck up his nose. He'd gone from the Prince of Darkness to Steve Martin without missing a beat.

Her wariness disappeared and she laughed. At that, he smiled openly, and she was dismayed to see him become even more beautiful.

"I don't know why God played this little trick on me," he said, watching himself intently in the glass, straining to see his profile, as if he were looking at it for the first time. "He gave me a face women

54

fall in love with, and I have to consciously make an effort to keep from hating them for it. They always expect something from me that I can't give, so I rescue them from themselves instead. Just once I'd like to find someone decent who can love me without constantly needing something in return."

He gave his image a last, longing look. "But I'm lucky. I can walk and talk at the same time. Most models can't do that; they don't know what to do with their hands."

He held out his hands and silently invited her to examine them. They were wide and powerful like her father's: the kind that looked natural working with wood and in dirt.

"I've got peasant's hands," he said, outlining his fingers. "Ugly. Useless and ugly."

Before she could disagree, he stepped close to her and caressed her face. "What are you thinking?"

It was more a command than a question.

Cross felt the wave of pins and needles start at the top of her scalp and flow down over her shoulders. This was a moment in which to prove herself, an impromptu performance.

"If I were a sorceress of high degree," she said, so seductively she faltered, "and could do anything, I would transport you to a deserted tropical island for one year and give you music to inspire tranquillity, books to teach you about love, works of art so you would be surrounded with beauty, and a wishing stone. Eventually you'd let go of all the hurt, and any time you felt afraid and needed to be held, you could make a wish and I'd be right there."

She couldn't tell if her statement intrigued or disgusted him, for he at once fell silent, regarding her with shining eyes.

They did not speak for the rest of the walk back to the gala, which gave Cross room to think. She should have known better than to say something so trite. The man probably interpreted her fantasy as an attempt to humor him, or perhaps he was offended by it.

His jacket hung heavily on her, and glancing down, she noted its color and texture. It was beautiful and very expensive. Automatically she brought the sleeve to her nose and inhaled his smell. What would it be like, she wondered, to be loved by him?

Cross dismissed the idea. What could she be thinking? He had made his feelings about women clear.

On the deck, she removed his jacket and handed it to him. "Well, there are a lot of people inside who would give their eyeteeth to meet you."

Without replying, he stepped onto the tram and pressed the lever.

The smooth whir of the motor filled the air between them. The tram had traveled only a few yards when he turned to her. "I've found what I need," he said with resignation. "There is no reason to look further."

The next afternoon she was tying up string beans, when she saw a man's shadow fall on the soil to her left. Instinctively, she cowered close to the ground and screamed.

Indifferent to her fear, he held a plastic cup full of fruit salad out to her as a greeting and told her, with a hint of disapproval, that she was asking for trouble by keeping her doors unlocked.

When invited on a tour of the house she had designed herself, he seemed reluctant, as if he were afraid of discovering something that might evoke feelings or admiration for her. Before he could decline, she pulled him into the main room, where he gazed through the oversized skylight that made up the ceiling, then let his eyes travel slowly down the spectacular glass walls. Smiling his tight, closed-mouth smile, he suggested curtains.

She moved ahead of him to the studio where she proudly pointed out the cleverly hidden reading loft, and broke her own rules by allowing him to see her canvases in progress.

Disregarding the canvases and the loft altogether, he simply frowned and asked what kind of things she read that she felt she needed to hide. His tone made her feel ashamed, touching off the memory of how her father had whipped her with his belt after he found her in one of the greenhouses studying a book on nude figure drawing.

At the alcove where she hung her own favorite paintings, he told her he thought her talent was incredible, and asked in the same breath if she really painted them herself. He wondered if perhaps there might be a male "ghost painter" behind her work; it was that good. His audacity shocked, then fascinated her. He was like a child begging for help, and changing in a moment to a severely critical man who projected onto her his own inadequacies and prejudices. Again she felt pity for him, which, she told herself, was the only reason she didn't throw him out posthaste.

He glowered at the photographs of her ancestors over the fireplace, murmuring fragmented statements about the burden of having invisible trains of other people's histories following one through life. With great deliberation, he hurried past the library and into the kitchen, where he suggested she make him a drink.

She was both amused and saddened by his discomfort, although when she confronted him directly about it, he told her that she, like all women, had a vivid and faulty imagination.

The way he had of twisting everything she said into something negative, then making her feel guilty about it intrigued her. His mood swings were considerable, going from rancorous to whimsical, hell to spring daisies. Without ever waiting for a reply, he constantly asked what she was thinking and never looked at her directly.

Once, when her gaze briefly wandered to his hair, he rushed to the hall mirror. Running his hands through the chestnut mane, he touched his cheekbones and then carefully inspected his face, as if searching for imperfections that might suddenly have developed. If he had found anything wrong, she was sure, it would have sent him over the edge.

He continued to stare at his image in the mirror, and with a straight face he told her it was important to maintain an austere persona on camera because it was a proven fact that the general public never took seriously anyone who smiled.

As she watched him primp, so obviously taken with himself, she was convinced once and for all that her initial gut-level impression from the night before had been correct: unbalanced, unhappy, and gay—no two ways about it.

Later, sitting in the garden between the lettuce and the basil, he pushed her back and tried to kiss her.

Confused, she laughed and struggled briefly to get up. "Wait a minute, aren't you . . . I mean, I thought you were . . ."

Without delay, he began the classic the-woman-I-am-involved-with-is-just-a-friend-now story.

"But—"

"See, I met her at a time when I was desperate for somebody, and she was so alone and needy and she—"

"But I thought you—"

"Of course, the romance only stayed for a little while. She's more like the good mom I never had . . . terribly dull and not very attractive . . . actually, the plainest woman I've ever known."

"But aren't you—"

"I haven't slept with her in two years, I swear."

"Well, actually, I didn't think you—"

"Of course, I'm the only friend she has in the world."

Cross had to bite her lip to keep from laughing. He'd thought she meant to accuse him of being involved or married; it never occurred to him that she'd assumed he was gay.

There wasn't much fanfare. He'd asked her what she wanted before they began. She told him that you didn't offer a starving woman a menu—you simply fed her.

He pressed his mouth to hers and brushed her nipples with his fingers until her back arched and her legs opened. Without waiting, he fell into the space created for him at the center of her body.

As he entered her, he pulled his head back and scrutinized her face, speaking in his deep and tranquil announcer's voice, a voice that surrounded, then captured her, blocking out all other sounds. "I'm inside you now, filling you as we make love. You've taken me in."

They made love with a mad craving that went worlds beyond any passion she had ever known. Clawing at each other, each searched every opening, every inch of the other's body. He was a master, bringing her to high-pitched frenzy, letting her down, then bringing her up again.

She was completely lost to him, frantic to get enough of his mouth; if it lingered on her breasts or the palm of her hand or the softness between her legs, she grew impatient, almost jealous. It belonged on her mouth, where she could be trapped by his eyes. The only thing that stayed constant was the way his hands repeatedly returned to the soft place where her thighs and buttocks met. It was there they could both feel her body dancing a mad rhythm of its own.

When he tired, he moved within her slowly, teasing her while controlling himself with ease. Each time he entered her, he watched her body shudder with a look of superior indifference that seemed somehow to mock her pleasure.

As the sensations swelled and became more intense, she tossed and moaned as though he were turning her inside out. Yet with the slow convulsions of her orgasm, she found no calm, only a driving desire to have more of him.

He pulled her to her knees and forced her head down, thrusting himself roughly into her mouth and throat so that she could not breathe. When the initial panic subsided, it was replaced by a sexual madness so strong she climaxed again without being touched.

Picking up his rhythm, she breathed around him while he went on stroking her hair and cooing as if he were reassuring a child: "Good girl. That's a good girl. Good girl . . . good."

58

Toward the end, when his eyes tore into hers with that consuming intensity which heralds the final release, she was paralyzed by the vision of who he was and why he was there.

It was the beginning of a murder that would take nearly two years to complete. But then again, Michael was like that; he was slow, but very thorough.

6 Anyone who observed her with him knew how she felt. Tight mouth, clipped voice, and head held rigidly—it was clear she did not like William Scanlin, and that made him one of her unsatisfactory deaths. There hadn't been many—two, maybe three in her twenty years. Considering the thousands of deaths she'd witnessed, Cat figured, it wasn't a bad record.

By the time she finished cleaning her AIDS patient and had the usual sotto voce how-long talk with Doll, Mr. Scanlin, the congestive heart failure she'd counted on as challenging to her patience yet minimal-care, was circling the drain, so to speak, as his lungs filled with the fluid that threatened to drown him. To meet the obligations of her job, she had to beat death to the finish line and cheat him out of his own natural end. From the clammy quality of his skin, her sixth sense of impending danger told her she needed to hurry.

Transferring him from 510 step-down back over to 503 acute would take a chunk out of her time, and she still had to assess, bathe, change linens for, and medicate five more patients. It was a lousy way to start the morning.

Never having mastered solo gurney steering, Cat ran the end of

59

the heavy bed into the side of the water fountain, startling the souring Mr. Scanlin. One of the wheels rolled back over her foot.

"Son of a bitch!" he snarled. "What the hell do you think you're doing?"

"I'm transferring you to the acute unit," Cat snapped, momentarily irritated by the pain in her foot, "And please don't use that language around me, Mr. Scanlin. Understand?"

"Why, you . . . you can go to hell." Mr. Scanlin threw back the sheet and made a weak attempt at climbing over the side rails. The gurgling in his upper airway was clearly audible. "I don't need your bullshit. I'm getting the hell out of here."

On the monitor, his rhythm became irregular. Alarmed, Cat took firm hold of his arms and pulled him back onto the gurney. "Lie down, Scanlin, you're going to hurt yourself. You have to be treated."

Without warning, the man drew back his fist and let it fly, catching her just to the left of her windpipe. She fell against the wall, stunned.

Jowls dancing side to side, Mr. Scanlin rattled the side rails of the gurney. "I don't want help from filth like you. Leave me the hell alone!"

Enraged by his assault, Cat lurched toward him until the word "professionalism" fluttered across her mind screen. At that, she stopped, closed her eyes and waited for the anger to settle in the pit of her stomach. It was an arduous task to care for people one disliked, but no matter how abusive the patient became, the rule remained that a nurse was to maintain a sense of fairness and never let her own emotions interfere with her clinical judgment. As she suspected, Mr. Scanlin was going to test the limits of her self-control.

That illness brought on petulance was understood, but Scanlin's reputation preceded him like the rattle before the strike. As the previous chief administrator of Mercy Hospital, William "Scaly" Scanlin had been widely regarded as a miserable bastard. One month after taking the position, he closed administrative records and barred the public from attending hospital board meetings. At six months, he'd raised his salary to a few thousand shy of a quarter of a million a year. In his new contract, full-length black mink benefits included two new vehicles for personal use and mortgage payments on the modest seven-thousand-square-foot home he and his wife occupied.

Although he believed any person with ovaries was devoid of gray matter, there was a rapid succession of young and pretty secretaries, one of whom complained publicly of Mr. Scanlin's perverse sexual harassment.

60

"It was very difficult," the ex-employee tearfully admitted to the *Examiner* reporter, "trying to take dictation while dodging his hands or his toes coming at me from all sides, but I dealt with it. It was when he started in with the blindfolds and the ropes that I quit."

Scanlin seemed to thrive on upheaval and bad press. Actively involving himself in secret kickbacks and shady deals, he'd even gone as far as nipping at a few of the hands that fed him by setting up two clinics on the outskirts of the city, thus putting half a dozen of the physicians on staff out of business.

On the afternoon he was admitted to Ward Two acute, only three hours after the first time she single-handedly resuscitated him out of a flat-line EKG, he'd told Cat point-blank, "Nurses are little more than fancy maids with exorbitant salaries. I've always said if you make it a rank-and-file position, you can get nurses to do the work of six people, pay them peanuts, and then make them feel guilty for cashing their paycheck. If you really know the game, you can scare them enough so they never ask for a dime in raises. It's all in the technique."

Later, when he was stabilized enough to be transferred to the step-down section, he loudly bragged that he was the corporate party mainly responsible for "cutting the fluff out of the nurses' salaries."

Trish reluctantly resuscitated him in step-down the second time his heart came to a halt. Five hours later, he'd phoned the incumbent chief administrator to complain that "the little twit" would not address him as "sir," and insisted she be written up for insubordination and placed on probation.

In retaliation, Trish refused to transfer him to the acute section, giving the excuse that Scaly was simply too mean to die. No one even thought twice about arguing the point.

Following Gage's advice on how to deal with troublesome people, Cat took a deep breath and envisioned a soothing stream of warm orange light between herself and her patient. "Look," she said in as calm a voice as she could muster, "why don't you just lie down and be quiet. There are other patients here besides yourself. People just as sick as you. You can't—"

Apparently unaffected by the orange flow, Mr. Scanlin shook his fist in her face. "You don't tell me to lie down! You're a nothing. You're a goddamned—"

Cat gripped the side of the gurney until her knuckles turned white. "Stop it right now or I'll have to restrain you."

The man's color went from dusky, hypoxic blue to rage purple. "You good-for-nothing trash. You . . . you . . ." His eyes frantically searched the busy unit as he began to shriek.

"Help! Somebody help me. This imbecile is assaulting me!" Clutching the center of his chest, he vehemently mouthed more words, swung at her again, missed, and fell back on the gurney, panting.

Cat quickly tied the corners of the sheet together under the gurney to restrain him from hurting her or himself. When he realized he was pinned down, Scanlin went berserk. "I'll get you for this! I'll break you so you never work again."

Reasonably sure he could not get his hands free, she shoved her face into his until their noses almost touched. Her neck veins were severely distended and visibly blue. I think you're through spilling your poison around here, Mr. Scanlin. You have no power over me." As the orange light disappeared entirely, Cat added under her breath, "Christ, what a pig."

Scanlin's eyes grew large and dark. "Wha . . . what did you call me? A pig? Is *that* what you called me?"

Cat shrugged. "Hey, if the cloven hoof fits . . ."

The man howled, desperately trying to free himself.

Summoned by the commotion, Nora appeared in the door of 515, her gloved hands decorated with smears of blood. "What's the problem here? Are the big animals restless?"

With a melodramatic arch of his eyebrows, Mr. Scanlin pleaded in Nora's direction, "Get me out of here! This idiot is trying to kill me."

"Why, Mr. Scanlin," Nora said with overdone sympathy, "you can't really believe that's true. Why, this lovely nurse wouldn't hurt you for anything in the world."

Behind him, Cat nodded vigorously and mouthed, "Oh yes I would."

At that moment, Mathilde rushed by and took in the scene. She glanced at Cat. "So! What trouble do you make now, eh?" Without waiting for an answer, the stout woman took hold of the opposite end of the gurney and with the strength only those who work overtime can have, effortlessly sent it rolling through the double doors into the acute entrance hall.

Mr. Scanlin turned an imploring gaze on Mathilde. "You don't look quite as stupid as these other two dimwits. You get me out of here."

Mathilde regarded the wretched man, thought for a moment, and gave a resigned sigh. "Monsieur, I think with this attitude you are up the creek without a pot to piss in."

The job did have its moments.

· · ·

62

Cat watched him through the observation window of his room as he continued his pitiful struggle for air. The multitudes of medications and breathing treatments had done nothing to open his lungs. In sick hospital humor, Mr. Scanlin's condition, as indicated by the shape of his mouth, was an O about ready to become a Q. By the time she put the stat call into his doctor's exchange, his color was changing from putty blue to grayish lavender.

She alerted respiratory to a probable intubation and dialed Mrs. Scanlin to inform her of the change in her husband's condition. She had just written in the word "difficult" under the psychosocial column of his assessment summary, when his monitor alarmed with the sawtooth rhythm of a dying heart.

Training and adrenaline caused her to bolt for the crash cart and hurriedly lug the two-hundred-pound cabinet toward his room. Halfway there, she suddenly remembered who and what he was and stopped dead in her tracks.

Around her, the rest of the unit was in its usual turmoil. The other nurses were busy in their rooms, and the monitor tech-clerks had long since been cut from the unit's budget thanks to old Scaly Scanlin. It would be a few moments before the monitor alarm was noticed.

Calmly she pushed the crash cart the remaining twenty feet to his room.

At his bedside, Cat first checked for the nonexistent pulse, then made a fist and with all her strength, slammed the fleshy part of it into his chest. This initial intervention barely interrupted his ventricular fibrillation, strong in its deadly course. As he continued to seize, his eyes beheld her for a moment, then rolled back and disappeared into his very purple head.

Perfunctorily inserting a green plastic airway into his mouth, she positioned his head at the proper angle and pressed a bag mask over his nose and mouth. "So long, Mr. Scanlin," she whispered, pushing several lungfuls of oxygen into him. "Sorry there isn't more help, but we're understaffed today due to the low, "no fluff" salaries. Hope you don't mind the inconvenience."

Aware of each passing second, she prepared the defibrillation paddles with meticulous care, until the voice from the loudspeaker startled her.

Attention all personnel, code blue Ward Two acute. Dr. Cramer, seven-four-one-seven, stat. Dr. Cramer, seven-four-one seven, stat.

Ah. Someone at the central monitor bank was on her toes.

Cat leisurely placed the greased paddles in the proper place on his chest and with the click of a button, delivered a 360-watt jolt to his heart.

With the shock, his arms and legs jerked five inches off the bed. His right hand, now cold and wet, grazed her hip as it fell. Still holding the paddles, she watched the monitor and waited for the new rhythm to appear on the screen. It reminded her of when she was a kid and used to play with the Magic 8 Ball, waiting for the fortune to appear in the black window, completely prepared to believe in the answers.

On the black screen, his answer came up as an unclouded "No." Asystole. A flatliner. A stilled black heart.

She looked into the dilated and fixed pupils. "It's time to rotate the crops, big fella. It's the big game of musical chairs and you lose."

That was when the usual code blue pandemonium hit the door: The two respiratory people were first—one to bag, the other to set up the respirator. They were followed by two lab techs, one to draw the code bloods, one to run them to the laboratory; a profusion of nurses, one to continue chest compressions, one to record the events as they took place, one to be a general runner, one to start extra IV's and push meds, and another to confuse matters. There was a pharmacist to prepare the syringes of standard code drugs, and finally a wild-eyed, sleep-deprived Dr. Cramer, in his sixty-fourth hour of duty, lumbered in to intubate and referee.

Handing over the defibrillation paddles, Cat took a place in the corner to shout report over the noise.

He didn't make it. The way she saw it, his death meant one less evil influence in the world and one-seventh more time to spend with her other patients.

7 Stella was awake. Lately it was getting harder for her to tell whether she was or wasn't, but today she knew for sure because she could count through the pile of washcloths that lay on her lap and still come up with the same number five times in a row. Running a bony finger over a square of bleach-rough terry cloth, she brought it to her nose and sniffed tentatively.

Hmm, the hospital again.

"St . . . a?"

She strained to catch the low, muffled sound. Someone was more than likely calling her name. A hand touched her back and she pushed her rounded spine into the small warmth, like a cat arching up for a caress.

"St . . . a?"

The smiling face of a young woman came into her field of vision. Gratefully Stella returned the smile.

O youth, can you see that I am here? I am ancient, but I am still here.

"Can you tell me where you are, honey?" The nursing student was a sweet blonde thing of twenty-one.

Stella covered her toothless smile with a misshapen arthritic hand and watched carefully as the girl's lips parted and moved in their pink-sugar beauty. The pretty face was unlined and new, and the gold color of the girl's hair prompted an instant fantasy about wheat fields rippling like waves in the midday sun.

Without restraining herself, Stella stepped into the vision and wandered through the golden grain, sniffing the air for rain. She wrinkled her nose; it wasn't the wet earth smell that filled her nostrils, but the acrid old lady pee-pee stench, threatening to linger in her

65

failing olfactory glands forever. Stella blew the foul odor from her nose and answered the question she had not heard. "Yeech! Lousy Mercy Hospital Ward Two Dump!"

The student nurse clapped her hands in delight. "That's right!" she squealed.

"What?" What was the excitement? Had she won something? A year's supply of Metamucil? Hearing aid batteries? A pessary?

The girl put her lips to her ear and shouted in that particular monotone pitch people use with those who are blind, deaf, or retarded. "I said, you're right as can be, sweetie pie!"

The vibration of the noise made Stella's ear itch. Scrunching her shoulder against the side of her head, she pulled away. Why did they have to speak to her like that? Besides being old and hard of hearing, did they think she was crazy, too?

Stella twittered. She suspected they thought she *was* a bit off her trolley. That was most certainly why she was an inmate of Senility Lane in the Dump, waiting for an old gomer to kick off in another county-funded death trap so she could take his place. The last hag joint in which she'd taken up space had been closed down by the board of health—or was it the Endangered Species Protection Society?—over issues concerning fire hazards and dog food in the diet. She was of the opinion it should have had more to do with the old man across the hall who was found two days after he expired, gagged and tied to his bed.

Bored to distraction, she yawned. After fifteen years of imprisonment in a variety of foul-smelling medical institutions, she had come to the conclusion that the only difference between prisons and hospitals was, instead of making license plates, she had piles of washcloths to fold in order to keep her occupied and out of trouble. Stella had spent more than a few hours wondering what kind of trouble might possibly be available to her in a place like Senility Lane.

Not that she had any choice in the matter of where to go. Both her husband and her son had been lost in one nightmarish afternoon. The rest of her own kin had long since died out, and none of her friends had been given the option of waiting with her.

Somewhere on God's earth there was a towheaded grandson whom she'd cradled and sung nursery rhymes to when he was three hours old. It was the talk of the family the way they fancied each other right from the start. Nanmar Tella and Little Oats: a conspiracy of the very young and the aged, a private club of two members to which only the closest of family might, if they were lucky, receive a day pass.

66

Her clearest memory of the child was the day of his third-birthday party. Frightened by the rented camel and the noise from the hired band, he'd rejected his mother and father, refusing to be comforted by anyone but her. He'd clung to her as if she were life itself, never loosening his grip until she rocked him to sleep in the gazebo swing as she told him the Nanmar Tella version of how the camel got his hump.

Six days later, the sleeping child again lay in her arms at the grave sites of his father and his grandfather, and it was she who clung to him.

But she did not cling tightly enough, Stella thought. One month after the funeral, the boy's mother, a slight, scared rabbit of a girl, stole away in the middle of the night with the child and two hundred dollars from the safe.

Tacked to the upstairs bathroom door, on the back of her cowboy cookie recipe, the note was scrawled in her daughter-in-law's childish hand: "I took the boy and the money. Please don't call the cops. I need it for me and the boy to start new. Thanks and good bye."

Stella waited for the girl to come back on her own until it occurred to her that she had meant to sever family ties completely and forever. She'd been a fool not to have realized how jealous and hurt the boy's mother must have been over Little Oats' relationship with his grandmother.

After her own attempts to find the pair proved unsuccessful, she hired a private investigator. For the next two years, he chased down dead-end leads, all the while sucking the life out of the meager funds her husband's creditors had deemed sufficient to leave her.

In those first lonely years, Stella wove her grief through each of her days in a monotonous pattern, and waited for time to dull the memories.

But the pain and memory had not completely faded. Of course, Little Oats would be a man in his forties with a life of his own, but she couldn't help wondering if he had any memory of Nanmar Tella, or if he sometimes dreamed of a thin, gray-haired woman who rocked him in her arms and kept him safe from ferocious camels.

As the student wrapped the black nylon pressure cuff around Stella's arm, the flash of the girl's gold-filigreed necklace transported her in another dream to 1910. Her August honeymoon in Venice. In the alleyways along the canals, she watched the seventeen-year-old bride play hide-and-seek with her handsome gray-eyed husband. Hoping her voice could reach that far, she shouted into the memory, "Otis? How old are you there?"

The nurse briefly removed the ends of the stethoscope from her ears. "I turned twenty-one last week," she answered correctly for the man who darted across a courtyard and into the grasp of a massive granite lion.

His fine blond hair flew wildly about his face, and his cheeks were flushed with patches of red as if it were a freezing day. Laughing, he turned to wave, then disappeared behind the lion, taking Venice with him.

Stella waved a washcloth. "Otis, wait! I'm so tired. Wait for me!"

The rubber bladder of the cuff pinched the thin skin of her upper arm.

"Hold still, honey. Just a sec more and we'll be all done."

Stella blinked away the necklace's sparkle, concentrating on the icy touch of the stethoscope and the uncomfortable sensation of blood sluggishly pushing through the purposely constricted vessels of her arm. She had to be careful. She knew better than to ever let them think she was confused. Organic brain syndrome, senility, dementia, all meant death row. She tried to look alert.

"Hey! One twenty over seventy—not bad for an old lady, Stella."

Assuming the wise, soulful expression that the red-haired nurse had told her was the Astral Projection Practice Run look, Stella watched the girl jot down the information she'd gathered from her old lady body, and nodded knowingly. "Ahh, yes. Wonderful." *Who the hell cares?*

Seemingly fooled, the girl slung her stethoscope over her shoulder. "Don't forget to finish folding the washcloths, honey, okay?" She kissed the top of Stella's sparsely covered scalp and left her to her own devices, which these days were discouragingly few.

For lack of anything better to do, Stella idly surveyed her surroundings. There were six beds, three on each side of the room. Four of them filled with LOLs—that was the abbreviation the nurses used instead of coming right out and calling them what they were: Little Old Ladies. Loonies On Laxatives. Low On Longevity.

The end bed, the one closest to the bathroom, was stripped down to its cracked and yellow-stained plastic mattress. That had been Sarah's place until they came for her in the wee small hours and took her to the Eternal Care Unit.

Through the dark, Stella had watched them slip the naked, wasted body into the clear plastic bag and drop it onto a low steel table. The sight did not shock her or make her sad. She had been in enough nursing homes to know that waking up to find one of your roommates permanently missing was no big deal. For people like herself, death had lost its punch and become ordinary. Eventually everyone had to make the transition from the social page to the obituaries.

Sitting up in the middle bed against the far wall, Tillie picked invisible lint from her bedsheets, all the while delivering an unending stream of nonsense in a whispery monologue:

". . . and I worked so hard for that connection, but you know, I've always been a poor sleeper. Nothing means anything now, I mean women and girls just fade away to widdle tiddle and sometimes I wonder that so many of them start out that way. I don't know how I could ever keep it up, and always looking for that connection . . . the connection I fought for. Fathers can run and do anything they want and wasn't it the French boys who came here wearing dead men's coats? I ask you that . . . and in the end, after it gets dark and cold, do you think the nuns will allow us to have coffee and . . . oh, you know, those things, what are they called . . . ah yes, politicians . . . for dinner?"

Stella wondered if Tillie was disappointed that the bedsheets never talked back—but then again, for Tillie, maybe they did.

In the two window beds facing each other, Shirley and Virginia, both immobile and in the no-return stages of senility, wordlessly competed for the title of most offensive. With reckless abandon, Shirley picked her nose and deposited whatever goodies she mined on her side rails, while a rather talented Virginia simultaneously passed wind and squished lemon Jell-O and Cool Whip through her gums, allowing the small globs of transparent gelatin to waddle down the front of her gown.

After a moment of deliberation, Stella pointed at Virginia. "You win! You get the prize of a free burial for two just outside beautiful downtown Las Vegas!"

Virginia stopped squishing long enough to smile and breathe an airy, Miss America–like "Thank you," then returned to her Jell-O.

The vacant faces of the women upset Stella. She did not want that to happen to her; she wanted to go out at least knowing she was on her way.

She wheeled herself over to the windows with the bars across the bottom half, locked the brakes and pulled herself up to peer over the top rail. She didn't mind the iron grating so much as some of the other old people; she knew there was plenty to fear in the world as it was now.

A patch of sun broke through the fog and soaked her shoulders and arms with a relaxing heat. Staring past the bars, she let a smile

69

rearrange her wrinkles for no other reason than that she was tired of the void and it was too late to weep.

On the busy street corner below stood two young women dressed in business suits waiting for the light to change. Both held identical computer terminals in front of them like pregnant bellies.

A sign of the times, thought Stella, allowing her eyes to close. She wondered what young women talked about, now that they were free to say and do whatever came into their minds. How different it must be to talk about computers instead of recipes and colicky babies. Or to be free to lie with a variety of men without shame or fear of scandal. . . .

On a satin quilt she lay bathed by the flickering light from the fireplace, while a flustered young Otis knelt at her feet, awkwardly unbuttoning her shoes. It was taking him a very long time.

A sudden rush of cold at her throat forced her to shrug off the dreamy image. Alarmed, she realized the invisible thief was at hand again, sneaking toward her. The stillness that preceded him hadn't been enough of a warning this time. His approach was becoming more seductive, and she'd allowed herself to be pulled in again; the damned sun had made her a perfect target, wrapping her in its warmth, making her sleepy—susceptible to his tomfoolery.

Phooey! I've got to think! Think!

Stella snapped her eyelids open, pulled the wheelchair closer behind her, and plopped herself down hard.

Don't let him in again. Think! Save yourself.

She needed to concentrate on something, anything. Tillie was still talking to the sheets; sometimes that stream of consciousness—or unconsciousness—proved fairly amusing. Stella leaned toward the end of Tillie's bed to hear the old lady's nonsense, but all that came through was a series of muffled tones.

Turning the volume dials of her hearing aids produced a loud squawk followed by a repeated stabbing of high-pitched static. Stella angrily pulled the flesh-colored pieces of plastic from her ears and threw them against the wall. "Damned things!" she shouted, pounding her lap with her frail fist. "Lousy damned things!"

She was trapped inside a body that had turned against her. That her teeth were gone at the age of sixty hadn't even fazed her, but her failing eyesight had been the beginning of a whole different story. Her eyes, those wicked betrayers, denied her her most vital source of nourishment: Ferber, Lawrence, Dostoyevsky, Shakespeare, Poe, Thurber, cummings, Fitzgerald, the *New York Times,* and the *National Enquirer*—all gone to dry and yellowed pages of vague and blurry chicken scratches.

70

Talking books might have sustained her, but her ears were the next deserters, leaving behind Mozart, Beethoven, Berlin, the Beatles, Tommy Dorsey, and National Public Radio as just a series of vibrations and broken tones.

When her legs, hands, and back fell prey to arthritis, she gave up fighting and allowed herself to become a dog food–eating captive of the convalescent circuit.

Until recently, she'd managed to cope. But now there was the mind thief, threatening to steal her very thoughts and leave her in an endless succession of murky, winding dreams. Of all her body's betrayals, the mind thief frightened her the most.

He'd first gained access to her a year ago via the yellow pill the nurses gave her every four hours. The doctor carefully explained that he wanted her to be more "relaxed." Stella had a good laugh over that one—any more relaxed, and she'd be dead. As it turned out, relaxed was a thin hair short of coma. When she finally woke up enough to figure out what her name was, she only pretended to take the pill, cheeking it until the nurses left the room and then spitting it into her orange juice.

Not that it mattered anymore: by the time her head cleared enough to tell the difference between day and night, the thief didn't need the yellow admission tickets. He was already familiar with her, creeping up at any hour on cat-soft feet. To fight his intrusions was futile; within seconds, he could usurp her will completely and deposit her in the middle of any one of a thousand distressful memories. Of late she noticed with some degree of alarm that each time he took her, she returned feeling a little less like herself than before.

Now she felt him standing silent at her back, and stared at her hands resting on the green sill where the sun was pooling golden and warm.

Ignore him! I will not be diminished further.

Eyelids drooping slightly, she attempted to concentrate on the cracked mirror, the dripping faucet, the hospital-green walls, the smells—anything.

Recipe for sour milk cookies. Ah, let's see, one cup soured milk, three eggs . . . Our Father, who art in heaven . . . Stop this! Get it straight. Think!

Shadows of memories leaked out of dusty corners and began to bloom vividly before her.

No! Pay attention! Two cups sifted flour?

Tillie was saying . . . ? Oh yes, that old affirmation. Every day in every way, I'm getting better and . . . Concentrate, you old bag! Look. Think about hands. See the soft white . . . the pearl ring Papa gave me for my sixteenth birthday? It is so beautiful the way it shows off its luster of mauve, now pale yellow, now blue and oyster pink . . .

Wasn't it that clever Mrs. Murphy who just the other day said to Mama that in this day and age with pearls being the rage, a woman was classified in one of two ways: among those who owned pearls or those who dreamed of owning pearls?

And wasn't it Mrs. Murphy who also said Stella was the luckiest girl alive, what with managing to get engaged to the only son and heir of Redmond Otis Gallagher? Every dream she'd dared dream had come true, especially Otis. At the thought of him, her stomach turned into a sack of nervous jump frogs.

Everyone said Otis Gallagher was the handsomest young man in all of Madison County. And it was true—his face was undeniably good: fine gray eyes, strong aquiline nose, and masculine jawline. But what made her lose her heart was not his face; she was in love with his hands.

She wasn't sure when she'd first noticed them, or why they affected her so, but the very sight of them made her burn with the loving of him. Through them, she read his moods by the way his fingers moved or the way they rested on his lap. They told her what he'd done and where he'd been; they told no lies and had no secrets, save one. In that, they were true to him, giving no clues to the reason for his frequent sullen moods.

Never before had hands meant as much to her as these, and because of them, all the people she knew, or would know, were judged by the sight, the touch of their hands.

Oh Lord, please make him hurry! The ache in the vicinity of her stomach was getting worse, like a slipknot being pulled tighter.

She smoothed down the soft ash-brown hair and adjusted a hair comb. In the hall mirror, she searched her reflection boldly. Dark almond eyes, round face, and fair skin: she was not the prettiest girl in the county, but she was close to par with Otis Gallagher in wealth and social standing.

Stella ran her hands over full breasts to a waist that measured nineteen inches after her battle with the corset. Disregarding her mother's protestations that young women should not look like carved lampposts, she refused to allow her body to go to the soft pudding plumpness that was so fashionable.

She blushed as she recalled that her mother had seen her that morning without her dressing gown. The strange expression that passed over the older woman's face puzzled her, though she suspected that if she could have read her mother's mind at that moment, she would have understood the feverish unrest that lately left her tossing until dawn.

She had listened good-naturedly as her mother scolded that if a young girl insisted on wearing her corset so indecently tight, she should expect to suffer the unflattering thoughts and comments she would invite.

Not that she wasn't aware of her new womanhood—on the contrary, she was enthralled by it. The scrawny, twig-limbed Stella she'd seen in the looking glass all her life had metamorphosed into someone altogether new: a woman whose voluptuousness and innocence mingled and exuded from her pores like an exotic scent.

The sound of a new Model T drove her to the window. Discreetly peering from behind the green velvet curtains, she saw the lean figure jump gracefully from the auto and readjust his hat.

At the sight of his hands, the rope inside her moved, pulling tighter still. Contrary to every natural instinct, she sat on the settee and took up her embroidery, staring at the double pansy design but seeing nothing. All her thoughts were centered on the touch of his one open hand covering the curve of her back.

His footsteps on the veranda caused her to pull the handkerchief from her sleeve and blot the flush of moisture from her neck. Her breath stopped at the shrill ring of the bell.

And the bell rang again, and then again. . . .

Where was Dade? Why didn't she answer the door? She couldn't answer the door herself, it wouldn't be proper.

And the bell ringing a fourth time . . .

Oh Dade! She stamped her foot. What's got into that woman?

Dade's voice, that calm, deep sound, called her name.

Here I am! For God's sake, woman, answer the door! Have you gone deaf?

And the bell again.

He'll think I'm not at home and leave. Oh Dade, oh Dade, please.

Hands shook her. "Mrs. Gallagher? Stella? Mrs. . . . ?"

What's gotten into that colored woman, shouting so, and calling me Mrs. Gallagher? Lord, the woman ought to have the stupidness slapped out of her. Why, if Otis heard her . . . why, I'd die of pure mortification. Wait until I tell Mother. Wait until . . .

A cool cloth was pressed to her forehead. She forced her eyes wide to the glare of the sun, and the face of a white woman replaced the dark brown face of Dade.

"It's all right, Stella, it's me, Cat, the nurse."

Stella quickly checked her hands; they were the color of red clay, wrinkled and old. The pear ring was years gone.

73

Lightly touching the place it had once been, she understood . . . the thief had fooled her again and pulled her another inch into his world.

8 Cat waited until his mother left before she turned off his respirator and removed the connecting tubing. Attaching a T piece to the end of his endotracheal tube, she turned on the misted oxygen and set the apnea alarm.

The boy was asleep and dreaming, his eyeballs sliding around under his lids. She sat on the bed and felt his body heat as it gradually penetrated her hip.

Goddamn it to hell anyway. Seventeen years old and he wants to die? She and probably ten other people desperately wanted to know why he'd tried to end his life. And how the hell had he managed to find all the pills? Almost a dozen boxes on the comprehensive drug screen lab slip were checked off.

None of the pieces fit the usual adolescent OD profile. In the chart, the kid's personal history read like that of a model character out of "Ozzie and Harriet": a clear-cut product of a functional, somewhat yuppified existence.

The boy's mother seemed levelheaded, though appropriately concerned and confused. She'd told Cat he was popular with all the kids, especially the girls. At any time of day or night, large numbers of teenagers could be found at their home, along with an empty refrigerator. In fact, Mrs. Benner said, she was convinced there was a neon sign on their roof that read: "Welcome to Benners' International House of Adolescents—Free Room and Board."

As far as she could remember, that had all ended sometime around the first part of November, when Corky stopped bringing friends to the house and withdrew.

At first he was quieter, moodier, and less willing to discuss things with them, but they figured it was all part of the usual hormonal insanity that, like pimples, was known to erupt in teens from time to time.

By Christmas, he had dropped all extracurricular activities and refused to take phone calls. Out of desperation, they subjected him to a surprise drug screen, which came back negative. They were actually disappointed, Mrs. Benner said, because it ruled out any logical explanation for his behavior.

Still and all, the boy's parents felt the suicide attempt had come out of nowhere.

So, why?

Cat rested her hand on his bare chest and felt it rise and fall. His breathing was strong. When he awoke, she would extubate him and hope for an answer.

Inside the shell, Corky tumbled aimlessly, like a leaf in the wind. A hollow sound, like that of air rushing through a transatlantic tube, pulsated behind him. According to the rooster-shaped kitchen clock strapped to his foot, the weekly calculus test began in four minutes, and it was Mrs. King's rule never to admit latecomers. That meant missing the test, which meant he'd get an automatic fail, and that would blow his average and then Coach Henny would have to drop him from the team, and then they'd lose the state championships, and then the whole school, including Molly, would hate him, and his whole life would be ruined forever and ever. No one would believe the story about the monster that had reduced him to the size of an ant and imprisoned him in a pink shell that smelled faintly of Lysol.

The hollow whistling noise grew closer; the monster was in pursuit and gaining on him. Using all his strength, Corky hurled his body against the flesh-pink surface of the shell. As the walls crumbled, a sharp pain tore his throat and a gush of cold air filled his lungs. Whatever had been behind him was held back by the light of day.

When he opened his eyes, he was flying, his shadow sliding grace-fully over the roofs of his neighborhood. Dipping and soaring, he visited backyards, flew in and out of open garages, picked a perfect persimmon from the top of Colindorf's tree, and made the bell in St. Adolphe's tower ring by smashing it with the rooster clock. With the bell's clanging signal, the roofs abruptly peeled away from their rafters, leaving what looked like rows of dollhouses with their tops removed.

Corky sailed down over Andy Leland's house for a closer look. Inside, Mr. Leland drank shots straight from a liquor bottle while Mrs. Leland lay sweating under Mr. Colindorf across the street. In a pink lace bedroom at the end of the block, pale little Annie Kochman carefully placed a small ball of crack in the gaily decorated pipe she'd made in her under-twelve crafts class, and lighted up.

He changed direction and drifted, staring up at the blue ceiling until the sick feeling subsided. Within a few minutes, a strong gust lifted him up and over a fog bank and set him down six blocks away.

As he hovered over a large Victorian, he saw a hermaphrodite standing naked before a mirror, smearing clown white over its breasts and heavily bearded face. Quickening its movements, it painted on an absurdly wide red mouth, donned a bulbous red rubber nose, then slipped under a shower nozzle dangling from the center of the sky. Instead of water, streams of red, white, and yellow silk flowed forth, covering it in the uniform of a clown. Its small, round eyes shone with a dull luster when it pointed at him and laughed the deep, eerie laugh of a man.

At once, Corky forced himself to fly from the grotesque man-woman writhing in its silk cocoon, and headed toward an interesting 1950s bungalow that had pink flamingos decorating the front yard like so much gaudy lawn jewelry.

Through the bungalow's transparent walls, he watched as a 1950s June Cleaver mother cheerfully orchestrated a meal in her all-electric kitchen. In the living room, reading the daily news before a crackling storybook fire, sat a 1950s Ward Cleaver father attired in a plaid corduroy jacket with matching slippers. On the hearth rug lay a well-groomed blond cocker spaniel.

It was a scene of such perfect domestic harmony that it occurred to him the characters might be the test dummies used in the fifties to study the effects of a nuclear blast on humans in their normal environment.

Corky was maneuvering himself for a quick getaway when he caught sight of a familiar face through the upstairs bedroom window. A Dixon Ticonderoga No. 2 pencil clenched between her even white teeth, Molly Connover sat at her desk and stared at the wall the same way she stared at the blackboard in Mrs. Way's fifth-period English class—as if it were a screen filled with combination Walt Disney–

Mitchell Brothers daydreams. On the desk, *Crime and Punishment*, Mrs. Way's latest reading assignment, lay open at page 2.

Molly pushed back the waist-length blonde hair framing her salon-tanned, blue-eyed California girl face and lazily stretched her long legs. Scanning the perfect bikini body, Corky had to bite the back of his hand to keep himself from barking.

Molly leaned just the right distance forward on her left elbow to show off a large portion of her ample cleavage. His body chemistry went berserk. Without blinking, he stared at the cream-colored bulges of baby flesh pushing out from the lacy border of her brassiere like neatly licked scoops of vanilla ice cream nestled in their waffle cones. Firm yet ravishingly tender, those B cup mounds taunted him, pleading for one quick, accidental feel or a deliberate, slobbery kiss.

Molly caught him looking and blushed like a virgin. Giving him one of her little Christ on the Cross smiles, she pulled her blouse closed and pretended to go back to her book.

For a while he hovered on the wind, joyously happy knowing that Molly Connover and her breasts existed. That was normal—life as it should be forever.

Breaking the moment, a slight stir, an increase in the pulsing sci-fi movie sound track, made him shift his gaze to his right, to the bathroom window. Someone dressed in a clown's suit hid in the shower, waiting.

As he floated closer for a better look, the bathroom door swung open and a second Corky, a Corky clone, entered and walked toward the toilet to relieve himself, totally unaware of the threat at his back.

Frantic, the flying Corky yelled at his pissing clone. "Look out, dude! Behind the door! Get the fuck out of there, man. He's going to . . . He's . . ."

But the Corky in the bathroom could not hear him. He did not notice the clown slip out from behind the shower curtain, fumbling with the front of his balloon pants. The peeing Corky was thinking only of Molly Connover and breasts; a monster in a clown suit was the farthest thing from his mind.

Corky shrieked against the wind and drew the clown monster's attention away from his clone. The hideous face twisted upward, its evil red-rimmed eyes eagerly scanning Corky's body. Before Corky could move, an absurdly long black snake came from the clown's opened fly and wound itself around him, gripping like a boa constrictor, squeezing until he choked.

77

9 Looking greenishly pale under the harsh fluorescent lights of Ward Two's kitchen, Nora continued to complain as she mixed the granola and plain yogurt in a stainless steel emesis basin.

"So then he says, I swear to God he really did"—Nora crossed her heart and hoped to die—" 'What's a nice girl like you doing in a generally unrewarding and morally questionable job like this?' "

She stirred the contents of the basin, added another handful of granola, pulled out one of her own long blonde hairs coated with yogurt, and then stirred again, secretly pleased that her culinary creation would give Julia Child a complete respiratory arrest.

"So I say, 'Well bud, the way I figure it is, we're nurses because we've done something really bad in this life or maybe the last few. I mean *really* horrible things, like torturing too many flies when we were kids, or killing our whole family by putting ant poison in the iced tea. So, the only way to work off all that bad karma is to be a nurse.' "

Nora held a spoonful of the dreadful-looking yogurt mixture to Cat's mouth, making no move to actually eat the stuff herself. Obediently Cat accepted the concoction.

"Anyway," Nora continued, "the guy can't believe nursing is all that bad, so I tell him the story abut the dinosaur of a copy machine that lives in our report room. Three times a day, for up to forty-five minutes a shot, nurses, sometimes pregnant ones, sit in the 8-by-10 foot, nonventilated hole, breathing the black powdered toner that the damned machine spews out.

"I told him that when the nurses started to complain that their white washcloths turn gray when they shower, and their Q-tips come out black, the director of nursing blew them off. She said the manu-facturer who rents these things out to the hospital, guarantees that the stuff is totally safe for us to breathe, and that the hospital policy says the machines are safe—and cheap—so just drop the subject."

"I've got an even better one," Cat said, spraying an oat onto her chin. "About a month ago I overheard one of our nurses tell the supervisor she had to have an operation and needed two weeks off. The supervisor said, "You want *another* medical leave?! That really messes up the schedule!'

" 'I'm sorry,' the nurse said politely, 'but I've just been told they didn't get all the cancer the first time.'

"The supervisor didn't even blink. She just turned to the nurse and said, 'Well, it would seem to me you could pick a more conve-nient time to have this done.' "

Cat laughed until she noticed that a sad, beaten look had come over Nora's face. "God I'm hungry," she said. "It's miserable serving breakfast to everybody else when you're starving."

Nora nodded in agreement. "What I do," she said, using the spoon as a pointer, "is, when I deliver the tray and take the lids off the plates, I bend inward at the middle a little, suck in my cheeks, and let my eyelids kinda hang all droopy, trying to look as much like a *Vogue* model as possible. Then I say something in a starved, wavy gravy voice like, 'Do you think you'll want your oatmeal this morn-ing, Mrs. Smith?'

"If that doesn't work, I usually stick the spoon in the middle of it and pull the whole gelatinous mess out of its Mocha Mix nest. 'Oh-oh,' I say, looking as concerned as possible, 'I see you've ordered one of the poisonous porridge pops.' That usually does it—the pa-tient gives the tray the old hairy eyeball and turns the whole thing over to me untouched. I must admit, someone in the Pit makes de-cent toast, and the fresh fruit is basically safe."

"Personally"—Cat sipped her decaf laden with skim milk and sub-stitute sugar—"I wouldn't touch anything that came from the Food Pit." She took another mouthful, winced, and tried to ignore the fact that the granola was getting mushy. "I mean, have you ever read the description of the Pit that's in the hospital propaganda booklet?"

Nora shook her head.

" 'Nutritional Services'—a misnomer if I ever heard one—'is where the patient's delicious food is expertly prepared.' What they leave out is how the dieticians have their masters in the art of extract-ing and discarding every bit of flavor and nutrition from the four

79

basic food groups, specializing in opening canned vegetables, then cooking them down to paste. Last year they apparently took first prize in the Grand National Powdered Potato Glue-off.

"The pamphlet ends by saying—and I quote here, 'The Nutritional Department is situated in the bowels of Mercy Hospital, right next door to the Department of Mortuary Affairs.' "

"Sounds like the correct location for the kitchen," Nora said. "I mean, considering what the food actually tastes like. Did you know that the infamous *they* did a study on the nutritional value of hospital food, and they discovered that if a person were to eat nothing but hospital food for six months, he would die of malnutrition?"

Cat dried her coffee cup and hung it on the peg that had once been marked "Richardson" but had recently been edited to "Bitchardson." "Well, Nora, thank you for sharing that with the class today, and now I think I'll go warn the patients about the killer lunch trays. After that, I will extubate the teenage OD, put Stella on the commode again, turn and clean Detlef, put the AIDS patient on a cooling blanket, serve the dreaded lunch trays, see if Lucy Cross is awake, do everybody's meds, do second checks on the OD and Walker, turn and clean Detlef, ditto for my AIDS man, and on and on and on *ad infinitum*, and thank you, Scaly Scanlin, you wretched son of a bitch, for setting me back two hours."

"Yeah," said Nora. "Can't say I'll mourn that one."

Cat leaned heavily against the kitchen door. "Let's face it, Nor, the idea that our medical system is some sort of all-powerful benevolent mother that's required to spread an equal share of love to everybody is bullshit. When we take care of a hateful person, something inside of us recognizes them as a thing gone bad and rotting; it's human instinct to sidestep it, ignore it, and get the damned thing buried as quickly as possible."

Cat wondered if it was a sign of aging that she had a tendency lately to go on about things like some windbag philosophy professor emeritus.

After a molasses moment, Nora shrugged indifferently. "Yeah, so?"

That set them off laughing, until Nora aspirated an oat and choked. Wiping the laugh dew from their eyes and the choke spit from Nora's chin, they moved on to the burned raisin toast Nora had pilfered from the breakfast trays. Cat spread a thick pat of margarine over the charred bread and was automatically reminded of the way burned flesh absorbed ointment. Quickly killing the thought, she picked out all the raisins and carefully placed them, one by one, on Nora's toast.

Raisins, she explained, looked too much like prune progeny, and that said it all right there.

"By the way . . ." Cat lowered her voice and glanced suspiciously at the corners of the ceiling as if to make sure there weren't any hidden microphones. "You didn't by any chance see that guy who was looking for Lucy Cross this morning, did you?"

"You mean the black curly hair with the unusually sweet face and the cream-your-jeans smile?"

"You noticed."

"I couldn't help it since there were about five other females doing heavy breathing after he showed up. He's the investigator for the Lucy Cross case. He's supposed to find the psycho boyfriend who tried to kill her."

"Hmmmmm."

"No, he's not; I asked."

Cat cocked her head innocently. "Beg your pardon?"

Nora dried the emesis basin and set it in its hiding place in the empty fuse box under the paint-by-number Renoir. "Not married, forty-four years old, four years divorced, no kids, a smart-ass mouth, lonely, and from what I could surmise in a few seconds, unbelievably bright. Just your type."

Cat suddenly became absorbed in wiping down the already immaculate cabinet doors; she didn't want to ruin her long-standing reputation as a forlorn, asexual old maid. "Sounds like you got to him first. Finders keepers."

"Your smug and unruffled attitude needs work, darling. You know the only men I like are the extreme left fielders, the ones that grow feathers and fur instead of hair."

Interrupted by the nurse alert bell, both women moved quickly into the hall.

"Well, horsepoop." Nora sighed. "My new admit is here and I didn't even tell you about what happened last night. How about dinner at Angelo's?"

"Sure, if we survive the day." Cat headed toward Stella's room. "What's your admission?"

"A three-hundred-and-fifty-pound pneumonia, complete with bedsores running over with staph-infested pus the color of the yogurt we just ate."

Cat blinked several times and swallowed hard. Sometimes, even after all the years of feces, urine, vomit, and blood, just a description would get her.

"Now *that* was really lovely, Nora. Very clear. Excellent mental

81

image. Why don't you use it in your charting? 'The color of the yogurt my friend and I ate for breakfast.' I think it will thrill the chart reviewers."

Nora's whinny echoed down the hallway.

10 Stella had a heavy-cream sort of calmness about her that reminded Cat of the sensation of swimming in a warm pond on a still summer's night. Not that a lot of the older folks didn't have similar qualities, but Stella seemed to have just a tad more life force shining from her eyes. The woman was rich with an inner knowledge born of years of patience, though Cat's intuition contended there was a persistent dark spot in the center of Stella's ninety-five-year-old soul which the old lady had not been able to erase.

Choked into semipermanent incapacitation by their own red tape, social services dragged their heels finding her a new home. She had been temporarily placed in Turf Tundra simply because there was no place else for her to go.

In hospital jargon, Stella was an LOL classified as MA in NAD, or mentally alert and in no apparent distress. That meant she was minimal care, requiring nothing other than help moving from bed to wheelchair and back again. In terms of healthcare, Stella's main problem was that she was old, broke, and needed more of people's time than was available, especially since time in a hospital was at a premium.

Cat was well aware of the hospital budget efficiency game, wherein care was rationed out to the patient according to a perverted sliding scale of who's who at the bank and the insurance companies. At the bottom of the scale were the elderly, and the unwritten rules regarding their care were strictly enforced.

Rule 1. Don't waste your time. They're going to die soon no matter what you do. Save your time for the younger ones who still have plenty of chips left to play with.

Rule 2. Don't waste the frills. Nine out of ten don't have any money. Medicare doesn't cough up much, so save the frills for Mr. Bigbucks.

Rule 3. Don't waste hospital beds. Move 'em out, ready or not. Save the beds for paying customers who won't stay so long. Keep the faces on Senility Lane moving.

In the hospital corporation's eyes, old folks were not equal, period. Phrases like "quality of life" and "life expectancy" made the over-seventy crowd sound like superannuated nuisances: subhumans you patted on the head and called "dear" or "honey" because using real names made them seem too much like real people who'd lived real lives. The system was criminal, geared toward putting the elderly out to pasture to die.

Going against the grain, Cat guessed she liked the over-seventy crowd the best. They were easy. Been-through-it-already mellow. Ask one of them a question, get a straight answer. No fooling around. They didn't have anything to hide. The only old people she had a hard time with were the ones who believed the rules and gave up.

Cat stood next to Stella's Twiggy-thin body tucked into the ancient wheelchair and stared into the old lady's eyes. No matter what the corporation said, this was a viable human being with a mind, who had managed to survive.

"Aw, fuck 'em!" Cat said suddenly.

Stella slowly looked up at the big redhead with the gray eyes like Otis's. "Whatcha say, dear?"

Cupping Stella's better ear, Cat yelled, "I said, screw the bastards. Don't you agree?"

Stella gave Cat the thumbs-up sign. "You betcha, sister."

Cat laughed and hugged her, delighted by the old woman's willingness to hop on the bandwagon. "And who do you think we should be screwing today, Stel?"

"Whoever the hell needs it!" Stella shouted, ripe for a good old-fashioned brawl.

"Where're your hearing aids so I don't have to scream?" Cat screamed.

"Under the bed, under the sink, in the toilet—I don't know.

I pitched them"—the old woman waved in the direction of the door—"somewhere the hell over there."

On hands and knees, Cat retrieved the flesh-toned earpieces, one from under Tillie's bed and one from behind the wastebasket. After she had dug out the hardened earwax from the tubes, she replaced the batteries and fit the devices neatly into Stella's ear canals.

The paging system belched out a call for Dr. Cramer.

"God Almighty!" Stella exclaimed in wonderment. "I can hear."

"Isn't that amazing, Stel?" Cat said. "With just a little care and patience, you could hear everything and people wouldn't have to yell at you. You wouldn't have to be isolated from—"

"Save the lectures, girlie," Stella cut in, "I've heard them all by now, and besides, I have to use the commode."

Little old ladies urinated more than anyone on earth. Having more than two LOLs per patient assignment could turn a nurse's shift into a nightmare. The only thing worse were LOLs on diuretics. Ladies of Leaks.

With Stella safely placed on the rolling potty chair, Cat pulled off a length of toilet paper and absently wound it around her fingers. Older patients especially were seldom bothered by her presence when they took care of their bodily functions. She'd probably had thousands of conversations with patients while they defecated, urinated, vomited, passed wind, bled and died. People expected that of nurses. They were counted on to be intimate strangers who never turned a hair at anything.

"In nursing school, they used to call this an after dinner rose," she said, holding out the wad of toilet paper, which, if you scrunched up your eyes and went into a stone stare, actually did look like a white rose.

The old woman took the tissue and cleaned herself, pulling it back out to inspect it—another human trait found mostly in the elderly. Cat was never really sure what they expected to see.

What Stella did see at that moment was Cat's feet. She squinted to make sure she was seeing correctly, a stricken look crossing her face.

"Are those shoes the right size for you, young lady?" she asked politely.

Cat nodded quietly and blushed.

Stella whistled. "Oh. Some kind of operation?"

"No, I inherited them from my father." Cat measured the old lady's urine and checked the odor and clarity for any signs of infection. "But my mother used to tell the neighbors the doctor dropped me on my feet and all the growth hormones fell down into my toes."

84

"What hogwash!" Stella clucked her tongue in sympathy and settled back into her wheelchair.

"I know. But you wouldn't believe how many people there are walking around Boston today who still believe it."

Using a wet, soapy washcloth, Cat carefully washed the woman's hands. "Okay now . . . what are we going to do with you, Stel?"

Stella thought for a while, at first scanning the ceiling, then tracking the path of the soapy washcloth. She studied the redhead's large, elegant hands and smiled. They were capable and strong, like the woman herself.

"I think the best thing," she said, wiping her hands dry on the towel Cat handed her," would be to throw me down the laundry chute and be done with me—that's my guess."

"Oh no, uh-uhn . . . too easy. We've got to come up with something better than that, Stel." Cat took one of the arthritis-sculptured hands into her own freckled amazon mitt and squeezed gently. "I mean, go at it from this standpoint—if you could do anything, what would you want to do?"

Staring down into her lap, Stella shrugged. "Nothin'."

"Well, at least you didn't say you wanted to die."

"Yeah, well, that was my second choice."

"Oh come on, Stel, I mean really, truly, and honestly, what would you like to do for the rest of your life? You're too full of it just to sit around waiting for your three meals and the Grim Reaper."

Stella gummed the side of her tongue and let some spit dribble out of the corner of her mouth. She was hoping the woman would go away, although she knew from experience redheads were stubborn as blueberry stains. All in all, she was glad this one wasn't one of those deathly pale redheads who looked so skeletal; that kind always made her think of the Holocaust newsreels.

After a while, Stella checked out the nurse's face; the carrot-top wasn't going down easy. "You really want to know?"

"I really do."

The old woman worked her mouth, flicking invisible crumbs from her lips. "More than anything in the world . . ."

"What, Stella? What do you want?"

"The thing I'd give my eyeteeth to do? If I had 'em?" She didn't want to, but she couldn't help letting a smile break at one corner of her mouth.

"Ummmmm, yeah?"

"I want to learn how to throw a ball like a man."

Cat knew that where there was piss and vinegar, there was hope.

11 Carefully peeling back strips of adhesive tape from the boy's peach-fuzzed face, Cat let the air escape from the cuff of the endotracheal tube and quickly pulled the long plastic piece from his airway. He retched once and his Adam's apple bobbed, moving the smooth skin of his neck. The death grip he held on the bedcovers turned his knuckles white, although his distress did not seem to bother his redheaded tormentor.

"Come on. Give me some big, deep breaths!" the woman growled in gestapo fashion, making him wonder if he was caught in a "Hogan's Heroes" nightmare.

The large fräulein leaned over to adjust his pillow, her substantially proportioned breasts blocking his view.

"Do you hear me? I want biiiiig, deeeeeeep breaths and I want them now!"

She placed two green oxygen-blasting prongs into his nostrils and proceeded to methodically wash away the black lines of tape residue from around his mouth with a hot washcloth that smelled of alcohol and soap.

Unable to suck in enough air past the fire in his throat, he turned quietly hysterical, the adolescent code of bravery not permitting him to blatantly signal his distress by screaming or crying. He twitched pathetically as a silent-panic rash covered his body.

The redheaded Brünnhilde was still unmoved.

"I'm—" He stopped, pushed over the boundaries of bravery by the sound of his voice, or rather, the lack of it. *I'm fucking dying!*"

"Nope," Cat said calmly; extubation panic was not uncommon.

86

"You're about three days too late for that, kiddo. Almost, but not quite—your mother found you before you made the grade."

She slipped her arm around his shoulders. "Try to relax and take slow, deep breaths. I'll give you some ice chips for your throat."

The boy wiped his front teeth with his tongue, closed his eyes briefly, and let his tense muscles sag.

Cat spooned ice chips into his mouth.

Savoring their chill, Corky let several whole chips slide down his throat. For a few seconds, the fire was extinguished.

"How long?" he croaked, greedily accepting another spoonful.

"Let's see, you came in Thursday night, so that's five days if you count today. Nobody's really sure why you're still alive. You took enough pills to kill a workhorse, let alone an assortment that would have kept the entire 1969 graduating class of Berkeley *and* UCLA in a stoned-out coma for months."

She stopped scrubbing and looked him in the eyes. "You must have really been hurt to try something like this, but"—she slapped his knee and stood—"I'm glad you didn't make it."

His face dissolved into sadness. Breaking the moment between them, he focused his gaze first on her breasts then on her shoes. Startled, he mumbled something like "Holy hot dogs" and looked away.

She ignored the reaction, and emptied his urinary drainage bag into a clear cylinder.

"See the color of your pee? That means you're a little dehydrated. I'm going to let the rest of your IV run in, but then you've got to start drinking some fluids on your own so we can get that tube out of your bladder."

The teenager's hand shot under the covers and felt the silicone catheter protruding from the end of his penis.

"Oh shit, what's wrong with my dick?" Corky's hoarse whisper cracked with urgency. "Oh man, they messed up my dick!"

The boy's eyes were so wide Cat blinked for him. "Relax. Nobody did anything to your penis. We had to insert the catheter because people in comas don't usually knock off for bathroom breaks. This way your pee drains into a bag instead of the bed, since marinating in the stuff isn't exactly great for your skin. Not only that, but it saves wear and tear on the nurses and generally lets us know how well the kidneys function after having to filter all those pills out of your system. You can also have a slight fever so the more fluids you drink, the better."

Corky squeezed his eyes shut as if he were enduring the tortures of hell. "What's your name?"

"Catalina, like the island, but you can call me Cat."

"Okay, Cat, like please, I'm gonna go outta my friggin' mind if you don't take that thing outta there, like right *now!*"

"Okay, I'll tell you what, Calvin, I'll make you a deal. If I take that tube out now, you've got to promise to drink at least six glasses of water or fruit juice to get yourself peeing. Okay?"

He grimaced. "Calvin is *totally* tweaked. The dudes call me Corky. Apple juice with lots of ice, please."

"Hey man," Cat said, snapping her fingers and strutting, "it's like totally cool, Corky dude. Fluid replacement is on its way, so hang tight and be loose."

The teenager rolled his eyes and sank back into his pillow. The aftermath was going to be tweaked to the absolute max.

CALVIN "CORKY" BENNER: Ward Two, 500 acute. 1215 hrs:

Neuro: Alert and oriented × 4, PERLA, all reflexes intact, equal grips with good strength. Short- and long-term memory unimpaired. (After the deluge, the attic was found intact.)

Cardiovascular: Blood pressure stable. Pt. remains febrile at 100.2, color pink, skin warm and dry. Good pulses, no edema, negative Homans, no extra heart tones or distended neck veins. Normal sinus rhythm without ectopy. (A lively, kicking specimen.) Ran in last liter of D5W.45NS and heparin-locked IV.

Pulmonary: Post extubation: breath sounds diminished but all fields clear. ABGs good on room air. (Could blow a candle off a cake at ten feet.)

Gastrointestinal: Tolerating fluids well. C/O hunger. (Asking for a double-garlic, anchovy, and pineapple pizza.) Remains on clear liquids at this time. Abdomen soft and non-tender with hyperactive bowel sounds. (They talked to me. Passing flatus which rattled the windows.)

Genitourinary: Foley catheter removed @ 0930. (Pt. made nurse keep her eyes closed during entire procedure.) Has not voided at this time. (But we're waiting with bated breath.) Bladder slightly distended. (With the liter of D5W.45NS, five cups of H_2O and four cans of apple juice, why isn't the kid floating?)

Musculoskeletal: Sat up at bedside without problems. Noted badly scraped and swollen knuckles of right hand. Asked pt. if he'd been abusing walls lately. Pt. states these are old wrestling injuries. (Unadulterated B.S. unless he's been wrestling with concrete blocks.)

Psychosocial: Pt. quiet and cooperative but offering no explanations for suicide attempt at this time. Marked anxiety exhibited when visited by family. (The dude totally wigged out. Had to be coaxed down off the ceiling after mom and dad left.)

Plan: Will call Dr. Leffler regarding moving patient to Ward Two step-down and request psychiatric consult. (I won't hold my breath on this one either.) Will encourage pt. to express his feelings. (Definitely still holding my breath.)

C. Richardson RN

The chart reviewers found Ms. Richardson's unusual style disconcerting, improper, horrifying, sometimes useful, and generally entertaining.

"Yeah, yeah, yeah, so whaddaya want? This is Dr. Leffler. Somebody paged me? Oh Jesus! Oh! Son of a bitch . . ."

"Hi, Dr. Leffler? This is Cat in Ward Two. I called about two patients. First, Mrs. Cejaka? Can we go ahead and extubate her? Nora thinks she's overdue for extubation."

"No. Uhn-uh. No— Jesus Keeeeerist! Look at that! Yiieee . . . WHAT! Penalty? Interference? Whaddaya kiddin me? NO WAY! He never touched that motherhumpin' son of a bitch! *How* many yards? That son of a—

"Ahhh, the answer is no on that, Pat. The old lady doesn't have the strength to cough up her secretions."

"Sorry, Dr. Leffler, but that's not true. Nora was cleaning her tube this morning and Mrs. Cejaka coughed up a mucus plug with enough force to stick it to the ceiling. Her color is great, she's been stable for over two days, and I think—"

"What? Oh man, oh Jesus. Hey, Bob, hit rewind. I gotta see that again. Was it an incomplete pass? Was it? They called a what? Son of a bitch!

"Hey, look Pat, when did you get your medical degree? I'm the doctor here, and I don't want her extubated—she's too weak."

"The name is Catalina, and I think the nurses taking care of her twenty-four hours a day happen to know how the patient is doing better than someone who sees her for five minutes every other day. The lady unhooks herself from the respirator each morning and walks around the room doing exercises with Richard Simmons! How can you tell me—"

"Whooooeeee! Way to go, Montana! Look at that son of a bitch go! Holy shit! Sweat, you motherjumping suckers! *Yeah!*

"Hey, look Cantina, don't question me about this matter. I'm the doctor—I happen to know what's best. Therefore, I'll say it one more time: I don't want her extubated, and when I do, I'll come in and do it myself. The nurses don't have any business doing that anyway."

"Catalina Richardson, not Cantina or Pat or even Carol, but that's okay, Dr. Leffler, don't worry about it. We'll just tell Mrs. Cejaka that she has to wait until you've viewed all the videos of the football games you missed this last season before she can be extubated. Of course, by that time her trachea will be rotted away, but what the hell.

"And moving right along to my second set of requests, I want to transfer the Benner boy to step-down as soon as possible, and I was hoping you could call in the psychiatric consult now. His ABGs and vitals are good except for a temp of 100.2. Before I extubated him, I got a sputum specimen for culture and sensitivity and as soon as he gives us some urine I'll get a C and S on that too. He appears to be pretty depressed so I think if we could get somebody in right away to talk to him while he's still—"

"YIIIIIIIIIEEEEEEEEESHEEEEIT! Did he get the ball? *Who* got the ball? WHO THE HELL'S GOT THE GODDAMNED BALL? Rewind! REWIND!"

In the background, a chorus of male voices roared a variety of curses.

"Dr. Leffler? Hello?"

"Why the GODDAMNED HELL don't they pull that asshole offa the damn field? What the HELL are they doing out there?"

"Dr. Leffler? Did you hear—"

"Yeah, yeah, sure. Use your nursing judgment, Maureen—that's what you girls are paid for. Do whatever you want. Listen, honey, I gotta go . . . there's a real emergency here. Bye."

Placing the phone back on its cradle, Cat sighed, wondering for the millionth time why she hadn't taken her mother's advice and gone into cleaning toilets for a living.

Corky was watching "Mr. Rogers' Neighborhood" and appeared to be enjoying it. Cat had never been able to account for people's tastes in television viewing, although there seemed to be certain patterns: Bored by the news and the stock reports, nine out of ten high-powered business execs could be mesmerized by the morning cartoons or any of the game shows. Old ladies loved to watch "Geraldo" and movies in which overt sexuality was displayed, while old men preferred "Oprah" and sitcoms.

No hospitalized human, as far as she knew, ever watched daytime soaps.

90

Holding out a new plastic urinal, Cat purposely blocked the adolescent's view of the screen, on which Mr. Rogers was in the process of closing the show, singing the "Tomorrow" song while neatly hanging up his famous cardigan sweater.

"Well, kid, the good news is that as soon as Dr. Barza comes up to talk to you, you're going to the step-down unit. The bad news is that if you don't pee now, I'll have to shove a catheter back into your bladder." She put a sinister amount of emphasis on the word "shove" without feeling any guilt whatsoever.

Corky grabbed for the urinal. "I'll pee." The gravelly voice was smoothing out, ready to fall to the edge of sand level.

Cat drew the curtains around his bed and began packing up his belongings—the bedside kit with toothbrush, Kleenex, and mouthwash, and a plastic bag containing the clothes he had been wearing on admission: gray baggies, neon-orange canvas belt, black T-shirt with the logo *Skate on Haight*. As usual, there was no footwear. It was her experience that most people attempted suicide barefoot.

She listened to the silence coming from the other side of the curtain. "It might burn a little at first, but that's all. Just let 'er rip, kiddo."

She leaned against the wall and wiped the inside corners of her eyes. An offensively ugly gray ball of makeup mixed with mucus stuck to her finger. Making a face, she rinsed it off under the faucet. After that, she adjusted the Velcro bands on her running shoes, braided her hair, snapped the band of her underpants, and clicked her incisors together in time to an unnamed tune which had been brewing in the back of her mind since she woke up that morning.

"I can't do this while you're standing there," Corky said through the curtain, sounding mortified. "Like, I mean, I can hear you twitching or whatever it is you're doing over there."

"Oh, sorry. I'll run down and get you a set of P.J.'s. I'm going to let the water run into your bath basin over here. The sound might help you get started."

"Umm, yeah, okay."

Behind the curtain, Corky listened to the water trickling from the faucet and imagined himself under a warm waterfall. He felt his bladder full and pressing, then relaxed and let go.

Not a drop issued forth.

His mind exploded in I-read-it-in-the-*Enquirer* flashes of panic. What if the tube blocked him up so he could never piss again? He'd heard of people dying from urine backing up into the blood. Worse yet, what if he had to have an operation and have a tube in his penis forever?

91

Sweat broke out between his eyebrows at the atrocious visions. Maybe—he felt like ralphing—maybe he'd burst something and have to pee out of a hole in his stomach or—argh!—maybe even his leg. He had to pee or they'd put that catheter back in, and there was no way in hell he could take that again.

He glanced briefly at his penis, then concentrated on the gold and yellow labels of the remaining juice cans sitting on his bedside table. When the light broke, a wide though not very innocent grin spread across his face.

In the dark linen closet, Cat dug through the soft flannel bath blankets and came up with one complete set of pajamas. She next picked out a patient gown and slipped it over her uniform, folded up the hem to form a large pocket, then tied the corners together tightly around her waist. Shoving her hands inside the large pouch, she leaned against the wall to sort through the information she had gathered thus far. The kid could use five more minutes to pee.

All right. So far, the kid was awake and already showing signs of putting up adolescent-strength resistance against letting anyone know why he wanted to die. None of the information she had gleaned gave her the sense he was a suicidal type; there had to be a specific and horrific reason.

So, where were the clues?

Cat again went over her initial conversation with the boy's mother, fine-combing every word. Twenty-three seconds later, she jerked herself away from the wall and made a beeline for Calvin Benner's chart.

Amidst the hectic bustle and noise around the main nurses' station, Cat flipped open the gray plastic chart to the section marked "Medical-Social History" and plodded through Dr. Leffler's tightly linear hen scratches.

Family Hx.: No siblings. Normal growth development. Usual childhood diseases.
Patient is a healthy-appearing, well-developed adolescent male in his senior year of high school. He is active in sports, excelling in baseball, basketball, and wrestling. Patient maintains a B average. Hobbies include backpacking, surfing, skiing, and girl watching.
Dec. 80—appendectomy
Jul. 83—tonsillitis

Jan. 85—pleurisy
Apr. 86—wrestling injury: separated left shoulder.
Dec. 86—Drug screen as requested by parents, negative.

Cat closed the chart feeling a general uneasiness. The subtle flip of her stomach and the tug behind her eyes were warning her to listen to her intuition.

As she watched the chaos of the unit, her eyes filled with tears.

The urinal was one quarter full: 250 cc's. Cat could see that the boy was pleased with himself: the corners of his mouth were turned up slightly. It was his first positive expression since his admission.

"Great job, kiddo, you're a real pisser," Cat said, pouring 60 cc's into a specimen cup.

Corky nervously twisted his fingers. "Hey, wait a minute— what're you gonna do with that pee?"

"Well, I thought I'd have the laboratory tech divide it up into small portions and send it to all your friends with insulting notes and sign your name to them."

His face fell.

"Sheesh, the kid has no sense of humor. Lighten up, bud—it's just going to the lab for a routine test."

He thought for a minute, then motioned her closer. "Bring it over here for a sec, will ya?"

"You want to see your urine specimen?" Cat shrugged and set the cup on the bedside table. "Well, that's okay. I once had a cousin who used to get off on peeing into hot-water bottles and selling them at football games to old ladies with cold hands."

He raised his eyebrows, pulled the cap off the cup, and gulped down the specimen. "Ahhhh, that's some awesome brew. Bring me the rest of the bottle, wench!"

Holding her stomach with one hand, Cat covered her mouth with the other. "Oh my God, tell me you did not do what you just did."

"What do you mean?" he said innocently. "This is killer home-made stuff. It's supposed to make your hair shine." He shoved the cup under her nose. "Here, have a swig."

Cat pushed the cup away, but not before she got a strong whiff of apples.

"Why you swamp-sucking little rat." Playfully she grabbed the boy by the neck of his gown and twisted the material. "Not only did you get me but you still haven't peed! What the hell am I supposed to tell

93

Dr. Leffler, you little creepola? Ooooh, just wait until I catheterize you, buddy. You won't walk for a week!"

Corky raised his hand.

Cat rolled her eyes. "What? What do you want?"

"When you're done, could I get another urinal? I have to righteously pee."

When he was through and the specimen safely on its way to the lab, Corky smiled again, though not very much. "Until I was about ten years old, I thought my pee was carbonated."

Cat's smile was uncertain. "Huh?"

"You know, like when a guy pisses, it hits the water all foamy and there's a lot of bubbles? Well, see, I thought—"

Cat's initial howl of laughter startled, then encouraged him.

"If you think *that's* funny, when I was in the sixth grade, I was taking a shower one night, and I'm soaping up, sort of checking things out down there like a regular curious kid, when I see this, like, you know that ridge line down the middle of my testicles?

"So, having heard the usual playground version of the facts of life, I put two and two together and come to the slightly messed-up conclusion that my parents had me castrated at birth.

"Totally freaked, I go charging out of the shower like some kind of raging animal, all soapy and pissed off and crying, and I run screaming into the living room, where my parents are entertaining a couple of business associates of my dad's, right?"

Cat bent at the waist, her laughter advancing now into wheezes. Corky allowed a small chuckle to escape.

"So there I am in the middle of the living room, all naked and totally bummed, wailing and flailing away. ''Oh, why did you do it, Mom and Dad? Why did you have my balls taken out? What did you do with my balls? Didn't you know I wanted to have kids someday? What about your grandchildren? Oh shit, my balls, my balls, they've cut off my balls.

"I went on all weirded out like that for a while. I remember my parents and the two business people just kept on sitting there frozen like they were permanent residents of Suspended Animation City for the whole time I was raving.

"My mom snapped out of it first and literally picked me up and carried me to my room. Finally my dad had to come in and show me that his balls were exactly the same as mine, before I'd calm down. He still had a hell of a time trying to convince me that *everybody* had

94

that line down the middle of their balls. Total bummer. Man, I thought it was probably some sort of weird family trait going back to the Dark Ages . . . like hairy earlobes."

Holding on to the sink for support, Cat gasped for air, wiped her eyes, panted for a moment, then started in again with an even louder wheeze. She was pounding the wall when Nora stopped in. Staring at her friend for a few seconds, Nora looked to Corky for some explanation.

He shrugged. "What can I say? She's, you know, like totally stoked."

Mercy Hospital was quiet. For a few moments, no one was being born or trying to die, pain was suspended, the doctors had returned to their offices, the nurses were all charting, even the overhead paging system was silent.

In his new room, Corky stared out the window through the middle side rail. Tentatively he moved one leg. The feeling that his body wasn't his own had returned, sending him into the panic's grip. The feverish strange body sighed.

Everything sort of smells like spilled Pine Sol. I wonder if the smell can get into your lungs and cause cancer, or what about the blood or even the brain? Could I go nuts from just the smells in this place?

He sniffed the air again. Alcohol smells now replaced the Pine Sol.

Nah. These people work here every day for years and years, and they seem pretty normal, except that shrink, Dr. Barza. Man, what a lame. Wonder what zoo they sprung him from?

He shifted his gaze to the activity on the TV screen. The sound was off, but he'd known since he was three years old that a person needed no more than the IQ of an ant to figure out the situations. He guessed the sexy brunette turning heads as she bounced down a crowded street was probably making a point of her shining, manageable hair, her sheer stockings, or her full-figure support bra with heavy-duty eighteen-hour straps.

Wonder how old that nurse is? Jesus, I couldn't believe she actually was gonna look at my dick to take that tube out. She probably does that all day . . . holding guys' dicks and fooling around with tubes. Wonder if she's married. Wonder if her husband knows she does that.

Killer tits . . . What was it Coach Henny said? More than a mouthful is wasted . . . No, wait. More than a hand in the bush is two on a breast . . . Shit, that stuff doesn't matter now anyway, man. You can just forget that noise.

Not a bad body for an old lady, except those feet. Awesome. Bigger even than Eldo's. Love to see those puppies in the raw. Smithsonian donations for absolute sure. Wonder if there's the same correlation between the size of a chick's feet and her bazooms as there is between a guy's feet and his dick.

He held up a hand that still didn't feel as though it was his, studied it for a minute or two, burped, cupped it to his mouth to test his breath, then returned it to its twenty-four-hour-a-day job of drumming out rhythms to the endless songs playing on the jukebox in his brain.

Boomin' face but too much makeup. Could tell by the way she looked at me she's got a thing for me. Wonder what she thinks about me.

Self-disgust mingled with his anger and he slammed a fist that felt nothing into the side rail, causing the TV control to jump. In response, the screen went blank.

Chill out, dude—she knows why you're here. She knows you tried to off yourself. I mean, face it, man, that is a total fucking desperate move.

Nobody is going to buy Mom's story about me having mono. Everybody'll find out what happened sooner or later, and they're all gonna want to know why. I can tell just by the way they look at me here, they're all wondering—and they don't even know me.

God, I wish they would have let me die. I mean, what the hell am I supposed to say?

Nothing, dude. You don't say a word about that.

I promise. I will not break down and tell them—nobody! Not the shrink or that nurse or Mom. Can't even imagine what Dad would say. What a complete bummer, man. He'd really hate my fucking guts forever. If even one person knew, my life would be shit. I'd have to move to Siberia or someplace. Forget college, forget the new car at graduation, forget everything.

He pressed his fingers into his temples and tried rubbing out the heavy feeling.

Man, if anybody at school found out . . . At least now I can just say I'm depressed.

But what am I depressed about that would make me kill myself? It's got to be something solid so nobody tries to guess.

How about that some girl from out of town that I was sort of in love with got married to some other dude, and it really messed up my mind?

Nah, might ruin things with Molly if that got around.

Hey, sucker, you think she wants some lame who goes around trying to kill himself? You really think she'd want to hang out with a . . . with a . . .

Blow it off, man. Her parents will probably ax your ass even if she doesn't.

Never mind that stuff. It doesn't matter. It's nothing compared to the real thing. Maybe everybody will forget it after a while?

96

Maybe not. Shit, man, sometimes I still think about what happened to Bart Hatch in freshman year. Nobody ever forgets shit like that.

Man, I've gotta stop thinking about this shit—it makes it worse to think about it. I need to think about other stuff. Like taking that part-time job at Denny's, or I could start working out at the gym really hard, or I could go skiing every weekend, or maybe join the spring track team. Except then I'd have to see Adam or Coach Henny or Jason, and they're all normal. Nothing like this would ever happen to those dudes.

But why not them? Did I make this happen to me?

He started to shift onto his side, when a thought arrested his movement.

What if it happened again? What if . . .

He dropped onto his back and shielded his eyes with the crook of the arm that wasn't really his. His stomach rotated and bounced into his throat, making him sick.

Jesus. Why the fuck me?

I wish I could go back in time. I wish I would have known. I wish . . . I wish I was dead. They'll all wish I was dead when they find out this noise.

Aw, man, why didn't they just let me die?

12 Walker was dreaming he was a contestant on "Let's Make a Deal." The show was staged in the lobby of Mercy Hospital, and Monty Hall had just directed him to turn his attention to a row of doors marked 1, 2, and 3. Walker removed his oxygen mask and was asking about the prizes, when the voice of Jay Stewart boomed from the paging system in a tone of suppressed excitement.

"Behind one of these doors, Mr. Peter Walker, you'll find . . ."

A curtain over the information desk swung back to reveal a jar in which floated a pinkish-white brain. One of its lobes was darkened with something that resembled tomato black rot.

A clamor of oohs and aahs went up from the audience seated in the emergency waiting area.

Monty Hall held up a hand for silence, and Jay Stewart continued. "Yes, Peter Walker of San Francisco, California, it's the trip of a lifetime . . . an all-expense-paid cancer of the brain valued at two hundred and twelve thousand dollars in medical bills, one to two months of seizures, and a load of excruciating pain before death!"

Walker shifted uneasily, not wanting to seem ungracious, but, well . . .

"Or, Peter Walker, you could win . . ."

Another curtain opened in front of the men's room.

". . . an incredible course of cancer of the liver with metastasis to . . . everywhere! Value? Two hundred and eighty-five thousand dollars in medical expenses, six months of being sicker than hell, and even more excruciating pain than brain cancer!"

Walker nodded uncertainly.

"And our final prize . . ."

Carol Merrill, attired in a low-cut nurse's uniform, pranced onstage carrying a rhinestone-encrusted shoe box.

". . . is"—there was a drum roll—"a . . . FAB . . . U . . . LOUS . . ." Jay Stewart's voice rose and broke now with the excitement.

". . . CANCEROUS . . ."

Several nurses in the audience wrung their hands and sobbed.

". . . MOLE on the right little TOE! Value? Fifteen thousand dollars in medical expenses, one amputation, and special shoes for the rest of your life!"

Ripping off the cover of the box with dramatic flair, Carol Merrill pinched the puny, discolored digit between her forefinger and thumb and held it up for the spectators' approval.

The audience went crazy, shouting and leaping out of their seats.

"This is your last chance, Peter Walker . . ." Jay Stewart was back in control, his voice taking on an edge of warning and intrigue. "Is it door number one, two, or three? The choice is yours!" No longer willing to have their responses ruled by cue cards, the audience wailed their encouragement.

"Pick door one!" some of them screamed, brandishing their stethoscopes. "No! No!" the rest of them shouted. "It's door number three."

No one was yelling for door number two, he noticed. That was enough for him; the little toe was definitely behind door 2. He opened his mouth to speak, when Monty Hall suddenly turned and dismissed him with an air of contempt. "I'm sorry, Mr. Walker, but you didn't guess and your time is—"

"Number two!" Walker shouted over him. "I want number two!"

Monty Hall turned to the audience wearing a should-we-make-an-exception-just-this-once? expression. Mass hysteria ruled the day.

Receiving the go-ahead from Monty, Carol hurried to the door marked with a gold-sequined "1," pulled the knob and enthusiastically beckoned him to come and see what he'd chosen.

Herded forward by a bank of three television cameras, he desperately tried to explain that she'd heard him incorrectly; he wanted door number two. Number one was definitely not the toe.

His face fell. Through the doorway was nothing more than an endless black void. Cautiously backing away from door 1, he felt someone rush up from behind and push him into the vortex. As he fell through the dark, all he could think of was that by some horrible mistake he had been given the brain cancer and was rapidly losing his faculties. But then again, maybe the network had pre-planned this real-life tragedy, hoping to elicit thousands of sympathetic, droolly letters from the home viewers. Why else had he been the only contestant required to wear a hair shirt?

"Number two!" he yelled once again, his lungs aching for more air. "I said NUMBER TWOOOOOOOOOO . . ."

"Do you have to go to the bathroom?"

Walker heard the feminine voice and thought it must be Carol Merrill. She was going to tell him it had all been a hoax and he was actually going to receive the toe as a consolation prize for being such a good sport.

"I told you number two. Did I get the toe?" He was coming up through the mist.

"I said, do you have to pee or move your bowels? You were screaming 'number two,' and I never know which is which. Some people mean pee when they say number two, some mean the other. Which is it for you?"

He opened his eyes and looked into the face of a redheaded Carol Merrill.

"Hi. Remember me?" The attractive face smiled down at him. "I'm Cat, your nurse. How are you? Do you have to go to the bathroom, or were you having a bad dream?"

He wiped the sweat from his face with the corner of the bedsheet and blinked out the rest of his stupor.

"Bad dream. Whew!" He pulled himself up to face the woman he'd christened "Bigfoot" on his last admission.

"Hi. Yeah, I recognize you from my last chemo here. You told the X-ray lady to go back to hell."

Cat recalled the incident. The cool, dark-eyed witch in X ray had clicked off a chest film without telling anyone in the room she was going to shoot. It was something the X-ray techs at Mercy Hospital did frequently. When Cat complained to the techs about it, they all used the standard rationalization: "Pssssh, a little X-ray scatter never hurt anybody—you get more radiation by crossing the street on a sunny day." What they forgot to add was that the street they referred to was on Three Mile Island.

When she pressed administration to enforce the safety policies or at least issue X-ray badges to the nurses for routine-level checks, she was told that any move made to correct the situation would not be cost effective.

"Oh yes. I remember now. She was the same one who followed me to my car one day with the fluoroscope and threatened to zap my ovaries *and* my tires if I didn't stop complaining. The ovaries I could live without, but I'd just bought four new whitewalls, so we're all still getting zapped on a routine basis. Now, tell me about this dream of yours."

"It was about 'Let's Make a Deal.' I picked door number two, where I could've traded in a pair of cancered-up lungs for a cancerous little toe."

She noticed that his shoulders, which a year ago had been broad and muscular, were now shrunken, caving inward toward the rotting center of his body. His death-bright eyes gave notice that his time was limited. His labored breath and dusky coloring indicated Thursday night or Friday as departure time, but the part of his spirit that was visible said something was hanging him up and he was not quite ready to go.

"Oh yes. Wish dreams. I know them well." She adjusted the oxygen flow dial on his mask, watching his expression closely. "If we could only make them come true, we'd all be able to fly, turn our inlaws into broccoli, or get rid of lung cancer on a bet."

"Yeah. Nice." Walker stared out the window at the black billboard, until a coughing spasm shook his whole body. He used the muscles in his shoulders and abdomen to facilitate each breath.

She touched his arm and caught his eyes like a magnet. Her question needed no voice.

100

He held her gaze for a moment, then turned his eyes toward his hands, which were busy twisting the top sheet. "I'm fine. I'm . . . fine."

"And I'm Flash Gordon. What's wrong?"

The directness of her was like a knife at his throat. He began to sweat, and the claws tearing at his lungs became a searing pain pulling at every fiber of his attention.

"Get me some Brompton's," he choked. "I need a Brompton's." In his own pleading voice he heard the desperate voice of every wino who had ever come into his bar and begged for a drink. Horrified, he recalled the faces of the ones he'd turned down. Had they all known this fear?

When Cat returned with the liquid narcotic, Walker jerked himself into a sitting position and hastily drained the medicine cup. For a moment he was confused, not knowing what to do with the empty cup, until she took it from him and he fell back into his pillow, exhausted.

"Are you ready for more, Walker?" she asked softly.

He looked up at her, puzzled. "What do you mean? I'm not supposed to have any more of that stuff for another three hours. The doc change the order?"

"What I mean is, are you ready for the big guns yet?"

His throat went dry, turning his voice to a whisper. "No! Uh-uhn. Don't need it. Fine . . . I'm fine. Not bad, anyway." He tried forcing a smile, which stumbled and died before it hit his mouth.

The mattress sagged under the weight of her body as she sat down on the bed next to him. He was glad for the nearness of her.

"Tell me what's going on inside."

"What?"

The narcotic's first wave washed over him, lifting him up, away from the place of fear. He stopped shaking and studied the curve of the woman's waist. He wanted to crawl into her lap and caress her. Sadly he realized there was nothing even remotely sexual behind the thought.

"Is there anything you want to talk about?"

"No. Uh-uhn. Fine. I'm fine."

"Okay. It's just that you seemed frightened."

The wave subsided a little, but stayed on in his chest, holding back the burning. He could feel drops of sweat running down his back in small streams.

"No. Fine." Walker wished she would stop looking at him as if she could reach inside and pull his thoughts out into the open.

The woman remained silent until he couldn't stand it anymore.

101

"It's . . . that sometimes I . . . well, there's this black hole kind of feeling and it's . . . I can't see what's at the bottom, but I think that if I let myself fall in, I'll somehow stay there forever, but be conscious the whole time, and it'll be an eternity of nothingness. Then I'll . . ." He stopped.

Cat tilted her head. "You'll . . . ?"

"I don't know," he croaked, starting to cry. He wished the woman would make the fear stop. Through the haze of his tears, he caught a glimpse of the billboard and shuddered. Instead of letters, there was a hideous bleeding red mouth opening wide. It wanted him. Its breath poured over him, sinking into his lungs, making the pain unbearable.

Closing his eyes against the mouth, Walker let himself fall into the open circle of the woman's arms.

13 Cross snored softly while Cat made a careful study of her. Despite the cuts and bruises lining her face and neck, hers was the type of exquisite New England face that graduated from quality places like Vassar: a dark Meryl Streep made even more attractive by an overbite.

A thick layer of silky black hair slid over the young woman's face. Cat recalled reading in the junky tabloids left in the nurses' lounge that Cross had a habit of hiding behind the curtain of her hair because she was so shy. With one finger, she gently pushed the hair behind Cross's ear and exposed the freshly sutured laceration that ran down her cheek.

Her gaze fell on a set of teeth marks deeply gouged into the bridge of the woman's crushed nose.

Bitten? Cat pulled back, disbelieving. What kind of man bit a woman in the face? In stunned curiosity, she lifted Cross's green hospital gown.

The woman's small body was a sea of broken ribs, bruises, and deep scratches, but it was the missing chunk of flesh from the left breast that transformed the strangled feeling in Cat's throat into a state of blind fury toward the man who had caused such brutal injury.

Cat picked up the report sheet marked "NOT FOR PUBLIC INFORMATION" in large red letters across the top and bottom. It was the usual famous-person protocol: No slips to reporters. Be on the lookout for exclusive-photo seekers dressed in medical personnel uniforms. Report all phone inquiries as to patient's condition to proper authorities.

In the middle of the sheet, under the heading "Marin County Sheriff's Office: SECURITY PRECAUTION—WATCH FOR THIS PERSON," were two photos of a man she recognized instantly as the Blazzie's Touch of Passion perfume model. In the publicity photo he stared boldly, almost defiantly, into the camera, the flawlessly handsome face and bottomless light blue eyes sending a flagrant message of sexual promise with a hard edge.

Under the second photo, a police mug shot, appeared the name Michael E. Lake.

Cat read the patient information card:

"Ward Two, 505 acute. Multiple trauma.

CROSS, LUCY: Age: 31. Marital status: divorced × 1, no children. Occupation: artist. Family: one married sister in Denver. Personal: Patient lives in Muir Beach Canyon. Injuries caused by live-in boyfriend (see report sheet). If there is any change in patient's condition, contact: Nathan Keplin, agent, and Inspector Padcula, Marin County Sheriff's Office."

Taking a pencil from her pocket, she wrote in the word "celebrated" before "artist." After all, the woman had an international reputation as the youngest, most talented painter to come out of the United States in years.

She stroked Cross's face and smiled sadly at the irony of being in a position to care for an abused woman who, at one time, had given her comfort when she herself felt abused.

On a misty November night years before, she had wandered the streets of Sausalito in search of sanctuary from the alcoholic lover who had taken to hurling stemware along with his verbal insults. She stopped to rest in front of a gallery, and saw the Cross painting.

In the watercolor, a woman stood at a window bathed in lambent early-morning light. Her head rested against the glass so only a quarter of her face was visible, but the easy posture of the figure and the hint of a dreamy gaze allowed no doubt in the viewer's mind that the woman was deep in reflective serenity.

The following day, Cat returned to the gallery to bask in the passion of Cross's work. Her art was not reserved only for those who, by merit of a sensitive eye, were set apart. Through her paintings, Cross created a force to stir the spirit of all who had lost sight of the deeper life within themselves.

Now Cross's left arm, the fingers swollen to twice their normal size, lay elevated on two pillows. Tenderly palpating the woman's wrist, Cat counted the feeble pulse, racing like a bird's heart under her fingers. The respirations, too, were shallow and fast, and the blood pressure cuff was sizes too large. She would need to use a pediatric cuff in order to register any kind of accurate reading.

The woman stirred and murmured Michael's name.

"Cross?"

The eyebrows lifted, straining to pull the lids apart.

"Wake up, Cross. You're *not* going to let some creep destroy you. Do you hear? You can't ever let anyone hurt you like this again. Cross?"

Cross opened her eyes, tried to focus, then drifted off again.

Cat picked up the woman's unbruised hand and held it. "Wake up, Cross. You don't have to be afraid anymore."

Aware of another presence, Cat turned to find Inspector Padcula watching her from the doorway. She noticed he was no longer smiling.

Whether it was the face without the smile, or the expression itself, she wasn't sure, but the look was intense. Intense *what* was the question. Whatever it was, it was unsettling.

"You know, Red," he said with tender admiration, "you wear the haunted look of someone who has stared the beast in the face and survived." A half-strength smile appeared. "Not many of your caliber still walking around."

Before she could say anything, he adjusted his glasses and headed across the hall to the elevators. A second later, he stopped and turned to face her, "You weren't easy to find."

She watched him walk backward for a few yards, noting that he missed the elevators completely. Trying for a smooth recovery, he

104

located the nearest door, awkwardly took three more steps backward, and without further ado pushed through the emergency exit, thus setting off alarms throughout the building.

"Well, I'm glad you knew who you were looking for," Cat whispered after him, "or you might have missed me and the beast altogether."

14 It was one of the best restaurant drops Cat had seen in years: a collision of two large trays loaded with full dinner plates and wineglasses. The waiters who went down with them were lying one table away, bleeding through several layers of linen napkins.

Having been jump-started into happiness by a bottle of good Chardonnay, Cat and Nora had no inclination to reveal their expertise to any of the attending restaurant personnel, although, out of guilt, Cat did walk over and assess the situation.

"It's okay," she said on returning to the table. "No major arterial gushers."

Barely looking up from her spinach calzone, Nora picked up her story where she'd left off.

"So there we were. His obnoxious dog has been contained in the closet, the phone is turned off, the door securely locked. And we're goin' at it like Tina Turner on coke—a real Tennessee Williams kind of scene, all sweaty hair and hot breath, and I whisper in this husky, moist voice, 'Where's the condom, lover boy?' "

Nora sat back. "Well you'd think I'd asked him to violate his mother on the Phil Donahue show."

Cat choked on her tortellini and furtively looked around the restaurant. Nora had a voice that carried like Ethel Merman's at Carnegie Hall.

"And he says—get this—'Oh man, you aren't one of those condom freaks, are you?'

"So I give this authoritative and disappointed sigh and explain the obvious. 'No,' I say, 'but I *am* crazy about living. I'm a nurse. Every day I take care of people who are kicking off in a mega-ugly way because somebody couldn't be bothered to use a rubber.'

"Of course, by this time his male member has melted like so much Silly Putty left out in the sun, and he gets all little boy huffy, like I told him he had to wear his sister's flowered bathing cap in the pool, and he says, 'Aw, that's only fags. Only drug addict faggots get AIDS, not healthy heteros like me.' And then he started rubbing against me, smiling, like he's been given special immunity but no brains, whispering this incredible bullshit about how I take my job too seriously and AIDS is just a CIA/PTL plot to keep people from having sex and thus keep the population down and restore religious oppression, and on and on until he gets to the part about plots designed to kill off Third World countries."

Out of the corners of their eyes, the couple at the next table watched Nora viciously attack the end of her calzone with her fork. The woman shifted nervously in her chair and looked away.

"Okay. So now I'm really pissed. The guy is obviously a total dick-brained moron, and my Italian temper surfaces through the atmosphere of creamy wet thighs and heaving breasts and I say, 'Bullshit, buster! Straight people, including women and little kids, are croaking all the time and I ain't gonna be one of them. The inside of this body has a dress code, buddy, so unroll the latex or forget it!'

"By this time the guy has not only forgotten it, he's unleashed the pit bull from the closet, thrown my clothes into the hallway, and is on the phone trying to talk somebody named Dixie into coming over and taking care of his unmet needs.

"Dodging the pit bull, who seems to have more than a passing interest in my left leg, I run out to the hallway to retrieve my clothes and the next thing I know, the door has been slammed . . . and locked on my very stark, naked buns."

Pausing for a healthy bite of calzone, Nora continued with a full mouth. "So there I am, it's midnight, and I'm trying to rush the hooks and eyes together on my bra before anybody comes upon me, no pun intended, when the elevator opens, and lo and behold, guess who issues forth from the movable box?"

The next-table couple, having been unable to ignore Nora's rising voice, stopped chewing and openly waited for the answer.

106

Cat bit into a flaccid carrot stick and leaned forward with a wide, toothy smile. "Go on, hit me—who?"

"Of all the bizarre and kinky people in this city that it *could* have been—an old blind bag lady, Margo St. James, a group of gay men, a tourist from some remote, unheard-of country where nudism is the order of things . . . but uh-uhn, for me, it has to be none other than Dr. Gerald Gillespie, chief of medicine of Mercy Hospital, accompanied by his wife no less."

Cat clapped her hands in delight and let out a high-pitched scream-laugh, which momentarily drew attention away from the injured waiters still lying on the floor behind them. Unnerved by the noise, the woman at the next table whimpered and dropped her fork.

"Perfect! What did you do?"

"I squatted down and put my panties over my face." Nora rested her chin in her hand and gazed thoughtfully over Cat's shoulder. "You know, I still don't know why I did that, but I think it goes back to my childhood or something.

"And here's the strangest part. They didn't miss a step. I mean, nobody even slowed down or gasped or anything. As they passed, Dr. Gillespie said, 'Good evening, Ms. Carmotti,' and I replied, 'Oh, good evening, Dr. Gillespie,' just as if we were at a cocktail party. I mean, I couldn't really tell if they were staring at me or not, because the all-cotton crotch part was over my eyes, but it *sounded* very normal."

Cat doubled over with hard laughter and snorted, slipping inch by inch out of her chair. An increasing number of people from nearby tables glanced over at them the same way they might have looked at a couple of psychotic chickens roller-skating down Montgomery Street at high noon.

Their waiter approached with an air of careful distrust. "Is anything wrong, miss?"

Nora nodded and smiled amiably as Cat fell to her knees under the table. "Oh, no. Everything's fine. As a matter of fact, we'll have one cappuccino and two Mount Vesuvius surprises, please."

Doubtfully, the waiter looked at Cat as she gripped the edge of the table and tried to pull the rest of her body up.

"You sure she's okay?"

"Well, she's not really okay, but there's nothing you or even the Salvation Army could help her with. Thanks anyway."

The waiter withdrew from the table, walking backward as if he were afraid of turning his back on them.

"Anyway," Nora continued, "as soon as I was fairly sure they were out of sight, I finished dressing and made it out of there. Okay, so then it's about one-thirty and I'm three blocks from home and everything is fine and I'm thinking about how great it is to be alive in this wonderful cosmopolitan city, right up until I turn the corner on Hyde Street, when out of nowhere I hear this thundering roar behind me. I think it's either got to be an earthquake or a runaway cable car, so I hit the ground—only to find myself eye level with an old drunk curled up in a doorway. Slowly he opens one bloodshot eye and gives me a deprecating once-over. 'Man,' he says in this totally disgusted tone, 'you can *always* tell when they're from the East Coast.'

"With wounded pride, I sneer him into a crouch, brush off the sidewalk goo, and pick up my pace a little, not daring to look around because the roar is steady and seems to be getting closer. Then through the noise I hear catcalls. Of course, that gets my curiosity up and I kind of *peek* over my shoulder.

Nora drained off her glass of Chardonnay. "It was the perfect ending to a typical Nora Carmotti night; approximately twenty Hell's Angels are spread out behind me, not one of whom weighs under two hundred pounds, and they're making these rather interesting proposals having to do with perverse group recreational activities involving me and them.

"Anyway, to make a long story short, I end up backed against a big trash bin at the end of an alley crammed with garbage and cockroaches.

"So there we are and I'm sweating bullets, telling these thugs that I'm pregnant and I've got AIDS *and* tertiary syphilis and that my husband is the chief of police and my brother is head man of the mafia. Of course, all this is doing is giving them a good chuckle. Then all of a sudden, I look real hard at this one guy in the back of the group and I start shrieking at the top of my lungs.

"'*Norman?*' I scream. 'Norman Nosenchuck, is it really *you?*' " Nora paused and gave a wildly happy smile.

Bewildered, Cat stared blankly. "Who the hell is Norman Nosenchuck?"

"He was my anthropology professor at Cal. Anyway, he recognizes me and calls off the hounds, and there's a lot of hugging and back-slapping and I ride home on the back of Norm's Harley.

"As it turns out, the guy is supersweet. The way he tells it, he was on a book research project two years ago which involved the political and religious beliefs of modern-day radical outlaw groups, and joined the Angels as a guest observer rider, then ended up staying because he liked the group's sense of freedom.

"He immediately divorced his wife and two kids and now he says he's found the true meaning of life."

Spooning the rest of the Chardonnay over the chocolate lava spout of her erupting Mount Vesuvius surprise, Nora tentatively took a bite while Cat waited, ears buzzing, lips numb from two glasses of wine.

"So, we have a date for Thursday night to see Pavarotti at the opera house!"

Nora glanced up in time to catch Cat's shocked expression. "Hey, I *like* him," she said defensively. "I really do. He's sensitive and a gentleman and . . ."

"Sensitive gentlemen," Cat said dryly, "don't ride outlaw Harleys and gangbang young women."

Nora waved her hand. "Oh *that*. That was just part of the Angels' public service message to women to make them more aware of the dangers of walking alone at night. They weren't *really* going to rape me—they just wanted to scare some sense into me." She thought for a moment. "You know, it's actually a great idea."

"Jesus." Cat shook her head. "Now I've heard everything. You are actually going on a date with a Hell's Angel who was going to gang-bang you, and then you tell me—"

"*He wasn't going to gangbang me!*" Nora cried just as their waiter returned with the check. The man started to say something, thought better of it, and went away.

"Come on, let's get out of here," Cat said, noticing that the couple next to them had apparently asked the waiter to move them to a table on the other side of the room. "We're giving the place a bad reputation."

Parked in front of Nora's apartment house, the two women shared an expertly rolled joint, fully aware, though unconcerned, that they were committing an infraction of the laws of California. They were making a conscious effort not to let the conversation fall into the usual delayed-response, dull-witted, monosyllabic answer category. They'd also decided to stick to the present rather than fall into profound reminiscences about previous lives.

"I'd really like to get Stella into Bresford Place." Cat stared at the streetlamp, keeping close tabs on the warm, druggy sensation creeping up her thighs, turning them into jelly. "At least they'll do something for her instead of just letting her die in a puddle of her own pee."

The impact of the drug on her buttocks rooted Cat to her seat.

"But I think out of my whole group this week, so far it's the kid and Cross that bother me the most."

Nora held in the smoke and raised her eyebrows.

"I don't know," Cat replied. "It's just a feeling I've got about that kid. If he even *thinks* somebody is going to ask him why he tried to kill himself, he gets that weird look—a mixed bag of innocence, panic, fear, and guilt."

Nora released a long tube of smoky breath and handed Cat the remainder of the roach. "What do you think happened?"

"Not positive and don't want to say until I know. I'll tell you this much though—I think I'm catching Gage's second sight, because while I was trying to figure it out, I actually saw the whole scene in my mind." Cat paused, took a hit, and coughed. "It was gruesome."

"Tell me. Tell me." Nora bounced up and down in her seat, fully reverted to the age of nine.

"Nah." Going with the backward flow, a twelve-year-old Cat sucked on the end of a half-undone braid. "I don't want to start ugly rumors."

"Aw come on, pretty pleeeease? Tell me? I promise I won't tell, cross my heart and hope to die in a horrible head-on accident on the Golden Gate."

Cat shook her head, a stubborn pout settling in around her mouth. "Nope. Not yet."

"All right, then," Nora sniffed. "I won't tell you about the strange experiences I've had with Almond Windmill cookies."

Cat smiled and let out a choppy stream of illegal smoke. "This morning Gage told me something evil is going to happen, something about a silver light tracking me down and . . . oh hell, I can't remember my own middle name, right now, let alone all that voodoo shit."

"Your middle name *is* voodoo, my dear. Hell, you're as taken in by all Gage's psychic crap as I am by the call of the male animal. You eat up every word that guy hands you."

"Not really," Cat lied. "I wouldn't know a psychic vision if it came up and bit me, never mind whether it was good or evil, but there's something about Gage that . . . I don't know how to explain it; he draws me to him. I will admit though that I'm almost convinced the man really *was* my mother at some point in time."

"Well, personally, I wouldn't trust Gage with my pet snail." Nora managed to get up a bristle through the lazy drug haze. "The guy's an uptight creep, and I know I'm supposed to be nice to him because he's a handicapped minority, but I mean, you could call Alan a handicapped minority for that matter, and nobody feels they have to be nice to *him*."

110

"Yeah," Cat said, "except Gage only has one handicap."

"Well, all I can say is, remember to keep yourself open to the right stuff and closed to the bad."

Cat fixed Nora with dilated pupils. "Jesus, that's exactly what Gage said!"

Nora coughed and rubbed her front teeth. "My teeth are numb," she stated casually, trying not to notice that the "Why Be Normal?' sticker in her corner of the windshield was moving verrrry sloooowly toward the middle.

"Wait. Why did you say that?"

"I don't know," she answered thoughtfully. "I think because I have soft teeth, and whenever I get stoned, the smoke seems to—"

"No, I mean about staying open and closed."

"Oh that. Well, because that's one of your major problems. You have a gift for cutting off things that are good for you and leaving yourself totally wide open and vulnerable to the things that have danger written all over them."

Cat nodded, trying to ignore the rubber band feeling of her lips. Tentatively she pulled up her lower lip, relieved that she could not make it touch the tip of her nose, but concerned about the unnatural way Nora's hair was moving by itself.

She was suddenly aware of an impending respiratory arrest, as the rush of drug-induced paranoid panic caused her to take large gulps of air. Her eyes darted, looking for the hidden narcotics agents.

"Speaking of vulnerable, where *did* you get this joint, Nora?"

Nora shrugged, refusing to look down and confirm the three spiders crawling over her shoes. She was, however, relieved that the giant red ant tracking them seemed paralyzed by the Thing under her seat. "An old lover of mine from Baja. He grows it in a mixture of cow manure, refried beans, and diet Seven-Up." She kicked at one of the tarantulas and looked at Cat apologetically. "It's gotta be the chemicals in the diet Seven-Up. Just ride it out, it'll be over soon."

"You know what really flips me out?"

"Wouldn't be spiders, would it?" Nora asked, almost hopefully.

Cat shook her head, relieved she wasn't the only one having problems. "I can't figure out why Cross won't snap out of it."

"Emotional shock," Nora said. "You know, kind of like sleeping all the time when you're depressed?"

"I suppose." Cat willed her lips to behave. "But why would a talented, beautiful, and intelligent woman like Cross allow herself to be beaten repeatedly by some jerk?"

Composed, Nora casually slapped at the spiders, now making webs around the hem of her coat. "Oh come on, Cat. You, out of all

111

of us, should know the answer to that. You've read enough of those ugly love books to choke a horse. Personally, I get turned off just by the titles: *Women Who Love Too Much and Too Long, Men Who Love Women Who Love Too Little and Too Many, Women and Men and the Pets Who Loved Them Too Much*. God, next thing it'll be *Children of Men and Women Who Loved Too Much Yet Not Enough*."

The wind pushed through the partially opened window and whipped a sheet of Cat's copper hair back from her face. She thought she smelled burned toast, and was suddenly ravenous for Mexican food. Thank God there was no food within reach. Her thighs were safe.

Nora sniffed the air, convinced they'd parked over a sewer. It was more than likely where the spiders, who were now finding their way out of the back window, lived.

"You know, I've come to the conclusion that we've all got our quirks. For instance, Trish doesn't mind dealing with vomit, but Mathilde hates touching urine or blood. I refuse to take care of junkies, while Laurel actually enjoys dealing with alcoholics. All these awful things are absolute facts of life, but for our own personal reasons, they affect us differently.

"However . . ." Nora looked Cat straight in the bloodshot eye. She was only a little disturbed that it appeared to be a good two to three inches lower than the other one. "Are you aware of how sucked in you get by assaulted women? I mean, Cat-o-lina baby, you *really* let them get to you."

Unable to hold her friend's nystagmic gaze, Cat concentrated on the Mensa member windshield decal moving a millimeter at a time toward the "Why Be Normal" sticker on the opposite side.

"You know my history, Nor," she said quietly. "It's pretty easy to figure that one out, don't you think?"

Nora was well aware of Cat's history. Everyone in the North End neighborhood of Boston knew that the Richardson household was troubled. The austere Frank Richardson was a pharmacist whose searing bitterness ran so deep no one dared say more than what was necessary for fear of bringing up the redheaded man's bile.

How anyone could have loved the tall, ugly man was a mystery to the neighbors, though love him Emily Richardson did—to an obsessive degree. It was true that he did not drink, or indulge in sampling his own wares, and he was a good provider. But he did have one vice: utilizing everything from fists to coat hangers, or whatever was within reach, Frank Richardson liked to inflict pain on Emily.

When Emily's sister insisted she leave him, Emily was horrified at

112

the idea, as if it were a blasphemy against nature. He was the man she loved, the man she had married for better or worse till death do them part. She would never leave him and that was that, although she might not have taken the abuse so passively had she not had an outlet for her own anger. Whatever abuse Emily suffered at her husband's hand she took out in kind on the only one of the three daughters Frank Richardson showed a fondness for.

The January wind pierced the heavy silence of the car.

Cat smiled in the dark. "Yeah, Nor, I guess it's sisterhood in the same club—mangled self-esteem, addiction to abuse. It's like a disease.

"I mean, I've never liked booze, and I've even got my limits for smoking this stuff, but when it comes to obsessions with certain men, I've not only got my mother beat but I've graduated from that game Magna Faux Pas. Loving men is a difficult business for women like us." Cat let her eyes wander back to the halo around the streetlamp, her mind reeling off dismal scenes from her past.

Her first marriage had been for love: love of an alcoholic newspaper reporter with a wandering eye. Young and naive, Cat endured the other women and the drunken rages for nearly four years, until he left her for a whore named Beverly who worked Fisherman's Wharf.

Brokenhearted, she ran away to Petaluma, chicken capital of the world, to get back to nature. Renting a converted coop on the outskirts of town, she drove herself to forget by adding to her normal work week a job in the Petaluma clinic on weekends. It was there she met the gangling, quiet railroad engineer.

He'd come in for a bad case of burning on urination. The lab reported gonorrhea, which he swore right to the end he caught from a toilet seat in the San Luis Obispo station house.

No matter—he worshiped his gentle redheaded rescuer, carrying her about the coop, the two of them billing and cooing *ad nauseam*. For two years, her heart was on fire with love, until she woke one morning with an unusual burning not in her heart, but in her lower, second heart.

This time, it was a toilet seat named Lenora.

Hit harder than by the breakup of her marriage, Cat mourned to the hilt—unable to sleep or eat. Things were in a state of emergency by the time Nora drove up one weekend and found her in a suicidal delirium.

Nora arranged for a visiting counselor, who told Cat she needed to emotionally kill off her meandering engineer. Mentally staging an elaborate accident, Cat visualized a twenty-one-car derailment in which he was rectally impaled on his own throttle.

The next day, she ate three square meals, packed her belongings, and flew the coop back to San Francisco with Nora.

Her third major relationship was strictly for sex. Ten years her junior, he could have easily played the part of the mule in a Tijuana whorehouse. It was he who initiated her to the world of erotica, introducing tricks one could do with another's body that she hadn't even dreamed possible.

After one year, the juices of passion were abruptly dried up when, in the middle of a particularly lusty session, a naked woman of Swedish descent slipped from their closet and joined in on the activity. Linda, her deviant young lover explained, was a close friend whom he had invited to surprise her with a rousing round of Three Can Be Fun.

The fourth relationship had started when they were eight, and, driven by illogical juvenile urges, he'd thrown the remainder of a chocolate ice cream cone at her front door. Four years later, they shared their first slow dance at St. Joseph's Hall and their first kiss on the same front porch where she had long since scrubbed away the sticky fragments of his Double Devil Fudge cone.

On prom night, they kissed on the crepe-paper-festooned bridge and, swaying to the theme of *Moon River*, vowed to remain sweethearts forever, no matter what or who else happened to them.

Living on opposite coasts made it easy to keep the embers of romance smoldering with the occasional offbeat postcards carrying sweet, nostalgic phrases and the periodic phone calls during thunderstorms or after earthquakes. In the off-seasons between relationships, on the occasions when she returned to Boston or his law practice brought him to San Francisco, they always managed a romantic lunch or dinner, complete with tantalizing kisses and passionate embraces of promise.

One April, in a candlelit corner of a Boston pub that smelled strongly of fish and rancid grease, they decided a twenty-five-year courtship was sufficient basis for happiness. The next day, during the worst blizzard in Massachusetts history, the die-hard bachelor and the failed romantic were married.

His newlywed-jitters excuse was plausible for the first six nights he fell asleep in front of the TV. The migraine that never ended was okay for the next ten days, but when he hit her with the I-contracted-a-mysterious-sleeping-sickness-in-Hawaii story, she went against the advice of the editors of *Modern Woman*, and confronted—nah, she

114

preferred to think of it as it was—she pressured and harangued him to tell her why he wouldn't—or couldn't—cash in on his conjugal rights.

His long, dark history of impotence, coupled with his even longer, darker secret of child molestation, tripled by a strong deficiency of certain physical appointments, led Cat to swear off marriage forever.

Next came a series of torrid and completely unsatisfying affairs, each of which left her a little less able to touch the memory of tenderness.

"Let's face it," Cat said, I've attracted pricks right from the beginning. Even in kindergarten, Billy O'Hara used to tell me he loved me just so I'd give him my peanut butter and jelly sandwiches, and I fell for it every time, until my mother noticed I was losing weight, and called the teacher.

"Christ, I never learned. Even the last fiasco was like a replay of *9½ Weeks*. But on the brighter side, I can say that at least now I don't have to worry about someone lying on top of me at six a.m. dropping bombs like 'Oh by the way, I won't be back tonight because I'm getting married this afternoon.' "

Cat hesitated. "I think the worst part of my relationships—or should I be realistic and say 'relationshits'?—was how they all started out loving me and then overnight they'd change; it was like going to sleep with a prince and waking up with the toad. I was so stupid— continually diving into the pool without looking to make sure it was filled, always coming away with major heart cord injuries. That's why I don't . . . It's why I'm so . . ." She sighed. "Never mind."

Lightly rubbing Cat's shoulder, Nora mentally said no to further drugs and to the retina-purple Thing innocently winding itself around Cat's size 12's.

"I know and I'm sorry, Cat. You didn't deserve any of that abuse, but you can't just cut out that part of living. You threw out the baby with the bathwater, and you don't have to. You're a bright, attractive lady with a good sense of humor and a great heart; you need to find somebody a little offbeat and weird, just not *too* weird. Don't you realize how much you've learned from your previous disasters? Not only that, but in the last four years you've had enough therapy to make anybody lose her mind. When you fall in love this time, it'll be different. You'll know how to—"

Cat turned on Nora, gray eyes flashing. "Oh don't give me this there's-still-hope-for-love crap, Nora," she said bitterly. "I mean, come on . . . what are the statistics in this area? Five women to every one single, straight male? You stick to your Not Quite Normal Nor-

115

man types and leave me out of it. Anyway, I'm done with that whole mess. The chances of my falling in love again are about as real as me growing antlers."

Nora was not put off so easily. She'd dealt with Cat's Joan Crawford–chilling, but no-stick temper for years. "Really? Well, what about the smiley cop? You trying to tell me he didn't do anything for you?"

"Not a thing," Cat lied.

"Yeah, right, Catalina, and don't hurt the duck while you're at it."

"Huh?"

Nora blinked, refusing to give credence to the antlers suddenly sprouting from Cat's head. "Don't you remember Timothy Mahoney?"

The name triggered a mental Polaroid of a wiry, snot-nosed little boy with Frank Sinatra ears wearing a navy-blue Catholic school blazer.

"Oh yeah, the kid at the end of Columbus Street with the six brothers and the ugly fat sister?"

"That's the one. Well, whenever he got emotional about anything, he used to go down to the Commons and throw rocks at the ducks. They finally sent him away to relatives in Idaho or Iowa—anyway, it was someplace that didn't have ducks."

Cat gave Nora a sideward, who-let-*her*-in glance.

"Come on, Cat. Just give it a chance, would you. Please?"

"Forget it," Cat said with renewed stubbornness. "He's probably got six girlfriends, all under the age of sixteen."

"Wrong. I told you he's lonely. More than likely he sits at home at night watching old 'Brideshead Revisited' tapes and eating canned burritos because that's all he knows how to make."

"Dream on, Nora. With a face like that, he ain't sitting home. Not only that but he probably doesn't like redheads. He probably likes twenty-two-year-old blondes who are five feet tall and have neat little breasts, tiny feet, and no freckles. He probably—"

"I don't want to hear it. He's probably a wonderful guy who'd like to meet a nice lady like you. Let's just drop it, okay?"

Cat nodded. All right then. So what? She was more than aware of the fact that she had always loved out of a need to love, not because she had found the right person. It was a long shot that Nora might be right. He had *seemed* nice, and he had come looking for her and said those sweet things about surviving beasts. And if he was, in fact, bright and lonely, well . . .

A warm wave of sensual awareness started in the region of her

116

solar plexus and spread slowly outward in all directions. The very electricity of it caused her to take in a sharp breath.

Nora gave her an odd look, smiled, then absentmindedly resumed rubbing her teeth.

For several minutes they said nothing, listening to the foghorns through the drug buzz in their ears. Nora thought about looking for a nail file in her purse, but her hands had been rendered useless.

Cat broke the silence. "You know, it's really true what you were telling me earlier."

"Uhnnn?" Nora laughed, tried to flick her fingers a few times, and gave up. "God, where did your mind get off to now?"

Cat considered for a moment and resumed. "You know what we were talking about today about paying off all the bad karma when you're a nurse? Well, I realized that we probably take care of a thousand lifetimes worth of bad karmic debt."

Nora brightened. "Hey yeah, and I'll bet in our next lives, we automatically become spiritual leaders. Hell, do you think that maybe Jesus and Buddha were nurses in their former lives?"

"No doubt in my mind," Cat replied. "Listen, you only have to think about what we do every day. There we are slaving in the filth of the human condition for peanuts, giving everything we have for the salvation of our fellowman."

"God, you make it sound like we're headed to Calvary."

"Very close to it," Cat said, suddenly animated. "Just look at today. You worked twelve hours, starting at three a.m. You ended up with a total of eight patients, two of them acute care needing constant supervision. Now you tell me how the hell you're supposed to single-handedly watch two people on ventilators, give meds to eight patients, give eight baths, change eight beds, tend to eight sets of intravenous lines, do eight complete physical assessments twice, deal with a minimum of twenty emotionally, and, in some cases, mentally, incompetent, over-egoed doctors, do complete and legally sound charting on eight charts, serve and collect meal trays twice in a four-hour period, and tend to the cares and fears of not only each of the eight patients but the multitudes of walking wounded known as the patient's family?"

Nora opened her mouth to comment, but was cut off.

"Furthermore, you end up doing housekeeping's job, plus pharmacy, plus laboratory, plus the clerk's, because they either no longer exist or they're as understaffed and overloaded as you are. There's no more float pools, no more LVN's, no more nothin'—just us, the tender, loving angels of mercy all fluffy and sweet, who, according

117

to the major networks' TV programs, don't really do anything but primp, make silly or fatal mistakes and chase after the doctors trying to get them into the linen closets."

Nora weaved a bobby pin through her left eyebrow. "Yeah, but who cares? You know as well as I do, Cat, that every business has an unfair downside and until you get totally fed up, there isn't anything to do about it except quit."

Cat shook her head and massaged her temples. The afterglow headache was threatening to make itself known. "Okay, except what *is* the end point, Nor? Besides the workload and the politics, how many dying kids can you hold, and how many relatives can you ache for? I mean, is there a limit some higher power gives each one of us according to what He thinks we can take before we crack?

"Nursing requires dichotomy. On one hand you have to be the altruistic, compassionate angel of mercy, yet you can't let others' suffering or the overwork and politics affect you *too* much, lest the superhealer clinician side becomes ineffective, and the caring part of you hardens and burns out.

"And of course, unless you're an automaton, the day eventually comes when you can't take the pressure for one more second and you find yourself ready to walk out the door in the middle of a shift. Then you see someone in pain and you know you have the ability to eliminate that misery, or the code bell goes off and it's sweet old Mr. Jones, and you're convinced that you'll be the one who will make the difference whether he lives or dies. Then you remember you left some little old lady sitting on the pot and worry that she'll fall and break a hip if she tries to get back to bed without your help, and you think, 'Well, okay, just this once more,' and—boom—you've signed up for five more years of traumatic bonding."

Cat glanced casually at Nora. "Do you ever get like that?"

Nora nodded, unable to blink. "Well, the way I see it, constant chaos creates a damp sanitorium and refuge for the wounded sane, but allows and, indeed, promulgates insidious mildew of the demeanor which is often resistant to psychiatric disinfectant. *That's* the real problem here."

Cat's expression turned to one of mingled hurt and indignation. "Don't you ridicruel me too, Nora."

Her words hung in the air. At once both women collapsed in hysterics, unable to stop until they were slapping the dashboard with floppy hands made weak by laughter.

Jolting upright, Nora tried to look honestly alarmed. "God, do you realize we have to get up in three hours and go to work?"

"Jeez. Try to get a little relaxation and all we've done is defurt the peapose."

Hopelessly lost to the influence of the drug and lack of sleep, they were swept off into another chorus of cackling.

With only two hours and forty-nine minutes left before they were to report back on duty, they fell asleep where they sat with smiles on their faces.

15

8:15 p.m.

Walker held the overlooked pink sweatshirt to his nose and breathed in his nine-year-old daughter's smell of kid sweat and sneakers. Closing his eyes to the terrifying black billboard, he focused on the image of her face, dreading its fading.

The kids, of course, never realized that their existence was primarily the result of his overzealous sexual appetite for Joyce, and Joyce's lack of attention to details. Nor did the boys know that there was an incompleteness to his feelings about them, as if they'd been sprung on him one day and he never got over the surprise. Not that he didn't love the boys, but Zoe, well, Zoe was different—most like him, least like him. A sensitive-natured kid with a warm heart, she understood people inside and out and they knew it. Like the morning he found Will Gekas, their postman, bawling like a calf and pouring his guts out to her on the back porch steps.

She never asked for anything in return. He'd noticed that right away, when she was still an infant. Joyce said he was imagining

119

things, but he felt attached to Zoe by the roots. The moment he laid hands on her huge, slippery head and eased her from her mother, he knew she had been assigned to have a hell of an effect on him.

There was a lot about her he still did not understand, like the fact that she preferred to be alone, and her saintly patience, which sometimes drove him crazy, but he respected her more than anyone he knew.

Like tonight. Joyce brought the kids in to visit and there were the usual polite, strained, shit-he-looks-bad-but-don't-let-him-know-you've-noticed conversations with the boys. "You look great, Dad." (Did Joyce tell them to say that, or did they know enough to lie on their own?) "We really killed San Jose's varsity team, Dad. I need new sneakers, Dad. I've got my driver's permit, Dad. Can I borrow the car, Dad? Can I go to the Winter Prom with Virginia Bradley, Dad? Can I stay out till midnight, Dad? When are you coming home, Dad?" (How did their mother get around not telling them *that* part?)

Then there was Zoe. Sitting silent, expressionless, knobby knees all twisted and melted into sticklike elbows, never taking her eyes off him for a second.

In the middle of Garrick's enthusiastic if somewhat embellished description of his winning free throw, she climbed onto the bed and pressed her cheek to his.

"I love you so much, Daddy," she said, then climbed down, straightened her skirt, and left the room. She hadn't given him a chance to say anything. Zoe was like that; when she had something to say, she said it—no beating around the bush, no room for discussion. It was her own little way of taking care of pressing but tender business. She was independent and that seemed strange for a little kid, especially a girl, but then again Zoe definitely knew her own mind, which was more than he could say for himself.

Walker looked over at the billboard displaying the horrible red mouth and shivered. She'd die better than me, he thought. She'd die without fear of going into that hole. Zoe would let go with real style. Zoe would know exactly who she was and what her purpose had been.

8:15 p.m.

For two hours, Stella lay awake praying the thief would steal her away to sleep, but he let her down when she needed him the most, and left her to winding, odd thoughts. Tillie and Virginia had long since been drugged into open-mouthed stupors, with only a

120

random word or a fluttering of sheets to interrupt their deathlike quiet.

"Mama?"

It was Tillie. Eighty-four and calling for Mama. Jesus. The complete cycle of man wasn't a lot of public television hogwash after all. It really did go from gumless formula-sucking, crawling, mewling, and puking to gumless formula-sucking, crawling, mewling, and puking. Life in an upright position took place somewhere in between.

"Mama?" Stella echoed, trying senility on for size. It felt a little odd, but nothing she couldn't get used to.

"Mama?" *Oh, Mama, how I loved you.* "Mama?" *Remember the stories you whispered to me each night? You wove the golden threads of your imagination around my innocence right up until the night before I married. I can still remember them, Mama. I remember "The Rabbit and the Moon," "The Owl and the Wind," "The Ragamuffin Boy," "The Almond-Eyed Girl." I remember them all.*

All your stories were so gentle, but mine . . . Oh dear, now my *stories would've made your hair stand on end and your heart sicker than any disease. It's a good thing you died before you heard even one of my stories, Mama.*

Stella moaned. Without warning, the bad picture-memory flooded up and stared out at her from Tillie's white bedspread.

The October day was so bright every detail of the scene was illuminated. It was the perfectly normal attitude of Otis's left hand resting on the open window of the driver's side of the car that prompted her to step forward and look, even though she didn't really want to.

In order not to stain her new polka-dot peau de soie pumps, she stepped around the pool of dark blood forming under the car. It did not register in her mind as unusual. Just as long as Otis's hand, that part of him she loved better than the man to whom it belonged, was visible, everything would be all right.

Arms pressed to her sides, breasts touching the warm metal of the car, she peered into the front seat. Behind the steering wheel, Otis sat up, his head thrown back. His eye were open, staring at the streaks of fresh crimson that decorated the gray mohair headliner.

For some moments, she regarded the delicate throat and face peppered with round, purple holes. Allowing her eyes to wander down his white linen sleeve, she found he had meticulously folded the cuff halfway up his tanned forearm. On the inside of the shirt was a laundry mark. It read GAL-28.

She rolled the cuff down one turn to hide the stamp, then thinking better of it, decided the police would want everything exactly as she

121

had found it. Calmly she returned the cuff to where it had been and patted her husband's cold arm.

She sat down on the running board and lowered her head between her knees. Only when the buzzing was completely gone did she stand and look again to reaffirm the lingering image of Otis.

When she felt strong enough, she looked beyond her husband to her son.

Still wearing the nubby felt hat, his handsome and noble head was slightly bent toward his father in the attitude of someone who has not heard what has just been said. The look on his face was one of distressed perception. The front of his blue-striped shirt was decorated with seven neat, purple circles. An eighth had been made through the middle of his smooth, ivory-white forehead a quarter-inch below the hatband.

She was glad she'd never thought to look down into the seat, grateful she never saw the bloody mess of severed and mutilated genitalia. The newspapers reported the particulars in detail; the key word they'd used to describe the double mutilation-murder was "unnatural."

A disturbance of the light caused the bad picture to fade.

Silhouetted by the hallway lights, a young girl, whose outline resembled that of the child on the Morton Salt containers, stood perfectly still in the doorway, her skinny spindle legs bowed under the thin dress. Her features remained hidden in the shadow.

"Hello?"

The voice was small and tentative. At the sound of it, Stella's heart turned over.

"Hello, darling. How are *you?*"

There was a short sigh. "My father is sick."

"Oh. I'm sorry." Stella paused, then added as half question, half statement, "You're sad."

The child said nothing at first but lifted her head slightly, her attention roused.

"Yes." There was resignation in the young voice.

"Mmmm, I know all about that."

The silhouette took a hesitant step into the room, one hand still holding on to the doorjamb.

"You do? Why do you know about that?"

Into the frame came the dark outline of a thick womanly hand gently tugging at the child's sleeve, pulling her away from the door. "Zoe! What are you doing? Come out of there! Let these people sleep —they're sick."

122

At the last second, before she disappeared altogether, the child looked back, yearning. "Wait for me. I might be able to come back tomorrow."

"Wonderful. I'll be waiting. Sweet dreams of roses, little one."

"Sweet dreams to you, too, old lady."

11:23 p.m.

He felt okay, a little weak and feverish, but at least he could say he was breathing and pissing without help. It was the boredom that was making him nuts.

Tiptoeing to the door, Corky held his breath and peeked down the hall. The nursing station was deserted. In fact, there wasn't anybody anywhere. To make sure, he did his cat-coughing-up-a-hairball imitation and croaked, "Help, help, I'm dying," a few times. No one came forth to save him.

He guessed that somewhere the changing of the guard was taking place and the two shifts of nurses were meeting for the sole purpose of gossiping about the patients.

He imagined a crowded locker room and an assortment of well-filled bra cups and lace slips, shaved and talced underarms, and damp wisps of neck hair. The air would be thick with the scent of Opium. He imagined himself sitting on the corner of the makeup-littered counter listening to the opera of idle feminine chatter going on about him.

"Oh yeah, and then there's that tweaked-out retard guy in bed 512-B who tried to kill himself and failed." (The uptight, skinny nurse with the gnarly black hairs all over her face said this, curling back her mustached upper lip.)

"You must mean Corky Benner. He's like a total lame." (The fat blonde nurse who smelled like she chewed garlic gum.)

"Yeah, except he's so handsome. He looks exactly like Bruce Springsteen. I mean, I really got turned on just looking a him. I wonder what his problem *really* is? I wonder if my sitting on his face would help?" (The outrageously excellent Oriental with the knockout ass and legs.)

"Oh, he probably got some poor girl in trouble." (The old broad with the southern accent who wore the "Trust Jesus—He's White" button pinned to the inside of her uniform.)

"Nah, he's probably on drugs." (The black swing shift nurse with the torpedo tits and the pink wart.)

"He's got *total* pimple death all *over* his forehead." (The cute fluff

123

with no brains who caught him squeezing the huge, inflamed third eye between his eyebrows after dinner.)

"Who cares about pimples? He's probably a real jerk who has a two-inch dick, can't get his shit together, and doesn't have any friends he can talk to." (The hugely fat one whose thighs looked like bulging cellophane bags of tollhouse cookies.)

"Let's face it, he's a fucked pup. A total cop-out asshole, and we wish he'd done it right." (The chorus.)

Anyway, he guessed it was probably something close to that. Angrily he slipped off the flimsy hospital slippers and threw them at the window. So what? What did he care what a bunch of girls said? Big fucking deal. What did they know about it anyway?

Inching around the doorjamb, he hugged the wall and crept silently toward the double doors marked "Ward Two—Acute" some sixty feet away.

A moan from the room across the hall grabbed his attention. Room 519. The sign on the door read: "ISOLATION! DO NOT ENTER!"

AIDS probably. He'd seen the man watching him. All bones and sores. Dying from AIDS. Totally gross. God. It was sickness to the absolute max.

Corky broke into a sweat and moved toward the next room. He wouldn't let himself think about the man with AIDS. It would make the panic come back.

From the darkened doorway of room 518, he caught a glimpse of an open mouth, drooling. Above the sound of even, harsh snoring, someone was crying "Mama" over and over. In spite of himself, he leaned in and sniffed.

Disgustorama. Piss 'n' crap. Worse than a park outhouse.

An old lady, concentrating on peeing, sat on a toilet chair with wheels. Spellbound by the sight, he did not move until Stella glanced up and waved.

Her toothless gums glistened as she grinned, unrolled a length of toilet paper, and wiped. "Hello there, handsome," she said.

Corky waved, caught himself, and quickly moved on. God. Totally weird. Staring right at an old lady while she took a whiz. Hello, handsome? Sheesh. An old lady talking like that? Bizarre.

He held his breath to guard against the strange and horrible smells emanating from other rooms and sprinted the remaining distance of the hall.

At the double doors, he peered through the windows and made a hasty check for alarms.

Clear.

Sucking in his stomach, he slid through to the acute unit and darted to the first darkened room. Again he scanned for the enemy. Seeing no one, he reentered the hall and glanced back into the room where he'd just stood: 500. His old room. Now empty, the place looked like a torture chamber. Large and menacing-looking hoses jetted out of the ceiling while shiny canisters with tubes running to black and chrome dials hung along the walls.

At the bedside was a gray machine covered with more black dials and knobs. He recognized the machine as the one that had breathed for him. Disgustorama. Totally gross. The thought of it going into him made him gag.

He walked on, passing another room that emitted foul stenches. Room 502. Fat lady, head shaved and a gray breathing machine connected to her via a tube coming out of her nose. The noise of the thing bothered him. It was similar to someone using a bicycle pump. In a lounge chair next to the bed snored a huge, Viking-type dude in a doctor's coat. The name tag read: "Dr. Cramer, Cardiology." Twitching involuntarily, the guy snorted, mumbled "Catechols?" and resumed snoring.

504. Old man ralphing into a yellow plastic bowl. The smell was beyond anything he'd ever known—sort of like old farts and morning breath wrapped in a Stri-Dex medicated acne pad.

506. Frankenstein. A young dude with steel tongs screwed into the sides of his shaved skull was strapped to a bed that stood on its end. The dude stared vacantly into space, his arms and legs jerking spasmodically.

"Psssst! Hey dude, what happened to you?"

"Uhn . . . uhn . . . uhn."

Oh. Blender brain. *Coma II.* Total bummer.

508. Empty or maybe just too dark to see. The silence in the room was unbroken. Maybe somebody was dead in there. Maybe they died of some kind of disease that was transferred through the air by spores from the fungus growing all over the hospital.

In his haste to get away, he tripped over a wastepaper basket, spilling its contents all over the hallway. A pencil-thin strip of bloody tissue rolled out of the gauze and stopped an inch from his bare foot.

With the reflexes of an athlete, he leapt to the other side of the hall and gaped back at the thing, horrified. A tapeworm for sure. He could see the eyes looking right at him. Oh gross. It was a frigging tapeworm that had almost touched him.

Immediately the hospital became a place full of unclean and infec-

125

tious dangers out to get him. He ran blindly down the hall and turned in what he thought was the direction of his room. Instead of seeing the double doors, he found himself inside a spacious room with huge windows and a 180-degree view of San Francisco.

The brass plate on the solid wood door read: "505 Private." Private. Had to be someone important or very special.

The room smelled like lemons and was furnished much like a hotel room. One bed, an easy chair, a private bathroom, and an end table holding a regular-looking table lamp. Fans and flowers were printed on the wallpaper in a repeating diagonal pattern. The only telltale evidence of a hospital was the distant sound of the fat lady's respirator coming through the wall. *Click, whoosh. Click, whoosh.*

It was hard to see who or what was occupying the bed. For a few seconds, he allowed his eyes to adjust to the dim lighting, then stepped boldly to the side rail for a closer inspection of something he thought he might have fantasized.

But it wasn't a fantasy, it was true. Lying on the bed, sleeping like Snow White under glass, was a righteously gorgeous girl. Different from—more excellent than—Molly. Any day.

He swallowed hard, fascinated by her face; even with the broken nose, cuts, and bruises, she was totally beautiful.

She'd probably been in a car wreck. He leaned closer and saw her broken arm. Yeah, definitely a wreck. Probably went through the windshield.

A surge of tender pity swirled inside him. "Hey! 'Scuse me. Are you asleep?"

The girl groaned softly.

Getting up the nerve, he gingerly uncovered her uninjured arm and picked up her hand. He worked the printed side of the hospital identification band around her wrist to the light:

"Cross (Lucy). Pt. #11248 N.F.P. Dr.s Gladstein / Snyder."

Lucy? Lucy in the Sky with Diamonds.

For the first time in months, he felt a joy he'd thought would never be his again. Made brave by the resurgence of feeling, he unlocked the side rail and sat next to the girl's frail body. The weight of him pulled the sheet down, away from her. Exposed to the soft glow of the bedside lamp was her breast, rosy pink nipple and all.

Drawing back, he took in the whole picture: the fabric of the sheet and the naked, living breast twenty inches away from him. He'd never seen anything so superior in all his life.

Prompted by a rush of emotion and hormones, he kissed her lips, hesitated, and quickly kissed the top of her satiny, warm breast. He focused on the small, even marks.

126

Then he whimpered. Oh fuck.

Teeth marks?

Rape?

The violence of the word jerked him off the bed, a repulsive scene playing over in his mind, getting mixed up with something else. Something ugly.

No! Please, no!

His mind reeled. For *her* to be hurt like . . . like *that*? Fuck man, no! No! Lucy in the Sky with Diamonds hurt by some piece of shit filth?

His heart beating in his throat, Corky retched once and began to shriek.

11:25 p.m.

Cross did not recognize the odd noise that was like breathing some-how. *Click, whoosh. Click, whoosh.*

She wanted to open her eyes and find the source of the sound but did not want to face whatever was there. Everything hurt. Her head, her ribs, her arm. Maybe it was best to stay in the dark.

Someone kissed her and was sitting next to her, touching her arm, or was it her breast?

Oh, Michael. Michael, please help me.

But it wasn't Michael. It was someone crying. There was a jarring of the bed and then women's urgent voices sounding as if they were filtered through cotton balls.

Maybe they needed help. Maybe it was Michael.

Open your eyes, Cross. Stop hiding.

I don't want to. I'm so tired, and it hurts.

A feeling of slow-motion unreality pulled her back to that first day after they'd made love. Without explanation, Michael had left sud-denly. Retreating to her reading loft, she analyzed their every mo-ment together, trying to make sense of the man's hot and cold moods, and his crazy, off-the-ceiling energy.

Sense, however, was not to be made of anything. Simply thinking of him sent miniature roller-coaster rides from her vagina to her throat and inflamed her with the powerful and unruly vitality created by new sexuality.

She ran from the loft to her studio. She would paint something magnificent for him. It would be a painting created by the muses born within her, parented by love's first joy. Cross laughed and corrected herself: Let's face it, Cross, you mean lust. Lust. Desire. Salaciousness. Hunger. Need.

The oil paint waited for her brush. Pastel colors. Cross pastel paintings.

But wait. What had Michael said? That her use of pastel colors was beautiful but . . . like an old cliché? Was that the word he'd used or was it "overdone"?

Her work had been criticized before by the masters, but this felt a million times worse. Was it true? Was her use of pastel colors passé? The artist's sickness, chronic self-doubt, made her blush. Why hadn't Nathan told her? How could he have let her go on embarrassing herself?

A moan of physical pleasure escaped her as she pictured Michael's eyes during their lovemaking. The rush of her desire brought with it an idea.

From her palette, Cross rubbed away every trace of pastel color. She would please him, thrill him, make him privy to the wild and free part of her soul.

Deliberately Cross slashed the canvas corner to corner with a bold stroke of deep Venetian red.

Tuesday

16 Sweat covered him like a flimsy sheet. In the sluggish bored time, there was nothing to do but bathe in the music Doll brought him and continue waiting. From the earphones, Vivaldi's *Four Seasons* created images which would normally have led him on to daydreaming. But today he resisted the desire to slip into other worlds. Today he was disturbed by the beautiful young boy across the hall who had wept most of the night.

He shifted his weight on the cooling blanket and glanced once more across the hall. The sight of the boy lounging in his bed took him back to the free years—that brief time before God's scourge began.

Those were the days of the bathhouses. Thrilling. Blatant. Addicting for a young man so long kept prisoner in a Bible Belt–town closet. Fifteen, sometimes twenty faceless men in one evening.

Just leave the door open, sweetmeat, and don't forget your towel. Like a small prayer before and after meals.

Then there was the night Doll walked in and closed the door on that part of his life forever. Like all beginnings, the crossover from orgy to monogamy was not easy, but Doll's patient love seduced him from his addiction.

Not that it saved him. It was too late, even then: too late to stop the Black Plague picking them off ten, then a thousand at a time.

Lord, why hast Thou forsaken us?

He rolled his eyes. Oh do come *on*, darling, don't you remember

131

the motto? The only life worth living is the one that is risked. He'd risked and lost. But life was, at thirty-six, too short. Then again, death was so fond of young, vital men—was it not? Hadn't he walked a hundred times in one day past the low, black granite wall in Washington, engraved with all those thousands of names? And whenever he went to the airport, didn't he slow the car to pay heed to row upon endless row of white cross markers in the military cemetery, looking for all the world like ghostly platoons marching before their noble leaders?

He could easily have been one of them; the disease of politicians being as senseless as the one he was dying of. Or at the very least, he could have been among the scores of young sons lost to car wrecks, drugs, or street warfare.

Except he would not give in to playing the fatalist. He did not believe he couldn't have been a survivor. God, what he wouldn't give to be an old man one day—an old queen full of stories and mischief and young, sweet boys.

He sighed as best he could, which was really like an aborted yawn, and closed his tired eyes. No, his death was not timely or fair, although he was able to take some satisfaction in knowing he had provided his father the fulfillment of his life's ambition of triumphing over Mother. Father was right all along—Mother, in perfecting the maternal art of sissification, *did* knot the apron strings tight enough around her only son's balls to make them rot away and fall off. He'd never had a chance.

Ahh, Mother. So cloying, those moist, fat hands always on him, caressing, invading, demanding. And that oiled voice of hers, whispering about Father and his dirty needs, then telling him how beautiful he could be if he would just hold still for Mommy to wash his pretty face and comb his lovely hair. Her little beauty was going to put them all to shame, and wouldn't he let Mommy smear a teeny bit of Mommy's lipstick on his full, pretty mouth? And didn't he adore the way Mommy's silky slips felt on his baby skin? Did he love his Mommy? Didn't he know he wasn't supposed to want to escape? Their love was special; their love was invincible. Mother and son forever.

He tensed, caught himself and swallowed bile. Anxiety pinched the back of his throat as he waited for the wave of cramps. Mercifully, the sharp-taloned devil in his guts remained asleep.

He hadn't told anyone, not even Doll, about the laughing.

It happened on his way back from the Castro Street clinic. The purple and black results slip, which bore his birth date, private code number, and the abbreviation "POS" in the lower right-hand corner, was neatly tucked into one back pocket. A partial list of one hundred and five past contacts was in the other . . . and those were only the ones he could remember on the spot.

Say baby, are you absolutely positive?

Yes, terminally so.

There was so much to think about and feel, he didn't know which emotion or fear to start with.

Take it from the top.

Doll—did he have It? Would he leave?

His job, the insurance benefits—could they, would they fire him?

His students—he'd have to . . . No, change that. He *wanted* to tell his students, eventually.

His plans—What about his dream of founding a school for gifted kids? Who could substitute and take his group of teens on the tour of Greece next summer? What about learning the rest of love?

Son of a bitch! *Who* did this to him? What gave God the right to do this to any fucking body?

He stopped in front of a playground full of children and listened to the constant twitter of their tiny, lively voices; it was like standing in the middle of an aviary.

Children. God's creatures—the defenseless innocents, blank pages open for the imprint of those passing through their lives. It seemed atrocious that some of them would fall into the care of others capable of damaging them so severely. But they did, and there wasn't anything to be done about it except to try to repair the damage later on.

Through the blur of tears, he thought he saw Mother waving to him from the other side of the jungle gym. Grossly obese in that disgusting pink cashmere suit with the mink trim, she wore a Jackie Kennedy pillbox hat set absurdly to one side of her overdone beehive. The material of the suit pulled tight over the bulk of her mammoth arms as she beckoned him to come to her.

Mother. The demon in his life. Her and her goddamned Bible.

Breaking into a run, he slammed his fist into the schoolyard fence, making it jingle like a series of bells. He was aware of a pounding behind him: her footsteps gaining on him, still refusing to let him be. All that lumpy, sweating mess grabbing at the back of his jacket, missing by inches. Her piglike grunts sickened him, reminding him of the dreaded mornings she would make them breakfast in bed, crawling in next to him and crunching, sucking down toast and jam and cream cheese by the fistful.

133

When the last drop of adrenaline was spent and his legs would not go another step, he stopped and spun around to face her.

In victory Mother stepped toward him, confident that he was hers and the Lord's forever.

He had only one defense against her now. He pulled the HIV test slip from his pocket and held it in front of her eyes—a vampire's victim brandishing a crucifix.

Here! See? My ticket to freedom, Mother. My ticket to peace.

An expression of profound distress instantly replaced the one of triumph and her pockmarked chin quivered violently, reminding him of a small burrowing animal.

I'm going to die, Mother, and you can't come along. I'm going to a place where you will never see your precious pretty boy again.

Mother's chin animal quivered harder, setting off in him a wail of hysterical laughter. He laughed until he cried, until the little animal disappeared and he knew he had won at last. . . .

The IV pump made a changing-gears kind of noise, waited a few seconds, and belched out a series of coded bleeps.

The redheaded nurse hurried into the room, mimicking the sound of the machine an octave lower so that her voice and the pump were in harmony. Adjusting the machine, she stared at him, then ran a bare hand through his hair, smoothing it back from his face.

"You okay, bub?"

He blinked and closed his eyes. No.

"Are you feeling worse than yesterday?"

His eyes opened and said yes, worse.

She nodded. "Well, me too. I did a lot of bad things last night instead of going to bed, and I'm worse too. Of course . . ." She shrugged. "I'm not *quite* as worse as you, but then again, I don't get any of the nice drugs you get either. I have to depend on suspicious street people or Ripple for my highs."

A left-sided half-smile appeared. She's crazy, he thought. I've got a borderline personality for a nurse and she's going to make me live another day if it kills her. He considered laughing at that but decided he couldn't afford the effort. He had to conserve his energy, although it seemed strange that he would need energy to die.

Cat pulled on a pair of exam gloves—or hand condoms, as she sometimes thought of them—and took a deep breath. "All right then, onward it is for us very *un*christian soldiers. We're about ready to pull you out of the gotten-worse category and demote you to only-feeling-bad classification."

"Yuhn." He gulped for air. "Thank you for your kind . . ."

Kindness. Almost got it all out—five words in a row was too much.

"Funny you should mention that," she said, unwrapping the isolation pack containing his bed linen. "I was just talking about my kind last night. Terminal nurse types—worse than creamed chipped tuna on . . ."

He stared past her, his pupils dilated in bewilderment. Scarcely lifting his head, he squinted in order to determine whether the doorway was obliterated by a giant cloud of brightly colored balloons or he had begun having noteworthy hallucinations.

The helium cloud was anchored by a pair of tennis shoes.

"This Professor Dean's room?" The voice came from somewhere inside the cloud.

Speechless, Cat swayed at the magnificent sight.

After a brief silence, the balloons bobbed. "We're gonna have to let these things go pretty soon," said the bodiless voice. "There's ten bunches here and I've got two more packages besides and they're kinda heavy. Couple of candy stripers had to help me bring them up on the freight elevator. We're creating a safety hazard by blocking up the hallway. Do you want me to release them in here?"

Springing into action, Cat pulled in the balloons and let them float to the ceiling. When all one hundred bright rubber globes were set free, the ceiling could no longer be seen.

Unballooned, a squat, bullnecked deliveryman stood in the middle of the room nervously juggling a clipboard, a clear plastic box containing about ten cassette tapes, and a large, twenty-pound box of chocolates. Handing the boxes to Cat, he stepped to the side of the bed. "Sign here," he said, placing the clipboard close to the sick man's face.

With detached interest, Cat stood back and watched the deliveryman slowly become aware of his surroundings. He checked out the wasted body, smelled the death smell, and within a matter of seconds, found the neon-orange "PRECAUTION—AIDS" sticker over the bed. He snatched the clipboard away from the hands he'd placed it in a second before and stiffly stepped back to the door.

"AIDS?" The man glared at her with savage eyes half bugging out of his head. "You mean this fucking fairy has AIDS and you let me come in here with all this contamination? You let me touch his things, breathe his air? You and that fairy ought to be fucking shot!" He sped heedlessly down the hall, leaving in his wake a trail of puzzled stares.

Cat glanced back at her patient and held out her hands. "AIDS-phobic—notoriously stupid people."

135

Undaunted, he shrugged. "Yuhn. Doesn't bother . . . me. Much like . . . uhn . . . being a Jew . . . in Nazi Germany. We are the unclean. The undead, like vampires."

She opened her mouth to protest, felt the protective surgical mask at her chin and the latex gloves on her hands, and hesitated. "But it's only the flesh," she said. "The disease doesn't change the spirit of the person inside."

"It does . . . to some. They lose faith . . . uhn . . . in others."

A string from one of the balloons caught in her barrette. She pulled the balloon—a green one—from the ceiling and read the inscription: "Dr. Dean—Miss your sharp, right-Engeled reMarx. Joel Skinner."

A white one with a red rosebud read: "Professor Dean, wish you were here. We all miss you muchly. Nancy Rucinsky."

Inspecting a dozen more at random, she found each one inscribed with a different name and line of endearment.

"Your students?"

"Yuhn."

"What did you profess?"

"Poli sci . . . at Berkeley."

"I'll bet you were good."

"The best."

"Modesty in moderation. That's what I like to see."

He fought the giggle down. "Uhn, don't make . . . me laugh."

At that they laughed, even though they both knew it would turn him blue and start the diarrhea. But having once been children, they also both knew that forbidden laughter was the best laughter.

Chewing on a nut-sprinkled caramel roll, Cat selected a tape from the plastic box, slipped it into his cassette player, and placed the earphones over his ears. There was a moment in which he strained to hear, a second of surprise, and then his face spread into a grin.

While he listened, she bathed him, gently scrubbing around the areas of fungus growing on his feet and legs. It was like washing down a laboratory skeleton. His ribs, prominently displayed through the thin skin, reminded her of a birdcage.

When she looked up at him again, he was crying.

Without protest he let her take the earphones, which she placed over her own ears.

" . . . quantum theories and all that useless hype. So, that's all I've got to say for now. Maybe at break I'll buzz over to San Francisco and pay a visit if you don't mind and if they'll let me in to see you. Anyway, there's a line of people here who want to say something too, so this is Rick Jason signing off."

There was a silence for a moment. Then the same youthful male voice came back on, only lower. "Take care, Prof. We all really care, you know?"

Next came a young woman's cheerful voice. "Hi, Dr. Dean, this is Iris Collier. I really wish you were here with us. Your sub isn't anywhere near as good as you are and he can't even tell a joke properly. I don't know how . . ." There was a long pause. "I really wish there was something we could do, you know? You were really—I mean, you *are* really such a wonderful man . . . we really, you know, *got* it when you lectured and, ah, we really feel such a loss because you were more than just our teacher. You gave us so much of yourself and we loved . . ."

Cat removed the headset and handed it back to him. "This is very special," she said. "This is the richest gift anyone could ever receive."

Later, after dusting his feet, buttocks, and armpits with baby powder, she turned him gently onto his side, changed the linen on half the bed, rolled him over the lump, and changed the other half. In the middle of helping him make brushing motions with his toothbrush, she felt him hook his hands in hers and hold it there.

"Do you think . . . I'm . . ." Gasp. "Does . . . what I am . . . disgust you?"

Ashamed, she blushed and dropped her gaze to her lap. "No, not now, but I used to feel that way once. We're jealous, you know . . . we women. There aren't enough men to go around as it is, and we feel cheated. But that was before I came to know who you are. Delicate and sensitive like women—no different."

"No different," he echoed. "Good truth." He nuzzled her hand and held up his arm to show off the patchwork of black and purple bruises. The IV she had started the morning before was still good.

"Well done IV. First one . . ." Suck in air, chest heaving, working overtime. ". . . that's lasted more . . . than twenty-four hours. Thank you."

From a roll of silk tape, Cat ripped off a three-inch strip. It wasn't necessary, but she double-secured the catheter at the entry site anyway.

Her nurse side wanted him to go quickly, go to sleep and boom, be gone. The unprofessional, selfish side wanted him to stay. There was something to be learned from him, and soon this lifetime of knowledge would cease to be available.

"Well, how about we try going for forty-eight hours more?"

He stared at her. "Why would I want to do that?" The question

137

was neither depressed nor resentful; it was simply that he had made his peace and was ready to go.

Taking another cassette from the box, she pushed it gently into his hand. "You can't leave until you've let all of them say goodbye."

In that fuzzy unreal world six miles left of exhaustion, Nora walked into and partway up Dr. Gillespie's feet.

Startled to attention, she groaned. "Oh God, anybody but you!"

Dr. Gillespie's oversized face swiveled on a nonexistent neck. "Get off my bunions," he growled, last night's bourbon still clinging to his breath.

Overly apologetic and not quite in her right mind, Nora knelt down and began brushing off his shoes, until the man pulled her up sharply and steered her into the Ward Two kitchen. Quickly he closed the door behind them.

"Listen here, Carmotti." He pushed his face so close to hers she could see the bottoms of his pores. "I'm well aware of the delicacy of this situation and I trust your discretion. Let's just forget about the other night. You forget you saw me with Mrs. Sauerborn and I'll forget I saw you in . . ." He paused. ". . . in that incriminating condition out in the hallway."

Nora covered her face at the memory, until the full meaning of what he had said filtered through the cobwebs. "Wait a minute. I thought . . . Mrs. Sauerborn? You mean the woman you were with was Dr. Sauerborn's wife?"

Dr. Gillespie clapped a pudgy, antiseptic-smelling hand over her mouth. "Jesus!" he said with urgency. "Keep your voice down, will you? Look . . ." His voice turned cold. "If you want to continue working here, keep your mouth shut about this." He released her, opened the door with a flourish, and pointed a threatening finger. "Not one word—not even to your dog."

"But I don't own a—"

The physician waved his hand. "I don't care. This is the last word. Understand?"

Nora nodded, trying to suppress a gratified smile. Cat was going to love this one.

Looking like a lost Great Dane, Nathan Keplin loomed over Cat and waited for her to acknowledge his presence. Annoyed by his expectant patience, she stubbornly stuck to the task of finishing her morning charting.

138

Nathan shuffled his feet once or twice and increased the volume of his breathing.

She turned her body as far away from his presence as she could and proceeded to write the same sentence twice.

He wrinkled some paper and tapped his fingers.

Her concentration was going. She forgot the patient she was writing about and had to look at the name on the back of the page to refresh her memory.

He sighed a long, forlorn sigh.

She reluctantly swiveled in her chair.

"May I . . ."

The words died on her lips as her eyes grew wide. The older gentleman before her wore a chartreuse-and-orange-plaid suit, a forest-green vest, and a tan ascot.

". . . ah, help you?"

My God, where did he find the outfit? Had to be either Salvation Army or Savile Row. Did his mother know he was out in public dressed like that? Liberace had competition.

The man knit his eyebrows, which vaguely resembled a weathered thatched roof. "Yes, I'd like to see Cross. Lucy Cross," he said with a slight British accent. "I'm Nathan Keplin, her agent. I think I'm the only one allowed in to see her." He held out a grocery bag and a thick pad of drawing paper. "I've brought some paints and pens and things. I thought they might help bring her out of it. I didn't know what else to do." He hesitated, and for no particular reason they both looked down at his white Air Jordan high-tops, which were only a half-size larger than hers.

"Is she fully awake yet?" The question was couched in hope.

Cat put the chart back in the chart wheel, then stood to face him. The kind, wrinkled look around his eyes softened her toward him. "I believe we're making progress in that general direction." She stopped, aware that she had suddenly developed a British accent.

It was one of her numerous bad habits to unconsciously mimic people's accents. Once, she'd spent an evening with Mathilde, an Australian rancher, an anesthesiologist from Georgia, and a German car mechanic. By the end of the night, everyone was convinced she had missed her calling as a linguist or a multiple personality.

She mentally reset the dialect dial to her own Bostonian pahk-the-cah-ovah-theah station and continued.

"She woke up around four this morning, and asked for a tube of cadmium red and a number twenty-nine brush. At four-thirty, she asked if we had any more gesso or rabbit-skin powder, and at five-thirty, she woke up long enough to take a few sips of water and complain that her head and arm hurt. She then asked what had happened to her, who stole her new roll of canvas, and how long she was going to have to stay in the academy infirmary. Without waiting for answers, she went out again."

"That's my Cross," Nathan said, his eyes beginning to water. "I'm glad she's back. I really couldn't bear to lose her."

"Well, don't worry about it anymore," Cat said, not a hundred percent sure he shouldn't. "She survived. She's got to have a strong will to come out of something like this." She took his arm. "Why don't you come with me and we'll see if we can bring her out of it. People respond to the voices of those they love more than any other stimulus."

When they entered Cross's room, Mathilde was busy restocking the linen supply cabinet. Cross remained in a restless sleep.

Shyly Nathan stepped close to the bed. At the sight of Cross's bruised and lacerated face, his eyes grew huge with alarm.

"Ah, don't worry, monsieur," Mathilde said, seeing his dismay. "She is coming up and out now, I think. She is only depressed. She will wake up for you soon, wait and see."

Mathilde ran an eye over his outfit, removed her gloves and rolled them into a ball. With a backhand jump shot, she landed them in the wastebasket seven feet away.

"Please, monsieur, I must say, it is so refreshing to see a man who dresses with such flair. Quite commendable to you, monsieur." She took a step toward the man and touched his lapel with an expression of complete admiration.

Nathan bowed and kissed her hand. "Enchanté, mademoiselle."

Blushing like a schoolgirl, Mathilde took a few mincing steps to the door, skipped once, and disappeared down the hall.

Sitting on either side of the bed, Cat and Nathan wedged the injured woman securely between them, both cradling her small shoulders.

"It's time, sweetie," Cat said, shaking Cross gently. "It's time to rise and shine."

Michael was there, touching her, saying goodbye as usual, although that wasn't the reason for her tears. It had more to do with the knot in the vicinity of her psyche that needed rubbing out.

A warmer, lighter touch confused her, pulling her from the dark as her body was lifted up and held.

Michael? Is that you, or is this going to be one of those nightmares where only the images linger? She could not remember if he'd left her again, and moaned in her sleep. For her, the saddest thing wasn't his leaving, but the coming back and leaving again.

It felt late. She must have overslept. It had to be Wednesday morning because it was Tuesday night that they'd had the ugly scene over the *People* magazine interview. She had kept it as a surprise, hoping that the little bit of new publicity would please him and make him see that she was still in demand and, to some people, still worthwhile.

Never for a moment did he lose his inscrutable smile, even after he started lecturing her in that barely controlled tone. "Nice" people didn't allow themselves to appear on the pages of a smut rag famous for advertising whores and other perverts. Obviously, he added, losing the smile, someone had her pegged correctly.

That was when she'd made the mistake of trying to defend herself. She knew better than to disagree with him, knew that it would set him off on a tirade, bringing up his venom and catapulting them into a violent scene. She knew all that, but pleaded with him anyway to please believe, for once, that she really was a good person.

Even after he'd dragged her by the hair to the mirror and pinned her neck with his arm, she kept on insisting that she wasn't all bad.

Squeezing her neck tighter, he demanded she look herself in the eye and admit she was nothing more than a slut, a worthless bitch, a waste of his time. She held off until she thought her temples would burst. And when she finally did look at the reflected image, she saw only an unhappy child who had lived all her life with the loneliness of never knowing love.

She managed to go as far as repeating a phrase that came easily to the girl in the mirror—a phrase she had said so often for her father: "I promise. I promise I will try to be better for you."

Michael broke the mirror with her forehead.

She began again. "I am a . . . worthless . . . a worthless . . . but I will be better, I promise."

He rolled her face into the broken glass and shouted until the veins in his neck were two long balloons.

She began again. "I am a worthless waste . . . and a bad . . ."

In a bloody shard of mirror, she caught sight of her favorite painting and stopped. It was one of her first serious works, a small impressionistic study of a garden. At the time it was painted, she had only begun to know her true power as an artist, able to make her colors mean something beyond tone or pigment.

A bad person could not have created that garden.

141

Rebellion welled inside her against Michael and her father.

"I *am* a good person!" she yelled defiantly. "I am an artist and my work brings joy to people. There are people who love me, people who care about—"

The force with which he snapped her head back and threw her to the floor immobilized her, so that for a moment, she thought he'd broken her neck. She realized with a small sense of satisfaction that she had the presence of mind to test her toes and fingers for movement.

Michael ripped her dress and forced himself into her, his fingers digging into the flesh of her buttocks.

Even through the violence that followed, she was fascinated that his eyes still held her. Yielding to him, she thought if she loved him through it, she would break down his wall of hurt and he would stop.

But he did not stop. His eyes left hers and pain seared through her left breast. When his face reappeared, his mouth and chin were smeared with blood.

"Come, you little whore," he said in a peculiar voice, one she had not heard before. "Come because it's the last fucking you'll get from me." He held her head in a vise grip as his pace picked up and he broke into the rhythm that heralded his own orgasm.

When he lay still, she slid cautiously out from under him and cupped her injured breast, searching with her fingers until she found the gaping wound. Using the wall for support, she stood up wondering what to do next.

Wash off. That was the logical thing to do. She would wash herself and tend to her wounds. She took a teetering step toward the bathroom and was sent reeling into the dining room table by the impact of his boot against her spine.

The first time she saw the hunting knife was the split second before it slashed across her cheek. In a daze, she watched more of her blood drip onto the light oak floor. The striking contrast between the yellow and the red held her attention until the shock of a kick to her solar plexus took her breath away.

Cross crawled toward the door to the garden. If she was going to die, that was where she wanted to be. Before she made it even halfway, Michael grabbed her legs and straddled her again, even more enraged that his body would not provide him with his first choice of a weapon to hurt her. In his frustration, he bit the bridge of her nose, then pressed his thumbs into her windpipe.

At that moment, it occurred to her that part of her *wanted* him to kill her. To die at his hand would be the ultimate submission, proving to him once and for all that her love for him was the ultimate love.

But her body, now recognizing itself to be in severe distress, rebelled and she struck out at him blindly. He'd killed so much of her spirit, what more could he do to hurt her?

As if he read her thought, he jumped forward, and with the force of both feet, snapped the bones in her arm.

When she regained consciousness, she was on the bed and he was doing something to her with the knife, but she no longer sensed pain. She had dissociated from her body, and was watching the goings-on like a mildly interested spectator. The last solid thing her memory saved was the sound of her head being smashed into the corner of the bed frame.

The rest appeared in chimeric sequences: watching herself inch to the phone, hearing herself whisper to a faraway voice that demanded easy things like name and address.

Then there were men in sky-blue shirts gently moving her and calmly demanding more complicated answers—answers she could not remember giving, just as she could not remember the town in which Michael had been born, or how he'd found her cabin on that day they first made love. . . .

Overwhelmed, Cross began to cry in her trauma sleep. The deep sadness she felt over the loss of Michael melted into and married the darkness of her dream.

Cross gave in to the movement, this floating in someone's arms, secure and cared for. Close to her a woman's low voice coaxed.

"Rise and shine, sweetie. You have a visitor." Cat held the tearing woman, and nodded to Nathan to speak.

"Darling? It's Nate, dear. You're really not being very polite. Please open your eyes and look at your lonely old dingbat, won't you?"

There was no response.

"Come out of it, Cross," Nathan said firmly. "It's time to wake up now."

Cross murmured but her eyes remained closed.

Cat used the control to raise the bed into a high back position and turned on the bedside radio. Strains of Debby Boone singing "You Light Up My Life" shattered the quiet of the room.

"She needs stimulation," Cat said. She's been cooped up without any sounds other than a respirator from the next room and an occasional nurse's voice. She hasn't been touched except for a bed bath and turning." Cat opened a window. "Lysol and alcohol swabs are about all she's had to smell."

Recruited into action, Nathan removed a tube of paint from the crumpled paper bag and smeared a gob of yellow oil paint onto a paper towel.

"Smell, Cross," he said, and held it under her nose. "Do you remember that smell?"

Cross opened her eyes and squinted.

Nathan spoke rapidly, running his words together as if he were afraid he might lose her attention before he could get everything out.

"Well, well, hello there, stranger. Let me see . . . ah, the garden is looking pretty natty and the Japanese cabbage needs looking after. You're the one with the jade thumb, darling. I certainly can't do a thing with it so you'll have to get out there and tame it or we'll have to plow it under and get a—"

"The garden." It was a definite statement.

Nathan was overjoyed. "Yes, darling, the garden. Do you remember?"

"Yes." She envisioned the purple, cream, and viridian-green hues of the cabbage plant. "I remember."

"Cross, do you know who this is?" Cat asked.

Lazily focusing, as if she'd had one too many drinks, Cross nodded. "Nathan."

Taking her in his arms, Nathan let her head loll on his shoulder. "Your arrival back to planet Earth is much celebrated, darling."

She patted his back and a drawn-out sob escaped her. "What happened? Where's . . ."

"You're in the hospital. You were . . ." Cat searched for the simplest explanation. The woman would be vulnerable; there was no point upsetting her and possibly sending her back into her dark retreat. "You were hurt by accident."

"Accident?" Cross strained to recall pieces of the dream, and remembered Michael's eyes. Growing pale with the fear that she had done something to drive him away, she disengaged herself from Nathan's embrace and tried to sit forward. Nausea waved over her. "Where's Michael?"

Nathan's jaw muscles tightened at the name. "Don't worry, darling, he'll never hurt you again."

Cross clutched desperately at his sleeve. "You have to tell him I'm sorry. Tell him I'm okay. Say that I need to see him."

Appalled, Nathan held her away from him, searching her eyes. Something in his gut bucked and he suddenly felt hugely depressed.

144

"Darling, he's gone away. He knows he's done a bad thing and he's run away. The bastard ought to be—"

Cat silenced him with a warning glance. "Don't worry about Michael right now. I'm sure he'll come as soon as he finds out you're here."

Cross bowed her head and cried some more as Luther Vandross sang the old maudlin tune "Anyone Who Had a Heart."

Nathan rummaged through the paper bag and brought out a pad of drawing paper and several sketching pencils. He placed them on Cross's lap.

"This is what really matters," he said, his voice stern. He tapped the pad hard enough to make the pencils jump.

"This is Lucy Cross, and Lucy Cross's life is her art. In her art there is to be found the higher purpose for our existence.

"You seem to have forgotten that you are one of the finest artists in the country, darling. You need to remember that what comes from you and onto those canvases has deeply affected many people."

Nathan waited. Cat stopped what she was doing and waited with him.

Cross stared at the pencils for a few seconds, then tentatively placed her finger on an ocher one, rolling it back and forth. One by one, the rest of her fingers approached the round shaft and, in an automatic, eager motion, accepted it into her waiting hand.

17 Stella pulled the covers over her head and pretended to be dead, a ritual she'd been practicing since the early years of her childhood. Farm life had been hard. Before her father made a success of the mill and they became members in good standing of the nouveaux riches, she'd spent her first twelve years sleeping three to a bed with her sisters. Faking death in such close quarters was the only escape into solitude, though she had come up with better escapes in better times. Now pretending to be dead was more like practicing for the real thing.

If she died anytime soon, her death certificate would read: "Boredom, complicated by too much idle time." She'd seen minds lying fallow kill off old people quicker than anything. Hell, maybe the redhead was on the right track after all, trying to place her in a new kind of nursing home. Maybe they would have one of those recording machines she could tell her stories to. And provided she could get her fingers to cooperate and her magnifying glasses to work, she might even be able to teach a few of the younger women how to tat —pass on the skill the way her Aunt Martha had passed it on to her eighty years ago. Some things could never be learned from books; people had to watch the way they were done—get their hands and eyes right on the thing to understand. How could anyone *write* about the hair's breadth twist of the shuttle as you brought the thread around an outside loop?

A burst of laughter from the nurses' station caused Tillie to cry out and hold on to a long, thin treble note. It sounded like a boiling teapot winding down. Old ladies' whimpering invariably created a despairing hole in Stella's night. She pulled the sheet away from her face and stared at the overhead light fixture. Dark outlines of fly and moth corpses littered the bottom of the institutional light cover.

Stuffing a pillow between her legs to keep the bones of her knees from bumping together, she thought of the ornate light cover on the ceiling of her and Otis's Paris bedroom suite. She laughed silently at the vision of herself on her back, legs spread and raised in that ridiculous pose, counting dead bugs. She had been patient, waiting for Otis to . . . to please feel *some*thing—just once, something that might make the touch and sight of her less repulsive to him.

She had come a long way from Mrs. O'Brian's Finishing School for Young Women, yet she knew little about the finer details of what was supposed to go on between husbands and wives in private. Whatever it was, she knew enough to know that Otis was holding out on her.

They settled in Paris, to be close to Otis's exporting business. Despite the gifts he lavished on her, and for all his gentle affection, when she looked in the mirror she could not find the dreamy glow her sisters had worn during their first years of marriage. The secret knowledge of married ladies was not to be hers. She knew without question from the timid way his hands moved when he touched her

146

that he loved her beyond measure. But loving her enough was not the problem; it was the *other* kind of loving that threatened to ruin them. Although his attentiveness appeared to spring from some bottomless well of passion, his pitiful attempts to consummate the marriage were infrequent, consisting of clumsy, embarrassing exertions which lasted at most two or three minutes.

They had been married only three months when Otis stopped approaching her entirely.

On a balmy Paris night filled with tears and self-recriminations, he'd broken down and admitted he thought the physical side of love between a man and a woman base and demeaning; that she should perform with him the same filth done by whores under the unlit arches of the Pont-Neuf made him retch.

Later, when he regained his composure, he tried to console her. He explained in his gentle way that children would never fit into their lives, and if there were to be no children, there was no reason for that kind of love. Their love, he said, was destined to be of a higher, more spiritual nature.

Stella stroked the forlorn head on her lap and murmured endearments of understanding, although she did not truly believe him. Otis had always been so much more sensitive than other men, she was sure that with patience and gentle persuasion, she would eventually achieve a full married life with him. The task would not be unlike that of mating a skittish mare.

Ironically, the fashionable lifestyle Otis created to keep her mind off the failings of their married love served only to fan her desire. In the cafés and promenades, she was surrounded by lovers, or those looking for love, while explicit gossip about the sexual escapades of this one or that one ran as freely as the champagne. Love could be found at any given moment in the milliners', on the lips of servants, and even in the vestibules of the cathedrals. The fear that she would prove no match for the clever, prying gossipers who might uncover her secrets outweighed her desire to make friends. The pressure of pretending to be the blissful bride of the handsome and successful American businessman made the endless string of dinner parties and soirees so torturous she was almost glad when Otis began his frequent business trips to England.

For weeks, often months at a time, boredom was her only companion in this meaningless life: rise at eight, read until noon, dress, eat breakfast, stroll the Champs Élysées, write homesick letters, consult with the servants on household details, dress for a dinner she rarely touched, then toss sleepless for hours in a lonely bed.

When a string of Otis's business acquaintances came calling, ostensibly to comfort the abandoned bride, she was flattered. She thought their concern over her welfare was admirable, at least until the chase-around-the-settee games began. She did take comfort in watching the gentlemen depart one by one, limping or bent in half from her right-elbow-to-the-abdomen maneuver. Of course, she never mentioned the incidents to Otis for fear of wounding his pride, and eventually forgave the lecherous adventurers, faulting them only on their ignorance of a farm girl's ability to handle large, bovine creatures.

She pleaded with Otis to take her with him to England or allow her to go home. Finally, when she felt she would die from the wanting of him, she abandoned patience and harshly accused him of having a mistress. He laughed at her, but she knew by his hands' anxious flight that he did not find the accusation amusing. Later, in the darker hours of the morning, she heard him cry.

From the towers of Notre Dame she gazed upon the city of love and romance, seeing only an elaborate cage. . . .

The squeak of a sneaker brought her back to the present.

"Hullo, lady. It's me again." Zoe stood in the doorway, bashfully picking at the blue plastic headband that held two braids of light brown hair back from her face. "Are you terribly sick and tired, or can I come in?"

At the sight of the child, Stella's body flooded with energy. In one motion, she pushed off the covers and hoisted herself out of bed. "Heck no, I'm not sick or tired, just bored out of my skull. Come in, come in. I've been waiting tea for you."

Zoe sidled up close to the bed. Unblinking, she stared into Stella's rheumy blue eyes and studied her wrinkles, lost in innocent fascination.

"What's your name, dear?" Stella asked, breaking the spell.

Never taking her eyes off the old woman's face, the gawky child bent her thumb back, stood on one leg, pulled at a braid, and bit at the tip of her finger. "Zoe Walker," she answered around the finger. "I'm the only one in my family excused from school because of our family crisis, you know. The teacher and principal feel the stress of my father's illness would interfere with my concentration." Zoe stopped to evaluate how Stella was taking the information.

"I'm very attached to my father, you know, so why should I pretend I was learning when I really was too upset to absorb anything? Besides, I'm the smartest kid in my class. I read the classics every night before bed and review one multiplication table just before I fall asleep. Since last October I've read twelve Nancy Drews and I can

148

do a long division problem in my head without making any mistakes, so I'm really not afraid of suffering in my education too much. My teacher says my brain muscles will stay strong as long as I read and do one math problem a day. She says reading and doing mathematics does for your brain what a Jane Fonda workout does for your body."

"Well!" Stella said, shaking her head in wonderment, managing not to smile. "Twelve entire Nancy Drew books, the multiplication tables, *and* long division! My, my, my! Quite a sensible solution to the question of education while one is incapacitated, I must say."

Zoe nervously pulled the edges of a faded pink collar together where the button was missing, cocked her head far to one side, and left it there for what Stella felt was an estimable length of time.

"So, what's your name?" Zoe asked, returning her head to its normal position.

"Stella Gallagher, but you can call me Stel or Stella if you'd like. Last names are too long and proper-sounding, don't you think?"

"Yeah, 'cept I like mine. Walker. Some people call my dad by his last name. It reminds me of Luke Skywalker, in *Star Wars?* Sometimes I fab-ri-cate—that means fibbing—and tell kids I'm his cousin, 'cept nobody but the first-graders believe me anyway." The girl pulled her foot up to her chin, stuck out a shockingly long tongue, licked the top of the multicolored sneaker, smiled, and, on one foot, twisted her body in a full circle.

Stella managed not to flinch and wondered who Luke Skywalker might be and if she'd ever had a spine of rubber when she was a child.

"I hope you don't think I'm rude"—Zoe stared at Stella sideways—"but just how old *are* you anyway?"

To get the child out of her pretzel configuration, Stella motioned her closer. "I'll tell you and nobody else 'cause we don't want this top-secret material to leak out." Looking first one way and then the other, she whispered in the girl's eagerly waiting ear. "I've been hanging around for ninety-five years."

Zoe's eyes grew large. "Ooooh, you're almost a hundred years old!" She gave Stella a conciliatory glance and patted the old woman's arm, further awed by the softness of the crepe paper wrinkles. "Don't worry, you don't look that old—you look more like you're only maybe around eighty-eight or so. Did you ever know Abraham Lincoln?"

Caught by the child's spirit, Stella couldn't help staring frankly into her eyes, delighted by the uneven ring of light gold inside the blue irises. Children—their logic was impeccable and their love was always so accessible. How many decades had passed since she'd been exposed to their sweet world?

As she waited for an answer, Zoe saw that the old lady was staring at her weirdly. She threw a wary glance first at Tillie, then at the door, as if to measure the obstacles and distance she had to cover in order to get to the hallway. She didn't really know any old people and wasn't so sure of what they actually *did*. There were stories about how sometimes they could do weird things. Like the time Sam's grandpa tinkled on the wall heater, and Mavis Greene's grandma ate a hole right through the middle of her birthday cake just before the party, so her mom had to fill it in with frosting and the leftover crumbs.

She hugged herself and took a small step back toward the door.

Recognizing the child's expression of wavering boredom and fear, Stella realized she'd been staring. "No," she said quickly to arrest the girl's flight. "Abraham Lincoln was a few years before my time, but I heard he was a great man. Which reminds me, how is your father?"

Zoe dropped her chin onto her chest. "He's very sick," she said, fidgeting with her collar. "He has cancer in his lungs and mesta . . . metas . . . a word that means the rest of his body caught it from his lungs. I heard the nurses talking about him to my mom. They said he was going to die soon. He's only forty-three years old, you know."

In the child's words, Stella recognized the inflection of some grown-up's voice—probably that of her mother. "Forty-three is much too young to be that ill. Forty-three is the very prime of life." She looked sadly at Zoe and lightly brushed her cheek. "It doesn't seem fair, does it, darling?"

"Mom says it isn't fair. She cries a lot. She and my dad were always kissing and tickling each other. My mom says that—" Zoe stopped, hunched her shoulder toward her cheek, and changed the subject. "How come you're in the hospital? You don't look sick except for being all wrinkly."

"Well, I'm just visiting until I can find a place to live. My old place was closed up."

Zoe spied the empty denture cup sitting on the bedside table and regarded it with curiosity. "I hate the hospital, don't you? It's all smelly and loud."

Stella nodded in agreement, wishing she could offer the child a treat. She made a mental note to ask one of the nurses to pick up a bag of lemon drops, then changed her mind. Hard candies wouldn't

150

do in the age of sugarless, superprotein gum and vitamin-enriched taffy.

"Well, I agree this place isn't any French perfume factory and they tell me the noise is enough to raise the dead, but I guess the smells and noise are all part of people being sick and getting well again. Don't you agree?"

As she pushed Stella's denture cup around the table, the child deliberated, her mouth held tight, her brow furrowed. Finally she nodded. "Um, well, I see how you might be correct in your ally . . . alga . . . allegrations on that matter." Unable to hold back, Zoe picked up the empty denture cup, cautiously sniffed the insides, and brightened. "Ooooh, minty!" Then, remembering her manners, she put the cup down and looked up at Stella to see if she was offended.

Relieved by Stella's smile, the girl took the old woman's hand and began a close examination of the fingernails. "So, what do you do anyway?"

"What do I do?"

"Yeah, like were you a teacher or something? You sound like Jane Eyre. That's Brontë, you know. You have a big bump on your writing finger, which means you write a lot, and you speak very properly and with good English too." Zoe ran her fingers briefly over Stella's blue-veined hand, reading the wrinkle braille. "You're kinda like Mrs. Valline. She's my teacher this year. She's really nice except she's not so old and you smell like pepper. I like pepper. It doesn't make me sneeze, you know, even when I put it up my nose."

Stella was titillated. "Oh my, do you put pepper up your nose quite often?"

"Well, not a lot but ummmmm, about, oh, maybe once a week. I do it at the dinner table," Zoe said proudly. "My brothers can't even do it and they're older than me. My mom doesn't like me to do it 'cause she's afraid the pepper shaker will get all snotty or something."

"I see. How many brothers do you have, dear?"

"Two," Zoe answered in the perpetually indignant tone of a youngest sibling. "Garrick is fifteen and Petey junior is seventeen but they're very immature for their ages, you know. All they do is think about themselves 'cause they keep asking Dad to give them things and do things for them and I don't think that's nice 'cause he's so sick and Mom says it makes him worry too much and that makes him sicker 'cause he doesn't rest very good."

Zoe stopped to take a breath and had another thought. "Hey! You know what my dad calls me sometimes?"

151

Stella shook her head. "Nope, but I'm sure it's a doozie."

"His pepperhead girl!" Zoe laughed, her hair glinting with rainbows of gold and pale yellow. "Isn't that silly? Pepperhead girl! Every time I think of that it makes me laugh, even when I'm supposed to be in serious conplem . . . comtep . . . compentlation."

Stella laughed softly and reached over to straighten Zoe's buttonless collar. The child tentatively leaned against the old woman's hand. On natural reflex, Stella slipped her arms around the tiny waist and Zoe rested her head against Stella's chest, looking into the woman's face briefly to make sure she wasn't hurting any old bones.

"You smell good. Like peppery vanilla," Zoe said, sniffing the thin chicken skin of the old woman's neck. Comfortable with the new intimacy, she rearranged herself so she was barely sitting on her new friend's lap. "My father's really sad," she went on. "I wish he wasn't so sad. I wish the scientists could find a cure for cancer and he could come home again. I . . . I wish he—" She ended her sentence abruptly and closed her eyes.

Stella stroked the child's head, barely touching the silk-soft hair. "You want to know what I think?"

A shrug. "Um, I guess so."

"I think you're very sad too."

Another one-shouldered shrug lifted Stella's arm.

"Maybe, but I can't let Dad know 'cause he'll worry."

Stella held Zoe tightly, taking in her warmth. "It's all right to be sad, little one. You're sad because you love him so much, and that's fine. Everybody knows what that feels like."

Without warning, the bad picture flashed over Stella's mind. As if to protect the child from her grisly vision, she shielded Zoe's eyes and spoke rapidly. "Whenever you feel sad and want to be with somebody who will understand, you come here and be with me. Okay?"

Zoe nodded almost imperceptibly. "Stella? Will you really talk to me sometimes?"

Stella tenderly pulled the warm, bird-fragile body closer and kissed the top of Zoe's forehead. "For you, I'll be right here day or night with my teeth in, waiting to talk your ear off."

It had been a long time since she had been kissed on the forehead and held by such a sweet voice. "Can you tell stories? You know, like old stories about the real Indians and cowboys?"

"Yup. About real brontosauruses and cavemen even."

Zoe looked up to see if Stella was kidding.

Convinced the old lady was the original, genuine article, she nestled in tighter, lulled by the sound of a strong and ancient heart.

Cat studied the last name and vocalized it several times so as not to make a mistake when asking for him. It was such an odd name. Padcula, Padcula, Padcula. PAD-Q-LA. What the hell kind of name was it? French? Jewish? Transylvanian?

A gruff, back room voice answered in the middle of the second ring. "Yeah, yeah, Marin County Sheriff's. Station Twelve."

"Er, hi." She immediately decided against the vulnerable, unsure tone, coughed, and changed over to an officious quality, the one least like her real self. "Ah, yes, this is Mercy Hospital calling for Inspector . . ." She plunged: "Pad-cu-la, please."

There was a scuffle; then hands clumsily covered the mouthpiece, although she could still hear perfectly well. "Hey Dracula, it's some broad named Mercy wants to talk to ya. You here?"

At once there was a series of clicks and a noise like a tomb door closing, then a smooth but quick "Padcula here."

"Hi!" Her energy level soared. She waited for a response and got the empty-tomb sound again. "It's Catalina Richardson here."

The dark tomb echoed her name. Her energy level plummeted.

"You know, the nurse over on Ward Two?"

"Ward Two?"

Ignoring the sudden death of her high spirits, Cat decided to take the easy, jivey way. "Oh, how quickly they forget those who are hard to find. Hey, you know, Blackie . . . it's me, eye to eye with the beast Tall Red."

He forced a skimpy laugh. His mind had been totally focused on one of the forty other matters piled on the corner of his desk. "Heh, oh yeah. Hi there. So, what's up?" (Tall Red the Clown? Red Buttons? Red McCarthy? Ward Two? The beast?)

A poor beginning. Cat decided to go for broke in the left-hand lane. "First of all, are you still smiling?" (Be playful, let him know you can be a kid.)

"Ahhhh, yeah, I suppose so." (Who *is* this? Can't be a solicitation from the Organization for the Socially Retarded—Christmas is over. Gotta be a crank call from the boys at the jailhouse.)

He was suspicious and withdrawn, like any truly stable and dry adult, Cat thought. She could even hear him thinking, Ah Christ, as if my day ain't long enough without these crank calls.

But she did not falter.

"Listen, I've got a question for ya. Don't your front teeth ever get sticky with all that smiling going on?" She held her breath, fearful he just might hang up; he could still be harboring an unpleasant

153

persecution complex caused by childhood pranksters who called to ask if the family refrigerator was still running.

But there wasn't even a millisecond's hesitation on his end. "Oh, I suppose," he said casually. (Okay, okay, I'll play. It'll pay me back for the hundreds of crank calls I made when I was a kid.) "Once in a while in the morning, I find bugs in the toothbrush bristles after I brush."

Her full laughter came quickly and easily, the way it used to when she was attracted to someone. Good. She'd brought him over to left field. Now what? A picnic lunch? No, just stick with the teaser— don't want him thinking you're over the edge . . . at least not yet. *Mysterious and Fascinating Lady* was the title of this movie.

"Well kid . . ." (Kid—that's good. Totally platonic, as in *"Me* affected by *you*? Ha!") "You'll be glad to know Miss Lucy Cross is with us A and O times four."

"Huh?"

"Alert and oriented to person, place, time, and thing."

"Oh, oh yeah! Hey, that's great, Red."

He'd just figured out who she was. She could hear the smile.

"When did she come around?"

The guard chain on his voice was loosening; the tomb door was scraping back and sunlight was steaming in.

"Well, she was in and out all night, but she really woke up about an hour ago." Cat waited a moment for a response, then, getting none, sensed that his mind had wandered elsewhere. Maybe he was a little slow on the uptake, or perhaps someone was there with him, a sultry Lauren Bacall seated on the corner of his desk, whistling softly. Cat imagined the ceiling fan, its blades rotating slowly, pushing the heavy perfume from the full breasts toward him . . .

"Oh yeah?" he said in that I'm-not-listening way people speak when they're engrossed in eavesdropping and trying to hold a meaningful conversation at the same time—hit-and-miss talk.

A tiny hint of anger flickered at the back of her throat. "Hey buddy, *you're* the one who left word you wanted to be called the very *minute* Lucy Cross woke up. Remember?"

"Oh, oh yeah, sure." There was silence again.

What was with this turkey? Had she been transferred to the right department? Were they being recorded?

"Listen, Blackie, maybe we should do a few neuro checks on *you*," she said with a mixture of impatience and mirth. "Can you tell me your name, the date, where you are, and the name of the current president of the United States?"

154

His easy laugh sent a shock of pleasure to her stomach. "Sorry, Red, I was searching for my file on this guy. Michael E. . . ." The name was left hanging while he sifted through some crinkly papers. "Ahummmmm. Yeah, here it is. Michael E. Lake, white male, thirty-six years old, six feet tall, one hundred seventy-five pounds, professional actor and model for"—he gave a low whistle—"Command Electronics, Suisun Cosmetics, Blazzie's Perfume, Gelteau Creations, Silk Kiss Products, et cetera, et cetera. All big-name companies, a list as long as your leg."

A swivel chair squeaked loudly and Cat pictured him: gun in shoulder holster, suspenders, tie loosened, glasses off. Her throat swelled.

"Boy, this guy's a real charmer. You want to hear the rest of this file, Red?"

Cat nodded eagerly. "Definitely, and don't leave anything out, even if it's confidential."

There was more shuffling, a louder creak, then: "Okay. In 1973 we have a dishonorable discharge from the Army for beating a fellow soldier's brains into oatmeal in a barroom brawl in Houston. The other guy is still in a V.A. hospital trying to learn how to put his socks on.

"After discharge, the dishonorable Mr. Lake went on to the University of Texas for a few years, where he made the Dean's list. In 1975 he married Mary Haven, a nice Mormon girl from Salt Lake who divorced him in 1977 on the grounds of mental and physical abuse. In 1980—"

A loud crash, followed by a louder howl and a torrent of profanities, cut the report short. Straining her ears, Cat thought she heard in the faraway distance choruses of whooping male laughter and tapping on glass.

"Hey! What happened? You okay, Blackie? Hello, anybody there?"

Then she heard the phone, being dragged over what sounded like a concrete floor. "Sorry," he said, back on the line. "Third god-damned time this month."

"What's the third time this month? What was all that noise?"

He took a breath. "Well, okay," he began reluctantly. "See, I have this sweet old mom who knows that I've been having a love affair with thirties and forties detective novels since I was ten, so a couple of years ago, she sent me this great 1940s swivel chair for my birthday, an exact replica of the one Sam Spade had at his desk. It's a world-class chair, except every once in a while I lean back a bit too far and the stupid thing gets away from me."

Cat tried not to chuckle and failed.

155

"The clowns here think it's real amusing too," he said.

A snort escaped her as she imagined a group of ogling cops pressing their noses against the glass of his office door.

"Yeah, real funny. They've got a monthly lottery going now, taking bets on what days my wonder chair and I will perform."

She laughed out loud.

"Anyway, not to go off business . . ." He cleared his throat and, ignoring the snorts of merriment coming from the other end of the phone, continued reading the police report. "In 1980 he was arrested on an assault and battery charge filed by a woman he was living with in Baltimore, but she dropped the charges. Then in 1983 he was charged with the rape of a minor in St. Paul, but he weaseled out of that one with a good lawyer and insufficient evidence. In 1984 he was arrested for rape and released because the woman refused to give a positive ID on him. In 1985 he had two more assault charges filed against him by two women he was living with simultaneously. They also withdrew the charges."

Inspector David Padcula sighed. "Man, this guy is a real charmer."

Cat was completely sobered now, her knuckles white from gripping the phone. "Sounds like this . . ." She bit her tongue to stop the truck driver adjectives. ". . . this ape needs to be taken out of the jungle and locked up for a long time. Any chance of that happening, Blackie?"

"Well, we're going to try. Do you think Ms. Cross is awake enough to talk to me?"

She's awake enough, but I'm not a hundred percent positive she can handle talking about what happened. You'd have to go slow with her for right now, like maybe asking simple questions that won't upset her.

"Believe it or not, she's still in love with the assho—with the guy and superprotective. If you can settle for that much until she's a little more with the program, you can see her."

"I will never understand why women fall for these abusive types." He paused. "You aren't like that, are you, Red?"

Cat was indignant. Hers had been an addiction to mental abuse only; the physical stuff left her cold. "Me? Psssh. No way. If any man even so much as—"

He did not let her finish. "See you in an hour or so. Don't let anybody push you around till I get there."

"Hey, wait a minute. Don't you want to know what she's said so far?"

"No thanks. I'll ask her myself and you can fill in details later. And if that doesn't work, I'll ask your soothsayer down in the lobby."

What? My God, not another one. "How did you know about *him*?"

"You mentioned him yesterday morning when I ran into you in the hall before your shift, remember?"

She did not. "Oh yes." After all, it had been Monday morning and she hadn't exactly been paying close attention to what she was saying —another bad habit she would have to break someday.

He laughed, which sent her stomach off on another ride. "That's okay, Red, you seemed like you were in a little bit of a tizzy."

"Tizzy? I don't get into tizzies—ever!" She faked bristling.

"Oh yeah?"

Trusting her finer psychic tuning, she heard the smile and a hint of playful seduction, as in, "I think I could work you up to a tizzy, lady."

She smiled back into the black receiver. "Welllll, all right, maybe I had a tizzy once ten years ago."

"Ummmmmm, I see, is that why you're twisting the garnet pendant back and forth on the gold chain around your neck? To protect yourself from tizzies?"

Cat stopped twisting her garnet pendant back and forth on the gold chain around her neck.

"I'm impressed as hell," she said, impressed as hell. Then, recovered: "Okay, smart guy, fourteen- or eighteen-karat?"

"Ah, very tricky, but not tricky enough, Red. Twenty-four-karat. You wear only twenty-four-karat because of your skin. It's very . . ." He paused. (Did he mean to sound so sensual?) ". . . sensitive."

"Jesus." Her freckles stood up on end and her guts tightened from the chill going through the pit of her stomach. What else did he know about her?

Something creaked. The wonder chair.

"When you've been on the investigations end of police work this many years, Red, you learn to notice everything, although with you . . ." The seductive tone was unmistakable this time. ". . . I think I would have noticed anyway."

He paused for a count of two. His timing was dazzling. "See you around one, Red."

Elated, Cat nodded and, at a total loss for words, let the handset slip from her sweaty hand into the receiver. As Nora would have said, she'd fallen in at least another foot and a half.

The thought of lunch left Cat nauseated—which was unusual. By the time noon rolled around, she was usually one-salad-two-sandwiches-plus-a-dessert ravenous. Today her greatest desire was to be alone in the think tank, locked in with only a cup of microwaved instant cocoa and a pilfered pillow. She needed to do a little mental monologing.

She pulled the Ward Two linen closet key from the hidden pocket of her scrub top. She'd paid a price for the precious piece of metal, bribing one of the housekeepers, an edematous overweight woman, with a two months' supply of Lasix, a carton of Nicorette gum, eight Valiums, a stethoscope, and biweekly blood pressure checks for six months.

Glancing around, she inserted the key into the lock and quickly let herself into the room. Set inconveniently in the middle of the ward, the long, narrow linen closet seemed to be part of a misplaced hallway, complete with a set of stairs that went to the ceiling. Cat figured it was the architect's way of either having a practical joke on the builders or satisfying his desire to create a bizarre though semifunctional sculpture.

The rectangular room, crammed with six four-tiered racks of folded linen, was pitch-dark. By feel, Cat took a pillow from the pillow bin behind the door, grabbed a fresh case, and inched her way along the wall to the last rack at the farthest corner.

When she had rearranged the flannel pull sheets into a comfortable mat, she maneuvered her statuesque body, along with her feet, onto the second shelf, folded the pillow under her head, and commenced dividing her thoughts into lists.

First thing: Gotta remember to put on fresh makeup before *he* gets here.

But why? If I'm not attractive to him as I really am, then he can just eat the big one.

Oh for Christ's sake, Richardson, shut up.

Okay, okay. Medicate Walker first thing. See if he'll take some IV morphine. Do noon assessment.

Check Stella after *he* comes by to see Cross.

David. David. God, what a great name. Never been with a David before.

Do assessment on Corky. Be more direct with him. He's a smart kid. He can take it. See if I can be tactful. (Tactful? Tactful? What the hell is that and why is it in my vocabulary?) Observe family dynamics if I can. Maybe I can get some more clues.

God, David. The guy has an incredible laugh. Matches the smile. A cop. Station Twelve—where the cops are hard and the criminals keep their backs to the wall.

She snorted. *Me* with a cop? A long shot, but isn't there something about nurses and cops always being cast together? Or was that firemen and nurses?

A strong contraction of pleasure rippled just above her pubic bone. She sighed. It was a sign that pre-limerance weirdness—that mildly troublesome stage of new relationships where one floats three feet above ground—was full upon her.

See if you can talk to him normally, Cat. Just be yourself like the love instruction books from the beginning of time tell us to be. Be everything that makes them want you—funny, light, brilliant. Don't appear too eager, and don't let your sexual appetite run away with your sense of propriety. Don't be such a hard guy. Don't slouch and don't be so—

Stop the tape, Mom. I'll be the way I want to be. What is this bullshit anyway? I can't really afford the time and I don't want to get hurt again, so what the hell am I doing? Forget it. I'm too old to be playing these kiddie love games, and besides, romance always disappoints you.

Except, do you realize he never even noticed your feet . . . not even once?

Yeah, well, maybe he's got arthritis of the neck, and besides, for these babies it only takes once.

Eyes fully adjusted to the dark, Cat stared at the underside of the metal shelf four inches from her nose and shook her head at her two sides arguing.

Please, please stop, will you? Let's get on with it, shall we?

Okay. Okay.

Check with Nora about what it was she needed to tell me. Sounded like a good one, except what could be so good about Dr. Gillespie?

Call social services and push the Bresford people to consider taking Stella. That one deserves a chance. Too young to ever have to die an old person's death. Not ready yet.

Find Doll—see if he needs anything.

A vision of Gage walking down the main corridor with Tom Mix crossed her mind, and was followed by an image of a white van fishtailing around a curve in the pouring rain.

Anyway, let's see . . . fish or chicken for dinner?

Boring. That's all I ever eat.

Pick up a pizza at Victor's?

Nah, too much grease and salt. Digging my grave with my teeth, as Aunt Helen used to say.

Hot oatmeal?

Too many calories after the toppings.

Yeah, except blue milk and strawberries don't have a whole lot of calories, jerkface.

Welllllll, maybe if I can find fresh strawberries.

Fresh strawberries? In January? Which planet did you say you were from?

Christ! Never mind!

Closing her eyes, she sank into her tiredness, feeling like a music box run down to its last dragging note.

Stupid thing to do last night. Grass kills six million gray cells every time you smoke. My mind just goes when I smoke that stuff. Don't know where it goes, but when it comes back, it's definitely carrying a lighter load. Don't know how Nora does it. . . . Then again, she's a couple of years younger and might have a few more gray cells to kill off—

Her thoughts were interrupted by an unexpected flickering of her mind screen: Gage held tight to Tom Mix's harness as he ran wildly through the rain in what looked like the middle of the woods. The absence of his dark glasses allowed her to see his state of alarm. Cat shook off the chilling image and blanked out the vision.

How about just a salad? Want to look slender. Need to run an extra mile for a while until this thing with old smiley pans out one way or another.

Instantly she imagined the two of them in bed on a Sunday morning reading the paper, her cottage cheese thighs draped over his muscular ones.

Definitely a salad—without dressing.

Wonder what to do about Corky. Maybe if I just come out and tell him why I think he did it?

Nah. Probably not a good idea.

Gotta remember to ask David about the—

The door to the closet clicked and opened.

Shit. If somebody found her in here—on a shelf—she was going to die.

(Hey, guess what? I just found Richardson on a shelf in the linen closet! Whaddaya think?

Probably playing with herself.

Yeah, knowing that one. Ya know, I've always thought there was something wrong in the upper deck. Doncha think so?)

Footsteps were tracking her down, headed right for her rack, as if they *knew.*

Damn! If she tried to get up, there'd be too much noise. Better to stay rooted.

160

Maybe it was the building architect come back to make amends? Nah.

Or Jesus, what if it was weirdo Dr. Cramer wanting to show her his back surgery scars and talk about catechols?

She crossed her fingers, praying that whoever it was would go away. But just in case they didn't, she thought of excuses.

"I felt sick and fell onto one of the shelves"?

Get real.

"Well, see, there was this crazy person from Ward Twelve who forced me in here and locked the door. I screamed and screamed for help but . . ."

Never mind. They're here.

Tom Mix nudged the side of her face with his cold, slimy nose.

"That you, Ms. Cat?" It was Gage's bumpy whisper.

"Gage?" How the hell did he find her? Whom had he bribed for a key and how much had it cost him?

Instantly relieved that she didn't have to explain about being in the dark on a linen shelf, she relaxed, chuckling to herself—the blind man would never know the difference.

"Whatcha doin' here in the dark on that there skinny little shelf?" he asked.

Cat's shoulders sagged. "Jesus, Gage. Hasn't anyone informed you that you're supposed to be blind? You aren't supposed to find people who are hidden in out-of-the-way places behind locked doors in the pitch-dark." She shook her head slowly. "I don't get it, Gage. I mean, if the CIA had been looking for me they would've had a hard time finding me here, let alone getting a copy of the key. Why are you picking on me?"

Gage sat down on the floor and rested his back against the staircase to nowhere. Tom Mix lay down next to him and yawned.

"I'm used to seein' in the dark, Ms. Cat. I got myself a built-in radar system could probably take me to the North Pole an' back. You forgettin' I been tuned in to you like a CB radio. I know you gettin' my messages some of the time."

Cat lay back down to stare at the top of the linen shelf. Oh God. The two flashes of Gage a second ago—did he do that?

"So what's up *now*? Do we get another jingle or what?"

Gage ignored her sarcasm. "I found you 'cause we didn't talk this mornin'. We needin' to keep close in communication for the next bit of time, girl. These be dangerous days for you an' other folk."

Only half listening, Cat wondered if blind people could tell when someone wasn't paying attention. She guessed that they listened to

161

breathing patterns, and made sure to take even, slow, *interested* breaths.

"Okay, Gage." She crawled off her shelf and nestled next to Tom Mix. "I give up. Run the whole thing by me one more time. What's the deal—something about bad stuff coming my way? Ken, the insane killer of redheaded nurses, is out to get me, right?"

Cat's throat constricted. What if the bad news was about David? Maybe he was gay after all. Maybe he hated redheads. Maybe he had a thing about feet. Maybe he—

"Girl, get that man off your mind for five minutes. There be plenty of time for him later. Right now you gotta listen to me, but you gotta hear me this time." He tapped her head with a long brown finger, producing a hollow sound. "No more slippin' an' slidin'. You gotta master your fear of your own power before it goes messin' things up."

Gage found her hand and took it into his. "Girl, this be His power and it won't hurt you 'less you ignore it."

Cat closed her eyes. *Was* it her fear of the unknown that made her hackles go up whenever Gage started in with his second-sight business? Certainly part of her did not deny the existence of psychic phenomena. As a child she had often had dreams that came true. Like the morning she informed her mother over breakfast that she'd had a dream about Aunt Helen going to heaven in a big green can.

Emily dismissed her daughter's prattle until the call came later in the day that her sister Helen had been killed in a head-on collision while riding the downtown bus. Rushing to the scene, Emily found the firemen still extricating the victims from the crushed green vehicle.

Her mother blamed her for the tragedy, calling her an instrument of the devil and a contaminant among good people. Cat was beaten severely and sent to bed to pray for her deliverance from the grips of Satan.

But no matter how many times she prayed and went to confession, her dreams continued to come true, confirming in her own mind that her mother was right. That meant she had to find a way to stop the dreams, and since dreams only came when she slept . . .

Each night, she tried a different method of keeping herself awake, like putting prickly rollers in her hair, or not allowing herself to have covers. She was the only person she knew who had actually trained to be an insomniac. When sleep deprivation began to interfere with her daily life, she read a book on how to remember dreams and did everything in reverse.

"You listen up now, girl." Gage squeezed her hand.

162

Cat examined the three of them huddled together in the dark, and felt herself yielding to him. In her heart of hearts, she knew there was nothing sinister about the man; if anything, he was simply a kindly though wayward wizard in disguise, and in his presence she felt protected and cared for.

"There be an evil man around here, Ms. Cat," Gage said and waved his arm in a wide, all-inclusive gesture. "His head be mighty mixed up 'cause the Lord didn't give him no love to feel with. The man got sick with all the hate that he been feedin' on his whole life.

"Right now the man ain't too far away. He comin' to do bad business with some people includin' yourself. You gotta be aware of his thoughts an' his energy, like you was with me a few minutes ago."

She felt him vibrating, the heat from his hands going into her. At first there was the physical sensation of the warmth, followed by a sense of something gone wrong. Her body turned warm, then hot, and she began vibrating along with him. Soon a presentiment of corruption mixed with despair pressed in on her and her arm hair stood up straight from the centers of her goose bumps. Whatever he was transferring to her was real, and it no longer mattered what mumbo jumbo it was born of.

"Do I know this person?"

"You do an' you don't."

Cat felt the sick depression ready to leap on the back of its older sister, bad news. The only man she knew but didn't really know was David. Could he be the evil force?

Gage rolled his head and sighed, released her hands and sat back. "It ain't *him*, Ms. Cat. He be a good man even though he ain't got patience for the power neither. You an' he been together for a heap of lifetimes."

"You mean we've been lovers before?"

"Not that, but once or twice you been brother an' sister, mother an' son. Once, you two was even kings fightin' it out with each other.

"This lifetime you an' he got some payback to do before you can get to bein' with each other. Me an' Delia went through it that way too. The Lord didn't give us much time together, but what time we had, we didn't waste." Gage quietly stroked Tom Mix's head. Cat closed her eyes again and tried to imagine the two of them. Delia's cherubic brown face had just appeared clearly, when Gage stirred and the image evaporated.

"But like my gramma used to say, whatever goes over the devil's back is got to come under his belly. Maybe this time you two gonna work out what you gotta work out for good."

163

A barrage of questions flooded her mind, but before she could get one out, Gage shook his head. "Your love life gotta wait. That be small fish next to what be comin' down the river. You gotta learn real fast how to be open to the power if you gonna be fightin' what I'm seein'."

Gage waited until she returned her full attention and sought her hands. Once again the connection created a circuit of energy that translated into a deep awareness of danger and the need for her to protect herself.

"Calm your mind like you was doin' just now before I came to find you, but do it even when you walkin' around doin' your life's business. You gotta be listenin' with extra ears, but hearin' only the words people ain't sayin', an' seein' only the things they ain't showin'.

"Kinda like how you know inside about what be wrong with the sick folks. The knowin' part be there all the time, but you listen to what your insides tell you even if somebody sayin' somethin' different."

"I don't know, Gage. I don't know if I can do this stuff. I mean, why *me*? There have to be other people around here who really believe in this spiritual . . ." She searched for the word, not wanting to upset him again. ". . . volunteer work who would be better at it than I."

"It don't matter, Ms. Cat. You been the one chosen and I'm your backup man. You gotta remember that you ain't never as blind as you think. You got more power locked up inside you than I even been allowed to look at. You a powerful force, Ms. Cat. You remind me of my Delia that way."

The room remained quiet until Tom Mix sat up and scratched the back of his ear with his hind leg.

"Okay," Cat said finally, resigned to the invisible task at hand. "What am I supposed to do, and when is this 'bad stuff' supposed to happen?"

"Just do what I already been tellin' you. When you lookin' at somethin' or somebody talkin' at you, open them inside eyes an' see what really be goin' on. You gonna see different an' hear different." Gage stretched one short skinny leg, then the other. "When you alone, put your mind to rest so it be strong enough to see them things that be hidin'.

"It helps to be sayin' a prayer over an' over to keep all them outside noises away from your head."

She screwed up her face. "Can't I do some kind of chant? That Christian stuff drives me nuts."

"Sure." Gage shrugged. "There be only one Lord. Don't matter what name you call Him.

"An' start payin' attention to your dreams; daydreams *an'* night dreams. Special dreams gonna be happenin' when you open yourself to the power."

Cat checked her watch and jumped to her feet. "I'm twenty minutes late. I don't even have a sense of time, yet he thinks I'm going to stave off the corruption of the world."

Gage rose slowly and majestically. Although he was several inches shorter than she, he seemed taller.

"All you gotta do is walk outta here like you be on time an' everybody gonna think just that. You gotta start thinkin' that way, girl. Be sure of your own self an' believe in your power. When you got it, flaunt it. Learn an' live."

Gage held his arm out for her to guide him from the room. As they reached the door, he turned. "An' you better stop smokin' shit for a while till this be passin' you by. You don't need that shit. Besides, it don't do nothin' but cloud your mind. Destroys your inner sight."

On impulse fostered by embarrassment, Cat gave the man a quick hug. "Okay, you win. I promise—no dope or booze until the Red Sea closes back up."

Grinning to his back teeth, Gage opened the door.

Together, the three of them emerged from the linen closet and into the bright light of Ward Two.

18 On several occasions during the last two years of Walker's fairly uneventful, quickly ebbing life, he had summoned the courage to face the question of who he was. Was he his body, or his brain, or his name, or the biological by-product of his mother and father's lust?

165

—and so on and so forth until he'd listed all the possibilities except the one that felt right.

And always, waiting at the end of the questions, was a limbo of paralyzing depression—a place in which he feared being trapped forever as a man without himself. Sometimes he could shake the gloomy feeling off by indulging himself in mindless activities like watching reruns of "Mister Ed" or "The Life of Riley" and poring over the stacks of old Sunday comics he kept in the basement. Sometimes, when Dagwood or William Bendix failed to bring him back, it would take a whole day and a good night's sleep before he felt normal again.

Now that he was coming into the home stretch, the question loomed larger than ever and he was no closer to an answer than he had been when he was fifteen and looking for God. Where was Mister Ed when you needed him?

The red mouth stuck out its tongue, then contorted as if it were trying to talk. Walker blinked a couple of times and looked away. He was not at all sure he wanted to hear what the mouth had to say right then, since a growing anxiety was running a close second to the pain in his chest in the race for his attention.

Walker glanced over to where Detlef lay like some stillborn tragedy, his intravenous lines dripping fluid into him, his pee bag full to bursting. It was simply water passing through, dropping off essential minerals and picking up leftover toxins from the last flush.

Had Detlef known who he was before they took out his brain? For that matter, what about Joyce or the boys or the down-and-outers? Did anyone else besides himself think about who they were and the meaning of why they were alive, or did they live day to day, eating, working, sleeping, reproducing, and leaving waste without ever giving it a second thought?

Not to be ignored any longer, his pain arrested his thoughts and sent him searching for the call button. He needed to be delivered from the claws tearing inside his chest.

Cat appeared, syringe in hand. "Looking for me?"

Out of the corner of his eye, Walker noticed that the red mouth stuck out its tongue at her.

"One Brompton's isn't doing it," he grunted. "I need a double shot."

"I read your mind." Cat held up the syringe. "This is the big gun. Morphine. Also called MS. You can have this much once an hour. I can give all of it now, taking a chance that it'll wear off before you can have another dose, or I can give you half now and half in—"

"All of it now," Walker said calmly, even though he was out of his mind with the fire raging in his lungs.

166

Cat injected the rubber cap on the intravenous line with his maximum morphine dose and watched the oily swirls race through sugar water toward his veins. Delivery routes to relief.

"You'll be better in a sec, Walker. Relax and let the morphine do its work."

As his pain careened out of control, the drug hit him head-on. He nodded toward the window. "Close the damned curtains on that mouth, will ya?"

Puzzled, Cat looked toward the window and saw the billboard. If she squinted, she could make out what might have been interpreted as a red monster mouth. She closed the curtain. In a painful death, she supposed, everything might have a way of turning macabre.

While waiting for Walker's fist to relax, she checked his not-so-vital vital signs and changed his bed. She had moved on to the other side of the room and was repositioning the seizure pads on Detlef's side rails when Walker raised his head off the pillow, squinted, then excitedly saluted the window. "Hey, Benny," he shouted, "Benny Newmann, how's by you?"

Cat searched the empty space next to where Walker's gaze fell. "What did you say, Walker?"

Benny Newmann emerged from behind the curtain and, hovering effortlessly in mid-air, did a few somersaults and came to rest hanging upside down over Walker's head.

Walker grinned, not so much at the antics, but at the odd appearance of Benny's fifteen-year-old face topping a grown man's body.

Benny tipped his sailor's cap and turned right side up to sit cross-legged on the air next to the bed.

Walker shook the ghostly hand offered him and flinched when it detached at the wrist and came off in his hand. The hand evaporated into a wisp of steam and Benny cackled like an asthmatic kid at his little joke, his mouth all silver braces and pink gums.

"Hey Benny, what're you doing here?"

"Well mate, I was reading through the public notices the other day and I see that my old buddy Petey Walker is looking to sign on with a crew, and I figure my fleet is as good as any, so, I fixed it with the higher ups that you can be with me. Welcome aboard."

Walker looked blankly at his friend. "What crew? What're you talking about, Benny?"

Cat brought her face closer to Walker's and stared into vacant eyes. "Walker? Who are you talking to?"

The rush in Walker's head drowned out the voice of a woman standing next to Benny. She was asking him something he couldn't hear.

167

"You'll have to wait a minute, Miss," he tried to say, although he had no control over his tongue. "I'm signing on."

The woman asked something else then faded away to white.

Benny bowed. "Styx River Tours," he announced proudly. "That's my outfit. Took over the business from old man Charon almost twenty years ago. I've got myself a fleet of nine boats that run the river twenty-four hours a day.

"How about it, Walker? Ready to come aboard?"

"Well I don't know I . . . I mean, I'm not sure what I'd have to do."

"Oh, you know, keep the boats shipshape, maybe take a few hardy souls up river, show them the sights, fulfill their sense of adventure."

Walker thought for a moment, warming to the idea. "Hell, Benny, you know I love boats. Don't you remember how we always used to talk about owning one of those thirty-foot Pearsons and sailing to parts unknown? Remember that raft we took up to. . . ." He trailed off, transfixed by the sudden appearance of three deer grazing on a lawn that had sprouted around Detlef's bed.

"Well then," said Benny, not paying the least attention to the animals, "is it a go? How about it, Petey? You want I should pick you up on Friday?"

From out of the bathroom, Detlef appeared, dragging his pee bag, like the ghost of Jacob Marley toting his chain of past transgressions. He made his way through the deer back to his bed, patting the animals as he went.

Not wanting to seem the odd man out, Walker acted as if the events taking place were perfectly natural. He had seen some barroom wildlife in his time, although this was another story. "I'd really like that Benny, but I want to talk to Zoe first before I commit myself."

Benny nodded thoughtfully as he filled the bowl of a corncob pipe with a tobacco mixture that smelled like drying apricots and the sea. When he had finished, he eased his legs to the floor and approached one of the bucks as casually as he might have a Honda Civic. "Okay, Petey. You talk to Zoe and I'll stop by again Friday morning early, say seven or so."

Hoisting himself onto the back of the deer, he waved and trotted bareback toward the curtain.

"Walker?" Cat pressed the cold cloth to his forehead and took his blood pressure once more. He was inching up—90 systolic. It was better than 62. She thought for sure she'd committed unintentional

168

euthanasia. If it hadn't been for his need to make last minute peace, she decided, it might not have been such a horrible thing to have done.

Walker opened his eyes and looked at the woman without seeing her. "Waiting for the next boat?" he asked.

Cat smiled patiently. "Walker, you're in the hospital. Can you hear me?"

He nodded and watched Benny vanish along with the deer.

"I thought we lost you there for a minute. You feel okay?"

"Yeah, I'm fine. Fell asleep is all. Except it didn't feel like I was asleep, and my old friend Benny Newmann was here and signed me up for a boat job starting on Friday. Then there were these three deer eating the floor and Detlef was walking around like normal."

With his sheet, he wiped the sweat from his face. "Whew, that morphine sure does funny things to your head."

A soft clanking from the other side of the room signalled that Detlef was having another seizure. Both of them stared at the pitiful sight of the man's pale hands flopping about on the sheet like fish fresh out of water.

"Pain gone?" she asked.

Walker took a test breath. "It's still there, but. . . ."

"But you don't care, right?"

"Right."

She moved to get up, noticed his look of uncertainty and stayed put.

"You still having a hard time with that black hole feeling, Walker?"

He chewed his lip and wished to God Zoe was with him. "Yeah. No. I mean, I don't know. There's a couple of things I need to find out first."

"Anything I can help you with?" She leaned toward him and laid her hand over his own where it lay, palm up, on the sheet.

The simple gesture threatened to crack the poker face he'd hidden behind ever since he was given a death sentence. He debated whether to tell her about his questions, then decided against it.

"No," he said. "I need to figure it out for myself."

In the nurses' lounge, Cat washed her hands and stared at herself in the mirror. They were pulling her in again as only the wounded could. Their need for her to care for and ultimately love them was what did it. Every time.

On top of that, it was only Tuesday morning.

169

Walking in the direction of Cross's room, Cat detoured into room 512. Sprawled out facedown on his bed, Corky reminded her of a prisoner counting down time in his cell. She stood still and watched him for a moment, debating whether or not to approach him again about what had happened. The way his foot pressed against the footboard and the deliberate twitching of his thumb told her he was not asleep, but aware of her presence and desperately wanting her to leave.

She turned away. Okay, kid. You win this time, but you can't escape forever.

Across the hall, Doll sat on the bed massaging his lover's feet. Lying on his side, earphones in place, Professor Dean grinned like a Cheshire cat. The balloons, affected by the heat, had dropped and now hovered a foot or so from the ceiling.

At the other end of the hall, Mrs. Walker and her daughter were headed toward Walker's room. Stubbornly resisting her mother's pace, the child stopped outside Stella's door and refused to budge, at the risk of having her arm pulled out of its socket. After a short interval of pleadings and debates with her mother, she was allowed to enter the room.

When Cat got there, she waited for Stella and the girl to finish beaming at each other before she interrupted.

"Need anything, Stel?" She could see that the old woman's face was more alive than ever, her eyes bright as bulbs.

"How about a good-lookin' man?"

"You and me both, lady."

Cat thought of a particular good-looking man and searched the nurses' station for any sign of thinning black hair and the glint of glasses. She would have to put a rush on.

"Be back in a little while with your pills, Stel."

"Yeah, well, I reckon I'll be here unless they need me out on the basketball court to teach 'em a few plays."

Cat made it as far as the acute-side doors, when a pair of strong arms wound themselves around her body and squeezed the wind out of her.

Accustomed to this particular assault, she studied the contrast between her own arm hair and the hairless forearms that hugged her. The two sets of arms resembled a couple of newborn mice lying on orange fiberfill.

"He's in the lobby," Nora said, releasing her. "Old monosyllabic

170

Gage has deviated from his taciturn nature and is talking the poor guy's ear off, believe it or not."

Obviously pleased, Cat flushed and tossed her hair away from her face. "Who's in the lobby?" she asked in an offhanded voice that fell flat on its face.

"The Prince of Wales. Who do you think, bonehead?"

Mindful of the rich joy dancing in her belly, Cat tried hard, though unsuccessfully, to suppress a smile.

"Oh, *him*," she said. "So what?"

"No reason in particular. I just thought you might like to pull on a lab coat before he gets here, since your nipples are about three inches erect."

Cat glanced down and groaned. Under the clingy scrub top, the little suckers were no more noticeable than if she'd had two wombats eating a pizza off her chest.

"Think about baseball," Nora suggested. "Maybe they'll go away."

Slipping a patient gown over the telltale bumps, Cat continued on toward Cross's room, paying close attention to the bits and pieces of conversation drifting around the crowded hallway. "Mobile eavesdropping" she called it, like turning the radio dial every few seconds to a different station.

". . . I'm going to do some pulmonary toilet on Mr. Sagepool, so cover my lights."

"Tell me, did you have many animal friends in Pittsburgh, Aaron?"

". . . and then the doctor says, 'Don't worry, the balls will cover your eyes.' "

". . . deep panic state. My feeling is there's been some major psychological insult, but the patient is unwilling to communicate at this time."

". . . catechols. They're our only hope."

"Well, I've always put mine in the sink until Sister Gerald told me they tasted better in the garage. How 'bout you?"

Cat approached the threshold of Cross's room, rehearsing her opening line. "Ah, Inspector Padcula I presume, jumping master of the killer swivel chair?"

Did she really want to be that flip? Maybe a professional approach would do better.

"Well, Inspector, Cross's neurological functions seem to have stabilized without any deficit whatsoever—no apparent loss of memory function short or long term. But of course we did intubate very

171

quickly and actually hyperventilated her so that even if a subdural hematoma had . . .

"Subdural hematoma? Ah yes, well, that is hemorrhaging into the subdura of the . . ."

Sure, okay, if he's into medical textbooks. How about a simple "Hi"?

Cat's swooshing Loretta Young entrance into Cross's room was abruptly aborted as her stethoscope caught on the door handle and choked her like a black rubber noose. The move was vaudevillian enough to make Cross pause in her sketching.

"Very charming entrance, Catalina," Cat said in her patronizing-piano-teacher voice. She did not dare look around to see if anyone other than Cross had caught her act. "And just how many years have inanimate objects been out to get you, Ms. Richardson?"

Cross smiled carefully, trying not to put a strain on the bruises and cuts around her mouth.

Cat was relieved to find that she and Cross were alone. Gage was probably still talking Padcula's ear off. Fine. It would give her some time to compose herself and break the news of his impending visit to Cross.

"How're you feeling?" Cat hugged the head of her stethoscope under her arm to warm the cold metal.

Cross resumed sketching. "I'm okay, thanks." The underlying tone of misery was hard to miss.

"Do your arm and head ache much?"

Cross briefly touched the plaster cast around the arm that ached like fire and shook the head that throbbed with every move. "Not at all."

Cat looked doubtful and tested the stethoscope. "Hmmm. Well, okay. I want to listen to your lungs for a sec, but I'll be careful of your ribs. They must be pretty tender."

Shyly Cross shook her head again and averted her eyes. "No, they aren't tender. I don't hurt anywhere, actually."

Placing the now subdued stethoscope on Cross's back, Cat listened to the faint, shallow exchange of air—the norm for someone with broken ribs.

"You're sure your ribs aren't sore? You don't need to be stoic in this place. I can give you some pain pills to take the edge off. Nothing heavy, maybe a couple of—"

"I said no!" Cross flared. "Really, there's no problem, thank you."

From her emergency room days, Cat remembered dislocated shoulders, kidney stones, and broken ribs as ailments that almost always caused pain of sweat-and-scream magnitude. She guessed

172

Cross was minimizing her injuries in order to minimize Michael's crime against her.

"Do you know if anybody's called about me?"

Opting not to answer the loaded question behind the question, Cat answered lightly, "Well, your sister has called every day, and there have been hundreds of calls from newspapers and magazines. Of course, Nathan checks in twice a day, and a woman from one of the galleries in—"

"I mean, has anyone else called?"

"You mean Michael Lake?"

"No, I don't mean Michael. I mean . . ." Cross's voice trailed off as she looked back at the sketch pad.

"Never mind. I know what you're asking. Michael has not called, nor has he been here looking for you, and I don't think he will, since I'm sure he's aware the police are searching for him."

The young woman's shoulders dropped, and Cat noted she did not take her eyes from the sketch. She took the tablet from Cross's hands and turned it to the light. The artist had captured the hard edge of Michael Lake's eyes.

Donning a pair of exam gloves, Cat checked Cross's numerous dressings. When she got to the one covering her left breast, Cat lifted one corner of the gauze and looked at the wound. Even after plastic surgery, it would leave an ugly scar, though nothing like the other, deeper one.

After the more significant of the wounds were cleaned and freshly dressed, Cat glanced at her watch. Ten minutes had passed. Enough time for *him* to finish with Gage, go to the men's room, clean his glasses and run a comb through his hair. On the ground floor he would, at that moment, be waiting for the slowest elevator in all of San Francisco to arrive and bring him to Ward Two. It was time for her to break the news.

"Cross, there's an Inspector Padcula on his way here to ask you some questions about what happened."

Cross stiffened and held her hands out as if she were warding off the devil. "I don't want to talk to anybody. Michael—he . . . he didn't hurt me, I swear to God. I fell off the roof. See, I was on my roof trying to hammer down some shingles before the next rain and I slipped and fell into the lemon tree." She forced a laugh. "God, you should have seen me, it was so funny, me holding on with my fingernails all the way down. . . ."

"Cross, it's okay." Cat's voice came out sounding as if there were a slipknot in the middle of it.

"No. No, it's not okay. I really fell. I—"

173

Someone knocked softly, respectfully. "Miss Cross?"

Cross shot Cat a look filled with her sense of betrayal. Then both of them turned toward the voice.

To Cross, Inspector Padcula was the evil bounty hunter: a menacing threat to the one she loved.

To Cat, he was an apple-cheeked Lancelot with a brand-new haircut.

Cat sighed. A fresh haircut on a man always left him looking so pink and sweet and fatter than she expected, rather like a heap of fresh baby fat all clean and innocent. The scraggly, well-broken-into-life length was more to her liking.

His eyes rested on hers. From across the room he caressed her with a look, one that exerted the lightest touch, yet it hit her like a physical blow. Inside she melted away like the Wicked Witch of the West. Oh God, she thought, trying without success to control the onrush of pheromones. Whip me, beat me, make me do bad things to the duck.

He touched Cross's shoulder gently and introduced himself as he settled in the armchair next to the bed.

She gave him a hostile glance and returned to her sketch.

Taking a notebook from his raincoat pocket, David Padcula wrote something. Over his shoulder, Cat noticed he wrote in such tiny letters one might think he had a secret.

"Miss Cross, do you know why I'm here?"

"Yes," she answered curtly. "You want to know where Michael is. You think he did this to me. You and everyone else I know—" her blazing eyes found Cat—"would like to throw him in some jail and let him die there."

She slapped her sketchbook like a frustrated ten-year-old, her voice nervous and fluttery. "Look, let's get it straight—Michael did *not* hurt me. I fell down the embankment of the creek behind my cabin. I don't know where he is, and even if I did, I wouldn't tell you. All you want is a victim to blame this on so it gives the reporters a good story and you can get your name in the paper. You want to be the easy hero, but it won't work, Mr. Padula or whatever your name is. Michael is very bright, Michael is . . ."

She breathed a sigh of sadness, winced, and sank back into her pillows, bracing her shoulders so as not to cry.

Cat sat down on the bed. "Cross?"

Cross turned away and glared at the wall.

"Cross, listen to me. Before you lost consciousness, you told the paramedics it was Michael who'd beaten you. Then a minute ago,

174

you told me you fell off your roof. And now you say you slid down an embankment. What would *you* believe?"

"He's a good man," Cross whispered stubbornly. "Deep down, he's really a good man."

David Padcula opened a manila folder and placed it gently on the artist's lap. "Miss Cross? This is Michael Lake's police file. It says he's hurt other women before like this. He's been arrested numerous times but never punished. It's all in here."

He glanced down at the file, then back at Cross. "We need your help—anything you can tell us that might help us find him before he hurts someone else. Any information you can give us about his habits, where he goes, who his friends are, what he does, things like that."

Cross did not respond.

Taking off his glasses, the inspector pinched the bridge of his nose and spoke as if he were suddenly very weary. "Look, I know you love him, but Michael needs help; he's sick. He can't control his violence. I've dealt with men like Michael my whole career and I know you aren't going to believe this, but you are very lucky he didn't kill you."

Cross pushed the file away a few inches, trying not to look at the report sheet. On top was a mug shot of the man. There was something about the eyes that made him appear a little crazy.

With her finger, Cross lightly stroked the side of the photo.

Padcula leaned close to her, creating a small, intimate space between them. "Michael Lake tried to beat you to death, and he almost succeeded. Don't you remember?"

Cross mouthed a silent "No."

Cat rubbed Cross's foot through the covers. "Cross, if you don't believe Dav—I mean Inspector Padcula, read the reports. The reports are facts about a man who hurts women over and over."

Cross looked from Cat to David Padcula. "Please, you have to understand, Michael is the way he is because people have hurt him. If he were to go to jail, he'd . . . he'd die. Literally, he'd never make it. I know you think he's a horrible man, but he's not, not really, not like a criminal. He has a bad temper. He doesn't mean it. Inside he's like a child who's lost and very scared."

Cross stopped. Cat had taken a small mirror from the wall and was holding it a few inches from her face.

"Look at yourself, Cross. Look at what this 'lost and scared child' did to you."

In spite of herself, Cross stared at the face in the mirror, touching the slash across her cheek as if she did not believe it was really there. After a minute, she pushed the mirror away and closed her eyes.

Tenderly Padcula cradled her hand, like the father of a young girl who's been told she didn't make the cheerleading squad.

The woman flared again, and snatched her hand out of his, although Cat could tell her rage had lost some of its fire. "He won't hurt anybody else but me. *I'm* the one he loves. *I'm* the one who caused this whole thing. I . . . I argued with him and he can't take that—he needed me to love him, not bitch at him. I shouldn't have talked back. I should have loved him better."

"You don't believe what you're saying," Cat said firmly. "I know you don't. Stop for a minute and think about what really happened. Get past that pretty face and see what he's done to you."

Cross lay back, exhausted. The dull headache that never seemed to ease added to her tiredness. "I want to sleep," she said bitterly. "You'll never understand. Please leave me alone."

Resigned, Inspector Padcula patted her arm once more. "Okay, Miss Cross. But if you change your mind and want to talk, call me." He took a card from his raincoat, wrote his home phone number on the back, and put it on her bedside table next to the phone. "Call day or night but if a dog answers, hang up—terriers are very nasty creatures when they get jealous."

He waited for a laugh, and not getting one, replaced his glasses and stood. "I'll stop in again tomorrow to see how you're getting along."

He touched Cat's shoulder and pointed to the door. "Miss Richardson, may I speak with you outside for a moment, please?"

Caught between feeling a need to comfort Cross and thrilling to his invitation, Cat looked from one to the other, deciding Cross would be okay for two minutes, and walked calmly to the door, clutching her stethoscope.

In the hallway, the second he looked at her, she went out of control. She imagined her face as a twitching mass of drooping, wrinkled eyelids and huge, fleshy nasolabial folds. Sudden fears cropped up that wild nostril hairs, matted with clumps of old snot, were hanging from her nose, while between the crevices of her teeth, black and dark green organic material suddenly gathered in a combined effort to sabotage whatever natural beauty she may once have had. Before his eyes, she had turned into Quasimodo.

Surreptitiously pinching the end of her nose in a I'm-just-thinking gesture, Cat felt frantically for nasal deposits and ugly bristles. Finding none, she vacuumed her teeth with twenty pounds of tongue-

176

sucking pressure, then smiled, making sure she showed only the tips of her teeth—just in case.

There's no point in panicking, she thought, even though the image of herself as reflected in the wide lenses of his glasses was, indeed, a strange and twisted sight. Take it calmly. Be yourself.

"Hi," she said, her lips trembling. She had meant it to be a low and intimate greeting; instead, it came out sounding like Yoda under water.

He took a step closer, and as he did so, his raincoat fell open, revealing the shoulder holster just as she imagined.

"Do you think you can talk to her, Red? The district attorney is going after this guy regardless of what she says or doesn't say, but it would help if she could give us some clues."

"Sure," she said with a wave of her hand. "I'd planned on doing that anyway." See, I'm no dummy even if I *do* look like Godzilla.

"Good. I hope the information I gave her about his other victims will wake her up." For a moment, he stared at Cat as if he were trying to fix her image in his mind, then took out his notebook and jotted something down. When he finished, he smiled and, unsure of what to do next, gazed at the floor.

And then he noticed her feet.

He opened his mouth to say something, thought better of it, and took out his notebook again instead.

It seemed to Cat that he wrote for a very long time.

When he finally put away his pen, he was grinning.

"Well, Red, I've got to run back to my office for a meeting or I'd force you to have a cup of coffee with me."

Cat tried hard to get her mind to move, to dip into her huge supply of snappy patter, but there was nothing on the tip of her tongue except blanks. It was pre-limerance insanity rendering her mute.

"Oh well, I don't do coffee," she said apologetically, wanting to kick herself even as she said the words. She undoubtedly sounded like an idiot. I don't *do* coffee? Christ!

He smiled peaceably, moved away from the wall, and straightened. In response to his movement, her unguarded stethoscope slipped from around her neck and landed on the floor between them with a dull clunk typical of cheap metal.

As she bent to retrieve the thing, a strand of her hair caught on his raincoat button—the one closest to his crotch area. Naturally.

Face-to-face with his fly, Cat grappled to catch hold of the unwieldy rubber and metal menace on the floor, at the same time attempting to untangle her hair from his button.

177

"Here, here. Let me help," he said, at first gently trying to unwind the strand, then plucking at it as if Medusa herself were climbing up his coat.

Three or four passersby paused briefly to stare.

"Hey," he chuckled, taking notice of the strange looks they were receiving. "If our jobs don't work out, I'll bet we could get a job in North Beach in one of those live-love-act places."

Cat snorted and started to laugh, which knocked her to her knees. Blushing to the point of burn pain, she gave a hard yank and separated from the button.

"Well, Red, that was good for me—how about you?"

Cat smoothed her disheveled hair and settled into an awkward silence.

He searched her face slowly, until he noticed her notice and began sidestepping to the elevator.

"You going to be here tomorrow, say about one p.m. or so?"

"Ah, yeah, sure. You'll be here then?"

"Gonna try." He paused. "Say, thanks for your help with Miss Cross. I appreciate it."

He was lingering. She was moving an inch at a time back into Cross's room.

"Anytime, Blackie." It had definitely been easier on the phone. At least her mind had functioned. She had to get a grip on herself.

He stepped onto the crowded elevator, peeked back, and waved a final time.

"Hey!" She yelled suddenly, and crossed the hall to wedge a foot against the straining elevator doors. The hotel elevator scene from *Barefoot in the Park* played clearly in her mind: he a bespectacled Robert Redford in a dark raincoat with a few straggling strands of red hair still hanging from a lower front button she, Jane Fonda in special-order running shoes striking a sexy pose.

"Whatever you do, David . . ." She paused.

The group in the elevator waited with him.

". . . try not to hurt the duck."

19 "Pssssst!"

Someone outside his door was trying to catch his attention.

For the third time, Corky ignored the insistent summons. The effects of the sleeping pill from the night before hung on, making him lazy and a little mean.

"Pssssssssssssst!"

Oh man! Angrily he turned his head and glared.

Perched in a wheelchair, grinning at him, was the same old woman he'd seen peeing the night before. In the light of day, he noticed that she looked a lot like the old lady in *Harold and Maude*.

The little kid pushing the chair stared at him noncommittally.

"Hiya, handsome." The old woman lifted her eyebrows a few times. "Catching up on your beauty sleep?" Clucking her tongue, she winked at him and motioned to her driver to move on.

The pair rolled out of sight before he thought to respond.

Corky stuck his fingers in his ears, made a wide, silent scream, then jumped up and commenced shadowboxing in the middle of the room just to be performing some action other than lying in bed thinking about himself. He thought about Lucy Cross and toyed with the idea of trying to see her again, or at least asking one of the nurses what had happened to her.

If he saw her again, he'd ask if they could just sit and talk. All the girls in his class said he was a great listener, and if Lucy wanted to talk, he would listen for as long as she wanted. No matter what she told him, he was sure he could help. They might even get together outside the hospital and just sort of hang out.

The idea jolted his thoughts from druggy fuzz into the realm of

179

vitalizing, gonad-charged possibilities. From there, he took a quantum leap.

Where to take an older, worldly woman could be a problem. She looked awesomely classy, like she probably had a million guys after her who owned hot cars and had shitloads of money. But, no problem. Some of the coolest things you could do with a girl didn't take a lot of bread, like Bill's Place on Clement for burgers and fries was considered *totally* excellent by everybody.

Except she's probably a vegetarian. Absolutely. She's too radically excellent not to be. Okay, so we'll go to Japan Center for vegetable tempura and then to the I Beam or Rockin' Robin's . . . No, wait. She was recuperating. We should go easy, like maybe take in the laser show at the planetarium or walk around the de Young or go up to the Palace of the Legion of Honor and hang out with the sculptures.

Yeah, for sure. She looked like a museum type. Quiet. Intellectual. Total nectar.

"Hey, champ, it's time for vital signs. Can I see you between rounds?"

Corky blinked himself back to reality. The nurse with the feet and the nice tits appeared out of nowhere—the one who had a thing for him.

He nodded a greeting and, in a flurry of alarm, remembered he was wearing loose hospital pajama bottoms. Sneaking a peek, he found with no small relief that the split front fly was closed. To play it safe, he pulled the drawstring as tight as it would go without hurting and retied it with a double knot.

When she'd checked his lungs, blood pressure, and temperature, he told her his throat still hurt, hoping deep down there was nothing she could do about it. The rawness of his voice made him sound older. While it lasted, he figured, he could probably get away with telling people he was twenty-two.

"You can plan on it being sore for another couple of days, kiddo." She noted his vital signs on her assessment sheet, and gave him a medicine cup containing two tablets. "Here's some Tylenol for your temp. If it'll ring your bells, we can start you on some warm salt water gargles four times a day."

Corky groaned and gagged, more for effect than for any real complaint.

"Hey! You expected perfect health after having a hard plastic tube shoved down your throat for three days? Give it time. Hasn't your mother told you patience is a virtue?"

180

"Oh man," he whined, returning to his dance-dodge-and-punch boxing routine.

Cat casually opened the boy's closet and at once drew back from the rank smell. Through watering eyes, she peered into the dark recesses, positive that if she dared to reach in, she would touch something that had died not too recently.

"Jesus, kid, what've you got in there? A favorite dead pet?"

Nonchalantly the teenager pulled out a pair of checkered high-top sneakers with the toes shredded out and threw them in the corner.

"I had my mother bring them. They're totally cool shoes."

Cat took his vacated place on the bed and watched him box for a minute or two, fully appreciating the solidness of his lean body and the soft boyskin covering it. How, she wondered, did he manage to hang together so well, considering everything that was going on?

"Dr. Barza talk to you?" she asked.

Corky did not stop boxing, although Cat noticed he seemed to punch the air a little more forcefully.

"Yep." He took a few more punches and circled around to face her. "Man, what a dweeb that guy is. He says to me, he says . . ." Corky fluttered his eyes and mimicked the monotone conehead voice. " 'No one can help you, Calvin, unless you are willing to communicate. Communication is the first step toward mental health.'

"I didn't say anything to that, so he starts ragging on me about how suicide is a *des*perate move, and if I'd actually succeeded, it would have devastated my parents and my friends *hor*ribly, and suicide is a *to*tally unresolvable death for the survivors, and all this other shrink shit. I mean, he was practically reciting from the shrink textbook of nerdisms."

Corky resumed boxing for a moment, then ambled from bed to sink, from sink to doorway, from doorway to closet, from closet to the other, unoccupied bed. He stopped near the bedside cabinet and picked several flakes of peeling paint from the wall.

"Oh yeah," he said, suddenly remembering more. "Then like out of nowhere, the dude starts talking about his forty-five-thousand-dollar Porsche and how cool it is to go a hundred and twenty miles an hour down Highway 280. Total bogus puke, like penis envy or something. I mean, like who cares?"

Cat smiled, imagining Dr. Barza going a hundred and twenty miles an hour in his famous, there's-not-even-a-fingernail-scratch-on-it black Porsche. The man was so anal retentive the small danger was probably the only excitement he had.

"I hope my parents aren't paying for this guy to drain my brain, 'cause it's not going to work on me. I'm not going to say like even one word to him."

"Did you tell him that?" Cat asked.

"What?"

"Did you tell Dr. Barza he couldn't do anything for you?"

"Sure!" Corky pursed his lips and lowered his eyes. "I mean, I didn't come right out and *say* that, but I didn't give him what he wanted either. I just sort of acted like I agreed with everything he was saying. He's such a dweeb he didn't even notice that I wasn't saying a fucking—"

Corky lightly slapped his own mouth. "Oops, sorry."

It's what Cat liked about the kid; he was so Boy Scout sweet at times. She waved it away. " 'S okay. I hear it all and sometimes I use it all too."

"That's cool," he said, his head bobbing like the dudes' downtown.

"So, what happened last night?" she asked. The question came unexpectedly to both of them.

Corky flushed, picking harder at the paint. He had peeled through a layer of institutional green and was getting through the songbird yellow. The shape of his scrapings vaguely resembled a rabbit's head.

"When?"

Cat said nothing.

"You mean last night?"

Cat rolled her eyes heavenward to indicate that she did.

"You mean in that girl's room?"

"That's the one."

Corky assumed an expression of innocence. "What about it?"

"You freaked. Why?"

"I didn't freak, man." The teenager bit his lip. "No way."

Watching him intently, she rubbed her thighs. "You were screaming when they took you out of Lucy Cross's room. Then you cried all night. You call that not freaking?"

"Somebody lied," he said, pretending to be indignant. "I didn't do any of that shit, man."

Cat debated whether to go hard-line, observed how he evaded her eyes, and decided to go with it.

"I don't think anybody lied, Corks. I think seeing Cross touched off something in you."

"No way." Corky's paint picking grew frantic. She saw that he'd scraped the top of his thumb to bleeding. "Something like what? What do you mean? Do you think . . . ."

Cat shook her head. "I think something happened to you, and

whatever it was was bad enough to make you want to check out permanently. Did you wonder what had happened to Miss Cross? Weren't you at all curious?"

"Nothing happened to me. And why should I be curious about some girl I don't even know? Man, you're out of your mind if you think seeing that girl made me freak. The only thing going on with me is I got depressed 'cause some girl broke up with me and I couldn't sleep and I took too many sleeping pills by mistake."

He winced at the lie. It was such a wimpy cop-out.

So what if it's wimpy, man? It's better than the truth.

Straightening to his full height, he stared at her defiantly.

She stared back until he looked away.

"Was that really it, Corks? Some girl splitting up with you?"

Corky chewed his lower lip, avoiding her eyes. "Sure was. A total bummer."

"Bullshit, kid. I think that seeing how badly Cross was hurt reminded you of how hurt you felt inside from . . . I don't know—whatever is really going on. You tell me."

He was sweating now. "Really, it was this girl named Molly who dumped me."

The overhead paging system interrupted. "Dr. Wilber, page two-nine-seven, Dr. Cramer, page seven-six." The operator sounded like a mother calling her kids in from the backyard fence.

Corky started pacing again, only slower this time. "So, what happened to this Lucy person anyway?"

Cat smiled as curiosity once again stepped over a dead cat. "She . . ." Cat hesitated, weighing patient confidentiality against the therapeutic value of giving out the information. It was, she decided, a day to break rules. "Just between you, me, and the bedpan? Miss Cross was beaten up by a sicko-type guy."

"Oh." His stomach ached as it rolled over a few times, crashed against his rib cage, and bounced back up into his throat. "I only wanted to know 'cause she seemed sort of cool . . . killer, you know, nice."

"She *is* nice, and young, and talented, and pretty, and hurting. Things like that sometimes happen to nice people."

"Is she gonna be okay?"

"I think so, but what about you? You gonna be okay?" *Talk to me, kid. Tell me where it hurts.*

"Sure."

"Okay, so indulge me—why did seeing Lucy Cross freak you out?"

"It didn't." He wished to hell he would stop sweating.

183

"It didn't? That's why you cried all night until Trish had to give you a sleeping pill?"

"The nurse lied." Corky walked to the sink and spit. "Is that dude across the hall a mo?"

Cat made note of the way he changed the subject before she could ask him to elaborate. "A mo? What's a mo?"

"You know, a homo." Corky sighed impatiently. "A homosexual. A fag. Does he have AIDS?"

"Yes, the man across the hall has AIDS, and no, Trish did not lie. You were given a chloral hydrate at three twenty-five this morning, and you were—"

"I want my room changed so I don't have to look at the mo."

Corky's neck veins were at once distended and throbbing. She could have easily counted his pulse from where she sat.

"He stares over here all the time. It gives me the creeps."

"Actually, he's a good guy." Cat stood to stretch her spine. "He's probably one of the nicest patients I've—"

"Oh man, I don't care what kind of good guy he is. He's a mo, and I don't want to be anywhere *near* where fags can be doing their fantasy-sex number on me. It's like mega-sick, man."

Cat nudged him away from the sink to wash her hands. "You're overreacting, Corky."

"Overreacting?" His voice was rising. "What do you mean, overreacting? You think I *like* getting stared at by some homofag? You think I want *him*"—Corky jerked his thumb in the direction of Professor Dean's room—"thinking about what he'd like to do to me?"

Cat sympathetically touched his shoulder. "Of course I don't, Corks. I didn't mean it like that."

The mattress came alive as the boy threw himself on his bed. When he spoke again, it was in a reasonable voice. "When am I getting sprung from this place?"

"Well, I think Dr. Leffler's plan is to keep you on this unit for the next day or two instead of sending you down to the psych ward, mainly because you're still running a temp. Dr. Barza will probably see you a couple more times and he'll more than likely have you attend a daily group where some kids your age get together to talk about what's bothering them. After that, my guess would be that you'll go home on Thursday."

"You mean they're gonna send me *home?*" He stared in disbelief. "Like *home* with my parents and . . ." He trailed off.

The magnitude of what must be threatening him at home made Cat uneasy. "There's a problem with going home?"

184

The teenager threw his pillow up to the ceiling and caught it with his feet. "No. I . . . I just sort of thought they'd send me somewhere else until . . . I don't know." He slid off the bed again and commenced doing the cool dude bop while beating out a rhythm on the corner of his bedside table with his thumb.

Unconsciously Cat tapped her foot to his beat.

"Home?" he repeated, far away. "Sure. Sure, that's cool."

Corky thought about the Sting tune he was tapping, then about Lucy Cross's breast, then about home and the danger that lay in wait for him there.

And Cat could only guess.

Stella was on the commode urinating when Cat dropped the four colored tablets onto her palm. "Last pills for today, Stel."

One by one, Stella held them close to her eyes. "The pink one is for the ticker, the green one is for my stomach, the yellow one is my water pill, and the purple and black is for my blood pressure."

Cat handed her the cup of water and watched as the woman proceeded with the Old People's Eight-Step Pill-Swallowing System: Line them up—small ones first, place smallest one at the very back of the tongue, drink half a glass of water, shrug, cough it back up, chew, shudder, and swallow.

"So, I see you've found a new friend," said Cat when she was confident that the last pill was being propelled safely down Stella's esophagus. She exchanged the water glass for a roll of toilet paper.

Stella nodded her thanks and wiped. "Sweet little Tinkertoy, isn't she? I see her father's not well."

"Not well at all." Cat helped Stella stand and pivoted her into the wheelchair. "Lung cancer. Advanced."

"Oh dear. How long does the poor soul have left?"

"A few days at most."

"Is he suffering?"

Soaking a washcloth with soap and water, Cat thought for a moment. "Well, the pain is somewhat under control, but it isn't only the pain he's suffering from; it has more to do with not being ready to let go."

"That's a shame. The young usually have a harder time with that than we do." The old woman let her hands go limp so the redhead could wash under the coarse and yellowed fingernails. "They're never quite ready to give up playing and go to sleep like us older children. It's that vexatious feeling that there's *more*."

185

The two women fell silent, watching their hands and fingers interact.

"By the way, Stel, social services is trying to get you into Bresford Place." Cat paused. "Do you remember about Bresford?"

"It's supposed to be nice, I hear."

"It's more than nice, Stel. It's got a lot of neat programs for senior citizens, like folk dancing and—"

Stella pointed to her arthritic knees. "Oh yes, that's me—swing your partner, do-si-do. Do they have wheelchair and walker-dependent ballets, too?"

Cat ignored the sarcastic remark. "Art classes, and photography classes, and programs where everybody participates in certain community services."

"Well, hoop-de-do." Twirling a finger in the air, Stella smiled at Cat's enthusiasm. "So, why don't *you* go there? Send me a postcard and let me know how it's going with you and the old fuddy-duddies."

"Come on, Stel, don't you care what happens to you?"

"What for? I'm just an old lady with nothing better to do than sit around holding up my clothes."

"That's absolutely not true. You're still a viable, worthwhile person with a future."

"You are a dear girl to say that to this old bag, but I'm afraid I wouldn't be much good to anyone."

Cat played an invisible violin. "I'd better get out my hip boots, Stel, because there's an awful lot of bullshit around here today."

Stella's eyes opened wide, then crinkled down with the cackle. "Your hip boots. Oh, that's very funny."

At the dirty utility sink, Cat measured and scrutinized the contents of the commode pan. Discarding the unremarkable urine, she washed her hands. She figured it was probably the fiftieth hand washing since her shift began almost eight hours ago. She inspected what she called her nurse's winter nails, momentarily depressed by the ragged, chipped ovals of dead skin that never looked nice during the cold months, and only sometimes nice during the summer, no matter what she did to them.

"The little one and I went exploring this afternoon," Stella said when Cat returned. "She took me to her father's room, but he started talking crazy to himself so we left. I'm afraid it upsets the girl to see her father like that, and of course, it would upset anyone but, well, let's see. . . ." Stella paused and wiped her rheumy eyes.

"Oh yes—after that, we sneaked over to the other side of the ward

186

and saw a young girl who was all banged up and drawing these lovely pictures of flowers and gardens. Then"—Stella held up her fingers, keeping count of the adventures—"we saw a lot of nurses and doctors doing that CPR business to some poor soul, then we saw a young fella whose bed was upside down and he had an ice pick stuck in his head, and then there were these two wretched patients hooked to—you know, those breathing contraption things. After that, we ran into a rather tall man, a doctor I believe, who was muttering to himself about cats and coal, or was it catty holes or—"

"Catechols," said Cat. "It's something that causes a chemical reaction. Dr. Cramer has this thing about them."

"Ah, I see," Stella said, then fell silent until Cat put a brush to the thinning mess of silvery-white fluff that reminded her of the insides of milkweed pods.

"I'll tell you, I made damned sure I never end up like that—hooked to one of those damned gizmos." The nonagenarian wagged a bony finger. "Heck, the first time I ever knew there was such a thing, I got hold of one of those living wills and told my doctor in as nasty a way as I could muster, I said, 'Young man, if anything ever happens to me and you don't respect my wishes, I'll come back from the grave to haunt you. I'm not going to hang around while you and the hospital makes money off my corpse. No way, José.' "

Laughing at the old woman's use of the youthful idiom, Cat finished brushing her hair into a sparse but neat bun, then stripped the bed and gathered fresh sheets while the old woman continued.

"Anyhoo, on the way back we saw the room with all the balloons, and a woman who nearly talked our ears off going on and on with this nonsense about her female troubles and describing all fourteen operations she's had on her tee-tee in the last year.

"If the girl hadn't been there, I would've told her a good man could take care of all her troubles better than any doctor with a scalpel." Stella appeared momentarily ruffled. "I reckon some women get to imagining they've got female troubles just to get a man to pay attention to them down there. I never understood women like that. It's as if they don't have anything else to put their attention on. It's not healthy."

Cat executed a crisp hospital corner and mused over Stella's statement; Nora had been saying the exact same thing for years about the ward's gynecological repeaters.

Listening to the old woman gossip, she couldn't help thinking that except for the need of a total body reconditioning, Stella really wasn't a bit different from any of the other younger women she knew.

In her first year of nursing school, she'd rejected the American perspective that the minute the outer packaging showed signs of wear and tear, anyone over retirement age automatically became a mental ward suspect, categorized as a feeble-minded and incompetent fool.

Her notion was that all old people led secret lives—even the ones who seemed lost to senility. In her fantasy, they waited for their doting younger relatives to disappear, then rehearsed advanced aerobics or Olympic pole vaulting.

She imagined a scene on the locked geriatric unit where one of the droolers and one of the vacant-eyed types were waiting for the attendant to leave. As the heavy metal door clicked shut, they gave each other sly, knowing glances and, in hushed tones, continued a complex debate on whether or not Sigmund Freud actually experienced a homosexual panic after he met Carl Jung, and what the deeper significance of the incident might have been.

Cat returned her attention to Stella's soothing old lady discourse. Stel was on finger number nine.

". . . then we stopped to say hello to that handsome boy next door. He looks like such a nice, polite boy." She took a sip of water and blotted her lips with a wad of toilet paper.

"By the way, dear, if you don't mind me asking, what is his trouble?"

"Hernia," Cat lied.

Stella clucked her tongue in a knowing way. "Oh yes, *those*. Now Otis used to have that *and* hemorrhoids, God rest his poor soul. Lord, did that man suffer!"

She motioned for Cat to come closer. "My papa used to say lots of water and a good stiff dose of castor oil kept the motors running smooth," she whispered. "Takes the strain off, you know. That's the secret.

"Something about that young man reminds me strongly of my grandson—from what I can remember of the little Tinkertoy."

"I didn't know you had family, Stel." Cat was immediately alerted to the red tape involved if previously unclaimed family suddenly popped up while she was trying to have the old woman accepted into a county-funded residence.

"Oh, I don't. Not really. Of course, my own kin have been dead for . . ." Stella thought for a moment, couldn't come up with the exact dates, and waved a hand at her poor memory. ". . . oh gosh, *years*. I lost my husband and son back in '43, so the only one that'd be left now would be my daughter-in-law and my grandson, but I

188

haven't seen hide nor hair of them since the little one was no bigger than a thimble.

"Little Oats is all grown up and probably has a family of his own now. I'm sure his poor mama made up some cockamamie story about his daddy's side of the family, so he probably never gave his old Nanmar Tella even a second thought."

"Wait—I don't get it. Why wouldn't she tell her son about his own grandparents?"

"Oh, well, *that* part of the story. . . ." Stella flapped her hand. "First you'd have to know that Otis junior married a simple girl he met on one of his trips for his daddy's business. She was a waitress in some roadside café and he fell in love on the spot—asked her to marry him by the time she served the pie and coffee."

Cat smiled. "It's romantic, you have to admit that."

"I suppose it was one way to get out of leaving a tip." Reaching over from her chair, the old woman smoothed out the wrinkles in the top sheet. "Well, we weren't at all surprised when he brought this little thing back from Arkansas that didn't weigh more than a sack of feathers. Otis junior was always dragging home stray cats or the runts from every litter on the block, ever since he was a boy.

"It scared the wits out of the poor girl to be any more than ten feet away from her own people. In her whole life I don't think she'd ever been more than two miles from home, and here we were living in the lap of rich folks' luxury in a big mansion in the Oakland hills. Otis junior had to teach her how to use the washing machine.

"She never said more than six words to me and Otis senior. We tried treating her like one of our own, but she never did warm up to us, poor little thing."

"You lost both your husband and your son together?"

Stella looked away. "Both of them, together. Yes." The bad picture came up, stung like a bee, then faded.

The flicker of pain did not escape Cat's notice. Over the years, she'd heard everything from fifty-year-old white lies to confessions of murder. She'd never believed in letting sleeping dogs lie—her curiosity made sure the hounds were always up and barking.

"How did they die?"

Even though she expected the redhead would ask, Stella still flinched at the question she'd avoided like the plague. Automatically she gave the answer she'd given for forty-odd years.

"Car accident. Both killed instantly. Thank God for that much, Amen."

"God, Stel, I'm sorry. That must have been horrible for you."

189

"Well, we all have to go on, don't we?" said Stella. "We all have to learn from what we're given, don't we?"

Cat slipped a fresh gown over the old woman's thin arms and noticed her breasts hanging like two shriveled albino prunes. She could not help wondering when they'd last been caressed by a man.

"What about your grandson? Did you ever try to find him?"

"Oh sure. Looked all over Arkansas for his mama's family, but never found anybody willing to admit they knew where she and the boy were. Those backwoods people stick together like tar and feathers."

"Well, what if he could be found? Would you want to see him now?"

Stella smiled sadly. "Oh, honey, I don't expect he could ever be located now. For all I know—"

"But what if he *was* found?" Cat insisted. "Would you want to see him?"

Out of the corner of her eye, Cat saw Alan standing in the doorway of Professor Dean's room. Above him, the nurse call light flashed in an eighty-beat-per-minute rhythm, indicating that the light had been on for longer than ten minutes.

Stretching on her toes, she saw Alan shake his head and walk back toward the nursing station. Professor Dean, his eyes closed and headphones in place, continued speaking to the empty doorway. She balled her fists and shoved them into her pockets.

Stella shifted on the wheelchair. "Well, I haven't thought about it for years. I wouldn't know what to say to the boy. I wouldn't think there'd be any point to it now. Maybe before, when I could've helped him with his schooling, but it's too late for that."

Professor Dean had just realized he was talking to himself and stopped. Cat guessed from the way he struggled to pull himself all the way to the edge of the bed that he needed to be cleaned and turned.

"I wouldn't be so sure it's too late," she said. "Maybe he has kids who need a great-grandma."

"Well, I just don't know, dear. I guess I'd have to spend some time thinking about it."

Stella scolded herself for being so untruthful. The dream of being surrounded by her own kin was not new to her. It was something she allowed herself to think about only when she felt strong enough to deal with the sadness that followed.

Across the hall, Professor Dean again searched for his call light.

"I gotta go, Stel. See you later. Push your call light if you need something, okay?"

"Okey doke," Stella said, watching the redhead run from the room. Always in a hurry, she thought. The whole damned world was in a hurry.

She figured it would be like that until the end of time, except just what in the hell was it they were hurrying *for?*

Under him, in the middle of the plastic sheet, lay a puddle of liquid stool.

Trying to control her rage at Alan's callousness, Cat pulled Professor Dean to the side of the bed farthest from the mess and washed the infected and sloughing skin of his buttocks.

He clicked off the cassette player and removed one earphone. "I'm sorry. I called before . . . told the nurse. . . . He must not . . . have under . . . stood what was . . . needed."

"Don't be sorry." Cat exchanged a soiled washcloth for a clean one. "It wasn't your fault. It was the fault of the nurse who ignored your request for the bedpan. I'll speak with him and make sure it doesn't ever happen again."

"No. Please. Don't want . . . any . . . one . . . to be . . . put out. Wasn't . . . his fault. Please don't."

It wasn't the first time she'd been put in the middle between an errant nurse and a patient who wanted to keep peace, even at the expense of his own comfort and well-being. But because it was Alan, and because it had happened so many times before, she would not let it slide by this time.

"Well, let me put it to you this way—if another professor was screwing up really bad, and you knew it was harming his students, and you also knew it wasn't the first time, what would *you* do?"

"But this . . . was . . . such a . . . small thing," he protested.

"But it isn't the first small thing."

He half nodded. "Ummm, I see."

She continued to scrub him, her anger against Alan building until she was clenching her teeth. She figured by the time she finished bathing Professor Dean and changed his bed, she'd have the strongest mandibles in town—either that or teeth ground down to nubs.

Preoccupied with her work and thoughts of Alan, she didn't realize until she'd left his room that most of the balloons had dropped a few more feet from the ceiling.

Alan was charting and biting his nails at the same time when Cat approached the nursing station.

191

"What's the matter, Alan, afraid of the balloons? Afraid you might strain yourself turning a ninety-pound man? Or maybe it's getting your rubber gloves soiled that bothers you."

Alan delivered an icy stare to the woman who probably outweighed him by twenty pounds. "I beg your pardon?"

"Bed 519 asked you for the bedpan and you walked away from him. I'd like to know why."

The nurse stood, his remote indifference reflected in his tone. "I honestly don't know what you're talking about. Do you?"

Cat blocked his way before he could pass. He was eye level with her breasts. Gripping her hands together, she consciously fought a long-held desire to pick him up by the shirtfront and hang him on any available hook.

"Unfortunately, my little cockalorum, I *do* know what I'm talking about."

Alan sneered and tried to dart around her. "And who the hell are *you?*"

In one agile move, Cat easily blocked him again. As she did so, she realized that people at the nurses' station were beginning to notice them. She turned her back to the stares to make it more difficult for the viewing audience. This wasn't meant to be a stage production.

"Look, Richardson," he huffed in a nervous, threatening way, "you'd better let me pass or I'll . . . I'll . . ."

"Ha! What are you going to do?" she baited. "Scream?"

From the peanut gallery behind them came a hiss, and for a split second she felt ashamed of herself for bullying him. Then she thought of the heartless way he'd treated Professor Dean, and rallied.

"I want you to explain to me why you ignored Professor Dean's request for a bedpan."

"I didn't."

"Cut the crap, Alan. The patient said you walked away from him after he asked for a bedpan, and I watched you do just that from across the hall."

"I . . . I didn't have time." Alan's color was high. "I was going to get someone else to do it but I forgot. Now get out of my way, please. I have to leave here on time today."

"You intentionally left the man in distress," Cat said, ignoring his demand. "You didn't try to find anybody. I mean, are you . . . ?"

She left the question in the air, with the sudden realization that Alan consistently refused AIDS patients. As a matter of fact, she couldn't remember his ever having taken care of one.

"Jesus, Alan, are you afraid of taking AIDS patients?"

The man squeaked at her like a cornered rat. "You're harassing me. Leave me alone!"

Mimicking Ralph Kramden, or was it Kingfish, Cat struck her forehead with the palm of her hand in disbelief. "What the hell is happening to this world? From a teenage boy, I expect this. From an uneducated person off the street, I expect this. From a nurse who is fully trained in how to protect himself from any communicable disease, I do not expect this."

The miserable, slightly ashamed expression on Alan's face made her soften.

"I mean really, Alan, what *is* the problem?"

Alan shoved his hands in his pockets and cocked his head. "Listen, it's in our contract with the hospital—I have the right to refuse any patient I don't want to care for, and I don't like taking care of those people with their nasty little disease. It's taking unnecessary chances. If you want to risk it for the sake of showing what an altruistic and compassionate humanist you are, great, go ahead! Personally, I'd rather be thought of as an uncaring asshole and live until I'm eighty than be dead in five years because I got splashed or stuck while I was being the perfect nurse."

The man's words took the wind out of her sails. He did have the right to refuse, and it *was* taking a chance, no matter how well you protected yourself.

She sighed. Alan was a small man with small values. His narrow point of view would not be changed by anything she had to say now or ever. She'd learned a long time ago that people in that bigoted, righteous frame of mind were as unreachable as deaf mutes without sign language.

The thought made her smile despite her anger. When she was fourteen, she had made two humiliating discoveries: one, that Chicago was not a state, and two, that the proper term was deaf mute, not death mute.

Alan was most certainly a narrow-minded, shortsighted death mute.

"Thank you for your honesty," she said evenly. "But the next time a similar situation comes up"—her words picked up steam and Alan shrank back—"don't use it as a way to make your statement of disapproval. Don't make anybody suffer because you've made some moral judgments—not in this unit, buddy, because if you do, and I find out about it, I'll make sure you answer for it."

Behind her, someone cleared her throat.

Looking over her shoulder, she saw Jo Atwood, the assistant director of nursing administration, standing stiffly at attention. Cat flinched and nodded in acknowledgment. When she turned back, Alan was nowhere to be seen.

"I need to talk with you, Richardson," Miss Atwood said in her low, even voice. "Think you can take a minute out from hassling the other staff?"

With her healthy, country-girl looks, Jo Atwood was an attractive woman, though it seemed to Cat she had taken pains to hide the fact under carelessly applied makeup and a shapeless military-inspired dress, complete with two brass stars on each epaulet. An unnecessary headband made crush marks in her sandy-brown hair, cut short on the sides and back.

Cat slumped. What had the administration found to ride her about *now*? Was it one of the people in the elevator? Had some SPCA radical complained about a tall redhead babbling about hurting ducks?

"Well . . ." she said uncertainly, searching the empty hall as if there were a pressing matter to be attended to just around the corner, "I suppose I could sneak into the conference room, but I've only got a short minute to spare. I have tons of work to do with my patients before report."

That was true: she had to say goodbye to each patient, and promise —in one or two cases, threaten—she would return the following day.

Walking toward the conference room, Cat recalled the period of time after her second divorce when she had gone to Jo to ask for a leave of absence. An emotional wreck, she'd pleaded with the woman to give her the time off in order to pull herself together.

"How could such a magnificent woman let herself be taken in by such a jerk?" Jo had asked, as if it were a personal affront. "And whatever possessed you to actually marry him?"

When Cat began to cry, Jo softened and slipped a reassuring arm about her shoulders. "Most men's egos can't handle strong women like yourself. It was *his* loss, Cat. He must have been blind not to see how lovely you are. Let it go. You're too smart to let a man like that affect you so much."

Cat took comfort from the woman's light stroking of her head until she felt the quality of the caresses becoming too tender and just a little too trembling. When she pulled back, it was evident that Jo's gaze was more than friendly.

Before she could move, Jo was kissing her.

Until that moment, Cat had never questioned her own sexuality,

194

and although she believed women were generally more advanced than men on an emotional and spiritual level, it had always been men who held her sexual fascination. Not that she didn't appreciate looking at a pretty woman as much as the next guy, but bedding one had not been part of her agenda.

Straight or gay, she considered women her sisters, her complete peers. She had never judged a woman harshly simply because her chosen lover was named Betty instead of Ralph. Certainly she had loved Nora more than she had loved anyone, but she did not have the capacity to fall *in* love with another woman, though there had been isolated moments when she was so miserable trying to relate to men, she almost wished she could.

Now, Cat cringed as she remembered how badly she had handled the situation. Her knee-jerk reaction of slapping Jo away had sent the woman running from the room in tears. After the incident, Catalina, being the coward that she was in such matters, avoided the woman the way she avoided Brussels sprouts.

Cat slowed a few steps before the conference room, wanting to kick herself. What a stupid choice, she thought, when the kitchen would have been so much more public.

Praying someone, anyone, would be using the room, she timidly pushed open the door and peeked in. There wasn't a soul.

"Ah, maybe we should go in the kitchen," she said, backing out. "We can talk over tea."

Jo marched into the room. "This is fine. Besides, I don't want to be interrupted."

Inside, Cat sought out an isolated corner chair and sat down while Jo circled the conference table, arms folded across her chest.

"Well, Catalina, you've been written up for insubordination once again." The hint of a frown played at the corners of Jo's mouth.

Cat yawned and studied the freckles on her arms. "And for what minor infraction am I to have my hands slapped *this* week?"

How boring. A week didn't go by without her getting written up by some threatened doctor or one of the policy-ridden nursing administrators for sticking her neck out for her rights as a professional or the rights of her patients. Other than a few matters of temper, the offenses were almost exclusively political in nature.

Miss Hurley was right behind you in the lobby parking lot yesterday morning, when she witnessed you making an offensive and lewd gesture to one of our esteemed doctors. Shame on you. You should be more careful about flipping someone off, especially when the director of nurses is watching."

195

"Big deal. Add this one to the pile." She stood to leave.

"Well, dear, this time, I'm afraid, it *is* a big deal." Jo paused, reluctant to disclose the bad news. "You see, this will be your sixth probation inside a twelve-month period, and that's cause for immediate dismissal without recommendation."

"Pssssh! Don't make me laugh, Jo. First of all, I'm a senior staff member in this hospital. Second of all, they wouldn't dare let one of their best nurses go, let alone in the middle of a nursing shortage. Third, they know me well enough to know I'd have them in court in two seconds."

"And you'd lose on all three counts, because first of all, you may be a senior staff nurse, but you are trouble and a rabble-rouser. You've also got too much power and you think you know too much. Second of all, nursing shortage or no nursing shortage, the hospital is letting nurses go left and right and replacing them with lower-cost help. Have you noticed how many new grads and imported nurses are on staff these days? You're premium salary around this place, and they'd just love to unload you. And last but not least, the administration has enough bad paperwork on you to convince any judge to not only fire you but keep you from practicing nursing for the rest of your life."

Jo rested a badly shaking hand on Cat's arm. "They're serious this time, Catalina. You keep bucking the system, and they don't like that. They're afraid you're going to spoil the rest of the apples in the barrel."

"You mean the rest of the sheep in the flock, don't you?" Cat said, and drew her arm away from Jo's hand without making it seem too deliberate a move. She did not want to encourage, yet she didn't want to upset the woman again.

Jo pulled up a chair opposite hers. "I'm thinking of misplacing a couple of the more recent reports. Not a lot, but enough to keep you out of administration's way for a while."

"Why would you do that, Jo? I mean, I know you're a nice person, and that you've given some of the nurses breaks, but the fact still remains, you're management."

"I don't want you to leave here, Catalina," Jo said slowly in the sad tone of a lover about to be abandoned. "I've admired you since the first time we met twelve years ago." She smiled. "You're a fighter. I was a nurse on the wards for eight years before I took this job, so I know what it's really like out there. I also know that some of the nurses count on you to speak up for them.

"I care for you, Cat. Very much. And I still want you." Jo blushed

196

and continued in almost a whisper. "I know you turned me away before, but I can't help but hope you might change your mind."

Her eyes steady on the carpet, Cat felt her stomach churn at the prospect of facing the hurt and hopeful look in Jo's eyes. No matter what end she was on, rejection had always been a major agony for her.

"Listen, Jo. I think you're a sweet lady, and I don't want to hurt your feelings, but I can't. . . . "

"Cat, please. Don't say anything now. You're nervous and so am I. Just think about it for now. Okay?" Jo hooked Cat's little finger in hers. "I really believe we could have something special. After we got to know each other, I think you'd realize how gentle we could be with each other."

Cat stood and moved toward the door knowing she was the biggest wimp in the world. All she had to do was make her position clear. Say she was strictly into men. Say she didn't swing that way. Just say no.

But she didn't. Yellowbelly. Pantywaist. Chicken.

"Cat?"

Cat's heel touched the wall. Mentally, she breathed a sigh of relief. What was it Dale Carnegie used to say about being in tight spots and being a major world class coward?—"Improve upon the worst situation"? She supposed she wasn't above just running out the door if it came right down to it.

Jo stepped close to her and was about to speak when Nora slammed the door open. At the same time, an announcement came over the paging system.

Attention all personnel, code blue Ward Two acute.

Nora took one look at Jo and then at Cat and instantly sized up the situation. Grabbing Cat by the hand, she pulled her out the door, shouting as they went, "Sorry, Jo. Code blue. Gotta run."

Side by side, the two friends sprinted a couple of yards behind the red-code cart.

"You get the mouth, I get the chest," Cat said, and laughed.

Nora flashed her a disgusted side glance. "Ya know, for someone who purports to have a simple, sedate existence, I have a feeling a documentary of your life would give the first thirteen minutes of *Raiders of the Lost Ark* a run for its money at the box office."

20

9:25 p.m.

At the end of a dead-end street, Tom Mix shook his coat free of mist and waited patiently for his master to open the door of the small cottage. Reading the edges of each of his keys, Gage chose the one with the most ridges and guided it smoothly into the lock.

Once inside, he went still, letting his other senses run a check on the dry, warm room. Satisfied that it was as he had left it that morning, he walked seven steps to the wood stove. Tom Mix's nails clacked against the slate floor, keeping time.

To Gage's fingers, the stove's satiny metal top yielded warmth on the low side of hot; the coals would need only stoking and two more quarter-logs to keep them both warm through the night.

Gage removed his navy watch cap and hung it on a rack near the stove. He was glad for the house and the fire, grateful for what he thought was an abundance of the best life had to offer, but then, in his simple life, anything more than a half-full belly was abundant.

The two-room cottage had been a godsend, and he could not have enjoyed the space more even if he had been able to see the panoramic view of San Francisco Bay that lay just outside the cabin's only window.

An artist had once come to his door to ask if she might take some photographs from his window. When she discovered he was blind, the young woman spent an hour describing the scene, explaining every color, every dimension, down to the finest details of the water's silver reflections and the shapes of the sails.

After she had finished at the window, he served her hot, strong tea and milk biscuits and begged her to go on. For three more hours, she gave him perfectly detailed pictures of everything within sight. The deep, shimmery browns of Tom Mix's eyes, the cream white of the woven wicker walls, the delicate flower patterns of Delia's crocheted curtains, the irregular and rough-cut slabs of gray slate used in the flooring, and even the colors of the hand soap—all were painted on the blank canvas of his imagination. By the time the woman left, he perceived the room in which he lived as a veritable palace of wonders.

Now, showered and dressed in a pair of clean long johns, Gage ate in a silence that was broken only by his occasional offers of bits of bread dipped in chicken gravy to the dog.

While he ate, he thought again of the young artist so blessed with the genius of creating beauty. She had given him a gift of immeasurable value. Yet whenever he sought her inside the sight, he was not strong enough to get past the heartache and upheaval surrounding her.

With the dishes washed and put away, he checked his watch cap for moisture. Finding none, or at least none that mattered, he stretched the soft wool over his ears, sat down on the edge of his cot, and switched on the radio.

Mozart's Violin Concerto no. 5 in A Major transported him at once to the warmth of a Mississippi kitchen where a skinny nine-year-old blind colored boy rolled out pie dough listening to the orchestras on the radio.

By the time he was two, his mother had suspected her youngest son's eyesight was fading by jumps and slides. Unwilling to let her child be enslaved by pity, she gave to him what meager education she had absorbed as a young girl working in the home of two cultured maiden ladies.

Pinning to her apron worn and tattered pages of whatever books could be begged or borrowed, the soft-spoken woman read to her son while they worked together doing the usual chores that were part of keeping house for eleven people. Through her, King Arthur, Puck, and Alice in Wonderland became his companions in dark but glorious adventures.

And there was always the music. Instead of jazz and the big-band sounds that beat out high-steppin' rhythms in the houses around them, his home was filled with the silken chords of the classical

199

music his mother loved. Her best pupil, by the age of fifteen Gage knew by heart the works of most of the major composers.

But as devoted as he was to his mother, it was his grandmother on whom he depended for guidance through what the rest of the family secretly referred to as his "fits." Only the old woman had known what to say and do when he had the visions, only she had perceived the true source of his light—until he met his sweet, round-faced Delia.

He recognized her as the woman he'd waited for and already loved the first time he heard her voice rise clear and sweet above the others in church choir. As for Delia, she knew he had the sight the minute she laid eyes on him. It didn't frighten her away as it did other folks, more than likely because she had enough of the power herself to make them spiritual kin. For twelve years, they grew so close in mind they couldn't tell where one left off and the other began. Theirs was a world of loving warmth until the Lord decided He needed her back. . . .

The announcer interrupted his reverie: Academy of St. Martin in the Fields. Gage sighed and repeated the name softly. Academy of St. Martin in the Fields. What a wonderful name for an orchestra.

Tom Mix circled on his old wool blanket, searching for just the right spot before lowering himself. Gage felt the animal's restlessness and chuckled to himself; even the shepherd was in on the receiving line of energy—from the red-haired woman to him to the dog.

Chewing briefly on his foreleg, Tom Mix yawned and settled his head on his paws. The only sounds to break the stillness were the music and occasional cracklings from the wood stove.

Gage paid attention to his breathing until the deep muscles relaxed, he could see a rapidly changing kaleidoscope in his head. The air pressed in around him and time stopped. Taking a long, slow breath, he shuddered once and went into the spirit.

Images crowded his mind. He chose one and brought it into focus. The red-haired woman rose from the floor and pointed in the direction of a man running. Gage followed him with his mind until the man turned suddenly and fixed him with hatred-filled eyes. The impact of the man's internal poison sent him sprawling back on the bed.

A bitter taste flooded his mouth as the eyes faded and were replaced by the rain-pelted figure of a terrified white boy. He moved the focus of the vision in order to see the boy's whereabouts but lost his concentration in an ocean of broken shells, sinking helium balloons, and a single cry for help.

He tried to swallow, but the bitterness of his spit made it impossible. He would have to wait until the sight passed to empty his mouth. Concentrating on his breathing again, he saw the blurred images crystallize into a searing streak of silver light.

As he reeled in the pictures one frame at a time, he was able to decipher shadowy hands fighting for control of the light, and then the picture was obscured by an image of the young artist, tears of blood flowing down her face into an empty shell.

He was running out of time. His respirations quickened, and he ran behind Tom Mix toward the fading light and into the murky brown that was his world.

When he could move, Gage emptied his vile spittle into the wood stove and slowly, cautiously stoked its contents. Wearily he eased himself under the blankets.

"Oh man, oh man. The hurricane be headed this way all right," he mumbled to the dog.

Next to the bed, Tom Mix groaned, already deep in sleep.

Feeling for the dog's body, the blind man found paws twitching in dream flight. He stroked the fur for a while, then let his hand rest between the ears of his partner in sight.

11:04 p.m.

Nights were the worst for Corky, especially if he allowed himself to think. Without the distractions of the day, nighttime was like a cocoon, encasing him, setting him apart from the rest of the world. If he let his guard down for even one minute, the panic, which was growing to huge proportions, became unmanageable. Thinking about it all made him feel like he was going to crack.

Corky exerted a constant pressure on the television remote control button, watching the channels flip, one after the other. As usual, the Tuesday night tube had nothing but pukeworthy garbage to offer: the news, the Spanish station, and an old movie he'd seen a couple of times before. It was one of the ones his parents got all weirded out about, as in, "Oh gee whiz, I remember *this* one, honey. Why, I saw this in CinemaScope with Biff Anderson," or, "Gosh honey, wasn't *Hawaii* the movie we saw (wink, wink) on our first date?"

Choosing from the wide selection of Strange Things to Do for Bored Teenagers, he balanced the remote control on his forehead, then, using only his face muscles, moved it down to his mouth and endeavored for several minutes to turn it off with his tongue. The TV screen went to gray on the fifth attempt to bounce the control off his front teeth.

A corner of the massive textbook his mother had brought bit into

201

the back of his right knee. A kindly though misguided soul, she'd said she hoped the sight of the text might entice him to actually study its contents. At the moment, the only thing he felt inclined to study was the book itself.

It was a masterpiece of high school art. Three sides of the page edges were beautifully done in a two-tone skull-and-crossbones design, and on each inside cover were elaborate sketches of Darth Vader, spaceships, breasts and buttocks, a giant phallus or two, a skateboard being ridden by a skeleton, a bleeding heart with a dagger through the middle of it, and two banners, one reading "Mr. Olson Eats The Big One," the other sporting "Drugs, Not Recycling."

Along its spine was the silver title *Learning Calculus!*

Why, he wondered, was there an exclamation point after the title? Was it to instill a subconscious excitement about learning calculus? Corky smirked remembering the bored-to-puking expressions worn by most of his calculus buddies. They were the good students—the rest of the class slept through it.

By rocking his body and then throwing his legs high in the air, he gained enough momentum to leap out of bed and landed on his feet, arms outstretched.

Around him, the spectators burst into applause. The Olympic judges held up their scorecards: 10.0, 10.0, 9.5 (the Soviets), 10.0, 10.0, 10.0. The gold was his!

Grinning broadly for the cameras back home, he clasped his hands over his head in victory. The CBS sportscaster shoved through the crowd of cameras and microphones vying for his attention. From every direction came pleas of "Please, Mr. Benner, look this way!" and "Hey, Corky! How about an exclusive interview with NBC?" A photographer was there to take his picture for the front cover of *Time*.

He spoke sincerely into the sea of microphones, wiping the hard-earned sweat from his brow.

". . . and most of all, I'd like to thank Mr. Jack Henny, my high school coach, for his encouragement, and my mom and dad for their support, and my totally rad wife, Lucy."

Stoked, Corky the Olympian hero ambled to the mirror and studied himself for a long time. Focusing out the zits and the half-strength stubble, he could see that his left side was best; it showed off the strength of his jawline. He doused his head under the faucet, then combed his hair straight back, jutted out his strong jaw, and clenched his milk-advertisement-perfect teeth.

He held the facial pose, pumped up his pecs and biceps, and slowly turned from side to side to catch a glimpse of his magnificent physique. Mr. Universe on review. *Totally GQ.*

The screaming, fainting crowd of stunning women broke through the security barriers and were inches away from his superb body, when the weird-shaped nighttime nurse waddled past, stopped, and did a double take.

"Should I even bother to ask what you're doing?" Laurel asked in a monotone.

Self-conscious, Corky instantly let his face and body slump back to their normal, everyday limits and mussed up his hair. "Nothin'."

"Want a sleeping pill?"

"Nah. Don't think I need it."

"Suit yourself, buster. If you need one, put on your call light. Gotta go get report. *Adiós muchacho.*"

The nurse went away and Corky returned to staring at his image in the mirror. He was blown away by how much he looked like Bruce Springsteen with his hair damp and fluffed out. Why had no one ever mentioned it to him before?

Across the hall, the AIDS guy with the earphones and the balloons looked like he was asleep . . . or dead. At least he wasn't staring over at him anymore.

Wedged between the tines of guilt and pity, Corky worried that he might have heard what he said about him. He didn't mean the dude any harm. Having AIDS was probably painful enough.

On the front page of the *San Francisco Chronicle* was a full-length photo of him in white lab coat, surrounded by a throng of beautiful women offering various parts of their bodies for his autograph. The banner headline read: DR. BENNER DEVELOPS CURE FOR AIDS. Three pages were devoted to the story, which featured a photo of him shaking hands with the President while his mother and father proudly looked on, and another of him receiving a kiss from his pregnant (with twins!) wife, Lucy.

Noiselessly edging into the main hallway, he knew it was going to be a highly risky mission. Because of his superior skill and cunning, he was now the last undercover spy left alive in the high-security Soviet biological warfare headquarters. The other six agents had been caught, used as test subjects for hideously painful, ethically question-able experiments, and disposed of in the basement.

Your mission, Double Agent Benner, should you choose to accept it, is to reach and facilitate the escape of one Lucy Cross, the brilliant United States biologist, held against her will by the Secret Red Army. If you are captured, you must instantly destroy all evidence and yourself.

Sliding along one wall to the next, Double Agent Benner made it to the prisoner's sector in record time. As soon as he stepped into the hall, he saw her sitting up in bed with a large pad of paper on her lap. Thank God she was awake, let alone alive. It looked as though she'd been tortured pretty badly. Walking toward her, he hoped, for the sake of millions of innocent Americans, she had not spilled her guts about the MJM-7 grand-horned-chigger-bite virus.

"Hi," he said, nervously glancing down at his fly drawstring, then casually leaning against her door. The very sight of her loveliness caused him to reshape his thumbnail to the quick with his teeth. "You awake?"

Cross's expression made him think of a child who, upon opening a long-awaited gift, has found only a pair of crummy old socks.

"I'm Corky Benner, an agent—I mean a patient from down the hall. I checked in on you last night, but I don't think you knew I was here. You looked pretty tweaked."

"Oh, yes. Tweaked. Thank you." Bitterly disappointed though she was, Cross made a gift of a half-smile to the young man who wore his interest in her like an oversized coat.

11:09 p.m.

From the radio, Michael Lake's deep voice surrounded her with a tranquil, sensual monologue about the secrets of passion shared by men and women in the night. When the Blazzie perfume commercial was over and the air space filled with music, she cried out and reached toward the radio, desperately wanting his voice to stay with her.

As she watched the floor indicator over the elevators, her face opened into a smile with each approaching car, then faded as it passed on to the next floor.

He'll come, she thought. He can't leave me now. How could he leave after they had shared so much?

It was raining and she ached for the sight of him—her crazy, laughing-in-the-corner hero. She marveled at how everything reminded her of some aspect of him: Someone's pink shirt prompted a memory of the first night they'd slept together, because he'd worn a flannel nightshirt of the same shade. The nurse giving her a bed bath brought back the time at the Sausalito Hotel when he'd washed her face and hands out of remorse over bruising her. Even the rain was guilty of reminding her of the bittersweet November day she'd tried to leave him and he had begged her on his knees to stay. She saw pieces of him in every face, in every movement. It had always been like that, even during their first year—the passions of their nights

204

would come up during her days like weeds sprouting up in an unruly garden.

She concentrated on the bad times, trying to find reasons to hate him, but her mind deceived her, hauling up the good memories and making them seem more perfect than they were.

What the investigator told her could not be true. Although she was never able to please him, Michael said he had never loved any other woman the way he loved her. She was his pivotal woman, his symbiotic lover. When they were together, the outside world did not exist. Without each other, they would not be able to function.

Even in the beginning, once her initial burst of creative energy passed, it became an effort to concentrate on work when she could easily choose to be with him. Like a child, he insisted she always be near him. Happily she went with him to studios and set locations, only to be left sitting in the car, staring at the door he'd entered, waiting like a well-trained dog for him to reappear.

When Nathan finally shamed her into demanding time away from him in order to take care of the neglected parts of her life, Michael would interrogate her for hours, sure that she was seeing someone else.

But no matter what she did, her supreme sin against the Law of Michael always came down to her failure to love him enough or in the right way. Even during their lovemaking she could not win; if she became too aroused, she was obviously a slut, and if she held back, it was absolute evidence that she had slept with someone else that very day.

Yet despite his accusations of her infidelity with every man, woman, and animal in town, he needed her desperately, and Cross had never been so needed in her life. Never before had a man loved her so much that he wanted to change her. With a critical eye, he went to work butchering her spontaneity, ridiculing her physical appearance, and mangling her sense of pride until he had finally shredded her spirit.

His rule and codes of behavior were so harsh that even a phone call from a friend was considered a major violation of his trust in her. Once when an old boyfriend phoned, she was so afraid Michael would use it as an excuse to punish her she lied when he demanded to know who had called. During his questioning her body betrayed her by hyperventilating.

It was one of his worst beatings.

From day to day she never knew which Michael would wake up beside her. Although the loving and kind Michael was scarce, she could not stop believing that if she loved him hard enough, one day he would stay and the other Michael would not come back. . . .

Past the elevators, at the end of the hall, a man looked around the corner and quickly pulled back.

Michael? Her heart was instantly in her throat. She squinted, cursing her contact lenses in the case on the bedside table. There wouldn't be enough time to put them in, and damn it, where were her glasses? The figure moved down the hallway, hugging the walls. The build of the shoulders and the coloring were Michael's. He had come to take her.

She made a whimpering sound and excitedly combed her hair with her fingers. Michael would yell at her for looking like a scum, but she didn't mind, she was ecstatic he'd finally come for her. All aches and pains were instantly replaced with her joy.

Would he get mad if she waved and got out of bed? Would he consider that trying to call attention to herself?

She sat back. It was better not to chance getting him upset again, especially since the *People* magazine thing was still fresh in his mind.

She sniffed herself. Did she smell okay? Would he start in with the tirade about her natural smell being like a whore's? Where was the perfume he liked?

What about her face?

The memory of it in the mirror instantly made her cringe. She didn't want him to see her like this. It would make him feel bad about hurting her and then he'd turn it around on her.

She relaxed when she saw that the man standing in the doorway was wearing the wrong clothes and had straight hair. This person wasn't hard like Michael. There was a sensitivity in this stranger's face that Michael lacked.

"Hi," the stranger said. She saw him nervously check the fly of his pajamas to make sure it was closed, then look back at her with puppy eyes. "You awake?"

"I'm Cross . . . My name is Lucy Cross."

"I know," Corky said, hoping he sounded cool and debonair. "So, how're you feeling?"

"Better, thank you. How about yourself?"

"Better too." He forced the briefest of laughs. She followed suit.

There was an uncomfortable silence, in which he tortured himself with self-deprecating thoughts. It was clear she didn't like him because:

He was ugly.

He sounded like a total dweeb.

He was too short.

He had wimp shoulders.

He had Dumbo ears.

His hair was stupid.

He didn't have a car.

He didn't have any money.

His nose was waaaaay too big.

And somehow she knew he was beginning to grow hundreds of tufts of fine dark hair on his back, as if it'd been planted with hair seed.

Cross weighed the pros and cons of inviting him to sit down. She was tired, but she didn't want to be alone either. And if Michael came and saw her with the boy, he'd accuse her of seducing him—but then again, it would be more like Michael not to come now. He was angry with her and would make her suffer for a few days longer.

She studied the boy with an artist's eye. He was built like Michael and even had a similar facial structure, except this boy had an innocent sweetness to him, especially around the eyes. Green eyes. And he wanted to talk to her.

Corky looked confused. "Well, guess I'll head back to my—"

Cross reached down to stop him. "No! Why don't you pull that chair over here."

Flashing her a grateful smile, he pulled the cushioned lounge chair closer to her bed and lowered himself into it without taking his eyes off her. "Well, if it's cool with you, I'd like to, ah, just, ah, maybe talk to you . . . if you're not too tired or anything?"

"Please. I'm feeling lonely, and . . . Oh, this'll be nice."

Corky was elated. She *wanted* him to stay? Did she say she was lonely? Did she say she thought he was nice? He wiped his palms against his pajamas, saw the streaks of perspiration, and crossed his legs.

"Yeah, I tried watching the tube, but there wasn't anything decent on except that old movie with James Dean and that famous actress where they strike oil and they, like totally take a shower in the stuff?"

She thought for a minute. "You mean *Giant*, with Elizabeth Taylor and Rock Hudson?"

"Yeah! That's it. What do you think? Did they use real oil, and if they did, how did they get it to come out of the ground like that at just the right time?"

Cross shook her head and realized the constant headache wasn't quite so bad anymore. Even her ribs had stopped burning. "Couldn't have been real. . . . Do you really think it was? Except how would they get it out of their hair?" She looked at him sideways. "You in school?"

"Yeah." He knew the next question, and having been at this crossroads before, knew he had to make a decision whether or not to lie. If he said he was at, say, SF State, he would also say he was twenty-five, and next he would say he had a part-time job as a stockbroker, and that he drove a new Jaguar XJ6, and that his apartment in Telegraph Hill was . . .

His dad's voice cut in with the old saying which, as corny as it was, had proved true all his life—"Oh, what a tangled web we weave, when first we practice to deceive!"

"Where?"

"Ahhhh, I'm a senior at Lowell."

That was it. It was all over. Send the baby back to his playpen.

Cross smiled as much as her injuries would allow. "Superior school. God, I wish I'd gone someplace like that." She looked at him with admiration.

"Oh, well, it's where my parents thought I should go. I've applied to Berkeley and SF State for next year. Eventually I want to go into . . ."

Corky paused. It was one of the biggest sources of irritation to his counselors and parents that he had no idea what he wanted to pursue as a life's career.

". . . aeronautic design." Mentally he shrugged. Sure, why not— he'd love flying kites as a kid.

"That sounds extremely interesting. Great choice."

There was a pause. "So, like, are you going to Berkeley, or what?"

"No, I graduated years ago. I'm an artist now."

The boy nodded. "You mean like paintings or greeting cards?"

Cross laughed, delighted. It was refreshing to find someone who didn't know her. This boy was infatuated with Lucy the person—not some fantasy the reputation of Cross had created. With him she could be Lucy the gardener, or Lucy the normal girl, or Lucy the greeting card dabbler.

"Oh, I dabble in abstracts and some contemporary stuff—nothing exciting. It's enough to get by."

For a half-second they were quiet.

"So why are you here?" she asked.

He winced. "Operation on my, ah, back," he muttered. "What about you?"

208

"I fell down some stairs." She flushed.

Okay, Corker, she doesn't want to talk about it. Change the subject. "Uhn. Didja hear there's a killer storm coming in sometime tomorrow? S'posed to blow the roofs offa houses."

She nodded, hoping Michael was safe. Then she thought about the roof of the cabin. It would survive.

"What're you drawing?" He pointed to the pad of paper.

"Oh, some doodles, not really what I'm used to doing. I usually do big paintings, or murals."

"Can I see?" The boy was close, leaning over her. The muscles of his arm reminded her of Michael's; the masculinity of it, and the way it was placed on the bed brought up fresh and painful memories of their lovemaking. Reaching out, she almost touched him but realized it was not Michael's arm, only one like it.

Corky flipped through the pages of drawings of Michael's eyes. Michael's jaw, Michael's mouth, without comment. When he came to the one of her garden as seen through the French doors of her studio, he stopped. "This is really killer stuff," he said in earnest.

Cross blushed and smiled politely. "Thank you. Maybe you'd let me sketch you."

Using his jaw as a handle, she turned his head for different perspectives. He had a strong, manly face like Michael's, but his good looks were softer. She wondered if she could capture the sweetness.

Corky wondered if she could hear his heart. Her touch was so gentle he almost couldn't stand it. Trying to act cool, he took her hand in as brotherly a manner as he could muster and held it up, palm to palm with his. Lovingly he examined the tips of her fingers.

"Man, you sure got little hands."

Not really wanting to, she started to cry. Michael had often said that to her as a lead-in to his bed talk. He would kiss each finger, reciting, "This little piggy went to market, this little . . ."

Stricken with anxiety and remorse, Corky stood and leaned close to her. "Oh Jesus, I'm really sorry. What did I do? Did I twist something that was sore?"

Cross placed her head on his chest.

"If you feel sick or something, I'll go get the nurse for you. Just tell me and I'll run down to the room where they talk. I know right where it—"

"No," she murmured. In his concern for her, he was lightly rubbing her back. The warmth of his affection made her cry harder. It had been so long since Michael had touched her like that. "It's not that, it's because I want . . . because you are so nice and it's just that I wish . . ."

Corky sat on the edge of the bed and let her sob into his chest. Her unhappiness moved him until he felt like weeping himself.

"Hey, Lucy, Lucy in the Sky with Diamonds, it's gonna be okay. I promise." The warm wet spot on his T-shirt where she was crying was like a part of her inside of him. The funny thing about it was that he felt as if he would give his life to protect her, and just a few days ago, he hadn't thought his life was worth anything more than a few pills.

"It's okay. I'm here now," he said, patting her back. "You're too beautiful for anything to hurt you. That's all over now."

Inside the boy's arms, Lucy the normal girl longed to fall back to sleep.

When she woke up, the last two years would all have been a dream.

9:17 p.m.

While she waited for the washing machine to finish its cycle, Cat bit into a piece of burnt-black toast spread with unsalted cottage cheese and smothered with pepper and salt substitute. Chewing thoughtfully, she gazed out her living room window and watched the wind prune the trees of whatever leaves they had left.

The winters in sunny California had turned record cold over the last few years, and cold weather depressed her. It was another someday promise that she would move to a tropic island, live in a screened-in hut, eat nothing but fruit, and go barefoot—Rita Hayworth in sarong and nurse's cap.

Saph rubbed against her leg, squeaking his desire to be held. Taking the nineteen-pound white Persian into her lap, she kissed his nose, then wiped her lips free of any lingering kitty scrunge with the back of her hand.

Cats were Cat's thing and had been ever since she could remember. In her baby book, on the page titled "First Words," was a brief notation in her father's messy scrawl: " 'Kitty,' age: 10 mos."

Until early pubescence, when she discovered the merits of sex, cats had been the only source of comfort she had. She'd depended on the household cat to protect her from the monster under the bed who would eat her up the minute she fell asleep. Friends and family dubbed her "Cat Crazy" at the age of two and rightly so. For her, being in possession of a cat was a habit every bit as necessary as breathing.

She'd made best friends out of every one she owned, telling them all her agonies and secrets. She'd cried on their necks, laughed up their noses, spoken to them in coo-coo baby talk, and carried them around in doll carriages, baby packs, and tucked into various parts of her clothing.

The thousands of hours she'd spent observing them, she felt, probably made her some kind of expert on the mysterious ways of the feline. She was convinced they were the most intelligent animals on earth. Though she didn't always follow their lead, she trusted her cats' instincts. All she ever had to do to know whether a friend was trustworthy or a potential lover sincere was watch her cat's response to them.

There had been people in her past, usually dog people, who were jealous of her way with felines. They were the ones who spread the malicious gossip that cats were her familiars and that she chased them around the house with cordless hand mixers to make them behave.

Allowing herself to make a cross-species analogy, she thought of Saph as an older, wiser brother, one who frequently regarded her with love, pity, and some embarrassment.

Saph squeaked again with urgency and ran to the bathroom door.

"Great Saphenous Vein needs to use the water closet, does he?" she asked in her cockney-waitress accent. She was pleased the cat no longer chose to use the bathroom rug as his personal irrigation system project.

Following the animal into the bathroom, she waited until his body was done rejecting its unused portion of Little Friskies Seafood Platter and then gave him the flush command: "Flush, Saph, flush"—her own rendition of "Run, Spot, Run."

Still perched on the seat rim, the cat pawed the specially rigged handle until he obtained the desired result. The sound of the rushing water signaled it was safe for him to either get down or have a drink.

Preferring his water out of a tall iced tea glass, The Great Saphenous Vein jumped down in a particularly spastic-overweight-cat manner, dumping her shower cap and loofah collection half in the sink and half in the toilet.

For a long time she stared at a grayish, tired-looking loofah floating in the toilet bowl. It looked exactly like she felt.

After taking a moment to clean himself, Saph nonchalantly sniffed the wall, then rested his nose against it. Staring wide-eyed, he froze in this position. Cat leaned over to make sure there wasn't some microscopic creature on the wall holding his interest, then smiled her approval. She knew better than to think the animal stupid. It was clear he was having an out-of-body experience.

But the experience was short-lived: he was sent scurrying under the window seat as three loud rumbles shook the house. Throwing off her robe, Cat grappled her way into a densely elastic jog bra, and wiggled into her neon-pink spandex aerobics workout suit. She pulled on a pair of pointy-toed black cowgirl boots, and ran, howling 'Hee haw," for the laundry room in the back of the house.

The innocuous-looking washing machine was picking up speed as it went full blast into the heavy-duty spin-dry cycle. There was no time to lose. Turning her back to the washer, she jumped up and back, landing bottom first on top of the machine, which was now rocking heavily from side to side.

Holding on to the loading lid handle, Cat fought to stay on the machine and rode it all the way to the end of the cycle. When she dismounted she was happy; she'd firmed her fanny, saved the washer's motor, and if she ever visited a Texas bar, she'd be able to hold her own on one of those mechanical bucking bulls.

As soon as her only set of towels came out of the dryer, Cat lighted her row of candles and showered. Romantic, relaxing, and not too harsh on the cellulite, showering by candlelight was the one luxury she had to look forward to each night, since coming home to an empty house and a "O" on the message machine was no longer a treat.

In the middle of drying herself, she stopped, an icy ripple hurtling itself down her throat. "Oh my God," she whispered, and slumped down on the bed to stare at the white pubic hair nestled in the mat of dark auburn.

It was the last insult. So much for growing old gracefully. Cat tweezed out the offending pubie, placed it in the small zip-lock bag containing her first gray scalp hair, and returned the bag to her jewelry chest, which also contained a laminated actual hair from the actual head of Paul McCartney.

Stretching out her muscles one last time, she oiled her body, did toenail maintenance, twisted her hair into a French braid, and slipped into a pair of men's flannel pajamas. With lids half closed, Cat was amazed that she had enough energy to crawl under the covers and switch off the light.

The second her head hit the pillow, her eyes snapped open and her body surged with the energy of a six-year-old on an Orange

Crush high. She knew she was exhausted, but the sleep god was going to be coy, punishing her for allowing him in for only a few hours the night before.

Convinced her pillow was saturated with speed dust or thyroid powder, Cat fixed on the idea that being warm would make her drowsy. She would exchange her flannel top for a thick angora turtleneck. As she pulled it on over her head, she panicked the same way she used to as a child when the neck of a tight sweater got stuck around her forehead and she couldn't see. She was always sure that the bad men who lived in the closet (close relatives of the monsters under the bed) waited for just those times to use their sharp torture weapons on her while slobbering their bloody drool. When she turned eighteen, the bad men who lived in the closet changed into mad rapist psychopath murderers who were Naval Academy runaways and members of the Norman Bates Kill Some Girls for Christ Club.

Cat threw on a pair of thermal socks for good measure and slithered back under the dust-blue comforter.

The sleep god wanted her to know unequivocally that he could giveth and he could taketh away. Tonight he was taking.

Listening now to the creaks and groans of the house settling, she was sure it contained something more than what was visible to the eye. There was the glass poltergeist, for instance—the one who had cracked all fifteen windows in the house and was currently working on her one set of dishes. Not that anything so stupid would bother her, although it was a poltergeist of the malicious variety. Cat recalled the night she told Nora about him. They'd laughed about it until the wineglasses they were holding sailed ten feet across the room and smashed into the ceramic pencil holder. After that, Cat never mentioned it again.

Giving up on the idea of sleep, she turned the light back on, rolled over onto her stomach, and sifted through the odd assortment of books piled on the floor next to the bed: *Gray's Anatomy, Ulysses, The Fundamentals of Judaism and Buddhism, So Long and Thanks for All the Fish, Rosie, I Ching, Alice in Wonderland, Dante's Inferno, The Tin Drum, Psychology and Alchemy, The History of Eroticism: Volume 3, The Revenge of the Lawn, The Skeleton Key to Finnegans Wake, Interview with the Vampire,* and *Hollywood Wives.*

At the bottom of the pile lay a thick, untitled clothbound book containing her own collection of random thoughts and phrases that took her fancy. She'd developed the habit of writing certain things down after Miss Geibel, her high school English teacher, told her

213

that one day she would be a great writer if she kept a daily log and stayed in an upright position when in the back seats of cars.

She smiled at Miss Geibel's misconception of her, the irony being that everyone, including the faculty, had voted her The Girl Most Likely To the first day of her freshman year, and four years later, out of a graduating class of a hundred and eighty girls, she was probably the only one who hadn't.

Even Bunny "Cyclops" Alvord had done it. ("You just aren't *juicy* enough, honey," Bunny had told her in the ladies' room one day while picking the perpetually present, perpetually red pimples on her forehead. "You have to be *juicy* for boys to like you.")

Opening to a page from 1968, Cat read:

> *Monday. She was one of those people you would not want to look at if you had just taken LSD.*
>
> *Friday. Oh my God. I am so embarrassed. I was so tired from studying all night for the cardiovascular section test that this morning when I walked into the Emergency Department, I was in a daze. I saw this old geezer on the gurney and he felt very cool, so I told him I would get him a warm blanket. I talked to him for a minute more, rubbing his hands and stuff, and Dr. Rothstein asked me—in a very uptight way—what I thought I was doing. I told him I wanted to get the guy warmed up because he was freezing and he didn't look so good, and Dr. Rothstein got that very snotty attitude that makes all the students want to rip his balls off, and he says . . ." When you get him warmed up and talking, let me know because he's been dead for almost an hour."*

Cat flipped through to 1980.

> *Friday. Imagine a man who calls his genitalia "Big Bob and the Twins" and you have pictured last night's blind date.*
>
> *Monday. Mrs. Petri died today anyway, so that's the end of that. I cried like crazy at lunch. Later, I stared into my other terminal patient's eyes and was taken with how handsome he is. I wish he could have been my lover instead of a 32-year-old dying man.*
>
> *—As normal as anything, Dr. Long looked right at Mathilde and said, "Honey, if you ain't a grinnin' while you're a pickin', you ain't playin' the banjo."*
>
> *Thursday. Coming back from lunch, I saw the drunken parents of the beautiful little boy who strangled himself with the curtain cord. They were being hidden away in the Meditation Room. I wanted to scream at them, although when I think of the children I have murdered inside my own body, am I really any better than they? The whole scene made me heavy in the head.*
>
> *Tuesday. Saw a man hiking alone on Mt. Tam last weekend wearing a T-shirt that read, "I am not the Trailside Killer." Sad.*
>
> *Friday. I miss the man's loving. He was like a Chinese puzzle.*

Cat went to 1986 and read:

Wednesday. When sex becomes as boring as sewing eyebrows on assembly-line puppets, it's time to quit.

—He looked like he'd been terribly scared by the hackings of life.

—I had the old Russian woman as a patient today (the one with the legs like a runner), who sang me the words to "Let Me Call You Sweetheart." When she was done, she pushed the hair out of my eyes and called me Veronica Lake.

—I asked Dr. Lavine if the patient's electrolytes were okay and he said, "Sure, his electrolytes are fine—but can you dance with them? That's the question."

Thursday. The one thing cockroaches love the best are human traits.

—There is no deep and lasting joy in this one-personed sex business, I'll tell you that for sure. Sometimes I miss having a lover. Without one, my bed doesn't feel friendly anymore and it was such a loving bed.

—I can relate; Lizzie Borden was just having a really bad spell of PMS.

—Nurses; always on the edge waiting for the next crisis.

Sunday. Termite wings litter my driveway one day a year.

—I should have quit after I learned how to write my name.

Cat made a new entry on the first unmarked page toward the back of the book.

Tuesday. This group is different. Yes, I know, they're always different, but this group is a special kind of different. It's nice to have the drudgery spiced with their originality.

Here we go again on the love-go-round (I think) after so long a time. (It has been four or so years since you-know-who.) Do I dare? Gage told me this man and I are meant to be. Shall I believe him?—I think I might.

He saw my feet and didn't say a word—not a smirk, just a tiny startle reflex. This is a good sign.

Switching off the light, Cat closed her eyes and slowly slid down under the covers. She knew the sleep god was reeallly pissed when, fifteen minutes later, she found herself humming old Seals and Crofts tunes and tapping her toes against the footboard.

The vision of the fat joint in her inside jacket pocket loomed up to invite her over to its side of reality. Wellll, she might maybe take one, small half-hit . . . nothing to even get glassy-eyed over. She imagined herself lighting up, lying back, and letting the drug do its magic-sleeping-pill number on her brain.

Then she imagined the six million cells gone . . . pfffft, the foggy partial memory losses, the paranoid panic attacks over the creaking door and he's-on-his-way-to-get-you fantasies, the puffy red eyes,

215

not to mention the eight-pound weight gain from her frenzied rape of the refrigerator.

No. She'd promised Gage. It wouldn't help, and besides, why would she want to have any more of those vivid Eisenhower-kissing-Khrushchev-during-the-Hula-Hoop-contest dreams?

Fine, fine—except she had to have something to keep her from using the heating pad.

During her one and only visit to a holistic clinic, Dr. Feelgood broke the news to her that her dependence on a heating pad for sleep induction for the last thirty-five years made her a heating pad junkie. Solemnly he warned her of the grave dangers of electromagnetic fields bombarding her back and delicate organs: of the thousands of heating-pad-dependent people in the world, every last one was going to wake up some morning with a Jell-O spine and failed kidneys.

She didn't doubt it for a minute. Going through heating pad withdrawal was harder than she'd bargained for. Sleepless, she'd taken to tossing and turning; and when she couldn't stand it, she cheated and lay on top of the electric blanket, hoping it wouldn't count.

Cat concentrated on the point of white light in the middle of her third eye and chanted until she found her mind sunning itself on a topless beach in Nice. She resumed chanting.

Three minutes and twelve seconds later her imagination took her to a sleazy hotel where she watched Dr. Gillespie and Dr. Sauerborn's wife commingle, their flaccid, psoriasis-riddled flesh smushing into a ball of two slightly different-colored Play-Dohs. It seemed a blasphemy against nature.

When she stepped from the chauffeur-driven Bentley parked under the Eiffel Tower and into the Arms of Inspector Padcula, wide awake, she gave up.

Surrendering to the I-can-get-by-on-three-hours energy rushing through her, for the next hour she talked out loud to David Padcula in the dark of her room, trying to impress the man on the ceiling with all the exceptional things she was and yet still be modest. His imagined answers and questions kept her chatting until she caught sight of Saph watching her intently with an expression of infinite compassion.

She made her apologies to Saph for disturbing his sleep, got up, and pulled the heating pad out from between the mattress and the box springs. She contemplated the three heat settings she'd renamed Lite Doze, Twilight Sleep, and Drool. Turning it to Drool, she placed it under her low back and lay down again.

216

Catalina Padcula. Yuck.

Was he really a suitable companion for her? Was he who she sensed he was? And if he was, was he the *right* one?

The damaging heat drug soaked through her dying nephrons and into her weakening spine. Relaxed, she twitched a few times, woke herself up out of the first layer of sleep, fell back down, and went into a dream about riding the back of an airborne dolphin through the deserted streets of Boston. On the sidewalk running alongside them was Tom Mix, keeping them both safe from the world's harm.

Wednesday

21 Around four a.m., the red mouth began saying some pretty odd things.

"If you're not in the know, you can't go." That was the first thing it said. Then it went on to singing old commercial jingles: "Use Ajax, the foaming cleanser ba ba ba ba boom," and "Use Sominex tonight, and sleep. Deep and restful sleep, sleep, sleep." And on and on until it began firing questions like, "What years did the Yankees win the Series?" and, "What makes you think *you* can get on this bus, bozo?"

At some point while it was still being nice, Walker asked it to tell him Blazzie's secret, but the mouth rubbed against his shoulder with its bottom lip and drooled on him.

Walker shut up after that because the bloody fangs had grown to an even more menacing size and their razor-sharp edges were closer to his face than was desirable for comfortable conversation.

The pain was driving him out of his mind all right. Aside from providing him with hallucinatory entertainment, the drugs didn't do much except make it a bit easier to breathe, by maybe a sixteenth to an eighth of an inch at most.

Just after his six a.m. dose of morphine, a waterfall came to life, cascading down from the corner of the ceiling over Detlef and spilling into a pool next to his bed. Walker was awestruck at the sight of Benny riding over the top in a rubber raft marked "Styx Whitewater Tours."

Benny smiled broadly and waved, his braces gleaming in the sun. "Hey Walker, whatcha' doing?"

Walker smiled briefly and without much enthusiasm. The red mouth had soured his mood.

"Come on, Petey, get with it." Benny rowed to Walker's bedside. "Say bud, do you remember one of your less fortunate customers by the name of Ed Bailey?"

"Ed Bailey?" Walker searched his memory to put a face with the name, but without knowing the man's drink and his hard luck story, he was at a loss. "Can't say I do."

In the manner of Ralph Edwards, Benny made a sweeping gesture toward the waterfall. "Ed! Ed Bailey, come on out here and say hello to Petey Walker."

From behind the waterfall appeared a pale, thin man wearing clothes that were wrinkled and much too loose. He held his hat in front of him, anxiously twisting it with sweaty hands. He nodded shyly at Walker and made his way toward the bed. With every step, the wrinkles in his clothes got worse.

Up close, the man seemed familiar, but Walker still wasn't sure which of the down-and-outers Ed Bailey was. He didn't have the hollowed, gaunt look of the late-night desperate group; this man wore the softer, defeated expression which belonged exclusively to the early evening depressed crowd.

"You remember Ed now, don't you, Walker?"

Walker squinted. "Can't say for sure, Benny."

"What say, Ed? Want to refresh Walker's memory?"

The down-and-outer pulled at his hat a final time and laid it to rest on Walker's feet. "I was the vodka with a dash of tabasco man."

At once, Walker remembered. He had indeed been one of his early evening depressed crowd, though depressed was an understatement in Mr. Bailey's case.

"One time, when I was thinking about doing myself in, you told me a story about a man who blew off half his head and lived the rest of his life in vegetable hell. That story put me off the idea for good.

"Another time when I was hitting bottom again, you gave me seventy bucks out of your own pocket and offered to let me sleep on your couch for a few days until I got myself together." He paused and winced as if an old pain had come over him then lowered his voice so that Walker had to struggle to hear what he was saying. "You told me to go back home and make it up with my wife and kids." Ed Bailey looked down at his hat. "After seeing what you had, I knew it was the best advice I could get.

222

"Heck, all us barflies knew you were good for a free one and an honest listen. The only ones you ever turned away was the ones that needed to be chucked out." The man smiled, showing bad teeth. "Some thought you were an easy touch, Mr. Walker, but every one of us gave you due respect."

"I appreciate your kind words, Mr. Bailey," Walker said, pursing his lips. He leaned toward the man. "Perhaps I could ask you a favor?"

"I'd be honored to help you out, Mr. Walker."

"I was wondering if perhaps you know who I am?" The question sounded ridiculous even as it left his lips. He pinched the sweat from his chin and stared closely into the man's eyes: eyes the color of weak tea.

Ed Bailey wiped his mouth. "Well, I'm no intellectual giant, Mr. Walker, but it seems to me and the boys that it's what's in your soul that makes you."

Minutes passed and Walker felt unable to move. His mouth went cotton ball dry and he blinked back the black spots dotting his vision. "Okay, so, who is my soul?"

The down-and-outer picked up his hat and ran a gnarled hand over the top of his head before putting it back on. "Well sir, your soul is like a block of whittling wood. You shape it and smooth it out into whatever you want it to be. At the end, it's what use you put the thing to."

Ed Bailey began fading rapidly from the feet up. "You don't want to be worrying those things to death, Mr. Walker. You've got to let them come to you natural."

With that, Ed Bailey was gone, hat and all.

When Walker turned back to Benny, he found himself in the raft on the widest river he had ever seen. Over Benny's shoulder he could see the mouth waving to him to come back. Walker gestured helplessly toward Benny.

Benny stopped rowing and half-closed his eyes in serious thought. "What are you afraid of, Petey?"

Walker let the sweat creep off him in rivulets without attempting to wipe it away. It was like the times he and Benny used to lie on the ant hills behind the old grocery store and see who could let the ants crawl on them the longest without scratching.

"I don't know," he answered. "I guess mostly of being lost forever without ever knowing who I was and what I meant."

Benny and the raft began to fade too, and he felt himself sliding into the river. The water was colder than he expected.

223

"No need to be afraid, Walker," Benny said, as his lips disappeared from view. "Swim straight ahead. Look for the simplest answers. They're like neon buoys. You can't miss em'."

Walker immediately sank like a stone to the muddy river bottom, folded like an accordion, then pushed himself up toward the light. At the top, he sucked in air and after a few shaky strokes, found himself sinking again. With his last bit of strength, he stretched his neck above the choppy surface of the water and whispered for help.

Wednesday was humpday, and two hours into her shift, Cat knew it was going to be one of those difficult, emotional days. Premenstrual. Not PMS militaristic cynical, but rather PMS soft and weepy. It was nine a.m. and she was fighting to keep from crying. She didn't know why; nurses were trained for all this.

She'd started with her morning care of Professor Dean, who was unable to talk to her at all, barely in before he went out again. Thank God Doll was there, valiantly cheerful, dodging the balloon strings, touching, massaging, coaxing him to take sips of water or juice every time he came out of wherever it was the dying went to get away from the laborious task of dying.

Then there were problems brewing with Detlef, who had stopped seizing sometime during the night and was no longer responsive, even to deep pain stimulation. Night shift reported his temperature was up to 103 and they'd put him on a cooling blanket.

Walker's pain was being held in check by the morphine, although when she peeked in on her way to Cross's room, his color was worse and he was sweating profusely. He had started talking to himself again.

Night shift said Corky had spent the night in Cross's room playing gin rummy, until they broke the game up at three-thirty a.m. It took most of her patience to get him up, showered, and fed in time for his therapy group. Moving the sleepy teenager along was like driving through molasses on the back of a slow turtle.

Stella had been on the commode four times, proving how effective her diuretic was. It was, in fact, where she'd left the old lady, hoping she could get Cross down to X ray and be back by the time Stella was finished.

The wheelchair sat waiting next to Cross's bed like a taxi with the meter running.

"No, I don't think I'm a better person than you," Cat said, as she held the weeping younger woman. "I'm merely telling you that emotionally I have been where you are once or twice in my life and it took me years to come out the other side. It's work. It's breaking an addiction that's worse than booze or drugs."

"I hurt," cried Cross. "You don't know how much I love him."

"Yes I do." Cat broke contact to hold the girl away from her. There was a point when too many tears muddied the mind instead of clearing it. "You're going to have to do the neurotic's waltz for a while—you know, two steps forward, four steps back. It's going to take time to disconnect your heart from him, but you have to do it if you want to get on with your life."

"But I don't want to disconnect. I want him." It disturbed Cross that her words, even as she said them, sounded awkward and hollow.

She slid off the bed, wobbled a little, and stared out the window at the massive rain clouds hovering over the city. The sun peeked out for one brief moment as if it were only kidding around. For scarcely a moment, everything spun away from her and her heart soared at the six or seven tones of gray and the one pale yellow spot of winter sun.

Not entirely trusting her legs, Cross took a few mincing steps and sat in the wheelchair.

Cat released the brake. "Let's start with basics. Basics are that deep down in your heart of hearts, you know for a fact Michael is bad for you."

"Didn't used to be," Cross said, flatly defiant. "In the beginning he was wonderful. You don't understand."

They were moving toward the door. "Oh, but I do, Cross. I told you, I've been on that roller-coaster ride more than once. I've had my heart ripped out too by someone I thought I loved more than my life. But that's the problem. For all the wrong reasons, sometimes we *do* love them more than ourselves.

"You let this man suck you in big time. After all, not only was he gorgeous and exciting, he was also the challenge of a lifetime. Then, because he doesn't know any other way to relate to women, he kept you on the edge, letting you think he might love you someday, but for various reasons, you were not quite perfect or remarkable enough for him right then.

"So, because you desperately needed him to love you, you abandoned your own spirit, trying to be that perfect person he said he wanted, when in fact, no one could ever be perfect enough for him."

Cat lightly tapped Cross's arm. "Don't you think you deserve to be loved just for who you are?"

Cross sat still without answering, the old sadness rising and falling within her. She tried to blot out the voices of Michael and her father telling her she didn't deserve anything at all.

At the door, a little girl stopped and faced them uncertainly. A tender part of Cross awakened and she smiled at the youngster.

Twisting a lock of hair around her finger, Zoe cocked her head to one side and addressed the woman she recognized as her father's daytime nurse. "I'm lost. Can you tell me how to get to my dad's room?"

Cat pointed down the hall. "Go past the elevators, then turn to the left and go through the double doors. He's four rooms down on the right side."

Zoe thanked Cat but did not make a move to leave. She seemed intent on staring at Cross with a mixture of pity and fascination.

Embarrassed by the child's scrutiny, Cross pulled her robe closer around herself. She wanted to say something to the little girl, something sweet, but the words died in her.

Zoe took a half step toward Cross and touched the arm of her wheelchair. "You're the lady we saw drawing." She spoke cheerfully, wanting to ease Cross's discomfort. "You're really very pretty, you know. When you get better, you'll be beautiful again, so don't worry. Your face looks exactly like Nancy Drew's and she has accidents a lot too, but she still stays beautiful." Having had her say, Zoe smiled broadly and walked on down the hall.

Cat laughed. "Well, Ms. Drew, are you ready for X ray?"

Cross did not answer but sat quietly with a faint, strained smile on her lips. She was envious of the child's innocence. She wanted to be like that again, to live a naive, uncomplicated life with the garden and Nathan and her painting. Like before. Wasn't that how Nathan categorized her life? Cross B.M. and Cross A.M.—before and after Michael.

When the elevator was between the second and third floors, the paging system activated with the sound of a throat clearing. Cat tensed.

Attention all personnel, code blue, Ward Two.

The adrenaline rush caused her heart to pound so hard it hurt her chest.

Who was it?

226

Walker? Oh God, and the little girl was on her way there.

No. He was a death-with-dignity patient.

Not Professor Dean—he was also a no-code.

Detlef!

"What's wrong?" Cross asked, sensing the change in atmosphere.

Impatiently Cat hit the Door Open button and wheeled Cross into the hallway two floors from their destination. "Gotta run back to the ward," she said hurriedly, pulling on the chair's brakes. "There's an emergency. I'll have someone else take you to X ray. You'll have to wait in the hall for a few minutes, okay?"

Without waiting for an answer, Cat fled up the stairs.

On the ward, the red-code light flashed over Detlef and Walker's room. The little girl was nowhere to be seen in the busy hall.

Why, she wondered bitterly, why couldn't somebody—just one little girl—be spared this bullshit?

"Daddy?"

Her father's slow, irregular breathing was labored and rasping. Once in a while there was no breathing at all, not for a long time.

Horror rippled through Zoe—something she had never experienced before in her life. With reluctance, she looked at the crowd of people around the other man's bed. The green oxygen mask usually covering his mouth had been kicked into the corner, looking abandoned. The way the nurses and doctors shouted over the man, let alone the violence of what they were doing to him, terrified her almost as much as the fact that her father would not wake up.

She held back until the lump in her throat hurt; then she began to cry. She was relieved that everybody was too busy to notice.

"Daddy?" she whispered. "Please, Daddy, please wake up. What's wrong with you?" Pressing her face to his shoulder, she noticed that his pajama top was wet and his hair was soaked, like in the summer when they hid behind the garage and sprayed him with the garden hose.

Someone shouted, "Clear!" and all the people jumped away from the other man's bed. At the dull thud, Zoe turned and through wet lashes saw the man's thin white body lift several inches off the mattress. His arm dangled off the side like a rag doll's. She thought it was the worst thing she had ever seen in her life.

Why hadn't she stopped with her mother at the gift shop? Why did things like this always have to happen when she wanted to show her dad what a grown-up she was?

"Clear!"

Waiting for the thud sound to be over, she squeezed her eyes shut until her head shook with the strain. "Please, Daddy," she pleaded. "Wake up. Don't be . . ."

She couldn't say it. He loved her more than anybody. He always told her that.

There was the click, and the sickening thud. In her mind's eye, Zoe imagined the man's white legs and arms coming off and falling to the floor, leaving big stumps all bloody with the blue veins hanging out.

Her father stirred and let out a thin cry for help. Funny gargling sounds came from his throat.

"Daddy?" She was desperate. Her whisper rose higher with her fear, attracting the attention of a couple of people working around the other man.

"Don't you do it, please, Dad."

She shook her father gently, not understanding why he did not wake up to reassure her. Taking a step back, she covered her ears with her hands as if she did not want to hear the sound of her own distress.

"Don't you do it, Daddy! I'M TELLING YOU, DADDY, DON'T YOU DARE DO IT!"

The Wednesday morning Mercy Hospital psychotherapy group was made up of three teenagers and one counselor. Tammy, the most outspoken of the troupe, curled her lanky body into a ball and squeezed as far into the corner of the couch as possible. Her pasty white face was offset by wide black lines surrounding her eyes and extending down from the corners of her lashes to her chin, where they ended in an unusual design of two fish kissing.

Curling the shoulder-length side of her hair around one of the spikes on her dog collar, Tammy continued her monologue.

"Wull, like you know, I *totally*, like you know, flipped out, you know? And, like I don't know *what* happened, but you know, like sometimes I just have to, you know, like *carve* on myself. You know?"

Tammy snapped her gum furiously, picking at the unraveled strings of her black fishnet jumpsuit.

Corky timidly raised his hand.

"Do you have a question you want to share with us, Calvin?" the counselor asked.

"They call me Corky," Corky said firmly. "What's carve on your-self mean?"

The counselor, a young man named Sandy, played with his mustache and nodded thoughtfully. "Fair question, Corky. Why don't you address that one to Tammy?"

Reluctantly, Corky repeated the question for Tammy, who was focusing her attention on twisting her ankle-length black wool cape into a large coil.

Tammy scratched the crew-cut side of her head and shrugged. "Wull, it's like, like you know, like carving on yourself. Like all the rad kids do it, you know, to see if you still, like bleed, so that, you know, you can tell that you're, like still alive." The girl pulled up a sleeve of her black leather overblouse and showed off the rows of scars. "I use a knife, you know, but, like some of my friends use razors and stuff 'cause they, like you know, get a nicer slicing action."

The cute chubby blonde, sitting opposite Corky, covered her eyes and gasped with a trace of pleasure, the way one might gasp on a roller coaster starting down a steep plunge.

"Mandy, why don't you tell us why you're here?" Sandy suggested. His thoughtful nodding continued without a pause.

Mandy giggled and hid her face with her baby fat hands. "I . . . well, I guess mainly I . . . " There was a short interval in which she rested from the strain of talking. Trying to think of something to say, Mandy flattened a gum wrapper on the arm of her chair, pressing it smooth with concentrated energy. "I guess my goal is to, ahhh, I guess mainly to figure out why I tried to kill myself."

Sandy's nodding became more pronounced, as if he expected this very answer. He was glad there were only three of them to deal with. Teenagers made him nervous. His own adolescence had been repressed—an unpleasant blur of oily hair, pimples, and masturbation. "And what have you come up with so far, Mandy?"

Mandy twittered some more, practically wriggled out of her chair, and peeked over at Tammy for help. Getting none, she shrugged and held up her hands as if completely baffled by the burdensome mysteries of her own life. "Well, I don't know. I keep thinking and thinking and thinking and I *still* don't get it."

"Don't worry about it, honey," Tammy said with an adolescent I-know-everything-in-the-world roll of the eyes. "I've been in this place for, like three weeks, you know, just like thinking about it, and like I don't have the foggiest, you know? You like totally never do either, so like, you know, just forget it."

229

Sandy turned his attention to Corky, who sat with his elbows on his knees, head bent low. "Would you like to share with us why you're here, Corky?"

"No sir," Corky mumbled slowly, feeling their curious stares shift, then bore into his head.

The silence weighed heavily upon them all until finally the counselor took in a long, disappointed breath. "Corky is here, Tammy and Mandy, because he tried to hurt himself. Dr. Barza and the other counselors working on his case feel Corky is very angry with someone, and turning the anger against himself was his way of handling it. Now, can either of you young women think of something to say to Corky that might perhaps help him get some of those angry feelings out?"

Tammy displayed her sharply pointed, black-polished nails by waving her hands around her head. "Okay, wull, like you seem, like super rad you know? And like I don't, you know, get it. I mean, like are your parents tweaked or what, man? Like do they just freak you right out of your mind or what? I mean, like *my* parents practically keep me in the closet, you know. I mean, like I could not *wait* to get outta there, you know? Like we are talkin' repression of this hot mama. Like Freedom train death, you know? I mean, like my parents are, like *to*tally from somewhere else, like you know, the living dead or something? They, like . . ."

Sandy cleared his throat. "We're trying to talk to Corky about *his* problems, Tammy. Let's focus on him for right now, okay? We can focus on you during Thursday's afternoon group, okay?"

The girl nodded, setting her miniature railroad spike earrings to swinging back and forth on her lobes. "Okay, so like, you know, how *did* you try to kill yourself, huh?"

Corky waited a few seconds, then solemnly lifted his head. "Pills," he said. "I took a bunch of different pills that were in the medicine cabinet."

"Oooooooh wow!" Mandy clapped in sheer delight. "That's exactly what I did too! What kind of pills did you take?"

Before he could answer, Tammy sniffed, regarding them with scornful disdain. "Disgustomatic, man. I mean, like that's just total cretinsville, you know? Don't you know, like pills, I mean, pills *never, never, never* work, man? Like totally till the end of time never. Puke. That's all they make you do, you know? Puke." Tammy came out of the couch corner like an unraveling ball of black yarn, suddenly happy to be alive and talking about her favorite subject.

"Like listen up, dude. Like if you *really* big-time want to do it up right, man, like you know, take your mom's butcher knife and slice

230

this . . ." Tammy contorted her neck, pointing to the jugular just next to where the railroad spike rested. ". . . right, like right here." She jabbed the correct spot several times.

The counselor was on the brink of breaking in, when Cat burst into the room out of breath and did it for him.

"Hi, ah, sorry to intrude, but I've got to take Mr. Benner to X ray now. They wanted him there ten minutes ago."

They took time walking to X ray even though it was time she could not afford. She had to get Detlef wrapped and to the morgue, and then there was Walker to medicate and the little girl to tend to.

Christ! Who was it said being a nurse was a piece of cake? Dr. Kildare?

"Man!" Corky said. He was running his fingers down his neck. "That was some bizarre and gnarly shit. Those people are totally insane. That girl? The one in the black with the hairdo?"

She nodded. Yes, she had noticed. No one could miss the girl in black with the hairdo.

"She *carves* on herself. I mean, she's sitting there showing us where to slit your throat if you really want to die?" The boy shook his head slowly. "Like disgustomatic, man. *Total* disgusto-puking-matic."

The large drain hole was placed directly in the middle of the tiled floor. Most people would consider that suspicious, Cat thought, especially with the water hoses coming from the ceiling and the cold-storage drawers built into the tiled walls.

Next to the door was a table cluttered with surgical instruments and a dozen metal basins. On one corner, lying on a grease-splattered Wendy's tissue wrapper, was a half-eaten hamburger and several stray onion rings which had lost sections of their breaded coats. A few feet away, an obese man wearing a clear plastic apron and green rubber boots snipped the heart out of the dead man's chest cavity and tossed it a few inches from the ceiling, then caught it in a stainless steel basin behind his back.

The organ hit the metal with a smart slap.

"Touchdown!" the man said, raising his eyebrows as if expecting laughter and applause. Getting neither, he lifted the heart out of the pan, and before she could stop him, drop-kicked it into the sink used for draining the blood siphoned from corpses.

"Stop it!" she yelled, and looked away stone-faced. Did he think

231

she could not be offended because she was just some jaded nurse who was supposed to have seen it all?

"I have a body here," she said as viciously as possible.

The fat man leered at her in an exaggerated once-over and whistled a low, seductive whistle. "Yessiree, sweetheart, I should say you do!"

As he laughed, Cat watched the rolls of his belly jiggle, her fingernails biting into the damp heat of her palms. Her control was slipping away. "Christ, what an insipid asshole!" she whispered violently under her breath.

The man glanced at her uncertainly, like an overfed lapdog who'd just done a clever trick but piddled at the same time. With some small satisfaction, she noted he'd begun to perspire.

"In the hallway." She pointed out the door. "Mr. Detlef Meltzer. They want an autopsy."

Growing immediately docile and obedient, the coroner's deputy lowered his head and stepped to the doorway. The man and the nurse fell silent as they stared at the draped gurney.

"It got a toe tag?" Indifferently he jerked his thumb toward the cart.

"Yes, this *man* has a toe tag," she said, and turned her back on him, hurrying to the peaceful quiet of the stairwell.

"And you'd better take care how you handle this man, mister," she called out abruptly over her shoulder in a steel-edged voice.

The deputy stared at her stupidly, weaving slightly in his spot halfway in, halfway out of the tiled room with the drain hole in the middle.

". . . and all the rest of my friends who come through here." She felt her eyes filling up, making it difficult to see.

"Do you understand?" she called back, hoping she'd reached something in him that was still salvageable. *"Do you understand?"*

The child was curled in Stella's lap.

"What is it, darling?"

Zoe shook her head without a murmur. Ever since the hard sobs had stopped, she had remained silent in her grief.

"It must be a very bad thing to have made you cry that hard."

A small hand wiggled along her stomach, disappeared to wipe away nose drips, then moved back to its roost. Stella searched her sweater pocket, pulled out a small square of lace-edged linen, and pushed it into the secret, warm center of the curled body.

The voice came from somewhere close. It sounded small and

232

frightened and miserable. "He's going to die." Zoe sat up to look at Stella with swollen eyes. "The other man in Daddy's room died, and they were doing all these things to him, making his arms and legs fall off, and I got scared because Daddy couldn't wake up. I tried to make him wake up to talk to me, but he wouldn't wake up, and he was all sweaty and he looked like somebody else. Even my mom couldn't wake him up."

The girl rocked in Stella's arms. "I'm scared," she said. "Why does this have to happen to him?"

Stella looked down at the little head, and her heart ached. "Some things just happen the way they happen and nothing we say, or do, or wish, can change it."

Zoe whimpered.

The master was making his presence known, the old woman thought. *Oh death, you hardest of teachers, can you not wait a little longer to dismiss this innocent pupil?* Stella picked up the girl's rocking rhythm.

"Once upon a time," she began slowly, carefully, "there was a wise old king who lived in the castle of the sun, and every day, as soon as the sun grew bright, the king and his many children would gather tiny pieces of sundrops and make stars to light the skies at night.

"One day, the king's youngest son, Starlion, came to his father and knelt before him. 'Father,' he said, 'it is time for me to seek my place in the world of men. May I have your permission to go?'

"The star king was very sad to see his son leave home, but blessed him all the same and gave him a magic rope, a magic dove, and a magic seed.

" 'I have no riches to give you,' said the old king, 'but take these gifts and perhaps they will be of use to you someday.' "

Zoe's breathing changed to an easy, regular pattern. She glanced up at the old woman as if checking to make sure she was really there.

"Starlion thanked his father, and the next day flew to earth on the tail of the fastest and brightest star his father had ever made in a thousand million years.

"Starlion landed in a village that was right in the middle of a big valley. Of course, being such a nice fellow, it didn't take him very long to make friends of the villagers, who were all good people.

"But Starlion soon discovered the villagers never had fun because they had to work so hard. So one day, Starlion decided he would climb the great mountains surrounding the valley in search of something to make the villagers' lives easier and happier.

"Taking the magic white dove, the magic rope, and the magic seed, he climbed the treacherous mountains for seven days, until he came upon a splendid smooth rock, sparkling in the sun. After he had rested for a time on its cool surface, Starlion asked the rock, 'Would you mind very much, o magnificent rock, if I were to take you back to the villagers, so they might rest upon you when they grow weary?'

"Well, the rock was very lonely (for only the mountain lion came to sit on it once every one hundred years to swish his tail at the moon), and it certainly had never been called magnificent before. So the rock decided the company and admiration of the world would not be a bad thing, and it agreed.

"But when Starlion tried to move the rock, he found it was much too heavy. Then, remembering the magic rope his father had given him, he took it from his belt and tied it around the rock. At one command, the rope pulled the rock from its resting place and sent it rolling down the mountainside and into the valley, where it came to rest next to the main road which wound through the middle of the village.

"After another seven days of searching, Starlion came upon a wonderful lake of crystal water. 'O beautiful lake, will you not come with me to the valley bed so that the people of the village might feed their land with you and refresh themselves in you and sail upon you to other lands?'

"The lake, tired of just the company of the fish and the wind, readily agreed.

"Starlion set free the magic dove, who flew to the center of the lake and flapped its strong wings very fast. Soon the water began to swirl and churn, until it flowed over the banks and down the mountainside into the valley.

"Throwing himself into the water, Starlion was carried along with the flow of the lake, which had turned into a lovely river.

"By the time he reached the village, Starlion was so tired from his long journey that he fell asleep, wet clothes and all.

"Soon, the magic seed in Starlion's pocket began to sprout. The roots grew and grew until the small sapling was much too big for the pocket and it fell out onto the ground.

"When Starlion woke up and saw the little sapling, he dug a hole and set it into the earth. Using pieces of the magic rope, the magic dove tied up the sapling's tender branches, and carried water from the river in its beak.

"Before Starlion's eyes, the sapling grew into a tall fruit tree, laden with sweet red apples, yellow bananas, green grapes, and any kind of fruit one could ever think of, from A to Z.

"When the villagers saw the tree of fruit from A to Z and the river and the rock, they were happy as could be. From that time on, their lives became easier.

"But one day soon after that, there came upon the land a terrible sickness, and Starlion was one of those who caught it and died.

"The villagers missed the young man very much, but whenever they gathered in the center of the village, they would see the colorful tree of fruit from A to Z and rest under its cooling shade and refresh themselves with its sweet fruit, and they would say, 'This is the tree which Starlion planted. What a good and kind man he was.' And the tree would stand as tall as it could, proud to have been planted by such a good and kind man.

"And when the people of the village walked along the long road to the neighboring villages, they would always stop to rest on the smooth, cool rock and admire its beauty. 'This is the rock which Starlion rolled down from the mountain,' they would say. 'What a strong man he was.' And the rock would sparkle, happy to have been set free by such a good and kind and strong man as Starlion.

"And when the people of the village came to the river to swim and fish, they would say, 'This is the river which came from the lake that Starlion set free. What a clever man he was.' And the river would ripple extra hard with joy knowing it had been brought to the people by such a good and kind and strong and clever man as Starlion.

"And after a few years, the tree of fruit from A to Z turned into an orchard which provided delicious fruit from A to Z for many villages, and the rock became a well-known landmark which kept travelers on the right path, and the river grew mighty and had many fish to feed the villagers and swift currents to carry boats all the way to the great oceans.

"For many generations, people remembered Starlion and what a good and kind and strong and clever man he was. To this day the villagers say that if you climb the tree of fruit from A to Z, or stand on the mountain rock on your tippy-toes, or drift in the right spot on the river, you can see Starlion in his father's great sun castle, making new stars to light the night sky.

"And the moral of this story is . . ." Stella paused. "Do you know what moral means?"

Zoe nodded sleepily. "Mrs. Valline told us. It means the lesson you learn from the story."

Stella smiled. "Yes," she said, "yes, very good. The moral of this story is that a man's life is not measured by its length, but rather by what he leaves behind."

235

Zoe was so still Stella wondered if the child might not have fallen asleep.

"My father?" Zoe said suddenly. "My father will always have me here."

"Yes, he will." Stella felt a deep satisfaction she had not felt for many years. "And he will have left behind a treasure of immeasurable value."

Walker was not fooled by the false-bottom gurney. After all, he had been an orderly once himself.

They had not even bothered to draw the curtains when they rolled the corpse off the bed and onto the cold steel tray. He wished he hadn't seen the way Detlef's head rolled from side to side, as if in protest.

The corpse had not looked like Detlef anymore without all the tubes coming out of every hole. All that life-support torture-chamber stuff was taken out of him as soon as the code stopped. Too bad they hadn't taken it all out while the old guy could still enjoy the relief.

One of Detlef's arms had caught at an unnatural angle behind him, and the orderlies lifted him roughly, shook him out like a sheet, and dropped him again.

Walker tried to turn away from the dead man's vacant cloudy eyes but found he could not. He could tell Detlef was still hanging on, looking for Jesus to escort him to the pearly gates.

As the gurney rolled past him, Walker thought he recognized someone else's face superimposed over Detlef's.

"Benny?" he whispered. "Benny Newmann, is that you?"

Detlef Meltzer–cum–Benny Newmann opened his eyes and waved. "Say, Petey Walker, how's by you?"

"Hey!" Walker called urgently. "Hey, wait!"

The dead men lifted their head. "Yeah?"

"So? So tell me—what's it like?"

"Well man," they said, "you just have to see it to believe it."

Somewhere, outside Walker's field of vision, the red Blazzie mouth laughed.

22 Cross thought the windowless and dingy X ray department resembled a well-equipped flophouse—either that or a cave. A technician stepped into the waiting area and studied the occupants without interest. On the outpatient bench, a man stopped reading *Sports Illustrated* and looked up to plead, by way of expression, to be taken next. At his feet, a boy who favored him closely played truck and auto smashup, oblivious to all but his self-generated engine noises.

Dismissing them completely, the technician walked with a noticeable limp around the corner, then came back a few seconds later pulling a gurney marked "Emergency Room." On it lay a deathly pale girl of ten or eleven.

Cross noted that no one accompanied the sleeping child—no distraught mother, no somber, silent father.

"This the overdose?" the tech shouted to the other end of the department. The answer came from behind the drab brown partition that separated them from the reception desk.

"Yeah. Check the name tag. Kelchesnie, Carol. Number 102671."

"Right. I'm gonna need help positioning her on the table. The parents here?"

The answer was flat and unaffected. "Can't find 'em. Looks like they didn't come in."

Cross looked at the waxen face and visualized the child alone, taking pills or some kind of poison off a shelf, hoping someone would pay attention.

The man across from her glanced over the top of his magazine and regarded the girl with an air of bored indifference, as if the child at his feet were somehow superior to this damaged one.

Through the side rails, Cross lightly brushed the girl's thin arm. It was covered with a filmy layer of old dirt.

"Ah, *excuse* me!" The technician fixed her with a hostile look. "Please keep your hands to yourself. This isn't a petting zoo."

Stinging with embarrassment, Cross pulled her hand away from the child and met the concerned gaze of the little boy, who watched her carefully, gauging how a grown-up handled scolding.

She hung her head, uncomfortable under the boy's scrutiny, and busied herself with making a crisp fold in the muslin sling around her cast. Several minutes later, her eye was drawn involuntarily to an approaching masculine figure. At the sight of the newly familiar face, she relaxed and smiled, surprised by the amount of delight she felt in seeing him.

"Hey! You got my six cents?" Corky sat down next to her. "I need it to pay the doctor's bill."

The boy had a spicy scent which stirred a clean, comfortable memory of drying herbs and flowers.

"What a pushy winner!" Cross teased. "Listen, I still say I'm the expert rummy player here."

"No way, man. You were making up rules left and right that I've never heard of before."

He was still elated over having made her laugh the night before. Twice he'd had to remind himself not to try and kiss her.

It wasn't until he returned to his room that he'd realized there had been whole blocks of time while they played cards that he felt normal; his internal unrest had retreated and lay dormant at the back of his mind like a rabid, but presently sleeping dog.

For the first time in months he'd slept two hours in a row, undisturbed by nightmares. He didn't want to think about what he'd do if his sleeping dog stirred again.

For the better part of the next hour, they waited together, he for his chest X ray, she for another film of her arm and shoulder. Unable to hold himself back, he expanded on the list of his positive attributes he'd begun telling her before the nurses forced him back to his cellblock.

He knew he'd told her he was a superior athlete, but did she know that he could bench-press 270 pounds? Did she know that he ran under a five-minute mile? Did she want to squeeze his pecs or punch him in the stomach? ("Go ahead. Harder. No, I mean be brutal!")

When he was on a roll, his comedic skills put Woody Allen to shame. Artistically, he had a sensitive eye, and musically, the piano teachers all said he had perfect pitch. As a scholar, well, he had *never* cracked a book in his whole twelve years of schooling. Brilliance came naturally.

Having convinced himself he was one hell of a highly evolved person ("See? Small earlobes"), he dared to break through boundaries. Gently he held her hand and added that he was a very honest and loving guy who could be trusted.

Somewhere between the story of his world-acclaimed perfect pitch and the one about doing an impromptu stand-up comedy routine in Golden Gate Park for five hundred people, he quietly admitted that the real reason he was in the hospital was because he'd tried to kill himself.

Touched by his confession and his naive embellishments, she wished she were seventeen again and starting over, or he were thirty-one and still unjaded. Between them she felt an alliance in which there was no room for lies or judgment.

She spoke hesitantly. "I hope you don't mind me monopolizing your time, it's just that I feel good around you. You take the pain away."

He soared. She was almost too excellent to be true. "Uh, like no problem. I'll kick back with you anytime you want."

Around them, the waiting room had grown increasingly noisy, and warm. Normally, it would have driven him crazy, but as long as she was there, he didn't mind at all.

Together, they were safe.

Doll heard the rolling cart and decided to look up as it passed. He knew, of course, what it was. He'd seen the rush of people and heard the commotion in the room down the hall; then twenty-five minutes later, he watched them walk out, very silent. A job not well done. Maybe next time.

Pressing the back of his lover's arm, he continued to massage the damp, loose skin.

Someday, he thought, this would be him, skin mottled with sores, shitting himself raw, then rolling down the hall on a steel table to the basement.

He pinched his lover's arm and the skin stayed peaked, like a little bit of molding clay. The dying man tried to turn his head but was too weak to finish the maneuver.

"What do you need, darling?" What gifts could he give to this love on his way to die?

"Uhn."

Doll searched for the need.

A wasted hand rose one, two inches and the finger bent, beckoning him.

"Yes, love, what? I'm right here, sweetheart."

"Hur . . . ry."

Out of habit, Doll grabbed for the green bedpan, then stopped, realizing that was not the need. The cassette tape was played out to the end. He reached into the clear plastic box, removed the tape, and exchanged it for the finished one.

"Last one, love," he said apologetically, not wanting to invite any more sorrow.

Cat's lower back burned from being on her feet so long without a break. Ignoring the stabbing ache, she singled out the narcotics cabinet key from the set of keys jingling in her pocket and fit it into the lock. Above her head, a bright red light flashed on and off repeatedly, signaling that the narcotics were being raided.

Among the various boxes and bottles piled together loosely on the three small shelves, Cat found the red and white box containing the morphine injecto-jet cartridge tubes. Removing one narrow glass cylinder, she wrote her name and the name of the drug and who would be receiving it in the register book.

Nora appeared and leaned back against the counter, arms folded across her chest. It was bad news: Nora didn't fold her arms across her chest unless it was news that was going to be upsetting.

"There are two acute admits; one from recovery room and one from emergency. Gilly wants you to take them both. She says you've got the lightest assignment."

Cat slumped and closed her eyes long enough to let the ball of anger explode and pass. Nora locked the cabinet and handed her back her keys.

"I know it's a major load. I'll help you as much as I can."

Cat was already figuring which of her patients could go without attention; certainly Stella was self-sufficient, except for getting her on and off the commode. Cross's dressing change could wait. There would be no noon assessment on either one, but who the hell read nurses' charting anyway? She'd ask Nora to make sure Corky got his first dose of antibiotics when he came back from X ray.

Walker was heavy, with all the medicating and the kids and the wife asking the walking-wounded type of questions. Professor Dean was heavy. She had a fleeting hope that he might go before the end

240

of her shift so her charting wouldn't take so long, felt ashamed, and retracted her wish. It wouldn't matter anyway, timewise; if it wasn't charting, it would be tending to Doll.

Detlef was done completely.

"Okay, so what's the damage?"

"Recovery room is sending up a fresh post-op patient of Dr. Gillespie's. A fifty-two-year-old male. Gunshot wound to the abdomen during a holdup. He's actually not *too* bad, except you've got to do Q fifteen-minute vitals for the first two hours and strain all his stool for bullets.

"The one in E.R. is Dr. Cramer's intentional Elavil overdose who needs monitoring and suicide precautions."

"How old?"

"Eleven."

Okay, she thought, calming herself, I've only got two hands and legs, and I can only do what I can do.

The prickles of sweat forming on her scalp told her she was going to do a lot more.

"Can't you pulleeeeeezzzz with sugar on top bring them back up to Ward Two for me? I am *swamped*."

The dull, impersonal voice whined back at her, "Sorry, but we're swamped too. You'll have to get them now because they're in the way down here. We have patients too, you know. We don't have the kind of staff you nurses have. We work just as hard as the nurses. Harder, in fact. You nurses think you're the prima donnas of the hospital, and you're not."

Both parties slammed the phone down simultaneously.

So much for remaining a calm and loving spiritual receiver, Cat thought, handing the syringe of morphine to Nora.

"Ten milligrams IV for Walker. I've got to retrieve Cross and Corky before they're trampled to death by the crowds purported to be besieging X ray."

Jogging through the west wing, Cat had just rounded the corner of the deserted procedures unit, when she saw Jo Atwood headed in her direction.

Jo motioned for her to wait up, advancing toward her. Cat had never seen anyone move so swiftly except in special effect. When she was less than fifty feet away, Cat ducked back around the corner and searched for a place to hide.

To her left, slumped against one wall, was Dr. Cramer. Startled,

241

he looked wildly around. "I want to talk to you about catechols!" he shouted.

Taking an immediate right, she ran down the empty hall until she spotted a cart full of soiled linen. On a Lucy Ricardo impulse, she stepped over the side, crouched down, covered herself with a sheet, and held her breath.

Seconds later, squeaky footsteps approached and stopped.

There was a sigh, and then the footsteps squeaked on.

Cat waited for the squeaks to fade out, and was about to disembark from the white plastic cart, when another set of squeaks, a bit slower than Jo Atwood's, came near and stopped.

There was whistling. Medical personnel didn't whistle—had to be housekeeping. Something heavy but soft landed on her back, and the cart began rolling.

Bumps. The elevator. Gravity said they were going down. Oh Jesus. To the laundry?

She pictured the giant washers with the enormous blades, the ones that did three hundred pounds of laundry at a time. She imagined them dumping out the carts one by one into the loading chutes, not really paying attention to what spilled out, not even if it was a hundred-and-forty-pound screaming redhead. With all the noises of the washers, no one would hear—not to mention that with all the bloody sheets and towels, no one would even blink if the water were to momentarily turn grossly sanguinous.

The elevator door opened. In the distance, she heard the hum of the washers. The cart rolled very fast—no, the cart *flew*—and the washers grew louder. The big blades were getting closer.

She was tempted to stick the corner of a towel into her mouth to muffle her screams, but she didn't know where it had been and she wasn't *that* liberated from bacteria dread.

The cart stopped so suddenly and with such force her neck crooked as the top of her head smushed into the side. The washers were very loud and the acidic antiseptic smell of the germicidal detergent blasted her nose.

The cart swung side to side, bumped into something solid, and tipped, causing her to slide to one end.

She had to do something.

What will it be, Richardson, the washer? You've ridden *on* them, never *in* them. Big difference. Or do you want to make a fool of yourself—again?

It was not a painless decision; the talk about her last escapade—getting locked inside the hospital kitchen refrigerator—had just died down.

242

"Wait!" she screamed, trying to stand under the weight of the load. "Wait! There's somebody in this cart."

The huge laundryman stepped back, struck speechless at the sight of a woman emerging from the bottom of the cart. After a few seconds, his mouth began to flap.

"Don't ask!" she said, shooting him a mean look. "And if you tell anybody, I'll have you castrated by that moron of a deputy coroner down the hall."

As she was climbing over the side, one foot precariously placed on the floor, the cart began to roll away, taking her other foot with it. The laundry person made no attempt to help her, which, of course, she knew he wouldn't since she had done such a good job of alienating him.

The big blades were snapping at her calves, impatient to make germfree mincement out of her, when a large, squarish hand grabbed for her.

"Need help getting out of some hot water, lady?"

She didn't need to look to know whose hand it was.

Of course.

David Padcula had come to save the day.

Cat blushed like mad, then shrugged. Yeah, so what? The Marx Brothers, Ernie Kovacs, Sid Caesar, Imogene Coca, Lucille Ball—they had been her mentors growing up; they were in her blood, like a close-knit insane family.

But he made no attempt to embarrass her. He did not laugh or make any references to the linen cart. All he did was ask her how she was doing and silently walk alongside her.

She was so relieved he didn't ask she decided to tell him.

"I was on my way to X ray to bring Cross and another patient back upstairs, but I saw this woman who . . . this woman who I wanted to avoid and I . . ." She hesitated.

What she really wanted to do was give him some kind of normal-sounding explanation as proof of her stability, but she could not think of one to cover rolling around in the bottom of laundry carts.

He laughed a wonderful, pleasant man's laugh, and she noticed that he was wearing a pale yellow pullover sweater and a tie of blue and gray. He looked soft and inviting.

"Look," he said, opening the door to the stairwell. "I really just came down to the cafeteria to get a cup of coffee. To be honest, I was a little surprised to look up and see you pop out of a laundry cart, but I'm sure there's a perfectly logical reason for you to be in there. However," he gently took her arm, "you are not getting away until you tell me about the duck. It kept me awake all damned night."

243

She restrained herself from looking him in the face; she didn't want to lose track of what she was supposed to be doing. "I can't right now—I'm really swamped."

At that moment, she hated her job more than usual. She wanted to be able to take a break like a normal person, to go with him for a cup of coffee without having other people's comfort and lives depending on her. There had to be something less stressful, where she didn't have to grow ulcers over who was going to die next and how she was going to deal with kids overdosing or soothe a tormented little girl watching her father's death struggle.

"Well, I don't need any long explanations, just something to tide me over until . . ." He slowed uncertainly. Her head was lowered, and he could see she was troubled. "Look at me."

She glanced up.

"How are you?" He asked the question in a way that eliminated the need for an answer.

"I know you," she said faintly. "Are you aware of that?"

"Yes, and I'm almost afraid because I think you really do."

She smiled widely, newly alive. If she had nothing more from him, this would be enough. "Now let's see. The duck. Well, that will take a little time, and I don't have any right now."

He was following her up the stairs at a brisk pace. "You're here to see Cross?" she asked.

"Yes." He was out of breath after only two flights. On the spot, he decided to start swimming again.

"Well, could you do me a huge favor?"

He nodded and smiled, trying to hide the gasps. Maybe he'd start running in the mornings again too. "For you, Red, anything."

Cat blushed. "I'll remember you said that. Cross and a boy named Corky are both in X ray waiting to be reclaimed by Ward Two. Would you get them and bring them up for me?"

"Sure. And the duck?"

"The duck will have to wait."

"The duck waits for no man."

"Will it wait for an eleven-year-old overdose?"

He adjusted his glasses and paused for a count of two. "For that, the duck waits."

Cat opened the door and pointed to her left. "X ray is down the hall three doors. Tell them you're picking up Miss Cross and Mr. Benner, and give the lovely woman behind the desk my very special regards."

She was on the third stair when he stopped her with his urgent, booming voice. "May I call you later? At home? To talk about the duck?"

And so it begins. "Sure. I live in Mill Valley, the home of the conscientiously aware and the terminally hip. I'm the only Richardson in the book who lives on Twill Lane. Beyond that, I'm the only person who lives on Twill Lane, period."

"Mill Valley, the home of the conscientiously aware," he repeated. "Twill Lane. The only one home. Got it."

As soon as the door closed, her body went numb starting just above the ankles. She covered eight flights, two stairs at a time, in thirty-nine seconds.

23

11:27 p.m.

After the ruckus died down, Stella lay on her side and stared at the puddle of water under the window. The colored fellow, determined as he was to climb out onto the ledge, hadn't had the common sense to close it after himself, and the rain streamed in until a nurse came to shut it and lead the man's dog away.

For the longest time, the poor animal sat as patient as could be waiting for its master to return. She didn't know what became of the Negro because he never did come back, but she hoped the puddle would dry before morning. It was a broken hip waiting to happen.

Nobody had common sense anymore. Hell, half of getting through life properly was having common sense and an iota of determination. It was a wonder that people without a thimbleful of either ever managed. Then again, there was such a thing as having too much of both. That had been one of her problems.

Driven by the storm's wind, sheets of rain beat forcefully against the windows, making a demanding, impatient clatter. *I know you're in there! Let me in!*

She thought again about the colored man and wondered where in blazes he'd been going in such a hurry. He looked too determined to be killing himself. And the way he was dressed, all in black? She sighed. He'd probably done something wrong and was trying to escape without being caught.

Oh, deception. Man could not live without his cupful of deceit. She hated being deceived almost more than anything, a throwback to the years when she was the favored subject for her brothers' practical jokes during their salt-in-the-sugar-bowl stage of development.

It had been that childhood sense of injury, mixed with her determination and common sense, which led her to stretch the limits of etiquette and finally shatter the maddening void that was her life in Paris.

Otis had become increasingly involved with and tight-lipped about his London business affairs, cutting her out of his life more and more, until she found herself seeking out the scandalmongers' prattle in order to keep informed of his doings. There were whispers about his involvements in shady deals with dangerous people and reckless entanglements with foreign governments.

None of which upset her. What troubled her were the murmurs about the man himself: that Otis Gallagher was somehow a peculiar and unsavory character. Where she had once been begged for stories about her husband, there was now an embarrassed silence when his name was mentioned. People regarded her differently, still friendly but less at ease. She often caught them staring at her as if she were some kind of curiosity.

His letters to her were always tender, devoted, and full of utterly plausible lies, but on the strained, rare occasions he was with her, he held himself back.

On the second day of June 1912, she awakened to the same life she had lived for two years. Time had passed and nothing had changed except she was one year sicker of it. Wearily she rose and went to the window.

Her attention was caught by the light from the magnificent Paris sky and the way it filled the cobblestone street below her. Across the boulevard, an old couple walked together, the sun riding the backs of their proper Sunday clothes. How many years together had they survived, she wondered, and had they made the connection between their spirits—man and woman?

Unfastening the buttons of her nightdress, she stared at the polished, pale skin of her body and ran her hands slowly, sadly, over herself. Outrage welled inside her at the neglect of the love she had to give. Nineteen years old. It was such a waste.

She clenched her fists to her temples as her anger broke and ran free, released.

In the lobby of the elaborate London hotel, she collected her thoughts by studying the ornate gold leafing on an ostentatious antique cabinet; it was solid, tangible. I am here, she thought, fingering the scroll work. I have dared to come for the truth.

She ascended the marble staircase with the firm and steady step of a determined woman. She did not expect the door to his suite to be unlocked, so when it swung noiselessly open, she did not enter right away but stood in the hall listening, suddenly regretting her presence there.

How could she? Had she no pride? She would throw herself at his feet and beg forgiveness for doubting him. Stepping into the foyer, she went directly to the drawing room. In the dim light she recognized his tweed overcoat, which had been thrown carelessly over a brocade divan. Parallel to this lay a long gray man's cloak made of the soft fine wool found only in the best bespoke shops of London.

Her stomach pulled tight. She had made a profound blunder. That was her thought the moment she heard his soft cries coming from behind the other door: whimpering and begging, then passionate, then frightened.

She shrank back from the sounds, suppressing a wild urge to cry out for him. She had accused him, but she hadn't really believed her own allegations. This was not happening, she thought. It was only one of her insufferable dreams. But she knew better. Unable to help herself, she listened to her beloved's fevered cries of passion.

Oh please, oh please, please. Yes. Yes, please.

Stella walked numbly toward the room.

She pressed her forehead into the heavy, cool panel of the door. "Otis?" she whispered, or maybe she didn't. It seemed unlikely she could have said anything.

Please. Please. Oh, please.

Pushing open the door, Stella stared into the candlelit chamber.

247

・ ・ ・

She never actually saw them. The layered shadows on the wall replicated the spectacle in a towering ghostly portrait.

As she recoiled, there was an instant memory of a sticky warm morning when, in the yard outside the chicken coop, she came upon two male dogs coupling. Curious, she watched for a while, then averted her eyes from the tangle of mangy, straining hips.

She asked about it when she returned with the eggs.

Embarrassed, her mother nervously evaded her questions, pretending to be too preoccupied with cooking breakfast to explain. But she stubbornly forced the question, further intrigued by her mother's tense reluctance.

"Sometimes . . ." her mother had replied at last, pouring out the hotcake batter. A splatter of grease bit her arm and she stopped to lick it off. "Sometimes animals turn strange on nature like that. Nothing to do about it but let them alone."

It was a subject never mentioned. Even the Parisian gossips blushed at the hushed references to the vulgar activities that sometimes went on around the *pissotières* after dark.

She felt her legs buckle and give way. As she lay immobile, her mind sought excuses to protect her from the reality in the next room. Of course it was a dream, she thought, a vile dream. She would close her eyes and imagine she was in Paris waiting for Otis to come home.

Except Otis was there, kneeling next to her in his nakedness. About him hung the faint scent of wax and sweet oil.

Stella, my darling, my love, he cried, over and over while his hands, those delicate creatures, caressed her face, her hair.

Stella, my darling, my love. It was his litany.

She was suddenly embarrassed for him. His smell, the shadows, the memory of the dogs, all made her want to cover him, to hide his shame.

There was a sudden warm rush of air, hurrying footsteps, a hushed, excited voice; then a door slammed shut and they were alone. She would have liked to die. She would have liked to disappear, but that part of her which turned on itself without reason made her look at him.

Otis crouched over her, still in a state of arousal despite his anguish. His was a face unknown to her—unveiled and flushed with the reflection of Eros' darker image.

Stella, my darling, my love.

Sweating above her in the faint afternoon light, he pulled at her

248

underthings with hands made clumsy from nerves. She surrounded his childlike hips with her thighs and tenderly took him in.

Stella, my darling, my love.

Please. Yes, please.

9:36 p.m.

Corky lay agonizing on his bed, jaws clenched tight, all thoughts obliterated except for those of his visitor. The way he'd just showed up. Fucking A, man. The way he didn't think anything of it, coming in like that to remind him, just when he was feeling nearly normal and safe. The way he just walked in and ruined everything. Son of a bitch. Should have killed him with my bare hands this time. Should have.

Now the perverted, "out there" feeling was back, crushing him down again until he could not see over the top of it. The burning in his temples and the sickness. And the hatred was worse than ever. The rabid dog was awake and howling.

Who was he trying to kid? It was never ever going to go away. He knew that for sure. People were going to be able to tell just by looking at him, like in that book they'd had to read in English about the woman who was forced to wear a letter *A* on her clothes just because she did it with some priest.

Getting off the bed, he picked up the new backpack the visitor brought as a present. The touch of it sent a squirmy, unclean feeling through him and he let it fall. The heavy canvas was contaminated.

"No hard feelings." Is that what the asshole said? Why hadn't he killed him? Bashed his fucking head in with the goddamned lamp?

He grabbed the backpack roughly and punched it, wrestling the frame until it bent in on itself; then he opened the window and hurled it over the iron railing.

Throwing his head back, he sobbed. Nothing was going to make him clean. Not Lucy, not his parents, not some goddamned puke-head shrink. He was through.

Why me? the wounded half of him cried out. *I didn't hurt anybody. I was okay before. Please make it go away. I don't want this.*

No use. It's over, said his gloomy, fatal side. *Everything has changed. You must get rid of it. You're destroyed, man. Totaled.*

But Dad said . . . Dad said everything passes. He always told me that nothing is forever.

Yeah, but Dad was talking about things like stealing a beer from the corner store, and getting kicked out of calculus for hitting the teacher in the back of

249

the head with spitballs. He doesn't even know about things like this. This is serious shit. There isn't any other answer. Gotta do it. Gotta get rid of it.

Corky held a pillow over his mouth to muffle the noise of his crying.

Dad? Please help me. Mom, Mom? God, I love you both so much. I wish I could be the way I used to. I wish I was the same as when we all went down to Disneyland . . . When was that? My sophomore year? Remember, Dad? Remember how we made Mom laugh so hard, she got Pepsi up her nose, and the man at the Matterhorn ride thought we were all stoned and I had to tell him you were my parents?

Mom? I wish you knew how much I loved you. You were the best mom out of everybody else's mom. I swear I was only joking about your clothes. You're cool. Don't worry.

Oh man, I'm gonna miss you guys. I'm gonna miss Coach Henny and Adam and everybody. I swear I will.

Barely able to see, Corky picked up the felt tip from the side table and scribbled on the back of his dinner menu.

TO LUCY CROSS:

Dear Lucy in the Sky with Diamonds,
*   You are beautiful. Don't let anybody hit you ever again, because you're too rad for that.*
*   I'm sorry, but I couldn't stay around. My life was turning into a pile of garbage and I couldn't get it straight.*
*   Hope you are happy someday because you deserve everything. I know you think I'm too young, but I really could have loved you. I think we would*

Corky ripped the paper to shreds and threw it into the waste-basket.

You've already gone through this, man, his depressed side reminded him. *Notes are bullshit. And besides, nobody will want to hear your noise after they find out.*

But I did love them, his wounded-boy side cried, allowing himself to break down again.

God, I love you all so much. I swear I do.

9:36 p.m.

Gage pulled the stiff hood of his ancient black rain slicker down over his watch cap and let Tom Mix lead him out into the storm. On the steps of the hospital entrance, the wind rushed into his face, pelting him with rain.

The ache between his eyes, which had been with him since that morning, suddenly grew worse until his hands shook so violently he dropped Tom Mix's harness. It was a clear warning that he should not leave.

"Go on back inside, Tom boy." Gage mumbled, searching for the harness. "We got business here yet this night."

As soon as he reentered the lobby, he felt the hospital settling deep into its more subtle second phase of metamorphosis. The obvious first-level change, the deceleration of noise and high-strung nerves easing down, began just after the business part of the hospital closed up and went home. The other transformation came sometime after the end of visiting hours and spread like an elusive ripple of tranquillity throughout the building.

On the evenings he kept the stand open, he found he could go into the spirit effortlessly, in sync with the relaxed pace of the people around him. During those times, he checked up on everybody: touching on the sick folks, listening to their thoughts, feeling where their pain lay and trying to ease it out.

That was how he'd found the artist who painted his world with her words. Her inner voice, muddied and fractured, had come through the sea of other voices in search of rescue from the constant pain.

The signal of distress came again. Like the artist's, it was muted, but in the foreground of his consciousness.

Letting himself into the Ward Two linen closet, he leaned against the wall and called up the spirit within him.

A secret, a lie, a wish to die . . . a wish to die.

Gage explored the shadowed corners of the spirit for the danger. Clear, then nebulous, the source of tension eluded him, choosing its own time to show its true nature. From the darkness came a stinging wind, and on it the muted cry came crystalline. He clapped his hands over his ears, deafened by the resounding cry of a boy.

Unaware of the stares from the people they passed, Gage, led by Tom Mix, ran through the halls and into the room the boy had recently occupied. He felt the boy's misery on the wind blowing through the open window. It had taken the form of a millstone that pulled the two of them down together.

He started for the empty window, then thought better of it. He couldn't walk into the center of the cyclone and expect to survive; he needed to approach the boy and the presence holding him cautiously, from a distance.

Gage stumbled to the window in the next room. He released the metal latch and crawled out over the bars and onto the wet ledge. Hugging the face of the building, he inched forward.

Eight feet away, Gage felt the boy's fear. In his mind he saw the young man, eyes closed, crouched on the ledge.

"Boy?" Gage's call, competing with the wail of the wind, was overtaken and erased. There was no time to lose; the boy was being consumed by the power of his depression.

Corky looked down into the street and readied for the jump. The millstone pulled him away from the wall. Below, the traffic light went from green to yellow to red. Trained response caused him to put on the brake and pause.

Gage shrieked over the wind. "Boy! Don't give in to it. On my soul, don't let the darkness take you."

Like a strong hand, a voice gripped Corky and his eyes snapped open. To his left an old black man, shabbily dressed, inched his way to him on the rainy ledge. He blinked the rain out of his eyes and squinted. He'd seen *The Brother from Another Planet* at the Roxie Cinema. Was he having a flashback? Was it normal to have hallucinations before dying?

"Is this real?" Corky asked.

Gage edged closer and reached out his hand in the direction of the boy's energy. "Boy! Get back inside away from the wind! Don't you blaspheme your life in this way! This ain't the way it supposed to be with you." His voice broke from the strain.

Corky searched for words. "I have to. You don't know anything, man. I can't live like this anymore. I have to do this."

With the boy's energy just under his fingertips, Gage saw the abominable images of his suffering. He pressed his face against the side of the building, and prayed: "Lord of Light hear me! I beg you to release the boy from this foul wickedness. Take this weight from his spirit."

With a powerful voice, the oppressive shadow howled back at him. It was not to be pushed away so easily. Corky again leaned out and crouched as if to jump.

"Boy! Listen to me. The wicked shall perish an' the good shall persevere. Don't you put shame on that. The Lord of Light don't want you to be doin' this."

The cold penetrated through the thin pajamas that clung to his body. "No!" he sobbed. "I can't live like this anymore. I have to."

"But it ain't your fault, boy. Your soul be beggin' to live. You ain't broke, only scraped up. You supposed to live. You gotta spite that shame inside of you—cut it away from you. That be the wickedness that be bringin' you harm."

The wind whipped at the black man, weakening his grip on the side of the building. With his last strength, Gage thrust himself against the viselike grip of the other power.

A huge force pushed Corky back against the wall. Finding a small protruding section of concrete, he grasped it firmly. He swung back in time to see the man lose his hold and stagger backward, into the sea of howling wind.

7:01 p.m.

It truly was, she thought, a dark and stormy night. The wind blew the garbage can cover all the way across the creek as if it were a very substantial Frisbee. Cat watched the flight of the metal disk without feeling anything one way or another about it, although she did murmur "Shit" when it hit the opposite bank, only because it was the type of situation that called for some kind of disparaging comment.

A few minutes later, it occurred to her to worry over the exposed garbage, specifically about the used tampons she was sure had by now been scattered all over the neighborhood. Everyone would know they belonged to her, and would discuss it for weeks to come over morning coffee. The corner store might even bar her from buying them. ("I'm sorry, Miss Richardson, but we'll have to ask you to put those back. It seems there's been a charge filed against you for tampon littering.")

She noticed that the corners of the windowsill were growing brown tufts of fine, hairlike stuff. She turned back to her book and mechanically read the same sentence for the fifth time: "It was as if another voice were speaking in her brain, taking over."

With the amount of time she'd put into it, she should have been into the next chapter, but she could not concentrate long enough to make the words mean anything. It was a clear-cut case of readus interruptus.

With a sigh, she threw the book onto the stack of ten other books and turned her attention to the rain sliding down the glass in smooth miniature waves. She summoned up the image of David Padcula. He hadn't called. Of course, she thought, he didn't say what time he would call, but how rude . . . How dare he wait this long to call— did he think she had nothing better to do than sit on top of the phone waiting for it to ring?

Obviously, he wasn't calling because she was waiting too hard. It made her feel like forty-two going on fifteen. Since junior high school, she'd probably spent weeks' worth of time waiting for some man to call. As far as she was concerned, any kind of waiting, but especially *that* kind of waiting, was an awful thing—worse than carcinogens to the body, like being plucked from the flow of life and put on ice for an indefinite length of time.

Jumping off the couch, she dressed in her warmest running clothes and briefly stretched in preparation for the five-mile run to the center of town and back.

Cat Richardson would not put her life on hold for any man; her life was bigger than David Padcula's measly phone call. And besides, she didn't want to be home when he didn't call.

She tripped out the door into Twill Lane, playing the David Padcula videotapes over in her mind. When she came to the gate at the end of the driveway, she made a sharp turn around the post on which her "No Jehovah's Witlesses" sign hung and returned to the house to change her phone message. "It's seven-ten. If you call," she recorded in a low, sensual, but respectable tone, "I'll be home in exactly forty minutes."

7:54 p.m.

He hadn't called by the time she returned. There hadn't even been a hang-up.

Twenty feet from the phone, Cat got nervous and slipped the remote handset into the pocket of her sweatshirt. She also tucked in a page of key words and witticisms she had jotted down, ones she was sure he would appreciate.

She would shower. That would bring on his call. It was a given that the minute her hair was full of shampoo with suds seeping into her ears and eyes, the phone would ring.

It didn't.

After her shower, she sat dejected in front of a large triple-power magnifying mirror examining her sixteen-inch-wide face. From enormous pores, she determinedly squeezed minute amounts of yellowish waxy-looking stuff, then plucked her nonexistent eyebrows and lamented the threatening crow's-feet.

There was nothing to do about the wrinkles; those she would live with, since she had ruled out the possibility of ever having a face-lift. She hated the way people looked afterward: stuck with wearing that constant, wide-eyed, tight-lipped expression of surprise, as if they'd just seen a famous person, or had recently been told there was a death in the family.

She glanced at her watch and sighed in disappointment. What was it Nora always said about a man who said he would call and never did? No calls—no balls.

8:32 p.m.

She was praying when the phone rang, which for Cat meant she was dancing wildly around the living room to whatever music happened to be cranking full blast from the radio. Turning down the theme song from *Flashdance*, she waited three more rings before she caught her breath and answered in her rehearsed Sunday conversation voice with the slight English lilt.

"Yes, hello?"

"Catalina Richardson?" The deep masculine tone of his voice immediately trimmed off her sharp edges.

"Yes?" she said coolly, as in "Do I know you?"

"This is David Padcula."

"Ahh, yes," she said, smiling, "the one with the rabid swivel chair."

He chuckled, a thin, distant chuckle. "I was going to call you earlier but I got caught up working on this Cross case and—"

"Oh, no problem. My evening is barely getting started. As a matter of fact, I just came in from doing my daily five." She wanted to impress him, let him know she was not the eat-bonbons-in-front-of-the-TV type of woman.

"Daily five . . .?"

"Miles. I run five miles every day, and I usually don't—"

"At night? You run after dark? Alone?"

She felt his smile fade. The swivel chair was also silent.

She hesitated. His disapproval got louder with every second that passed. "I carry a can of Mace . . . which, I might add, I know how to use. I take it you don't approve?" She felt her Irish hackles rising and the English accent returning. Goddamnit! Another arrogant, dominating male was going to try and tell her what she should and should not do.

"Well, let me say this . . . I'm willing to bet you're extremely capable of handling yourself in any situation, but if I told you I smoked a pack of cigarettes a day, and that I couldn't get cancer because I smoked only filtered cigarettes, what would you tell me?"

"I'd tell you that you had been misinformed and that I have seen a lot of people die of lung cancer who smoked filtered cigarettes."

"Okay, so when I tell you I've talked to a lot of rape victims who were carrying Mace which they knew how to use, you won't think I'm an arrogant, know-it-all male trying to lecture, will you?"

Cat let the slow warm feeling take over her throat. Okay, okay, so she liked him because he was fair. Big deal.

"Touché, Inspector Padcula, and hello to you," she said. Without

255

any reason other than being happy he'd called, she laughed from her insides out.

"Hi. You have a great laugh, Red." The infamous swivel chair squeaked in chorus. "You've got the wheezy, low-pitch kind of laugh as opposed to the high, nasal, gulping kind. I like that."

"Thanks. I hear your friend in the background. You must still be at the office?"

"Oh yeah. The office is my home."

Cat was too exact an observer to miss the tired, sheepish tone of his answer. Adding "workaholic" to her list of David Padcula descriptives, she immediately guessed it was at least half the reason why he was divorced. In her mind's eye, she saw a tall woman standing in a courtroom wearing the expression of a person weary of trying to change someone she knew now would never change.

"May I ask you a personal question?"

"Anytime, Red."

"Were you married to a tall, attractive brunette who wore her hair in a French twist and her eyes in oversized dark-rimmed glasses?"

"Ah, yes. Why? Have you met my—"

"And part of why you divorced was because she felt you didn't spend enough time at home?"

"Do you know Pamela?"

"Well, no. Like police, nurses have to be pretty observant. It's piecing things together like voice inflections, certain body language, stuff like that. It tells you a lot about people."

"Yeah," he said, "except I'll bet you had no idea what I was thinking the first time I met you in the hallway."

"Oh really? And what was that?" Cat held her breath, although somehow she knew he would not disappoint her.

"When you first turned around and looked at me, I thought, Well, David, here she is. What are you going to do about it? That's why I didn't talk much—I was bowled over by you. You've got a pretty powerful presence, Red."

"Is that why you didn't remember me when I called you at your office the very next day?"

He groaned and laughed at the same time. "Perfect example of my workaholic nature. One-track mind. I haven't gotten used to the idea of having someone as nice as you to think about. It's been a long time since I've *wanted* to take a break."

Unable to speak, Cat reclined on the window seat, then stood up and started pacing the length of the living room, all the while grinning. Not only fair but sweet.

"Yeah." His voice turned weary. "Pamela is an amazing woman but she didn't approve of my work, and to be perfectly honest, I don't blame her for divorcing me. It was hard on her.

"My job was the main source of contention between us. She resented the long hours. I wanted kids, but she didn't; she said my job was too risky and she didn't want to be left raising a family by herself. I couldn't blame her, but mostly she didn't respect my work and I couldn't live with that. As you can tell, my job means a lot to me."

"So, what made you want to be a cop?"

Cat heard him take a deep breath.

"When I was ten, my eight-year-old brother, Daniel, was on his way home from school one day, when a psychopath got to him and bashed his head in with a rock. The only witnesses were two of Daniel's friends who saw the guy run from under the bridge where he'd tried to hide the body.

"The kids couldn't give a good description and the guy was never traced. I spent the rest of my childhood reading everything ever written about crimes and the criminals who committed them. Eventually the police let me go through their files on Daniel's case and I did my own investigation and search. I didn't come up with much more than they had, but I knew from then on that law enforcement and investigations was all I ever wanted to do. I wouldn't want to do anything else, even now."

He paused, and the swivel chair wailed out a long, mournful creak, as if it were concurring with his story.

Cat mumbled an apology and fell silent, thinking how one man's life had been turned around and molded through a decades-old tragedy that took probably all of five minutes to happen.

"And that's not to say I don't love to play," he continued, "I mean, I'm not an anal retentive type of guy, but I really believe that what I do makes a difference in the balance of good and bad."

Fair, sweet, and decent. Where, the suspicious, nagging worm in her throat wanted to know, where was the major flaw? It had to be here somewhere.

"Say, do you like your mother?" She was so taken aback by her own question that they both asked "What?" at the same time.

The ugly-love books were having more of an effect on her than she thought. The last one she'd read suggested that one of the first things to find out about a prospective mate was how he felt about his parents . . . especially his mother. According to the author, he would be sure to view most women in the same way he did his mother.

257

"Sure. I love my mother. She's a doll. Both my parents are really nice people. They gave me all the basics: love, right and wrong, football, backyard barbecues, and the work ethic. Why do you ask?"

"Oh, just wondered if you held any grudges against your mom because of, you know . . ." She used a stage whisper. "The chair."

One more question, demanded the ugly-love therapist in her head.

"Do you have a hobby?"

A man's hobby, the books told her, reveals a great deal about his soul.

"Tell you what, Red. If I answer all your questions, will you promise to answer a list of my questions?"

What? He wanted to know about *her*? He didn't want to monopolize the entire conversation with stories about his wonderful self? Whoa! This was a switch.

"Not only will I answer every one of your questions, but I'll be so tactlessly honest, you may want to be careful to ask only those questions you really want the answers to."

"You're on. Okay, my hobby. I carve birds and small animals from wood . . ." There was a softening of his voice, a sensuality creeping in. "And sometimes, when I have the time and the muse is present, I bleed a little poetry onto paper. It's a kind of self-therapy."

Christ! Fair, sweet, decent, *and* sensitive? Cat suddenly felt like crying. Her suspicion worm retreated.

"Oh, by the way, I wanted to tell you that Michael Lake's car was found today at a truck stop outside of Santa Barbara."

"Hey, that's great," she said.

"Not so sure about that, Red. The waitress said he was there three days ago, left his car, and hitched a ride with a trucker going to San Francisco. The guy obviously knows we're looking for him, but he's leaving tracks a mile wide, so either he wants us to catch him or he's deliberately playing a cat-and-mouse game. I called the hospital and told them there's no need to panic, but that Ms. Cross shouldn't be transferred out of that private room and that it might be wise to be more aware of people milling around there. I'm trying to get through the political b.s. and red tape here to scare up a twenty-four-hour guard for her."

"Listen, Blackie, not to change the subject, but I just thought of something. Do you think you could get me a lead on finding a long-lost relative for one of my patients?"

"I can try. Who are we looking for?"

"A man in his late forties by the name of Otis Gallagher the third. His mother took him to Arkansas around 1943 or so, when he was three years old. The name of the county where the mother's family was situated is . . ."

She fumbled through the deep recesses of the suitcase that masqueraded as her purse, searching for the slip of paper Stella had given her. Frustrated by the jumble of contents, she dumped the mess out on the couch.

The yellow paper fluttered out at last, soaked with Aliage cologne. The leaking bottle would be somewhere at the bottom of one of the deep pockets.

". . . Nolan. Which is also the name of the family. The mother's name was Daisy Nolan Gallagher."

"Gallagher, huh? Otis Gallagher. You know, for some reason, that name rings a big bell. Hold on for a second."

In the background, the swivel chair went crazy as he strained to lift a twenty-pound, 2,047-page book off a shelf behind him. "I've got a reference book right here of criminal history."

"Wait, you don't have to do that," she said, alarmed the swivel chair might act up the moment he moved. "See, this guy isn't a criminal, he's somebody's grandson."

There was the sound of pages being turned. "Yeah, except I know that name. As a matter of fact, I think I might have even done a paper in college on . . ."

He snapped his fingers. "Ah! Okay, Red, I found it. Oakland, October seventh, 1943—two men, a father and son, Otis Gallagher senior and junior, were gunned down and mutilated by mobsters.

"Apparently, old man Gallagher was in the import-export business, and around 1936 he got involved with a couple of underworld bosses. By 1943 things got too hot for him and he snitched to the feds about importing narcotics for the underworld in exchange for immunity.

"The son wasn't in on any of the old man's underworld dealings, but he was unfortunate enough to be in the car when they got his father."

Cat was stunned. "She told me . . . Well, of course she'd feel like she had to lie about something like *that*. I mean, who wouldn't."

"Who lied?"

"Stella Gallagher, the wife of Otis senior."

"She's the one who found them," he said. "Says here, they were on their way to downtown Oakland, driving through an apple orchard about a mile from the house, when they were hit. The wife got suspicious when they didn't return after a couple of hours and went looking for them."

259

Cat heard a book, a big book, slap closed.

"The whole thing was front-page news back then."

"Do you think you could get a lead on the grandson?"

"I'll try, but only on one condition."

"Mmmmm?"

"First, you have to answer all *my* questions."

"Yeah?"

"Then you have to tell me everything you know about the duck."

10:15 p.m.

In the dream, Cat caught herself midfall and jerked herself awake. A tight, cold feeling ran through her, making her acutely aware of the vague uneasiness that had crept into her gut sometime during the evening.

Shaking off the sensation, she grabbed the tail of her fleeing drowsiness and went back into another dream, where Gage was lying death-still on an old army cot shoved into the corner of the morgue.

As she approached him, his body changed, folding and twisting until the metamorphosis was complete and he had turned into an egg from which a baby chick emerged still damp. Picking up the chirping creature for closer inspection, she was not at all surprised to see it had Corky's face.

It stopped peeping and began to whisper. "A secret, a lie, a wish to die . . . a wish to die."

10:25 p.m.

The phone rang, which pleased the insomnia god to no end, for Cat had defied him this night by falling asleep.

"Hello," she growled in her deep, mucus-coated sleep voice. "All I can say is this had better be either God or very, very good."

There was no reply.

When the phone rang a second time, she realized she had not picked up the receiver.

"Hello?" she said again, amused by her own voice; for some reason, she sounded like a truck driver from the Deep South.

"I'm sorry, I have the wrong number," Nora said, and hung up.

Cat giggled, took a sip of the soda water from the glass next to her bed, and cleared her throat waiting for the phone to ring again.

"Thunder Thighs Café, you eat, you pay," she answered.

Nora laughed. "How'd you know it was me?"

" 'Cause you just called and told me you had the wrong number."

"That was *you?* Jesus, I thought I dialed Billy Carter's private line by mistake. You asleep?"

"Yeah, and having the weirdest dreams."

"Oh, sorry, but I thought you'd want to know what drama just took place at old Mercy Hospital."

Wide awake, Cat sat up involuntarily and snapped the clear plastic tooth guard from her bottom teeth.

"What?"

"I called around ten to find out if they needed me to come in at three a.m. and Gilly told me that Corky Benner had tried to kill himself tonight by jumping off the ledge outside his window."

Cat could barely speak through her panic. "Is he . . .?"

"He's okay. Shook up but alive."

Cat's adrenal medulla began secreting epinephrine by the quartful. It was fight-or-flight time. Springing out of bed, she grabbed the pair of jeans hanging on the light switch and wiggled into them, cradling the phone against her shoulder.

"I gotta go, Nora. Bye."

"No, wait! There's more. Blind old man Gage is somehow the only one who figures out what's going on, so he runs up to Ward Two, climbs onto the ledge, and talks the kid out of going through with it."

Even though her breath was visible in the ice-cold bedroom, she was sweating as she pulled on an oversized green angora sweater.

"Gotta go, Nora. I mean it, I want to—"

"Wait! I'm not done yet—you have to hear the five-star ending. Gage loses his balance and falls off the ledge, but the kid sees it coming and grabs the back of his raincoat. I mean, are we talking escape by the skin of our London Fogs, or what?" At the sound of Cat's zipper, Nora hesitated.

"Why, Catalina Richardson! You sly trollop, have you got somebody there with you? Is that why you're trying to get me off the phone?"

"God, does your mind live in the gutter? Listen, I'm going now, Nora . . ."

"So anyway, everybody is okay and the kid is back on phase one suicide precautions and Gage was treated in emergency for scrapes and bruises. I think—"

"Is he still there?" Cat interrupted.

"Who?"

"Gage—in emergency."

"I suppose so; you know how long that can take. The last time I had to go to emergency for a tetanus shot, I waited three hours for one stupid—"

"That's it. Your time is up, Nora. Thanks for calling, but I really have to go now."

"Wait! What *are* you doing?"

"Remember Miss Elwanda's typing class? Well, now is the time for all good men to come to the aid of their party—I'm going to the hospital to check on Gage and the Death Wish Kid."

"Oh, for Chrissake, Cat!" Nora snorted. "Are you crazy?"

Precisely. Concentrating on breathing slowly, Cat winked at the insomnia god looming over her pillow and wondered why it had taken Nora so long to figure that one out.

11:05 p.m.

His arms folded tightly against his chest, Corky stared blankly at the ceiling, lost in his own world. She was beginning to doubt whether he'd even recognized her.

"Corky, you don't have to talk at all; as a matter of fact, don't say a word, but pull yourself together long enough to listen to what I have to say."

Cat made note of the boy's puffy eyes and pushed back the still-damp hair from his forehead. There wasn't a pill in the world for his kind of depression.

"Look, I don't know why you did this tonight. I'm no psychiatrist, but I do know you need to tell somebody what's going on. You're a wonderful guy. It shines from you when you talk sometimes and you don't think anybody's noticing. You're one of the special people in the world, and I don't want those who love you robbed of your specialness."

Corky stirred uneasily, tears rolling down his face. She felt her own eyes well up, and had to swallow the lump in her throat five or six times before she could speak again.

"Please, Corky, believe me—no matter how bad it is, it can be fixed. Nothing is so bad it can't be mended, I promise you. Okay?"

She stood, picked up his limp hand, and squeezed. "I want you to tell somebody—and I don't care who—about what's eating you, because if you don't . . ."

How did one threaten someone who has just tried to kill himself?

". . . because if you don't, it will end up taking you from us, and I don't want the bad guys to win."

262

11:41 p.m.

Gage allowed the woman to drive him home and grudgingly gave in when she insisted on fixing him something to eat. She did not ask what he wanted, but simply made do with what he had, serving him a meal of corn bread, sweet potato, buttermilk, and steamed spinach.

He appreciated the way she let him eat in peace, not talking his ear off, or overstuffing him the way most women were in the habit of doing. If he was still, he could almost imagine it was Delia there bustling quietly around him. Like Delia, this woman possessed a self-assuredness and an innate female sense of knowing what was right that, when mixed with the sight, became a very powerful combination.

They didn't talk much. They didn't need to. Between them was a new respect and understanding that would not be easily shaken.

Thursday

24 An age-spotted hand landed on the door handle at the same time Cat reached for the crescent of brass. With amazing strength and ease, the woman pulled the door open, smiling a knowing old lady smile.

She nodded at Cat. "You go on, young lady . . . go ahead."

Cat hesitated. She was uncomfortable about forsaking her ingrained New England manners by going before an elderly person, yet at the same time, she was aware her hesitation was keeping the woman standing in the damp cold holding the heavy glass door.

Patiently the old woman urged her through again. "Go on, go on. I've got more time than you do, dearie."

Cat hurriedly entered, leaning close to the woman so she would brush against the camel hair coat that smelled of old people—Effer-dent, Ben-Gay, and shoe polish. "Why do you say that—do I look as if I'm late?"

Inside the warmth of the lobby, the woman stopped to catch her breath, wearing the expression of someone who'd remembered an old joke. "Oh no, it's simply that old ladies always have plenty of time. That's why we go so slow; we've already moved our mountains."

The steel-blue color of the woman's thinning locks prompted a recollection of a childhood neighbor named Tante Elsa, who, each Friday night, gave Cat a dime and a slice of homemade kuchen to wash, tint, and pin up her silvery-blue hair.

On Saturday mornings, the ten-year-old beautician dutifully returned to remove the pins and artfully brush out soft blue creations. One such morning when her curiosity outweighed her breeding, she'd asked, "Tante Elsa, why do old ladies always make their hair blue?"

Alarmed, the German woman had hurried to the mirror and searched frantically through the silvery-blue trees for the offending blue forest. "Blue? Ach! Vat blue you see here on dis head? Vere is dis blue hair you speak of, huh?"

Cat blushed and excused herself by saying the light reflecting off the blue walls had confused her.

"Ja, ja." Tante Elsa had patted at the blue curls, reassuring herself. "It is a vunderful vite, like der snow on der roof."

Cat was tempted to call out after the old woman, "Excuse me, will *you* tell me why the blue hair?" But the old lady was one of those fast, steady walkers and had already made it to the other end of the south wing corridor.

Across the lobby, Gage's stand was open but deserted. She wondered if the rest of his night had been as disturbing as hers: spent tossing and turning through bad—no, dreadful—dreams, then waking on the other side of black.

She'd started out with a joke dream about Saph wearing a fake rubber nose and being written up in *Cat Fancy Magazine* as the amazing Cyrano de Bergerac of the cat world.

Then she had the recurring one about narrowly escaping the clutches of a group of termite control inspectors carrying daggers and guns, complete with the drawn-out, complicated chase scenes.

But the last dream—that was the beaut.

She was driving into someone's muddy driveway, when she noticed a puddle of water next to which was placed a flashing yellow caution light. Proceeding slowly through the middle of it, she immediately found herself firmly stuck. Before she was aware of what was happening, the Volkswagen tilted and rapidly slid, back end first, into the soft muck. Mud streamed through the partially opened windows, preventing them from being rolled up or down, and opening the door was out of the question.

In a silent hysteria of total helplessness, she thought briefly of Mary Jo Kopechne, cursed Ted Kennedy, and lay back to die. As the mud filled her nose and mouth, she was absolutely indignant over having to die in the prime of her life, and in such a ridiculous way.

The dream ended with a short obituary: *Catalina Richardson, Registered Nurse at Mercy Hospital for 21 years, died early Thursday morning after a brief encounter with some mud.*

She'd awakened with a total body jerk, breathing in the fur from Saph's huge belly, which was pressed firmly over her nose and mouth.

As she entered Ward Two, she saw Gage waiting for the elevator. In recognition, Tom Mix barked in her direction, causing Gage to brace his body in a defensive stance and spin around.

"Gage?" She touched his arm gently.

Letting his shoulders slump in relief, Gage led her quickly toward the linen closet. "I come up this mornin' to see how the boy be doin' and maybe talk with him, but he be in a psychological conference or some such thing."

The man removed a key from his pocket and, with swift precision, unlocked the door and pulled her inside. In the dark, he searched under his watch cap, withdrew a handkerchief, and wiped the sweat from his face.

"Okay, Ms. Cat, the time be here. That danger I told you about be standin' right behind you waitin' for you to slip up."

Automatically Cat glanced over her shoulder and encountered an innocent-looking linen rack.

"Dark force started up closin' in on me about five this mornin'. Can't you feel it, girl?"

"Well . . ." She nodded in agreement. "I admit I haven't been feeling right since last night, and this morning I had a really bad dream about suffocating under a ton of mud."

Gage sat on his haunches and drew her down next to him. "That'd be about right—the mud, I mean, closin' off your breath. The evil be thick, like mud. I tell you, a cold wind be blowin' through this place today." He shivered and laid his hand on her arm.

"You gotta take care, Ms. Cat, this be only the beginnin'. Be lookin' on the other side of closed doors, ready for anythin', you hear?"

Cat nodded. "I hear."

"Okay." Gage stood and opened the door. "You got the power, Ms. Cat. You equal to anythin' the dark side can throw at you. Like I told you, if you believe, it *will* be."

As soon as she walked into step-down, she knew Professor Dean was in his final process. The staff, to show their respect for the dying, were making an extra effort to create silence. Why people universally believed that the dying needed silence in which to die, she never understood. When she went, she wanted something loud. Music. Cannons. Obnoxious crickets.

In report Laurel said he'd become completely confused, then

269

stopped responding altogether, but kept his eyes open, hugging any balloon that fell into his reach. His fever reached a record high and he'd stooled all night. A few minutes after seven, Trish had called Doll to come in.

As she entered his room, her stomach did a soft somersault in protest; she did not want to watch him slip away. She took a sharp breath, then laughed. The balloons, now slightly shrunken, rested on the bed like a bright patchwork quilt covering a mound.

She paused by the sink and slipped her hands into a pair of exam gloves. "Hey bub, can you breathe under all that rubber?"

There was no answer.

Halfway across the room, Cat perceived she was alone, the absence of him having left a hole in the atmosphere a mile wide. For a moment, her heart ached and her breath caught in her throat. Brushing back the balloons, she searched his eyes, cloaked by an opaque film.

"Where have you gone, Prof?" she whispered. Taking his hand, she sat down on the bed, feeling the hollow despair of one accustomed to seeing death each day, but never getting used to the initial ache.

It didn't matter that she'd learned the basics of death long ago, heard all the my-life-passed-before-me and I-saw-a-white-light-at-the-end-of-a-tunnel stories, felt the absence, and sensed the hovering presence. She was still mystified by it, still strove to find an explanation to ease the despair. At times, she experienced a longing to escort the dying into death, or at least to the entranceway, in hopes of a glimpse of the hidden inner room where the final release of the soul takes place.

She wondered how he had been in the last seconds. Had he struggled to slow the process, resisted turning over his fate until the last breath? Had he struck out at the heavenly escorts presumably floating above his head? She cocked her head and stared at him. No. Not him.

She knew the difference. Often she prepared a body for the morgue in an atmosphere so fraught with unresolved conflicts or revenge she could have cut it with a spatula. He had gone in peace.

Blowing the musty odor of the deceased from her nostrils, she pushed the lids down over his eyes, taped them closed, and bathed him, gently soaping and patting dry the limp, cool body. She felt sorry for all the things he would not do, for those who had loved him, and those who would never know him at all.

She was wish-thinking of how he might have been saved, when someone entered the room and slipped an arm uncertainly around her shoulders. Nora or Doll she guessed, allowing herself to take a

270

few seconds of comfort from the contact before she opened her eyes and, in mild disbelief, pulled away to stare at the person consoling her. Overprotected by what hospital personnel referred to as a "paranoia wrap"—a double layer of isolation gowns, gloves, hair caps, and shoe covers—Alan leaned close. From behind antisplatter glasses, his eyes conveyed empathy.

"I'll do morning vitals on the rest of your patients so you can finish with him," Alan said through his triple-layer mask. "Do you have any eight o'clock meds to give?"

Her first impulse was to tell him not to bother, but she reconsidered. No matter what she thought of him as a person, he was still an insider, and who else was better qualified than an insider to understand exactly how another nurse felt when a patient died?

She handed over her report sheet with medications due for each of her patients noted in red. "Thank you. I appreciate this."

"Do you need help with him?" Alan nodded toward the dead man.

"No. Actually, he's my most stable patient right now."

Alan did not smile but scanned the report sheet in a starchy, businesslike manner and left the room.

By the time Doll arrived, she was tying the identification tag onto the corpse's left great toe.

"Were you with him when he went?" He was hopeful, pleading.

"Yes," she lied. Deathbed lies were the lies a caregiver learned early on to tell the ones left behind. "Did he suffer much?" "Did she ask for me?" "Was he peaceful at the end?"—they were all classified as questions that could be answered with justifiable lies. After all, said the unwritten rules, why should the survivors be made to spend the rest of their lives needlessly tormented by guilt?

Doll's handsome boy-face sagged. Supporting him by the waist, she eased him into the chair. "I'm sorry, Doll. Is there anything I can do?"

He took his lover's hands in his, chafing them as if to bring them back to life. "Tell me what I do now," he murmured. "Tell me what I'm going to do without him."

Having no answer, she slipped her hand into his while he cried into her shoulder.

Hand in hand in hand, they waited for his tears to stop.

"I don't know exactly how I knew it back then," Stella said, allowing Cat to help her to the commode, "but ever since I was a little girl, I knew it was the simple things that made life worth the struggle."

The old woman coughed into her handkerchief, then examined

what she spit out. "When I was, oh, I don't know, maybe five or so, before Papa made all his money from the mill, we didn't have much —no electricity, only an outhouse and the old wood stove in the kitchen. My mama really cooked and baked on that iron monstrosity. When I remember her, I remember her in two ways: stoking the stove and kneeling in front of it after a Saturday night wash, drying and brushing out that long gold hair of hers."

A girlish quality came to Stella's face. "You know, when you grew up with so little, the children made do, making up the most wonderful toys out of nothing—well, I should say what you people nowadays might call nothing. A blade of grass became a whistle to hail fairies and ghosts; a tree branch turned into a mighty sword to fight dragons, or a diviner's rod for finding underground waterfalls; and the wildflowers made the most beautiful bridal bouquets, perfect for an all-day dream wedding with mud cakes and river water tea."

Stella was silent for a while, her head shaking slightly, like a dandelion moved by a light breeze. Cat imagined the almond-eyed girl dressed in faded gingham, watching out for fairies and blowing on a blade of grass held expertly between two thumbs.

"Sometimes at Christmas, when Pa could afford it, each one of us would find an orange in our stocking. Winter oranges were a rare and wondrous gift in those days. Rare as hens' teeth.

"To us kids, that orange was like gold. I cherished it so much that my sisters would laugh at me, because I'd keep it for a week before I could bring myself to eat the darned thing.

"One year, I even covered it with lacquer thinking I could preserve it forever, but the fruit rotted beneath.

"I used to put it next to my pillow so I could take the smell with me into sleep. I used to dream about orange groves, with huge orange jewels set in green velvet leaves.

"By the time Mama could persuade me to have done with the thing, I knew every pore of that orange. And you'd better believe that I ate everything, rind, seeds, and all. Of course, I made it last all day by holding each bite in my mouth as long as I possibly could, not wanting to give it up to my belly."

Stella hunched up her shoulders and snapped her fingers. "Ooooooh, they always tasted so good! The very best. And I'll tell you this—for all the rest of my life, I never tasted anything so darned sweet and wonderful as those winter oranges again."

She paused, then pointed a skeletal finger in the direction of Walker's room. "She's like that for me."

Cat tilted her head to show she did not understand.

272

"You know, that little girl, Zoe. She's like the winter oranges the way she stares up at me all sweet and fresh from God. She's a rare gift; every day when she walks in here and smiles at me, it's like having my own winter orange all over again."

"You've got to be brave, Zoe," Walker said weakly. He held her pinkie between his fingers, memorizing its smallness, its warmth. Her fingernail was the size of a sliver.

"But I don't want you to go, Daddy. Why can't you keep on being here?"

"Ah, honey, you know why. I can't change that. I wish I . . ."

Benny Newmann, wearing a Chicago White Sox jersey, appeared and sat next to Zoe. He threw a baseball into the air, then caught it in his glove.

"I'm scared, Daddy." Zoe glanced over at the bed recently vacated by Detlef.

"Me too, my little pepperhead girl." Walker gave Benny a look and motioned him to go away.

"You are?" She twisted her thumb back and studied her father's face.

Walker nodded. "I don't want to leave you and Mommy and the boys. I wish I could stay here to watch you grow up. I wish I could stay to be a better person than what I've been. See, honey, I need to find out who—"

"But you've been the best dad ever!" Zoe's mouth contorted around the word "best." She placed a small hand on either side of his face and held it with a gentle pressure. "You're the person I love more than anybody. *Everybody* loves you, Dad."

He tried, but could not keep himself from crying.

His child hugged him. "Mommy said she married you because you were the best one. She said you were the only one she would've ever married because you were so much nicer than everybody else, and Melissa's father always says you're a fine man, and Mrs. Vanderskill told me she could trust you more than her own brother, and Joshua says he wishes his dad was just like you."

She kept on rocking him while he wept, her hand moving inside his.

"Daddy?"

"Yes, honey?"

"Do you want to know a story?"

"Mmmm."

273

Zoe settled herself next to him so that she could rub his head and concentrate on telling the story exactly as it had been told to her.

"Okay, here it is, so listen good." She coughed, swallowed, burped, and set her voice for the most interesting and Nancy Drew–like tone she could.

"You see, it's like this. . . . Once upon a time, there was a king who lived in the castle of the sun and he made stars to light the skies at night . . ."

Corky forced his mind to race, driving it places it didn't really want to go . . . like imagining what it would be like to do it with Tammy. Would he have to be careful not to smudge her chin fish? Would she have carve scars on her other, more intimate parts? Had she done it before with someone else, and if so, had he been a carver too?

Freddy, the hideous murdering freak of adolescent cinema, made a sudden appearance in his mind. Yeah, Tammy *would* do it with Freddy, or somebody like him.

Freddy laughed and started to move in on him, his tongue turning into the snakelike Alien, searching for the right place to strike.

Gripping his giant bullwhip, a present from Indiana Jones, he met the fiend in midair and twirled several times about the room, whipping the writhing thing into submission.

"Er, hi."

He hit himself in the eye. His nerves were still raw despite the round-the-clock mood elevators Dr. Barza had ordered.

Cross was watching him with shining eyes. She opened her uninjured arm and curtsied. "I walked here all by myself to get you. Aren't you proud of me?"

"Hey, that's good," he said. "You did real good."

"I figured when you didn't show up for our game last night, you were pulling the old hit-and-run trick, so I figured I'd come down here and pay up."

Cross opened her hand. In the palm lay a nickel and two pennies.

"Six cents plus interest."

Corky half smiled, took the change, and stared at his feet. "Thanks."

"Can you come down and let me sketch you for a while?"

Could he? Torn between life and death, depression and joy, he hardly knew what to think or do when he was by himself, let alone what to say to her.

"You might as well say yes," she said finally, pulling him to the door, "because I'm going to need help for the trip back."

Corky held her arm and let her lean heavily into him as he walked with her toward her room.

"A tough nose, but a great nose," she said, working on her fourth sketch of him.

Without moving a muscle, he thanked her and remained staring out the window at San Francisco taking its winter shower.

"You don't have to freeze like that, you know. You can relax— otherwise you'll look stiff and unnatural." She studied the sketch and erased the mouth that looked too much like Michael's.

"So, where were you last night? Couldn't you find your marked deck?"

Corky stared hard at her and decided she knew the real story; she was just trying to be kind. He was positive everybody knew about his attempt to jump off the ledge, especially after he'd caught the way the old lady shook her finger at him when he passed her room. He wasn't stupid.

Something pulled tightly in his jaw.

"What's the look?" She motioned him to return to profile. "I paid you the seven cents I owed you, didn't I? Don't you look at me like that."

He began to pace the room. "You know, don't you? You're just trying to be nice."

"What?"

"Oh man, you aren't going to tell me you didn't know about last night."

"No," she said, her smile fading. "No, I don't. What's wrong? What happened last night?"

He had come to stand next to her. "I almost killed myself by jumping off the ledge outside my room, but an old guy stopped me. I wasn't going to tell you because I didn't want you to think I was a total pukehead wimp and because . . ." He looked away. "Because you're the most radically beautiful woman I have ever known in my whole life and I thought if you liked me too, I could be, like normal, you know?"

For a moment, his raw honesty left her speechless. She stared at the sketch she had made of him, until suddenly he was on his feet and halfway to the door.

"Look, just forget it, okay! I've got to go. It was stupid to try and make you like me. I'm totally fucked up."

"Wait!" Cross stood and moved toward him. "I lied to you. I'm not in here because of an accident. I'm here because I let a man . . ."

275

She faltered. "I let a man beat me up. A man that I love. I let him abuse me in all sorts of ways and I still didn't leave him." She gently touched his face. When she spoke again, her voice was different: kinder and more tender.

"You're the first person in years that I've been able to talk to and be myself. You don't demand anything of me. You don't try to pick me apart or make me feel guilty about who I am or what I feel. I feel like you're the only real friend I've got."

Cross went back to her chair and resumed sketching.

"Look, please don't leave right now, okay? I can't handle losing the only person I can talk to."

Resigned, Corky sat on the floor next to her. "Great pair," he said, shaking his head. "As in the tweak twins."

When Cat came in ten minutes later to take their vital signs, they were laughing over a caricature of themselves wearing exaggerated smiles, she sporting two huge black eyes, and he with a gun to his head.

"I love you, Stella." Zoe stood next to her, her small hand resting on the old woman's arm. The child was not smiling or particularly tender—she simply had information to pass on.

Stella nodded, her eyes welling. "I love you too, dear."

Zoe shuffled and sighed, the smell of lemon drops and corn chips heavy on her breath. "Well, I have to go be with my dad. He really needs me right now. That's what he said."

Stella nodded again. "Good. That's the best thing."

Zoe ran to the door.

"Zoe?"

"Yes?"

"Be the best you've ever been for him. Then come and see me and I'll tell you a story about the owl and the little girl in the moon."

The suction catheter was full of white mucus.

"I'm sorry, honey," she said, knowing her apology made no difference to the gagging eleven-year-old struggling against her wrist restraints. "It's all over for now. All over. Take it easy."

Cat forced several extra breaths of pure oxygen down the child's endotracheal tube and stroked her cheek. "I know you're scared, but everything is going to be okay. We're going to take good care of you until we find your mom and dad."

276

The girl cried harder and bucked the respirator, triggering the alarms.

"You don't need to be afraid of being alone. There's lots of nurses and doctors right here to be with you. Just press that blue button when you need something, okay?"

The girl pressed the button.

"No, no." Cat pried the call button out of the child's grip. "I'm here now, so you don't need to press it—just show me what you want."

The child tried to talk, gagged, and set off the machine again. Cat hit the alarm silence, untied her hand, and pressed a pencil into it. "Can you write down what you want?"

The girl worked over the pad for several minutes, then handed it back to Cat. The scribble read: "Don't let them get me. I will die if I go back there."

Cat's eyes met the child's. Someone very old and very tired stared back at her.

Gilly appeared. "Catalina, I need you in step-down to take a rule-out pericarditis."

"Can't," Cat said without looking around.

"Got to," Gilly replied.

"Won't."

"Too bad."

Furious, Cat turned to her supervisor. "Goddamnit, Gilly! I've got the heaviest load on the unit. Walker's needing medication every twenty minutes, I've got suctioning and vitals on this one every thirty, Stella's on and off the commode, the angina patient, which, I might add, I took over for *you,* is constantly on his call bell insisting he's having a heart attack because he changed the weight of his underwear last month, Corky's—"

Gilly held up a hand. "Corky and Cross are fine, yucking it up. He's drawing flowers on her cast."

"Okay, great, then how about the DT's patient who's in four-point leather restraints peeing all over himself? What do you want from me, Gilly—blood? I'm beginning to think you've switched your allegiance to management's side. I mean, it isn't safe for any of these people. I can't be in eight places at once. Somebody is going to be lacking care. Somebody could die. Why don't you choose which ones you want me to let go and I'll follow orders, just like the goddamned gestapo."

She heard the melodrama in her voice, felt the laughter breaking at the edges of her mouth and tried to keep it back with forced bitterness.

"Just like Auschwitz, Gilly. That's what this place is. A real death camp."

Gilly snorted and covered her mouth. "Jesus, you really are part of the lunatic fringe, you know?"

Her anger renewed, Cat retied the girl's hand to the side rail.

"You know we'll all help out as much as we can, Catalina."

"Oh yeah, sure, right. Same old story, same old bullshit story. Nobody has time to help, Gilly. Maybe we should ask the families to pitch in. Maybe we should start teaching the patients how to do their own vital signs and what to look for on the monitors. Maybe I should teach this one how to suction out her own ET tube. How about *that!*"

Gilly left the room, walking in that stiff, uptight way known around Ward Two as the Official Nancy Reagan Broom Handle Walk. She was halfway down the hall before Cat made it to the door.

"Hey!" she shouted. "It's *my* license you're playing with, Gilly. *My* malpractice insurance rates. It's *my* bad back. *My* reputation. *My* sanity!"

Cat's guts tightened and that vague uneasiness she'd felt since the night before returned. Goddamnit!

And she wondered why she had death-by-mud dreams?

Walker was back out there, only this time he had some control over the situation. He was able to watch Zoe sitting cross-legged on the bed next to him, singing her Girl Scout songs.

> *"We're the girls in green*
> *who're always in the know.*
> *Always prepared,*
> *ready to help . . ."*

Walker's eyes snapped open. "You're in the know?" he asked.

"What, Daddy?"

"Do you know the secret about who I am?"

Zoe noticed her father was getting the funny look, the one she called the "D" look: D for dead. Be brave, she told herself.

"You're Peter Walker and you're my dad."

"Is that it? Is that the answer?"

Be brave. "You're the best one, Daddy. Remember the story about leaving goods things? I'm here. You're the best man on the whole block, Daddy. Don't worry."

Benny stood behind Zoe wearing a Girl Scout beret at a rather rakish angle over one eye. "You should listen to her, Walker." He

278

took a bite of the charred marshmallow at the end of his stick and threw the rest to the red mouth.

"She's giving you all the clues."

"If anybody found out what happened, I couldn't even begin to tell you what it would do to me . . ."

He was frozen again, forgetting to relax. Cross was having a difficult time with the brilliance of his eyes.

"Hey, I'm not going to tell anyone." She crossed her heart. "I swear to God and hope to die."

"You would never speak to me again; you wouldn't even want to be in the same room with me, I swear."

"I'm great at unconditional friendship. You could probably tell me you killed somebody and I wouldn't feel any differently about you."

Corky shivered, and she was shocked to see his face go ashen.

"In October I went . . . I was . . ." He stopped. "In October there was this—"

He ran to her bathroom retching. When he returned, he sat at her side, moaning into his hands. "I can't. My life wouldn't be worth shit. My father would hate me. Everybody will look at me like I'm . . ."

Wearily Cross smoothed down a few wild strands of wet hair over his ears. "Whenever you're ready, Corky."

The single red rose in the white pebble glass vase was for her. At the sight of it, her heart caught in her throat; then when Cat read the card, it changed from the place of love to the place of sorrow right next door.

"Thank you for being you and for all you have done. When it is my turn, I pray there will be someone there for me like you."

The note was signed simply "Doll."

Holding the flower under her nose, Cat breathed in its intoxicating fragrance and reread the note three times just to remind herself this was exactly why she did what she did.

"I don't get it. I mean, why would you pick somebody who keeps telling you you're bad news? I mean, there's a lot of dudes who would give their right arms just to be in the same room with you."

"Yeah, but see, it's who I chose for me. Those guys you're talking about would like to be with me for different reasons, and not all of them are good. Most of the men who want to be with me think I can . . .'' Cross thought twice about telling Corky who she was and why she steered clear of "star fuckers," the men who wanted her in order to further their own careers. ''. . . do something for them.

"Since my divorce, I had pretty much isolated myself with work, so by the time I met Michael, I was so lonely and needy that I gave him all the love I had immediately without seeing if he could earn it. I forgot to save anything for me. Besides, he's like my dad was in a lot of ways.'' She stopped sketching. "So I guess I tried to work out the problems I had with my father through Michael."

Absently she touched the healing red scar on her cheek. "That's why I chose him. That's why I took him back every time, even after he'd hurt me."

"But, I mean, you're not going to take the dude back *this* time, right?" Corky's voice was innocently hopeful. "I mean, not after he did all this to you?"

She did not know what to tell the boy who was measuring her expression, holding his breath for the right answer.

"This time?" Cross repeated, embarrassed by what she was going to say.

"This time, I don't know."

25 Mathilde watched in awe as the artist's hand glided confidently over the paper. The woman had done more than mirror the boy's image; she had managed to capture his spirit as well.

The nature of the relationship between the two was something to wonder about. Such an odd combination. Certainly, the woman was older than the boy, yet when they were together, they created a private world in which their age difference seemed insignificant. Of course, where she came from, no one would have given them a second thought; romances between older women and boys were commonplace, not even considered small fodder for the gossips.

Mathilde placed a peppermint drop between her tongue and her cheek, promising herself not to chew; she would let this one dissolve.

Not that she approved of such liaisons, but hers was not to judge. *Ce n'est pas la peine de se faire des cheveux blancs.* It was best to take the gourmet theory—age only mattered if one was a wine or a cheese.

"Come! We must go, Monsieur Corky. I promise this favor to Mademoiselle Catalina and so I take you to the therapy sessions now."

"Oh man, those people are so totally burnt." Corky slumped down into his chair. "This is the second time today. Can't you say you couldn't find me? I am so totally sick of hearing about Tammy's stupid carving and her pukehead parents and that other lame whose IQ is hanging in at the minus-points category. It's total bore-death, man, I mean, can't we skip it this once?"

Separating the unwilling teenager from the chair, Mathilde pulled him toward the door by the seat of his pajamas. "No! No! No! The doctor, he orders this for you. It is good for you to talk with the weirdo peoples, *qui*? I think it makes you feel normal inside your head to know there are more crazies worse than you, no?"

Cross waved him on. "Go on, go on. While you're getting your head straight, I'll get rid of the garbage from my sketch pads to make more room for my studies of you."

Corky moaned his reluctance as Mathilde dragged him into the hallway. "But you don't understand, you guys. These dweebs are like *totally* fried. They're so bad, they make you *want* to kill yourself. They're carved mutants from . . ." He had been hauled out of her range of sight, so only his fading voice could be heard. ". . . some other planet for rejects. Aw, man!"

Alone, Cross sorted through the sketches in her portfolio and drawing pads. Divided by date, they chronicled the major events of her life—the garden studies after her father died; the Santa Monica Boulevard sketches in her early postfame, pre-Michael, Los Angeles glitter days; the sketches of bold, brassy suns, sensuous swans, and erotic red phallic flowers in her beginning-with-Michael phase; the studies of the strange little blind man in his one-room house with the magnificent bay view, in the days of her first attempts to leave Michael; and finally, the pen-and-ink studies of Michael in the holocaust days of his beauty and his violence.

In a daring move, she weeded out all the sketches of Michael and tore them in half. The finality of the action panicked her. She did not want to close the door on him. Never would she find another man as brilliant or playful as Michael, let alone one who understood art as well. No man would ever be able to make her laugh as hard, even though she could not remember when the last laughter had been. No one could ever play her body the way he did.

And what other man would jump out of bed at three in the morning and drive two hours to find lemon custard ice cream for her, or, on a whim, drive her to New Mexico in search of some obscure Indian artist she thought was interesting? Who else would be as honestly critical of her and her work?

The unbearable times when he was crazy and vicious were, she decided, the price she had to pay for the zenith of highs. Life without him was unimaginable. What else was there for her? To spend the rest of her life in her cabin, painting and tending to her garden like a withered-up old eccentric? Sleeping alone, having love only as a memory?

A sketch of the boy fell out of the stack and landed at her feet. The sweetness stared up at her, forcing her to be gut-honest. Okay, so it was stupid to try and defend Michael; he had a tendency to be cruel even in the best of times. As Nathan said right from the beginning, Michael was a man unable to love—a devil possessed by a compulsive appetite for destruction.

She recalled a day at Sea Ranch when they walked the freezing, misted beach, and she had tried to explain how alive she felt being there with him, smelling the sea wind and watching the endless sheet of water join the sky until one was indiscernible from the other.

Timidly laying open the prizes of her innermost self, she couched the beauty she felt in words of love for him.

Michael savagely cut her off, then mocked her. He told her that playing the sensitive artist role made her appear ridiculous.

In that moment, as her hair mingled with his in the wind, she knew their differences were too wide to bridge. To be with him, she would have to make herself numb from the inside out. But to be without him was worse than death.

When Corky reappeared at the door a minute later, she was piecing together the torn sketches.

"Do me a favor, will you?"

In the hall, Mathilde, arms crossed over her chest, frowned and tapped her foot impatiently.

"Don't throw out those drawings of your garden, okay? I mean, I

282

think they're totally awesome pictures. I don't know what any of them are worth, but maybe I could buy one from you."

Pleased by his request, she studied him, ashamed that she had not allowed him the possibility of having a mature or sensitive enough eye for what she considered her best work. Was she so ensconced in the snobbery of the highbrow art world and out of touch with every-day people that she had forgotten that the appreciation of beauty was not a function of age, education, or bank account?

"You really like the ones of the garden?"

"They're my favorites. They remind me of you—sort of like a dream, but right in front of you at all times."

Mathilde regained her hold on the seat of Corky's pajama bottoms and pulled. Disappearing from view, he raised his voice.

"Hey! When I get back, you gotta sketch my pecs and my biceps, and maybe you could get the ripples on my abs . . ."

She waited for his voice to die out completely before she went to the mirror. Summoning the courage to raise her eyes, she examined the bridge of her nose and gingerly touched the wound on her cheek. They were Michael's brands, hers to wear for the rest of her life. Perverted as she knew it was, she felt a fleeting sense of pride. That he had left her with something of himself, even if it was his anger, gave her the feeling that she belonged to him.

Cross turned away from the mirror, changed her mind, and looked back at her image once more. Under the harsh fluorescent light, her romantic notion of the red scar dwindled. It was a disfigurement as ugly as the one her father had left on her spirit.

Hardening herself against Michael, she decided the scar would not be his brand, but rather a reminder of his vicious hatred of women and a symbol of her resistance against his power over her. She was resolved to cancel out the vision of his eyes always there, spying on her thoughts; she would find tools to clean out the room in her life which he had occupied.

She ripped the sketches of Michael into hundreds of irreparable pieces and flushed them down the toilet, feeling like a traitor, al-though she did not know who she was betraying. From the box of pastel chalks Nathan had brought, she lifted out a piece of dawn blue and amused herself by shading in the boy's eyes. Couldn't there be a man for her somewhere who was more like the boy? There were millions of men in the world—surely there was one who could break the spell.

The door to her room softly clicked shut and arrested her thoughts. Chilled by a cold rush spreading into her neck, she refused to raise her eyes.

283

For a time she studied the piece of blue chalk, made a final shading, and then, with an air of surrender, let it drop from her hand.

Nora strained, holding on to the delirium tremens patient, a retired gentleman presently under the illusion he was chasing after wild elephant in Tanzania.

Cat pulled the wadded, urine-soaked diaper out from under his wide, fat hips and examined the man's inflamed testicles, manipulating them as gently as possible. The patient, who was for the moment peacefully rambling on in his own version of Swahili, at once sat straight up and wailed like a banshee.

"Whoa! Whoa! Wulp! I say! She's got me by the nuts, Simbwani! She's got me good now! Shoot, for God's sake, shoot!"

Capturing the man's flailing arms, Nora and Cat reapplied the leather cuffs to his wrists and fastened them securely to the sides of the bed with heavy-gauge locks.

"I still can't believe you came back here last night to check up on the kid and Gage," Nora said, lifting the man's testicles while Cat smoothed a thick coat of bitter-smelling white ointment over them.

"Why not?"

Nora rubbed the side of her face against her shoulder. "I don't know. Seems to me you would have had enough of this place."

"But that's just it—I was off duty. When this place and the politics don't have any hold over me, it's okay; it's almost enjoyable to drop the super-healer-earth-mother role and act like a normal person around the patients."

Both nurses went silent, contemplating the new puddle of urine slowly forming underneath the squirming patient. Sheepishly he looked at Nora.

"Whoa? Wulp?"

Nora stuffed a thick pad of toweling under the man's buttocks and they started the process of wash, dry, and grease all over again.

"Yeah, but give yourself a break, Cat. Visitor or not, you're still trying to save the world, and if you keep it up, you're gonna burn yourself all the way out. The kid and Gage would have survived the night without your coming in to see them, but you couldn't let it be. Instead, you screw yourself out of a good night's sleep to come running to the rescue. I mean, what's the point? Do you want to end up like Dr. Cramer, skulking around the halls scaring the patients and whispering 'Catechols' to the walls?"

"Look Nor, I know they would have survived, but Gage is my

284

friend and he doesn't really have anybody else. I couldn't let him get on a bus and go home alone after doing what he did.

"And who the hell was going to take the time to sit down and really talk to Corky last night? His parents are totally freaked and don't understand why he tried to kill himself in the first place, and do you honestly believe Barza is going to roust himself from his ten-thousand-dollar custom-made bed that does everything but screw him, and leave his two-point-six-million-dollar house in Pacific Heights in the middle of a rainy night just to make an inpatient call on some traumatized teenager?

"Have you forgotten how the system works? You know as well as I do that the medical profession's way of dealing with those issues in the off-hours is to do exactly what Barza did—order that the kid be sedated around the clock so he could sleep in and deal with the situation at *his* convenience, not when Corky needed it.

"I understand how it feels to hurt like that, and I wasn't about ready to let the kid suffer all night without letting him know *somebody* gave a shit, and if that makes me crazy, then I guess I'm a real case."

Nora rubbed another glob of ointment over the patient's testicles. "But what about you, Cat? That's all I'm trying to get at. Don't you need to take care of you, too?"

Searching through the piles of linen for a proper diaper, Cat found a stack of sixteen pillowcases, three chin straps, a scultetus binder, and the empty plastic wrapper from a set of adult diapers. "Sure. Isn't that rule number one of the Rules You Were Never Taught in Nursing School: You can't take care of the patient until you've taken care of yourself?

"Granted, I don't do it very well, but I care about these people and I'm still convinced no one else can look after them as well as I do.

"And besides, with my personal life the way it is, who else do I have to spend my excess energy on?"

"How about Inspector Pandora?" Nora offered coyly, "I mean, yesterday I saw him standing at the end of the hall and my first thought was, my God, now there's a remarkable man just made for Catalina Richardson. Face it, he's the man of your dreams."

Cat shook her head. "What is it with your obsession over my reentering the world of relationshit misery? I thought you were my best friend."

Nora fluttered her eyes, and spoke in a deep Mississippi accent. "Why, honey, it's mah southern nature that drives me to dwell on the delicate and enjoyable matters of love."

"Oh for Christ's sake, Carmotti, you're about as southern as I am."

285

"You might recall, Miss Richardson, that ah was born deep in the heart of Georgia—"

"Not *in* Georgia, Nora, going *through* Georgia . . . on a train headed for Bigbone, Indiana."

"Schenectady, New York."

"Wherever it was, it was a weird place to go, and your mother shouldn't have been riding around on trains in her condition, that late in—"

"Trains were the only thing that helped her morning sickness."

"Then she should have known better than to get herself in that situation at all, *especially* after giving birth to your brother Harry. Any woman in her right mind would have stopped right there to spare the world."

"Harry was an accident."

"And how. Except what does your mother do about it? Have her tubes tied? Divorce your father and go into a convent? No. Your mother decides to populate Boston with five more warpos. I mean, I have never even heard of a family who, three times a week, despite snow, rain, or sleet, climb out onto their peaked roof, hold hands, and breathe exactly fifteen times in unison, to reap the benefits of higher-altitude negative ions."

"My mother read it in a *Ladies' Home Journal.* See, she believed that—"

Cat held up a hand. "I don't care. Your mother was the sickest. She contaminated all of you. You're all warped."

"I know." Nora smiled, pleased with herself. "It's really the only thing that gets me through life."

Cat handed Nora the jar of ointment. "Well, you just exercise that old sense of warpedness while you finish smearing the rest of that goop on our friend's jewels here. I need to run down and get another batch of diapers, okay?"

Nora slapped a huge gob of white ointment onto the man's exposed parts and curtsied. "Ah will do mah best, Miss Scarlett."

"Wulp. Wulp. Whoa!"

The smells coming from the lunch carts permeated the hall with promises of overdone chicken covered with thick, yellow-green gravy, and unnaturally shaped, soggy, and nutrition-robbed vegetables. For midday, the halls of Ward Two were unusually deserted and peaceful. Not that Cat had any complaints.

She reflected briefly on the DT's patient's testicles, then let her mind run the gamut from Walker being overdue for another shot of

MS, to David Padcula's voice, to the little OD maybe needing another suctioning, to the end-stage renal failure whose call light was on, to Cross's door being closed, to Corky being due back from therapy at one o'clock, to Stella playing solitaire, to the amount of chanting she had left to do, to the fact that Mathilde promised to—

Wait. Back up.

Starting in the lower region of her chest, a nagging feeling worked its way up to her temples: Lassie tugging at her skirt, trying to wake her up to the roaring fire outside the baby's nursery.

When she reached the utility supply cart, Cat couldn't remember what it was she needed. Ointment? Basins? Catechols? Fire extinguisher?

What the hell was it?

She felt as if she were in a vortex and closed her eyes to think. Something about the mud dream? No, that wasn't it. Gage warning her? Closer. About what?

Closed doors.

The blood drained from her face as she took off at a run toward Cross's room.

Cross did not have too look up to know who was standing over her. It was his breathing, his smell, his energy that always caused her world to stop for a beat whenever he entered a room.

Unable to hold off, she raised her head. The sight of him wrenched her heart. Michael had changed: older, tired, and something else— eyes that were his but not his, looking at her as if he recognized her but didn't know who she was. Fighting the temptation to look directly into the wild eyes, she focused on the coarse leer of his mouth and decided he had come to hurt her again, since she could think of no other reason for him to seek her out.

She stood and took a step toward the bed, trying to remember whether the call light was to the left or the right of the pillow. She had forgotten about Michael's uncanny ability to read her mind. Before she could take another step, he caught her wrist and put his face close to hers. His stale cigarette breath felt hot against her face.

"Oh, no, baby. Not this time you don't. This time Mikie won't be so stupid as to leave you a line for help." Pushing away the front of her robe, he pressed his body to hers. She could feel his penis hard against her.

"Oh baby," he said, twisting the sensitive flesh of her nipples, "I sure have missed you."

Cross made herself speak gently, praying he would snap out of it, or pity her, or at least remember that she had loved him. "I don't want this, Michael. I love you, but I don't want you to—"

"Shut your lying mouth!" Michael covered his ears as if he were being assaulted by his own noise. "You lied to me! You always lie! No more, Cross. This is the last time you're ever going to lie to me!"

He pulled the muslin sling from her cast and roughly stuffed the bulk of it into her mouth. Cross gagged on the stiff cloth. She wanted to beg him to take it out, promise not to scream, but all she could do was to make low, guttural noises in her throat.

"I thought about you, Cross," he whispered, rubbing his groin against hers. "I kept wondering if sluts begged for mercy before they died, or if they kept lying about how much they loved you all the way to the end."

In his eyes, Cross saw for certain that it wasn't a game to scare her; this time it wasn't going to be a few scrapes and bruises. This time he meant to kill her. She dared only move her eyes in search of a way to escape.

He caressed her face and hesitated over the laceration on her cheek. "How are you, Cross? I see you've got yourself a new sucker. A real young stud for you this time, huh, baby? I wasn't enough for you, that it? Or maybe you're going to tell me he's only a friend? That it, Cross? Were you going to tell me how much you love me before or after you fucked him?"

Out of her range of sight, he began fumbling between her legs while his other hand came to rest on her windpipe. She brought her knee up sharply, but he'd seen it coming and moved out of the way. With the back of his hand, he delivered a blow that sent her reeling into the utility sink.

She pretended to lose consciousness, hoping he would leave her alone, but Michael had come with a goal. Roughly he pulled her to her knees and hit her repeatedly, aiming most of the damaging force to her face.

She clawed at his jacket until the smell of wet leather filled her nose. It was the smell of her father's shaving strap, the one he used to beat her with.

A lifetime of buried loathing surfaced in an agonized growl. She despised this man with the force of one suddenly maddened by long years of having been made to beg for love.

Enraged by her outburst, Michael sank his fingers deep into her throat. Forcing her to the floor, he ripped the thin hospital gown from her body, pulled back to hit her, then stopped cold at the sight

288

of the bandage on her breast. Carefully he removed the gauze and stared at the wound as if he could not figure out what it was doing there.

Aware of his hesitation, Cross pushed him off balance and half crawled, half stumbled to the door. As her hand touched the handle, he seized her by the ankle and dragged her back to the other side of the room.

Cross bit down on the gag with the initial force of him. She was dry and could feel him tearing at the delicate tissue inside her.

"Now tell me how much you love me." He braced her shoulder against the leg of the chair to keep her from sliding away with each thrust of his body. "Tell me you're a lying slut."

With a final surge of hatred and fear, Cross twisted to get away from him, but he was like a steel bar crushing her, grinding his mouth into hers around the gag, splitting her lips so that the fleshy, iron taste of her own blood filled her mouth.

Unexpectedly, the harsh tone of his monologue changed and his voice went tender. The pressure on her throat eased enough for her to suck in half a breath.

"I missed you, Cross, even though you lied to me. I got so lonely. I was going to take you with me, maybe someplace warm like Mexico. Then I saw that punk in here and you all over him, like *she* used to be, and right then I knew I was going to have to teach you once and for all."

A strangled sob escaped through the gag that was choking her.

"You did it to yourself, Cross. You spoiled it." Michael stroked the side of her face. "You can't help yourself. It's in your blood. Women like you have to be taken out of the game. You understand, don't you, baby? I have to do this. You had your chance to be good, but you proved what you really are. You're a well of poison, and I'm going to be the one to dry you up."

In earnest, Michael doubled the force against her throat, cutting off her air completely. A second later, she was dimly aware of him at her nipples again, biting, hurting her until she thought she was screaming. But the scream was all in her head.

She wasn't sure if it was lack of air or the sight of the veins in his forehead pulsing Mediterranean blue that made her sick. It was easier to close her eyes and concentrate on other things, like how much her paintings would go up in value once she was dead, and how sad it was that she would not see Corky and Nathan again. She was glad her father was dead so he couldn't say he'd been right about her meeting a whore's end.

Some time passed—maybe an hour, maybe two seconds—before she was jerked back into awareness by a sudden sharp pain down where Michael was brutally thrusting into her.

Holding on as long as she could to the sound of the rain outside the window, she felt a warm tingling sensation creep into her temples as a hundred white spots took over her vision, then went to black.

Michael felt her go limp at the same time he heard the door slam open behind him. Abruptly he stopped what he was doing and turned.

Cat did not quite believe what she was seeing and wondered for the second time that day if she was in another dream, although this time she was certain she would not be allowed the luxury of waking up in bed. Cross appeared to be dead. Her pretty face was now grotesque: the dusky gray tinge, common to fresh corpses, had settled around her eyes, and the blood-soaked gag hung from her mouth.

Defiantly the man with the perfectly chiseled features moved out from between Cross's legs and stood, zipping his pants. He started toward her.

Wailing loudly enough to rupture blood vessels in her throat, Cat grabbed the metal-cased flashlight from the neuro assessment tray and charged, swinging it at his head.

"Code secure!" she screamed. "Call a goddamned code secure, stat!"

Michael gripped her by the hair and delivered a well-placed kick to her solar plexus. The blow dropped her to the floor.

He knelt down beside her and grabbed her throat. "Lousy bitch! You want the same thing our friend got? Come find me, or maybe . . ." His hands traveled to her breasts where his eyes settled on her name tag. He licked his lips and roughly shoved her away from him. ". . . I'll find you, Catalina Richardson, R.N."

At the door, the man glared once more at Cross's still form and backed into the hall. "You can tell Cross she's dead meat. Tell the slut to consider herself history."

Still paralyzed by the impact of his boot, Cat lay on her side and struggled to make her lungs work.

Michael had just made it out the door when two security guards rushed into the corridor from different directions, searching for the source of alarm.

Michael pointed to Cross's room. "In there!" he shouted over the din of confusion. "Hurry! There's a maniac in there!"

The guards drew their guns and ran toward the room while Michael pushed through the gathering crowd of gawkers and entered the elevator.

By the time Cat was able to speak, he had vanished.

26 "I say my baby been sick, lady. She need a nurse."

The disheveled sloe-eyed woman held out a tattered wicker flower basket for Cat's inspection. Covering the basket's contents was a handmade linen eyelet baby blanket. Covering the woman's thin arms were lines of new and old needle tracks.

"I'm sorry?" Cat said mildly, trying to keep her nausea at a controllable level. More than anything in the world, she hated to throw up.

"You a nurse, ain't ya? You gotta look at my baby girl. She been awful sick. She ain't taken no milk for three days, lady."

Although she appeared much older, Cat guessed the anemic-looking woman was only nineteen or twenty. She also guessed the woman was in bad need of a fix, the way she was vibrating, deep into that body dance hard-core junkies often do. She was having a difficult time holding on to the basket.

Instinctively Cat lifted the coverlet, looked in at the contents, winced, then dropped the blanket as if the cool white fabric had burned her fingers. The naked infant, no more than two weeks old, had obviously been dead for several days. The sight of the bruises, concentrated around the baby's neck and head, made her forget her nausea. A deep sorrow for the life that had never had a chance settled within her.

Drawing on her community service experiences, she had little dif-

291

ficulty figuring out the scenario: the sleepy newborn, fussed over like a prized doll, then left alone for hours—sometimes a day or two—cold, hungry, and wet in a makeshift cardboard box crib. And when the novelty was replaced by the realities of responsibility, the screaming infant beaten and smothered into quiet.

Cat swallowed the lump in her throat and pointed to the triage nurse. "I'm not on duty. Take your daughter to that nurse over there—she'll help you."

"But I gotta get outta here quick, lady," whined the woman. "Why can't you fix her? She ain't cried for three days and she been sleepin' all the time. All she need is some medicine."

"I can't help your baby," Cat whispered. The sickness in her stomach returned and grew heavy. "Take her to the nurse at the desk over there."

The woman shrugged, changed the basket to her other hand, and shuffled toward the triage desk. "Aw, this one wasn't no good nohow. Didn't play or nothin'."

This one? Did that mean there had been other babies, or did she mean to continue cranking them out until she had an infant who would care for itself and play pitch-and-catch?

Resting her chin on her hand, she continued to watch the emergency room chaos. There was no doubt in her mind it took a special breed to work emergency; you had to have a tougher skin than the rest, be able to think a little quicker, and be more willing to lend yourself to situations from scrapes to rapes without blinking an eye. Not that there wasn't some compassion among the group, but who had time for sympathy when you were standing ankle-deep in some eighteen-year-old's blood while trying to preserve the amputated limbs and keep the body from going into shock?

Her own emergency room experience had come during the hiatus between graduating from nursing school and receiving the results of the boards. Eager for work, desperate for money, she'd applied for and received a training job in a central Los Angeles emergency room.

She rode high on the excitement of the chaos until her first night of full-moon pandemonium, when one of the docs was shot in the leg by a patient who didn't like the stitching job he'd done on her hand. Shaken but not destroyed, she rallied her unflagging caregiving spirit and returned the next night, only to be told nonchalantly (the clerk actually *yawned* in the telling of the story) that a nurse had had her throat slit in the waiting room that very morning by another patient, who thought the wait too long.

When she went to the waiting room to call in her first patient, she was horrified to find the walls still splattered with the nurse's blood and the bottoms of her shoes sticking to the dark stains in the carpet.

But wasn't that the nature of emergency rooms and hospitals everywhere—to reap the harvest of man's violent nature and also of his frailties? And now here she was, a patient in her own arena, feeling somehow responsible for the death of neglected babies, not even an hour after having been assaulted. It was an insane way to exist.

She lay in the gurney garage, on a gurney designated as bed A, waiting for the X rays to confirm she had no broken ribs or damaged vertebrae. Even if she showed no evidence of injury, she would not be allowed to return to work for the rest of her shift. For legal reasons, the doctor said—in case she decided to bring a lawsuit against the hospital.

For several seconds after he put the idea into her head, she toyed with the idea of suing the hospital, then dropped it; no sense throwing logs into a burning barn. There were more pleasant topics to think about, like an unexpected free afternoon staring her in the face. If she'd won a four-hour free shopping spree at Gump's, she couldn't have been happier.

Her options of how to spend the rest of the day were limitless—go to Chinatown or maybe run Tennessee Valley out to the ocean, or there was always the library, or maybe she'd grab Gage and Tom Mix for an early supper in North Beach. He'd be full of good stories, perfect material for her daily log or her nightmares.

The side door opened and Nora appeared, anxiously searching the room. Cat waved to her, jolted for the millionth time by the blonde's seductive beauty. It still amazed her that men did not faint or at least fall down in the street at the very sight of her.

"Well," Nora began, after giving her a deeply felt I'm-reeeeally-glad-you're-okay hug, "for the longest time, I stood there holding the DT's guy's balls with him yelling 'Whoa, wulp, wulp,' until I started feeling perverted. At that point, I covered him with a few towels and decided to hunt you down and kill you, only to find out somebody had already tried to do that."

Nora faced her with a long, steady gaze. "It's true, isn't it, Cat? You really *do* have a contract with Stephen King to do the story of your life, don't you?"

Cat smiled, loving her friend. The lump in her throat grew to voice-choking proportions. "I didn't want to tell you because I figured you'd insist on being the detail consultant, telling everyone how you were the single most important influence in my life. And when they

293

made the movie, you'd want to be in charge of casting and, God forbid, wardrobe."

For a while Nora held her hand, not saying anything.

"How's . . ." Cat cleared her throat. "How's Cross?"

"Amazingly enough, she's pretty calm. She's going to have a few new bruises, and she sustained a small vaginal tear from the force of the rape, but one of the OB GYN guys fixed her up. That's it, really. Gladstein ordered her some Xanax. Corky's freaked—refuses to leave her side."

"What about Walker and the little OD? Who's taking over those guys? What about the guy with—"

"Cat, don't worry about it. You could be dead right now, and you're worrying about how the patients are doing?" Nora broke into a wry grin. "Tssssh, Jesus! You know, I'll bet you even worried about whether the jerk got away safely or not."

Cat pulled back. The instant flash of red temper trimmed her voice like a thin sheet of ice. "Hey, look, I want Walker to have a pain-free death and I don't want that little kid to suffocate. Who's going to get Stella to the commode every five minutes? You or Gilly have time for that? What about the guy in 509? I hadn't even done his vitals yet, and there wasn't any charting done on anybody. Who's going to—"

"Hey, Cat, calm down. Jesus! I mean, everybody's taken care of. We divided them up. I got Walker, Cross, the gunshot, and the DT's. Gilly got the OD kid, the underwear angina guy, and Corky. Mathilde got the rest. Nobody's complaining."

Nora's voice rose, her hands emphasizing each word. "Stop being so narcissistic. You *aren't* the only one who can fix people. The rest of us went to nursing school too, remember? Some of us even graduated."

"But listen . . ."

"Jesus God, no! Drop it, Cat. I mean it. Give it a rest."

Cat felt deflated and on the brink of caving in. There was too much pain around her. Everything was so screwed up and backward, and there was so much left to be done. Not able to fight the sadness, she began to weep, leaning into Nora, using the simplest excuse she could think of for her tears.

"I couldn't tell if Cross was dead or not. It was like one of my nightmares or something out of a movie and . . ."

. . . *and I'm so tired of this, Nor. For twenty years, I have lived a life where death and tragedy surrounds me, and my spirit has reached the end of its tether. My mettle has softened. I am starved to know the love and joy of the living. Tell me, my sweet, misguided Nora, where is my healer? Who will give care to the caregiver?*

Nora held her, cooing softly into her hair, which made her cry all the harder. Tears ran down her hands and arms to her elbows.

"Goddamn! That asshole was sickening. You should've seen him." She took a Kleenex from the box on the utility table and blew her nose. "He touched me, Nor—he actually put his hands on me."

Nora stroked the nape of Cat's neck. "It's okay now. You're okay. Inspector Smiles has posted a twenty-four-hour guard outside Cross's room. He's been interviewing everybody—even people who were so much as *thinking* about Ward Two when it happened."

Cat sat up abruptly, wiped her eyes, and sniffled. *"He's* here? Upstairs? Right now?"

"Uh-huh. In the process of grilling Corky, I think." Nora lowered her voice. "Do you know that the first question he asked when he got to the ward was if you were okay—not about Cross or Michael, but about you. He said he'd come down here to take your statement. Personally, I think he wants more than a statement."

"Oh God, I'm a mess." Cat unfastened her braid and fluffed out the soft waves around her face.

Nora's affectionate gaze rested on Cat's eyes. "Wrong. You should wear your vulnerability more often—it becomes you. You're going to make a lovely middle-aged bride."

Cat tentatively rubbed the painful area of her lower rib cage. "You *are* warped."

Digging into her pocket, Nora came up with a single key, which she pressed into Cat's hand. "That's my apartment key. You're staying with Warpo tonight."

Cat opened her mouth to protest, but Nora stopped her. "By order of the *poliziotto,* my dear. Smiley gave the order, and I figure it's about the best excuse for an overnight there ever was. Besides, I think you're getting too much of that Marvelous Marin nuclear-free-zone air."

"Wait a minute. Didn't you have a date with . . . Oh God, don't tell me you canceled your opera date tonight with Normal Norman Nosenchuck, the Humpbacked Harley Gangbanger. You know how much the neurotic caretaking side of me hates to be fussed over, even if it is by the warpo."

Nora held up her hands. "Don't worry, I know you better than that. However, take warning that I will be home early—you just make sure you have the popcorn and champagne ready."

There was a sudden flurry of subdued excitement at the triage

295

desk, enough to pull several of the staff from the trauma room. A doctor was in the process of prying the covered basket out of the woman's hand, while the triage nurse half pulled, half shoved her toward the meditation room.

"She must have a bomb in that basket," Nora said.

Emotionally exhausted, Cat let her eyes glaze over. "Well," she said absently, her stare fixed on Nora's scuffed white clogs, "I suppose you could say that."

Corky sat quietly next to Lucy and held her hand while she dozed. He wished the old guy holding her other hand would leave. It was taking everything he had to suppress the panicky feeling, which had grown uncontrollable since he saw Lucy on the floor like that, naked and totally wrecked. He tried to block out the thoughts about the blood on her legs and the way she screamed when she woke up. It reminded him of when his dog was hit by a car.

She would not let go of his hand, even when the investigator dude made her go over the story in detail.

Was there penetration? The dude asked her that. Fucking A, man. He'd really said "penetration" in front of everybody.

The fat, bald guard sat outside the door reading the paper and drinking coffee from a thermos. Every once in a while, he absently jingled the chain that hung off the side of his holster. A lot of good that dork would do, Corky thought. Probably some rent-a-dick who hasn't fired a gun in a hundred years. Probably doesn't even know where the trigger is.

After a while, the old dude made some moves like he was going to leave. He leaned over and kissed Lucy's forehead.

"I'll leave her to your care, son," Nathan said sadly, pulling on his jacket, which was made of a shiny pink and purple material with metallic threads running through it. Somehow it worked perfectly with the extra wide, lime-colored suspenders and the maroon slacks.

Corky rose from his seat, wondering how such an old dude knew about dressing cool. "Yessir."

"If she needs anything, tell her to call, or if it's easier, you can ring me." Halfway across the room, Nathan stopped and picked the sketch pad up from the chair. On top was one of the garden watercolor studies.

"Look at that, son," he said, holding it up for the boy to see. "She has a formidable and awe-inspiring talent."

"Like totally *awesome*, sir."

296

"I'd like to kill the damned dirty scum with my bare hands," the old man said, shoving the potential weapons into his pockets.

"Me too, sir, I'd like to kill the damned dirty scum myself, sir."

Unsure of what to do next, Nathan regarded the young man for a moment and nodded. "You're a good lad. Take care of her."

"Thank you, sir. I will."

Adjusting his suspenders, which didn't really need adjusting, Nathan left the room.

Corky cradled Lucy's hand, bracing himself for the next wave of panic. He moved his toes around in his moccasin slippers as a kind of reality check and sighed. What was really setting him off was that things were starting to get mixed up and really far out.

Like, for a few seconds, he couldn't remember his last name when the investigator asked him, and somehow he forgot that last night he had tried to jump off the side of the building, so that when he saw the black dude, he couldn't remember where he knew him from, and now there was this animal scumbag who had ra—hurt this person he loved, his Lucy in the Sky with Diamonds.

The roar of the panic wave came, searing through his head.

He was cracking up. Things had never been this weird before.

He leaned close to the sleeping woman and kissed the back of her hand. "Please wake up," he pleaded. "Please, Lucy, I gotta talk to you."

The panic gouged at his temples, making him want to scream. If he let himself go, he wouldn't ever come back to being normal.

Miserable, he laid his head on the bed next to Lucy's shoulder and counted her breaths.

One. Hold on. Two. Hold on. Just until she wakes up.

Cat was glad she wasn't actively bleeding or having any of her PMS-impatience screaming attacks. The hands of the clock had pushed ahead to 2:47 without a word from the X ray department. For some reason, they seemed to be keeping her films a secret. She tried not to think it was the X ray bitch from hell who recognized her name and kept putting her films at the bottom of the pile.

From the way the nurses rushed past her without ever making eye contact, she was beginning to believe she was invisible.

Everything was okay though; the second Vicodin was working to the point where she thought the piped-in Muzak quite lovely rather than an aural blasphemy.

Boredom had driven her to pay close attention to the world where the human condition paraded itself in the raw. Bed D received a man begging for something to numb the searing pain. His blind, burned eyes rolled upward as the nurses peeled away shreds of clothing, searching frantically for an inch of unblistered flesh through which to inject the morphine.

Bed F held a drunk who sat and stared at his handcuffs, probably, Cat thought, reflecting on his young and pregnant girlfriend lying still in the darkened corner of bed G. No one went near the drawn curtains. The dead did not require much care.

Bed B was a nun with asthma.

Bed C was a junkie.

Bed E was an overweight housewife complaining of pains in her heart.

The baby had been removed from the basket and wrapped for morgue pickup.

E.R. nurses never walked, she remembered; they ran.

At the other end of the gurney garage, she observed a bent, elderly man with Parkinson's nervously twisting his fingers next to bed J, which held a young, strikingly attractive, extremely pregnant, blonde and tanned surfer type.

The proud grandfather—no, great-grandfather—seemed distraught to the point of collapse. Within seconds, one of the emergency nurses helped the man to a chair in the waiting area.

"Your wife will be fine, Mr. Sturdevent," the woman shouted, making it easy to eavesdrop. "We'll bring her up to obstetrics in a little while. Don't you worry."

A vision of the old man and the young woman entwined on the marriage bed made Cat shudder. Oh yuck, she thought, repulsed. Had the marriage market for women gone *that* bad? Was this the future trend due to a society full of commitmentphobes?

Stethoscope and sphygmomanometer in hand, a first-year nursing student timidly approached Cat, begging for a chance to practice taking blood pressures. She gave her compassionate, all-knowing approval and relaxed.

As the young man awkwardly fumbled with the cuff, she smiled upon him tenderly, until he pumped the mercury to the top of the scale. Convinced her arm was going to fall off or sustain permanent nerve damage, she gripped the side of the gurney and bit her tongue.

The student released the pressure at a snail's pace, raised his eyebrows, and frowned. Unhappy with the results, he pumped the cuff up a second, then a third time.

Barely retaining her magnanimous demeanor, Cat told him it was the slight movement of his eyebrows that caused her systolic and diastolic pressure to shoot up twenty points beyond normal limits. She explained how patients used the nurses and doctors as their barometers, monitoring and interpreting every move, facial expression, tone and inflection of voice.

For instance, she said, did he know that when healthcare professionals whispered to each other in the patient's presence, it translated in the patient's mind to the fact that the patient had cancer or some gross, accidental disfigurement; a show of anger meant that somehow, somewhere, the patient had been incontinent during sleep, or that a horrible mistake had been made and the patient was going to die and the doctor's malpractice insurance was going to go up; bad jokes, raised eyebrows, silence, or forced, meaningless conversation meant death was imminent.

The effects on a patient waking to the sight of a priest at his bedside, said Cat, could very well be fatal.

When the student left, she glanced over to the vacant face of the elderly father-to-be. Focusing her attention on his black wing tips, she replayed snatches of the scene that had taken place in Cross's room.

Something wasn't clear, as if she knew she had forgotten the most important part of a story. It bothered her enough to make her stop thinking about it.

There was a light touch at her shoulder as the concerned face of Gage came into view.

"You okay, Ms. Cat?"

"Sure. I'm okay." *Ready for a nervous breakdown, but okay.*

Visibly relieved, Gage wiped his face with his handkerchief and smiled. "I knew it. You be strong as a mule. Stubborn like one too."

"Well, you've done it again, Gage," she said. "I found trouble behind closed doors."

"You been the one that seen it, girl. You been one that took on the bad an' gave it a fight." Gage appeared uncomfortable, then clasped her hand in a reassuring gesture.

"Oh-oh. What's the problem?"

"It ain't done," he said reluctantly. "This be only the beginnin'. This man, he got a lot of the evil spirit residin' in him."

"What else?"

"The worst part."

Cat's eyes narrowed. "Oh yeah? Like what worst part are you referring to? Give me some clues."

Gage seemed embarrassed. "Ain't no clues right now exceptin' what I already told you. You gotta be on your toes every second. Just know that man ain't done with you, girl."

"That's wonderful news, Gage," she said, watching the man in handcuffs pee into a urinal held by the student nurse. The student had forgotten to draw the curtain, and the whole room seemed to be staring in fascination.

"I know you ain't feelin' good right now, girl, but you gotta still be payin' the most close attention you ever paid in your life."

"Oh God," she groaned. "How am I going to know?"

Two nurses rushed by, shoving the crash cart toward the lobby.

"You just will, sister," Gage said, "I can promise you that."

"Mrs. Gallagher? Stella Gallagher?"

Stella gave the solidly built man standing before her a hard, sour stare. "No more. Uhn-uhn. Not again, good-lookin'. That'll be four times today, and that's too much for this Geritol-enhanced body."

David Padcula adjusted the black-framed glasses. "Sorry, ma'am?"

"No more blood. You fellas have sucked me dry today. Whatcha doing down there, supporting a colony of vampires or something?"

"I'm not here to draw your blood, ma'am. I'm Inspector David Padcula with the Marin County Sheriff's Office, and I'd like to talk to you for a minute if you aren't busy."

Stella regarded the man and his smile for a moment, then chuckled. "Well, I'm pretty busy breathing, but I think I can still listen while I'm doing that."

Inspector Padcula pulled up a wheeled chair that seemed oddly built but sitable. "One of the nurses here told me that you were—"

"The redhead with the feet," Stella said, nodding.

"Ah, right. Nurse Richardson. Did she mention that I was going to try and—"

"Nope."

"Ah, well then, how did you know it was Miss Richardson who told me that—"

" 'Cause she's one of those do-gooder activists. She'd be the only one that would find an old bag worth mentioning to anybody."

Stella motioned for him to wait a moment and adjusted the dial on her hearing aid. "Where was it you said you were from?"

"The Marin County Sheriff's Office. But you see, actually this isn't official or anything, ma'am. I'm just a friend of Miss Richardson's, and—"

"That's too bad."

"Pardon?"

"It's too bad you two are just friends. Judging by the looks of that ball of fire and the smile you got on you, you two should be making sparks instead of friendship cookies." Stella waggled her eyebrows.

David Padcula's pen suddenly began giving him trouble. First he stuck it in his eye when he tried to place it in the crevice over his ear; then it slipped off the back side of his ear and disappeared down inside his shirt collar. When he fished it out, it flew out of his hand and rolled under the bed.

"That device getting out of control on you, son?" Stella asked in a way that reminded him strongly of George Burns without the cigar.

Attempting to hide his smile, he retrieved his pen and sat back down on the chair, which rolled away defiantly, reminding him briefly of his swivel chair. "Ah, well, I'm here because Miss Richardson informed me that you had been unable to locate your grandson, Otis Gallagher the third, for quite a few years?"

"Yes, that's true," Stella said quietly, staring at the glare of his glasses.

"Well, I happen to have access to certain information through our computer system that allows me to, let's say, check federal tax returns and other records that are frequently used to locate missing persons, and I went ahead and—"

"This going to take a long time?" Stella asked, smiling a tight smile.

"No, not at all, I—"

"Good, because I have to use that commode you're sitting on there pretty soon, and I didn't want to be rude and interrupt you in ten minutes when you were getting to the crux of your story."

He looked embarrassed and cleared his throat. "I'm pretty sure I've found your grandson, Mrs. Gallagher."

Stella straightened, her heart pounding. "You found my grandson? Otis Gallagher? You mean you know where he is?"

"Yes ma'am. He's living in Greenville, Arkansas; owns an auto repair shop there. He's married and has four children."

"Oh," she said, making it sound more like a sigh than a word. She looked out the window at the drab overcast sky. I am not alone, she thought. I didn't dream it. My own flesh and blood exists on this earth. Otis Gallagher is a reality. I've got a reason to be here.

The man searched his inside jacket pocket and brought out a slip of paper, which he handed to her with an air of solemnity.

"This is your grandson's address and phone number as of April of last year."

Stella took the piece of paper with a trembling hand and folded it

301

into her pocket without even glancing at it. "Thank you," she whispered. "You don't know what this means to me."

She covered her eyes to think. What was she supposed to do now? All those years she'd dreamed about this moment, and now she could not think of what to do or how to feel.

To see her grandson and look into the eyes of her son and husband, to touch the past after so much time? She thought about the child in the gazebo, and the memory touched off a chain reaction of longing and sorrow. She was grateful when the man finally stood to leave.

"Well, I ah, gotta get back to work. I hope this helps you, Mrs. Gallagher. I know you've had it rough."

Stella looked up at him suspiciously. What did he mean by that? Rough? Had she had it rough? Not all of it. Smooth and rough, she supposed.

She offered her hand. David Padcula took it in his and gave it a gentle squeeze. She noticed that his hand was thick and muscular like the rest of him. Would her grandson have his grandfather's hands? A spontaneous sense of joy flittered through her, settling in her chest.

"Thank you, Mr. Pacula. I wish I could do something to show you how much I appreciate this." In her pocket, she fondled the paper key that would let her into her grandson's life.

"No problem, ma'am." He winked and took a step back. "But if you think of it, you could put in a good word with the redhead for me. And the name's Padcula."

"I'll certainly see what I can do, Mr. Padcula, but I think with that one, the direct approach is the best. Share a little spit with her when she least expects it. That always goes over big."

On the way to the door, the man tripped over his own feet.

"By the way," she said, "you might want to try to calm down a bit before you go for the redhead—they have a tendency to be skittish."

Thanking her, he departed, leaving her alone with Tillie and Virginia and the scrap of paper in her sweater pocket that threatened to change her life.

Cat was daydreaming she was a queen on her pallet watching the grisly events at the Colosseum, slightly removed from the proceedings. The Vicodin was now in full effect so that when Jo Atwood suddenly appeared at her side, it modified her tendency to leap off the gurney and run. Instead, she pulled the sheet over her head.

"Oh, Cat," Jo said, pulling the sheet down. "Are you okay?" She took Cat's hand and held it.

"I'm fine," Cat answered, dismayed at the woman's firm grip.

"You're lucky the psycho didn't kill you both. But . . ." Jo shook her head in a sad, resigned way. "That's men for you. They can be like animals."

Cat bowed her head and squeezed her eyes shut. After a moment, the small, sadistic spot at the back of her brain came alive and she smiled.

"Yes, isn't it the truth though, Jo?"

In mild surprise, Jo studied Cat.

"Yes, Jo, today I've finally seen the light about men and their disgusting habits. Just the thought that I ever let one of them . . ." She hesitated and blushed. ". . . you know, 'do it' to me makes me want to vomit. I'm so ashamed. And now this! God! Sick, sick, sick animals, all of them. It's an outrage to women."

"Why, Catalina," Jo stammered, "I'm . . . I don't know what to say. I mean, I'm sorry about what happened, but I'm glad you've seen the light about . . . everything." She trembled, still holding Cat's hand, and squeezing extra hard.

Suddenly giddy, Jo laughed. "What do you say, Cat? Is this a sign that I can at least hope for the beginning of a . . . how shall I say it? A lasting friendship?"

Cat lowered her eyes.

"Well, Jo, I've seen another, brighter light and . . . and I want you to see it with me." She looked up, her eyes sparkling under long dark auburn lashes.

Jo was breaking her hand.

"Oh, Cat. I'm so happy that you . . ."

"Yes, Jo, I want to share with you . . ."

"Yes, Cat?"

"I want to seek with you . . ."

"Oh, Cat, I'll make you so hap—".

"I want to have you bask in the rich warmth of . . ."

"Yes?"

". . . of the joy of Jesus, Our Lord, and hope that He will make you whole." Cat paused, bit her tongue very hard, directed her gaze to the ceiling, then back at Jo. The woman's face had stopped dead in its expressional tracks and was quickly turning pale.

"What?"

"You must tell me, Jo—and don't be ashamed—have you been saved?"

303

"Well, I don't know," Jo faltered, her expression limping badly. "I mean, religion is fine, but I never really—"

"Oh, Jo, we must bring you back to Jesus, Our Savior. You must be reborn into His gentle love." Cat leaned close to the woman, who was now struggling to get her hands free of Cat's grip.

"I pray He will forgive you your errant ways and guide you back into the fold of bad lambs who have been turned into angels of His bidding," she whispered.

Jo drew back stiffly. "I . . . I really don't know what to say, Cat. I mean, I've never . . . I mean, I'm not an atheist or anything like that, but—"

Cat covered her ears in alarm. "Oh! Please, Jo, don't ever, ever, ever say that word—it makes me want to pray right out loud for your salvation."

Confused, Jo tenderly took Cat's hands away from her ears and stroked the backs of them. "What word? What word offends you?"

"You know," Cat whispered. "The 'A' word."

Jo looked around, then back at Cat. "You mean 'atheist' is a bad word?"

Cat clasped her hands to her breast and bowed her head. "O Lord, forgive the one who has strayed so far, for she knows not what she says." Grasping Jo's hands in hers again, she lifted her eyes slowly in a desperate, pleading stare full of fear for the woman's salvation.

"Tell me the Lord's truth, Jo, do you pray?"

Wide-eyed, Jo looked helplessly around. "Well, I guess that depends on who's driving. I'm not sure I understand . . ."

Raising her eyes to the ceiling again, Cat bellowed, "We shall pray for our sister, Jo. Our Father who art in . . ."

Jo's head swiveled left and right, mortified that most of the staff and patients were either already gaping at, or still in the process of looking for, the raving lunatic.

". . . hallowed be thy . . ."

The assistant director took Cat's hand and patted it. "Ah, Catalina, I think you should try to keep your voice down. You're upsetting—"

Cat raised her voice another decibel, until it cracked. "Thy kingdom come . . ."

"Catalina? Please . . ."

At "Thy will be done," Jo said there was a situation on Ward Twelve that had to be tended to immediately, and left.

When she was gone, Cat held the pillow over her face and roared snorts of laughter.

304

The fold of bad lambs? God, had she really said that? Wiping away the laugh tears, Cat sighed. She was a bad little lamb who more than likely was never going to be taken into any fold in this life or the next.

At 4:25 p.m., almost four hours after being attacked by Michael Lake, Cat, clutching her supply of Vicodin, nimbly stepped out of the way of the high-speed stretcher coming into emergency.

The hydraulic pump on the automatic chest-compression machine was in full swing as its padded arm pushed in the center of the victim's purple chest at eighty beats per minute, which, by coincidence, exactly matched the rhythm of the indistinguishable Muzak tune floating inconspicuously through the air.

A large Iranian family trampled in after the gurney, wailing at the top of their lungs. She couldn't help noticing that when one moved, they all moved, reminding her of Woody Allen and his chain gang buddies in *Take the Money and Run*. They were obviously relatives of the thumper victim, which was too bad. She'd never seen anyone who came in on the machine survive, and for that reason always referred to it as the Automatic Death Pump.

The fact that her coat and purse were still upstairs in her locker meant walking through Ward Two and being assaulted with questions, advice, and even worse, sympathy. She thought of calling Nora on the lobby phone and asking her to bring them down to her, but decided what the hell and headed up the stairs, taking the first and second flights two steps at a time.

She passed several pairs of interesting shoes and ankles. With a certain amount of distaste, she reflected on a pair of white, spiked, four-inch heels, which were overstuffed with hairy, stockingless, edematous dimpled feet.

Obviously misplaced in January, the white shoes incited her to an instant of fury. Where did Californians get off thinking they could wear anything any time of year, as opposed to the East Coasters, who most definitely had narrowly defined winter and summer wardrobes.

Most of her young life had been spent caught up in the struggle of remembering which colors and fabrics went with which months. No one she knew in Boston would have been caught dead (literally) in white shoes or light cotton anything in January. It was sheer sacrilege.

On the landing between flights four and five, she caught sight of a pair of beautiful soft leather Italian loafers, the cuffs of a pair of charcoal wool slacks, and the black leather belly of her purse.

His quiet smile dazzled her and warmed, as her grandmother used to say, the very cockles of her heart. Standing before her, he held her parka and purse in a tenderly awkward way.

In a surge of emotion, she laid her hand on his sleeve, felt the rough wool, and without giving herself time for censorship, made the declaration.

"You are lovely, and I'd like to spend some time with you."

"My thoughts exactly."

She had a strong suspicion she would for the rest of her life remember the moment, the words, and the fact that he did not hesitate.

The duck was taking a beating. The idea made her laugh out loud at midspan of the Golden Gate Bridge.

"What now?" David Padcula asked, grinning like a big, self-satisfied high school kid on graduation night. He checked his rearview mirror and changed from the outside, death lane to the middle, safer lane.

"Just thinking about the duck."

He nodded and laughed. "Have we sufficiently maimed it yet?"

She found it difficult to take her eyes off him, enthralled with the way his face changed every time he moved. Giddy, she kicked off her shoes, not even caring if he noticed how much space they took up, and tucked her feet under her. Raised a few inches, the top of her head pressed firmly against the headliner.

"Okay, so the plan is that you're going to take me to my house and I'll pack an overnight case, then over dinner you want to take a report, then you'll drive me back to Nora's. Right?"

He did not answer her, but looked over his shoulder. "Look," he said, pointing toward the rear window of the ancient, bubble-style Volvo station wagon.

Behind them San Francisco floated majestically on a cloud of fog, looking a lot like a storybook city drifting in the sky above the bay. The Golden Gate Bridge, showing deep orange in the dusk, framed the spectacle.

He shyly touched a strand of her hair. "Do you know that right this second, your hair exactly matches the color of the bridge?"

She shook her head, fascinated by his fascination with her hair.

"Oh, my lady of the bridge, connecting one soul to the next, are you real or are you . . ."

306

She threw out the word "hexed" while he searched for a rhyme.

"Actually," he said, "I was going to say 'flexed.'"

At that, Cat accidentally snorted, which made them both laugh so hard he had to take the Sausalito exit in the name of safety.

"How would you feel if we had dinner now and went to your house later?" he asked.

She experienced a wave of mild perturbation. "You want to eat now? I mean, I'm still in my uniform. I thought I'd change into some normal clothes and we could eat in Mill Valley. Maybe something Italian?"

He hesitated. "Ahhh, yeah, okay."

Cat drew back, ready to leap. "I sense there's something wrong with that picture. Are you hypoglycemic or something?"

"Um, no. It's only that I need a little more time to prepare myself."

"For what?"

"Going to your house."

Cat's stomach flipped. Did he expect he was going to sleep with her? Is that what it was all about for him—just another smooth and easy one-night screw?

She set her jaw. Well, dickhead, you better think again. You had to go and ruin it, didn't you? You almost had me fooled. Well, that teaches me a lesson. I'm never—

"I'm worried." He peeled some skin from around his thumbnail with his teeth.

She stopped the silent tirade. Okay, okay, so he really *sounded* worried. "About what, David? I keep a clean house. Nothing's going to infect you or anything. I mean, you can use the toilet and run the water at the same time if your habits require that sort of thing. What seems to be the problem here?"

He smiled uncertainly. "No, no, no. It's not that, it's that . . . well, it's that I don't know about . . . Well, last night on the phone you told me how you relied heavily on your cat's intuition about people, and I guess I'm a little worried about meeting him. See, most cats are intimidated by my size, and I'm afraid he won't like me."

As the car floated down the hill into Sausalito, Cat stared at the man, his body blocking the dull radiance of the winter sun. The halo around him gleamed soft and gold.

This one was a limited edition, she thought. A real keeper.

Her taste buds were craving Italian; his, Japanese. The Italian restaurant was an hour-and-a-half wait and the Japanese one had a collection of thirty-seven dead bugs littering the front windows. Taking a gander at the bugs, he admitted raw fish was hard on his ulcer.

In the end, they settled for a place she dubbed the Healthier Than Thou Café—half restaurant, half health food store—where the condescending and physically fit waited for unhealthy and acne-ridden souls to come through the front door seeking treats like organic tree sap gum and frozen yogurt from clean cows fed from the farmer's table.

The menu was made up of foodstuffs with names such as wheat grass, spirulina, minted tofu heart, and royal bee jelly—items that to Cat sounded like the products of rare botanical diseases.

Under the disapproving stare of the glowing-with-health, back-to-Eden waitress, their diseased hearts pounded with guilt as they ordered the only nongluten items, tucked way down in the corner of the recycled paper menu: steamed clams and range-fed, organic virgin chicken smothered in bee emesis and fresh herb sauce. Deciding which superprotein drinks to have became a problem, due, in part, to the fact that the waitress's abundance of wavy armpit and head hair competed with the menu for their attention.

When they were served the organic wine, he made a toast to the most beautiful woman with size 12-EEE shoes he'd ever known.

She returned the toast, saying he was the only man she'd ever been out with who, when she looked into his eyes, made her feel as if she were looking into a giant fish-eye lens.

After that, they proceeded to dribble everything they put in their mouths onto their clothes, until his tie looked like a tablecloth at an Italian wedding, and her blouse resembled a Jackson Pollock painting. It was pre-limerance weirdness at its best.

While the melted-butter feeling played with her knees, she tried to keep her thoughts straight enough to answer his questions.

". . . about three minutes total from the time I walked in the room until he entered the elevator," she told him.

"And what was the reason you went into the room? I'm not sure I understood that part."

Forgetting he had traded his fork for his pen, David absently speared a section of lettuce from his salad and ate it off the ballpoint tip.

"Well, I'm not sure either." Cat daintily scooped out a steamed clam with her shellfish fork, slipped, and sent the clam flying across the table.

"Our psychic friend in the lobby has been warning me for days that something was going to happen and to be on my toes. So when I saw that Cross's door was closed, I just got this creepy feeling that she was in trouble."

David pushed his glasses up from the tip of his nose and wrote something in his official notebook. "Would you say it was nurdmal for you to have these kinds of—"

"Nurdmal?" Cat repeated. "Well, yes, I'd say it was nurdmal. I mean, I get the nurdmal amount of ESP stuff, I guess, and this was one of those times."

He laughed, nodded, and bit into his bread, nicking his thumb. "We use psychics in the department once in a while, usually to locate missing persons. I'm not sure I really believe it, but sometimes it actually seems to work."

"What's your middle name?" Changing the subject abruptly was part of her courting style.

He finished chewing and wiped his mouth without incident. "Joseph. What's yours?"

She took a sip from her glass of iced water, watching him over the rim. "Glover."

"Glover? As in 'lover' with a 'Gee whiz'?"

She nodded, went pale, clutched her chest, and let out an ear-piercing shriek. "Oh my God, I remember!"

Confused, he stopped his fork in midflight. The piece of chicken fell off, splashing virgin herb sauce onto his virgin wool sleeve. "You have another middle name?"

"He read my name tag. I knew there was something bugging me. He even said it. He . . . he said he was going to find me."

"Are you listed in the phone book?"

"Oh shit!"

"Including address?"

"Rat balls."

Taking out his notebook again, he wrote something, took in a deep breath, and let it out slowly. "In that case, I strongly advise you to stay with your friend Nora until we find this guy. Of course, I have an old army cot in my closet, but I wouldn't want to do anything that might jeopardize any future relationship I might have with your cat. I mean, we've only just met and I think he's withholding judgment, waiting for me to prove myself."

She beamed. *Any future relationship.* That's what he said.

After dinner they strolled arm in arm to one of the three posh Marin-style coffee shops and bookstore places that lined the street. Tempered by his placid, even nature, she found the mountain water-processed beans, low cal cappuccino (for spilling on Burberry's and the lamb foetus seat covers of XJ6's and Beemers only), enlightened espresso—and the rest of the specialized froufrou meant only for the yuppie designer table with the black place settings—hysterically funny rather than fodder for her usual tirades against the affluent snobbery that inundated the North Bay county.

Ordering two cups of regular decaf at three dollars a shot, she laughed cheerfully at the haughty attitudes of the people behind the counter. The place was too cool to know it was going out of business because of the outrageous overpricing.

They sloppily sipped their fake coffee as they browsed through the bookstore, she concentrating her attention on the metaphysical and biography section, he on the poetry and auto mechanics. After being separated for ten minutes, they met in the philosophy section.

He showed her a line from e. e. cummings; she shared with him the circumstances of Isadora Duncan's death. Neither one of them gave a second glance to the ugly-love books.

Later, at Nora's apartment, Cat waited while he shook the place down, turning on lamps, checking windows and other access routes. Dissatisfied with his inspection, she checked under the bed and pulled open closet doors to make sure no one was waiting on the other side.

When she took off her shoes and stood facing him, he thought she looked beautiful, although she was taller than he had expected.

He didn't dare look down at her feet.

"God," she sighed, eyes dancing, "I sure feel more like I do now than when I got here."

Smiling uncertainly, he thought about the way her mind worked —faster than a bat out of hell soaring over a very fertile left field. Of course, he already suspected she was smarter than God, and not just because she knew Tietze's extension theorem. Everything about the woman was distinctive—the way strands of hair curled out at the temples, then fell down and circled halfway around her neck like the collar of a soft wool coat, and the way she moved, like a sensuous tomboy, and the way she talked, sometimes nonstop, sometimes without saying a word. But it was the laugh and the fire of her that made her different from any woman he had ever known; she was more of everything and tougher than hell.

She was, he realized, going to be a handful, miserable at times to deal with. After his friends met her, they would joke about the old adage, "Never get involved with a woman who has more balls than you do." But it was right, and since it was, he was ready to give his heart to the redheaded and steely-gray-eyed world.

310

He tried to stare into her eyes, but she looked away and bowed her head.

"David?" she said eventually. It was more a statement than a question.

"Yes?" He yearned to kiss her, but didn't want to risk putting her off. She was a woman who would unlock the gate and still be cautious about opening the door.

"David . . ." She was mildly shocked to realize that her body had disappeared but she could still hear her voice. "I was wondering if . . . you would . . ." She felt hot, brushed her hair back from her face, and looked directly into the eyes that made her think of old, soft flannel shirts.

"Mmm?" Amazed at himself, he reached up and let his hand rest on the side of her face. More than anything he wanted to comb his fingers through the red silk. He found he could not steady his breathing.

Instantly she moved into the curve of his body. The fit was perfect, like a two-piece puzzle.

". . . if you would kiss me?"

He kissed her tentatively on the mouth. She leaned more into him, shivering as if she were cold, though the body heat between them was enough to melt the elastic bands of their underwear.

After the first lengthy kiss, they held each other. His chin, his neck, with the Adam's apple she did not have, were all she had to focus on. Something—maybe the sudden downpour or an increase in the amount of free pheromones in the air—was working its magic on both of them, causing feelings to seep out as slow and steady as a snake to a charmer's flute.

When she shut her eyes, she saw herself as a Road Runner–type cartoon character; screeching to a halt at the very precipice of a cliff, then running like mad in the opposite direction.

What was she afraid of? Hadn't she been the one to once tell a bawling, lonely Nora to find the courage to step out onto the floor and take a chance?

"So what if you get your heart broken by some guy who comes along?" she'd said. "At least you can say you've danced."

When they reluctantly tore themselves away from each other, her chin was raw from whisker burn and the bottoms of his glasses were steamed and smudged.

Feeling deeply disturbed in the region of his groin, he walked somewhat painfully to his car. He sat behind the wheel for a full ten minutes sniffing the sleeve of his raincoat where her perfume lingered.

In Nora's bathroom mirror, she examined her face and burst into tears, then hysterical laughter.

Two intelligent, stubborn, fiercely independent, middle-aged people were only slightly aware they had just invited each other to love.

27

7:22 p.m.

The changing of the guard had taken place. Corky wouldn't have noticed except that the one sleeping in the chair at present was overweight and had white hair, while the one sleeping there before had been overweight and bald.

That Inspector Barbequla dude seemed pretty cool, but he needed to get a better grip on the security he was hiring. These losers were okay for maybe a group of two or three really pissed-off nursery school kids, but anything beyond the level of Tammy the carver, let alone a maniac asshole, was definitely going to blow these guys' circuits all to hell.

Cross buried her head deeper into his shoulder, her fingers absently stroking the dark hair on the arm that was going numb from being in one position for so long. Weighing the possibility of losing the use of his arm against the idea of disturbing her, he chose to leave his arm where it was for the time being.

"If only I had been here, I would've killed the asshole," Corky whispered urgently into her hair. "I'd like to find him and kill him. I'd do it too." His mood began to tilt and shift. The roller-coaster cart was ready to head down.

312

"Lucy?" he disengaged himself from her and pressed his fingers into his forehead, trying to rub out the weird feeling taking over his head. "I'll stay with you. I'm going to sleep right here in the chair. We can play cards or you can sketch. Nobody's gonna make me leave this room, not for that bogus group or anything. That jerk is never gonna touch you again."

Cross gingerly prodded the newly bruised part of her neck. "That's right," she said in a strange, hard voice. "He won't because I won't ever let it happen . . . ever again."

He got up and walked to the other side of the room on rubber legs and closed the door. Concentrating on Lucy's face, he tried to stop the unsettling inner voice by imagining what it would be like to kiss her full on the lips, her nose pressed against his few whiskers.

What he really wanted was not to think at all, but the bizarre thoughts were scrambling in his head, getting him closer to the point of no return. He'd seen *Cuckoo's Nest* and enough of the PBS specials on insane asylums to recognize that much.

Alarmed by the change in his appearance, Cross pushed herself into a sitting position. "What's wrong? Are you sick?"

His mouth felt drier than a piece of dead wood. "I'm going nuts—like for real," he whispered. He tried to swallow, realized there was nothing to work with, and ran his tongue over his lips without moistening them.

Tell her now, sucker, or you're gonna die.

"Something bad happened to me. I . . ."

The unrelenting panic choked him. He tried to think of the consequences of telling her what was now forcing its way up and out of him, but the urgency of releasing the sickness took over his every thought.

Frightened by the magnitude of his anxiety, Cross gently coaxed him to sit next to her on the bed. "Everything is going to be fine," she said, searching his eyes. "Please, tell me what happened. Say it and get it over with. You won't die if you tell me, I promise. I won't let you."

He nodded in agreement and pushed back the shock of dark hair that had fallen into his eyes.

Say it now, man! Get it out!

"See, I'm totally losing it because of this thing that happened and I can't live with it, 'cause it's . . ." He started to cry, the intense kind of masculine weeping that always sounded so catastrophic. He wanted to hide, but if he moved away from her, there was no telling what would happen.

313

"... it's the worst thing ..." He stiffened again under the siege of another, stronger wave of panic and dug his fingers into his thigh. There was no pain, no feeling in his leg, as if his body were not his.

She's the only one. The only one. Say it now!

"I ... In October ..." He paused and tried to calm himself by taking little gulps of air.

She's the only one.

Under her hand, Corky's arm was cool and clammy. "Relax," she said, rubbing his arm as if to bring it to warmth. "Take a minute to calm down."

He took a deep breath, held it for a moment, let it out and began again, pronouncing his words precisely, as if even he were unsure of what was coming next.

"Last October, on Halloween, there was a costume party at this house in the neighborhood. The dude who lives there is a superjock type, you know—I mean, like he goes to a gym every night to work out and plays football with the guys on weekends and all that jock-type shit. Me and some of the other guys used to shoot hoop with him out in his driveway, and once in a while he'd treat a bunch of us to a Forty-niner game, or take us camping up at Yosemite.

"Anyway, he's got the whole package—drives this hot little Mercedes 450SL convertible, and has these totally awesome-looking girls coming in and out of there constantly like Grand Central Station, right? I mean, he seemed sorta cool, like everybody thought he was a totally radical dude."

Corky rose suddenly from the bed. "Oh man, I cannot be-fucking-lieve I am actually saying this out loud. I mean, I don't even let myself *think* about this."

Outside the door, a bell sounded. He startled, and in the same quiet fashion as before, Cross pulled him back to the bed. "Look at me, Corky. It helps to tell somebody. Tell me."

He put his hands to his temples and rocked back and forth slowly. "Okay. Okay. So me and my parents dress up like the Three Stooges and go across the street to this asshole's party. He's dressed up as a clown, which is perfect, and there's this big old keg of beer, and everybody is drinking and dancing and the music is cranked to the max, but all the neighbors are there, so there isn't anybody to complain. Then, like when the party is at total hyperspeed level, he asks me to help him with a new keg that he has stashed in the toolshed."

Lapsing into silence, Corky hugged himself and walked to the window.

Don't stop. Almost there. Almost.

For a moment he ignored the inner voice and watched the rain. He thought about when he was eight years old and had walked to the end of a high diving board for the first time. For one hour and thirty-five minutes, no one was able to talk him into moving off the end of the board one way or the other.

Somewhere, on the other side of the wall, a man laughed. *Go on, go on. Can't go back now.*

"And I said sure, no problem. The shed was way in the back about a hundred yards from the house. It's one of these real fancy sheds, you know, with a workshop and a place for a boat and all the garden stuff? So he goes into this closet-type room with the garden stuff, and I remember hoping he was finding a wheelbarrow in there, except pretty soon he comes out holding the clown suit in his hands and he's all naked except for the white face with the red mouth and the rubber nose.

"Right up front I thought it was a little weird, but I figured he was loaded and fooling around, so I started cracking up, and then he says he can't pull the keg out by himself because he's too drunk and he doesn't want to get a hernia or anything on account of some big basketball playoffs he's supposed to play in."

Corky stopped, absorbed by the scene racing through his mind. He had the idea of opening the window and jumping out.

You're there. Get it over.

His voice now sounded unfamiliar to him, as if it were somebody else telling her the nightmare. "And when I was lifting up the keg . . . then he started, you know, like fooling around wrestling with me, and then he got me pinned. The motherfucker was, like awesomely strong, and then he . . . he . . . ."

Corky looked at her, unable to swallow, feeling as if he were in a dream far away. ". . . and then he, you know, he like . . . he . . . raped me."

The room went to an electric silence, which was broken by his weeping.

When he spoke again, it was a horrible sound: rushed, half crying, half screaming. "I was such a fucking idiot, man! I mean, I didn't even know what was happening at first. Then when I realized what was going on, I went nuts trying to get the son of a bitch offa me. I wanted to kill the bastard, but he outweighed me by about ninety pounds and I couldn't get away.

"Since it happened, like, I've been trying to think of ways to kill the son of a bitch. At first I wanted to beat the motherfucker to death with my bare hands; then I was going to burn his house down or cut

315

the brakes on his car, but I figured in the end I'd get caught and then everybody would find out what happened."

Arms hanging limply at his sides, the boy looked at her as if he expected her to run out of the room in horror. "Don't hate me, Lucy. God, please don't hate me—you're all I've got."

Not knowing what else to do, she folded him into her, pressing him to her aching breasts and stroking his head as she would a child's. "I don't hate you, Corky. I couldn't hate you, ever. You didn't want that to happen. It wasn't your fault. You couldn't stop it."

She waited for him to speak, but he continued rocking in silence, hugging her.

"That man is sick. . . . Don't you see it? He hurt you in the same way Michael hurt me. He . . ."

Cross held him away and carefully wiped away his tears with the hem of the sheet. He made no move. He did not speak.

"It's not your fault. . . . It's not your fault. It's them, not us."

Something changed in his face. Gripping her like a life preserver, Corky climbed onto the bed, weeping helplessly.

Locked together, they rocked themselves to sleep.

8:10 p.m.

Sometimes there was an advantage to being a decrepit little old lady, Stella decided, especially if you enjoyed sleeping or hearing lurid gossip. If you were old enough, you were welcome to sleep twenty-four hours a day without question, or, if you wanted to, it was easy to horn right in on the most confidential of conversations without anyone giving it a second thought.

None of the nurses seemed to care that she parked her wheelchair right in the middle of their station and listened to the intimate and barbarous details of what happened to the pretty young girl down the hall. After all, she was too old to really understand the scandal, wasn't she? And besides, who would *she* tell anyway?

But she did understand and it depressed her. Why, Stella wondered, did the world have to be so vicious? Was no place safe? The thought momentarily roused memories of the world as it was in her childhood, when the sky was clear, and peace and quiet could easily be had at any given moment.

She didn't belong in the here and now. She belonged to another, earlier time. And oh, that poor, poor young woman. If only the world could have the old times back, when—

316

Pfffft! Who was she kidding, thinking like some pristine, white-bunned grandmother? It had always been a savage world; that was nothing new, especially in her life.

Using the aluminum walker, Stella hobbled at her old lady's pace to the sink and splashed cool water on her face. From the mirror, two watery, blue, almond-shaped eyes stared into her.

"You know us," they said. "We're the same eyes that watched your precious Otis with that other one on the night your son was conceived. We are the same eyes that beheld the disfigured bodies and faces of the two people you loved most, watched the life drain from them, death defying you to interfere."

Stella sneered scornfully at her mirrored image. "Well, what are you waiting for, Mr. Thief?" she said out loud, "Come on, let's have it! Playing hide-and-seek now, are we?"

Tillie glanced over at her and waved. "I haven't got it, Mama," she cried out. "The French girls took them all away."

Ignoring her, Stella moved slowly to the window and sat purposefully facing the subsiding rain. "Okay, Mr. Thief, you're on." She closed her eyes, freely inviting the bad picture, directing her memory to re-create the dark wine holes and the dank smell of drying blood.

But instead, she found herself catching handfuls of warm October wind, her nose delighting in the smells of berry and peach jam while the sun made diamonds from the tiny beads of sweat on her grandson's skin.

From inside the red-and-white-striped circus tent, the big band played children's tunes with a swing beat as grown-ups and children alike ate white frosted cake and scrutinized, with some trepidation, the camel serenely grazing on the lawn behind the seven-thousand-square-foot stone castle in Oakland modestly known as Gallagher Manor.

Servants in their bright attire ran from glass to glass pouring champagne or ginger ale and cleaned away bowls of swirled ice cream soup. It was the best, most successful party she and Otis had given that season, despite the disturbance at the front gates when the men in the black Ford got rough with the gatekeeper and demanded to be let in.

She smiled at the memory of how bravely Otis had handled the unpleasant situation. With a confident and sure step, he'd walked down to speak with them, although she did notice he unconsciously twisted his hands around one another. He'd made her wait at a distance, so when the four olive-skinned men got out of the car, she

317

could not distinguish their features. She did see however, that one of them, the one who hung back from the rest, carried a machine gun.

The one who was the leader wore a cream-colored suit and a Panama hat. He did most of the talking, dramatically gesturing with his dark, stubby hands yet mindful enough of her presence to speak in a low voice and tilt his head so the brim of his hat cut off the possibility of her reading his lips.

She recalled thinking at the time that the man appeared angry. Stella clucked her tongue and bit the inside of her cheek. Yes, he'd been angry, but he hadn't seemed angry enough for the revenge he had already decided to take on all of them.

When they strolled back to the party, Otis had been strangely quiet, all traces of his previous lightheartedness gone. She didn't dare ask what the dark men wanted; Otis had always insisted his business dealings were none of her concern.

Stella rested her head against the cold surface of the window, remembering the rest of that day, when their only grandchild blew out the three candles on his cake and Otis cried into her hair and whispered that he was sorry for cheating her out of a full life.

His distress had alarmed her. Thirty years after the fact she still worried he would find out about the lover she'd taken in Paris after Otis junior's birth. In her pain, she had not bothered to be discreet. She'd wanted him to discover the affair, hoping then to wound and perhaps jolt him into coming to reclaim her the way he had in London. But the breakout of World War I destroyed that possibility and forced them to return home. Starting over as the respectable, happy family, they were buoyed and protected by wealth and people's ignorance of the way they had lived in Paris. In still-neutral America, Otis grew richer and more remote, while Stella preoccupied herself with their son and the tasks of starting and leading community women's groups. . . .

After the men dismantled the big tent and the camel was led away, Otis had said something that meant little to her at the time, though later she would have to repeat it over and over—writing it down a half-dozen times until the police were satisfied: "I've cut them off, Stel. The bloodsuckers will have to find another warm corpse to drain. We're free of them now and no one can harm any of us ever again."

But of course, they did. Otis perpetually lived in a world of make-believe where one could play at high-risk games and never be injured. He hadn't realized you couldn't get rid of a nest of rats simply by making noise. And how could he? He'd never lived in poverty, so he wouldn't have known that rats bite when riled.

The worst of it was that they'd taken her son, too. Had Otis been so afraid that he thought the presence of innocence would protect him?

Stella shrugged and went to her bed. Ah, questions for the wind.

Tillie banged on her side rail with a spoon she'd filched from the lunch tray and hidden under her pillow. "I really didn't take it, Mama. Cross my heart and hope to die. It was the terrible French girls, Mama."

Smoothing back her hair, Stella searched the pocket of her flannel robe and found a hairpin, which she clumsily slid into her bun and patted it down.

The slip of paper with the phone number and address written in a very small hand lay on her bedside table.

Tomorrow, she decided

Tonight she would rest. Tonight she would be still, rummage around within and dust off a couple of memories.

10:34 p.m.

Gage felt the boy's release, and lay back on his bed to relax.

Closing his eyes, he listened to the high-pitched *hissssss* of tires parting rain puddles in the streets. For a brief moment, a penetrating wave of warmth went over his belly and groin. He smiled knowingly.

Yes, well. The woman was in love. That was good because it opened her, made her more receptive to the powers she normally shunned. As long as the loving did not distract her too much. In the area of romance, she tended to be high-strung and likely to lose her head over such things, though this man would keep her balanced. Spiritually, it was a suitable match for them both. Fire and water.

Tom Mix stirred and the air suddenly filled with the pungent scent of hatred.

There was an acceleration of space and time, and when the bitter taste flooding his mouth had passed, Gage was drawn to a dark spirit sleeping fitfully in a room of windows. The smell of a weapon close by made him uneasy. The black hatred that had been festering inside the wretched soul for years now ruled, and the decision to kill had been made.

He could have easily reached through the planes and inflicted great harm upon the man, for there was sometimes only a thin line dividing good and evil: the first lesson of the high priests.

319

Tempting himself, Gage spread out his hand over the man's head. From within the core of his soul, the power moved and twisted, taking force, changing. Fate was in his hands, seducing him to destroy. He could do it swiftly, effortlessly, better than man's weapons.

He faltered, and a dream took hold of him so quickly he could not gauge how far into the spirit he had gone. In the vision, his grandmother sat under the shade tree in the front yard skinning and halving peaches for the bubbling jam pot. Listlessly she removed a clean white linen handkerchief from the pocket of her faded lilac apron and wiped the moisture from between the rolls of fat hiding her neck. From another pocket, she pulled out two pieces of sweet divinity, ate one herself, and popped the other into his mouth.

"Child," she said in her low, steady voice, "always be keepin' youself on the outside of the power. It be fine if'n you work it wit' other folks, but you cain't never work it wit' you ownself. If you be tryin' to do that, it gonna turn on you, boy. An' if'n it turn to the dark side, it gonna be wantin' to grab you up and smite you down 'cause you been workin' for the Lord, an' honey, there ain't nothin' worse'n that to the Dark One."

She split another peach, dropped it into the pot, and pulled out two more pieces of divinity.

"You be sure'n keep clear of it as you be of a snake by the river. The power be a two-faced snake—it can be lickin' you, 'n' faster 'n you can say peach jam, it turn to bite you in the heart 'n' spread its poison afore you even knowed it bit you."

Wide-eyed, Gage quickly said "Peach jam" four times, making the old woman jiggle all over with her easy, wheezing laughter.

The laughter echoed loudly in his ears as a cold wind delivered him back to the side of the sleeping man. His head swam and he was aware of an ominous warmth in his throat, when the sudden anxious presence of Delia made him draw back. For an instant, he had half an idea that the power was testing him.

He moved forward to touch the cloth of the man's shirt. There was so much hatred, it threatened to choke him. Delia warned him to break the contact, but he barely heard her. With the deftness of a master magician, he reached out for the cold handle of the knife.

11:02 p.m.

By the third ring, Cat was swearing. "Where the hell did you put your damned phone, Nora?"

Fourth ring.

"The beer can," Nora yelled from the shower.

320

"What? I said, where's the phone?"

Fifth ring.

"The can. It's new. The tall can of beer right there on the desk, for Christ's sake!"

"I still don't get it, Nora." Cat's tone had a warning edge. "I want the *phone*. Where the goddamned hell is the goddamned phone!"

Sixth ring—the one people usually hang up on.

Nora turned off the shower and jerked back the curtains. "I said the beer can! The phone *is* the beer can! For crying out loud, pick it up and talk!"

Cat picked up the plastic replica of a can of Budweiser, tentatively put it to her ear, and said, "Hello?" From the end that read "Anheuser Busch, Inc." came the smooth voice of David Padcula.

"Hi. Just called to see if you were okay, Red."

She smiled and melted onto the desk chair. "I'm fine—speaking to you through a Budweiser can right now, but otherwise I can't complain."

"You need anything?"

Yes, you. "No, I don't think I need anything right at the moment, but thank you." Searching for something on which to doodle, Cat opened the desk drawer and took out a notepad on the top sheet of which was written: "Eyebrows at drugstore, bloto fruckspin x 2, bridge down, Hickey-Freedman suit, catechols?"

Quietly she closed the drawer and watched Nora, clad only in wet hair and a set of earphones, dance the cha-cha through the living room while sipping from a glass of champagne.

"Is Nora home yet?"

Cat nodded. "Definitely. Nora is home in full color, yes."

"Would you like to have dinner tomorrow night?"

"Yes, absolutely." Letting her head fall back, she saw a starlit sky but no ceiling.

"Listen, Red, I have to ask you this one more time. . . ."

"Umm?" She smiled, not believing her luck that this particular man had walked out of the dark and stormy night and into her life.

"Do you think your cat *really* liked me, or was he just being polite?"

After the second ring, Cat's answering machine clicked into action.

"Hi, this is Cat. If you're calling to leave good news or money, press one. If you are calling as a purveyor of gloom and doom, press two. If you're calling to leave a message of a mundane nature, press three-three-three-one. Now enter your Social Security number, divide by your date of birth, and multiply by your mother's maiden name. Thank you."

She waited until the irritating tone blew out her eardrum and left a goodnight message for Saphenous. Immediately after hanging up, she called again to retrieve her messages.

Someone had called but, instead of leaving a message, had breathed a few times into the receiver and hung up. Replaying the message a second and third time, Cat detected a whooshy background noise, like taffeta skirts made when rustled. The fourth time, she heard a faint disgruntled groan an instant before the connection was broken.

The call was definitely from a man, was not long-distance, and had been made from indoors.

She decided not to tell Nora—no sense in both of them being freaked. By the time Nora turned off the light and slipped under the covers, Cat was calm enough to sound cheerful.

"Well, tell me, how was Pavarotti and Norman the gangbanger of phallic-locomotor-symbol fame?"

The half-full water bed undulated as muffled waves betrayed every movement of its inhabitants. In the dark, Cat could barely make out the scratchy gray outline of Nora propping herself on her elbow. A faint odor of Pond's cold cream hung in the air.

"Very nice." The blonde brushed imperceptible wrinkles out of the thick down quilt between them. "I mean, he's different. Actually, I made love with him."

Nora's sheepish tone was probably, Cat thought later, due to the fact that she did not want to launch them into the same debate they'd been having for five years—her promiscuity versus Cat's born-again, strait-laced morality.

Before she could stop herself, Cat sighed the predictably huge, disapproving, disappointed sigh. "Oh, Nora. How *could* you?"

Nora followed the recipe by getting defensive. "I *wanted* to make love. I don't know—it seemed so much easier than making up excuses and false pretenses."

"That's my electric friend Nora," Cat said angrily, "always taking the path of least resistance."

"Hey! It feels good. It relaxes me. I *like* getting laid as much as the next guy." Nora now brushed the quilt furiously, as if the material were a breeding ground for mosquitoes. "And to be perfectly honest, if it weren't for some nosy, abstemious old bag lady and an untimely shortage of condoms, we'd still be in Grace Cathedral wildly getting it on."

Cat raised both her eyebrows and her voice. "I see. You did *it* in Grace Cathedral?"

"Calm down. It was the farthest away, most secluded pew in the whole damned place. I mean, it was behind a pillar, for Christ's sake!"

"Was the organ playing?"

"No, but it was being played—loudly, I might add." Nora sat up and tensed her shoulders, ready for the usual onslaught of puritanical drivel.

"God! how can you do that?" Cat fumed right on cue. "A Californicatrix—giving yourself away on the first date to every dick you meet? It drives me nuts. I mean, what's the meaning in lovemaking for you anymore? Where's your pride? Didn't anybody ever tell you that men will screw anything eight to eighty and not over three days dead?

"Don't you know that you ruin it for other women who want a relationship with these men? It's called sport fucking, in case you haven't heard that lovely term before. Guys get their rocks off without ever having to make a commitment. Then they go around thinking, 'Well hell, why should I bother having only one woman, and work through all the hassles of a relationship, when I can have it anytime I want with women like this?' "

Nora hung her head and was silent. Cat hated herself for lecturing, but she rationalized that she loved Nora and didn't want her to be unhappy. Except when she really stopped to think about it, Nora wasn't unhappy at all.

Was she jealous? In her heart of hearts, did she wish she could be as carefree and sexually unfettered as she once had been during the sixties and seventies? Maybe she was jealous that Nora had always had the ability to hold back just enough to protect herself from getting hurt. Cat had to give it to her; the woman knew how to sail through relationships without geting a scrape, but then again, Nora wasn't into commitment either.

Still, she could not put a cap on the negative feelings.

"*Why*, Nora? Why not be with some*one*, not a lot of some*bodies*? Why not keep it special? I mean, what kind of quality goes into relationships that are simply life-support systems for sex? God, you spend so much of your time getting laid I can't believe you haven't caught chest hair." In her own ragging voice, Cat heard the echo of her mother's whiny, one-pitch-above-normal ravings and leaned back against the headboard feeling miserable.

"First of all," Nora began, trying her best to keep the injury out of

323

her voice, "chest hair isn't contagious. Second of all, most men aren't so barbaric or stupid as to think that sport fucking replaces loving relationships, and I don't apply that disgusting term to myself.

"You paint me as having this cavalier attitude about sex, and I don't. Making love *is* special to me, Cat. Every lover I have is different; each one has a different touch or laugh or heart. I love men in that way. . . . They fascinate me. Their masculinity captivates me.

"And if the truth be known, Cat, I could make love twenty-four hours a day, seven days a week. I mean, it's not as if I get into the kinky stuff, like ben wah balls and nipple tethers, but it's totally thrilling to me. Making love is like nothing else in the world—it's unique unto itself."

Her eyes having adjusted to the dark, Cat focused in on the intensity of Nora's expression and laughed, despite the odd collection of frustration, jealousy, righteousness, and misery all sitting in her stomach like a bunch of lead ball bearings.

"Nipple tethers?"

Nora giggled. "It's true, you know—I've never had anything not real in me, but sometimes I can't believe some of the real things that have been in this body." She shivered, hugged herself, and squealed, falling back onto the bed. The waves sent Cat rolling from side to side.

"Okay," Cat said on a decidedly lighter note. "So you like Norman. But is he good for you? I mean, he's not a jerk, is he? He's not going to hurt you or anything?"

"What, are you my mother or something? I mean, give me a break, Cat. This is not going to be the father of my children. I'm enjoying him, not spending my life with him."

Nora was back on her elbow and slithering closer until she was in Cat's face. *"You* are the perverted one, my love. How the hell can a woman like you be celibate for four years? Now *that's* insane, not to mention radically abnormal. Don't you miss it? Don't you sometimes *ache* for it? I mean, it is a basic human need, you know. What do you do with that energy?"

"I sublimate, I guess—work and dancing, running, stuff like that. There's a lot to do out there, you know, besides screw: art, reading, sports . . ." Cat trailed off, aware that she sounded unconvincing.

"Some people consider lovemaking an art form as well as a sport," Nora said sweetly.

Covering Nora's face with a pillow, Cat held it until she screamed uncle. When they were settled again, Nora reached over and gave Cat's braid a gentle tug. "So?"

"So what?"

"How's Smiley Cop?"

Cat carefully weighed the various replies she could make against Nora's reactions and chose a low- to mid-key answer.

"I . . . I like him very much. He's nice. He's a lovely, gentle man, actually."

They fell quiet for a few seconds, after which there was a squall of choppy waves as Nora scrambled out of bed and stumbled over the frame. Without warning, she switched on the light.

"He's the one, isn't he, Cat?" she said, leaping onto the bed to fix her squinting friend with an up-close, intense stare. Cat blinked, trying to get Nora's face in focus.

Nora sat back on her haunches, dreamy-eyed. "I feel it. This is the one you're going to grow old with. You've been this huge, loving heart just waiting to leak all over somebody. I can see it in your face —you're a lovesucked puppy."

Cat rolled her eyes and covered her own mouth with the pillow, muffling screams of "Save me! Save me! Psychic on the loose!"

Nora knelt next to her. "God, I'm so happy for you, Cat. I was afraid you'd never love anybody again."

"Yours," said Cat, "is the working of a sick and deformed mind."

Flipping the light off again, Nora flopped back on the bed, sending the mattress into contractions. They were staring absently at the ceiling, when Nora tenderly touched Cat's hand.

"Cat?"

"Uhn?"

"Are you okay? I mean with what happened today. You haven't said a word about it since the emergency room."

Phantoms of the scene came to mind: the man hurting Cross, then the touch of his hand on her breasts and his breath in her face, and finally, the hang-up on her machine. "It's right there on the top of the heap, Nor, I just don't want to deal with it tonight." She gave Nora's hand a squeeze. "You know me—I need to sort it out by myself first, then bounce the results off you." And besides, she thought, there's this man that I'm half in love with and I'd rather concentrate on him.

"And what about you, Nor? I mean, here you are pushing all this lifetime-warranty-marriage shit at me, and I don't see *you* settling down. Cripe, talk about perverted? Here we have one Nora Carmotti, insanely involved with an extremely married man from the age of twenty-two to thirty-one, then, after being rudely dumped, pushing on to become a raving, promiscuous sex goddess making up for lost time."

"Oh, can it, Cat. I'm telling you something's coming for me," Nora

325

said. "I feel it, and I know for damned sure it's better than any coming I've ever had before."

"Ah yes, Cat said dryly, I quite understand."

Nora laughed and jumped to her knees again. "No. No. Listen. You know how Gage gets those sights of his? Well, I started getting this feeling about a few days ago when I was reading this article about an organization called Friends of the Turkeys and how two weeks before Thanksgiving, they turned loose thousands of turkeys from seventeen different turkey farms all over the country?

"Well, I read the article and got this feeling that something huge was going to happen to me . . . I mean, something life-changing."

Cat stared blankly at her friend through the dark. "Do you have any idea what the hell you're talking about?"

"Well, yes. What I mean is, I know how those turkeys must have felt when they were set free, and they probably realized right away that, hey, this is something really different, this freedom thing, and it's going to change my life to be out of this cage, and they probably all ran for the hills, knowing there was another, better life outside the confines of—"

"Nora?' Cat said, patronizing and sweet. "You didn't take your Thorazine this morning, did you, dear?"

"No really, Cat, I'm serious about this."

"Are you trying to lead me to believe that turkeys, with brains the size of an ant's ass, are capable of thinking all that stuff?"

"Well, of course, not exactly in human words or anything, but yes, I think they fully realized the implications of freedom and many of them probably had some premonition that their lives were about to be changed in some way as those people were cutting open the gates in the middle of the night." Nora's expression was Berkeley Campus Righteous Indignation circa 1968.

Cat closed her eyes, glad to know she was not the only one from another planet. "That's it."

"What's it?"

"This is the reason I love you."

"You love me because of the turkeys?"

"Yes, exactly. I love you because of the turkeys and because in 1981 you told me you were going to make a million dollars by collecting all the bright-colored hippie clothes from the sixties and giving them to old ladies in convalescent homes so they could make them into dazzling braided rag rugs. And last but not least, in 1977 you protested zucchini and onion abuse at Veg-O-Matic demonstrations.

"What three better reasons could one have?"

. . .

Later, one small toe and one not-so-small toe barely touching, they listened to sheets of hard rain spray against the windows. The sound had lulled them to the edge of sleep, when Cat snapped awake in alarm. "Nora?"

"Mmm?"

Cat leaned over to see if Nora was awake or talking in her sleep. Her long blonde hair was spread fanwise over the pillow, her eyes were closed.

"Nora, you know the red toothbrush on the back of the sink?"

For a full thirty seconds, there was a deep, thoughtful hush, then a slightly suspicious, fully awake "Yeah?"

"What do you use it for?"

After another, weightier silence, Nora lifted herself on her elbow. A small, lopsided grin made the white of her teeth barely visible through the dark. "I douse it with scouring powder and Clorox and use it to scrub under the rim and around the base of the toilet. Why do you ask?" Nora's small grin went from lopsided to widely perverse.

Cat's stomach spasmed and retreated into its darkest, deepest cave. "Oh, no reason." Without her really wanting it to, her tongue, that mischievous sleuth with a mind of its own, apprehensively explored the smooth surfaces of her teeth, searching out the loathsome, like a foreign pubic hair or (she gagged a little) a crust of some exotic bathroom soil.

A few moments later, Nora sighed and lay back down. "Listen, Catalina, if you haven't dropped dead by now, nothing's gonna kill you."

Friday

28

5:20 a.m.

Benny Newmann was on the midnight to six a.m. shift. It was a comfort to see his friend sitting vigilantly by his side, reading Marvel Comics or sorting out baseball cards and debating with himself as to whether he should trade his mint condition Willie Mays for Billy Thorpe's one-corner-wrinkled Mickey Mantle. It would be an extremely wise investment, Walker thought. A real steal.

Benny smiled broadly under the rim of the New York Giants cap, showing off his braces. Walker was mildly surprised to see the mouth floating close to Benny, contentedly chewing the remains of an old baseball glove.

"Hey bud, how's by you?" Benny asked.

Walker nodded. "Where's Zoe?"

"Home, asleep. Where else would a kid be at this time of the night?"

Walker threw a suspicious glance at the red mouth.

Benny placed an arm around the fanged orifice and shook his head. "Nah, this monstrosity ain't after your little girl, Petey. This thing belongs entirely to you, born the first time your mother didn't come running to change your nappy or stick a teat in your mouth. This is the thing that kicks your ass to make you think."

331

The mouth spit out a metal snap and smiled. "Yep," it said, or something close to it.

"So, if it's here to make me think, then why's it got to act so scary?"

"The best things in life ain't given away for free, pal," Benny said matter-of-factly. "There's gotta be something to get your brain moving: fear, pain, love . . . it's all the same."

"Listen, Benny, I'm still having a hell of a time figuring out who I am or what I was doing here." Walker tore his eyes from the mouth, which was slurping up the last bit of leather lace like a strand of spaghetti. "See, I'm dying and I can't rest until I know . . ."

A powerful flashlight beam momentarily blinded Walker. Two nurses, one blonde and heavyset, the other dark and small-boned, stared closely at his face. The portly one smelled of cheap perfume and cigarettes. The petite one set her fingers on his neck, feeling for something.

"Wanna make a bet on the time he goes?" asked the husky nurse.

The delicate nurse, who Walker thought might be Filipino, caught a bead of his sweat on her finger and sniffed it thoughtfully. "Seven a.m. change of shift," she replied blandly. "What are we betting?"

The big nurse mashed his earlobes, then opened his mouth and pulled out his tongue, which she took a long time to examine. "Ah, I'd say it'll be closer to noon meds. Betcha dinner at the Silver Moon or ten bucks flat out."

"Make it dinner," said the Filipino nurse. They shook hands and went away.

Walker looked mournfully at Benny. "I've got to find out who I am."

"You already know," said Benny and the mouth.

Confused, Walker stared at his friend. "I do?"

Benny Newmann nodded knowingly and pointed to the ceiling. Floating above Walker were clusters of people he knew; relatives, teachers, friends and neighbors, Lars his mechanic, Suzanne the secretary, the down-and-outers. In front were Joyce and the boys. Zoe stood off to the side, blowing kisses.

"Read it in their eyes, Walker," Benny shouted, now standing on the deck of a new forty-foot Mason. "That's your answer."

5:21 a.m.

Zoe awakened from her bad dream with the feeling that time had stopped. Tamis, the Cabbage Patch doll, sat happily in the corner of her own little crib keeping a watchful eye over Nita, the black Barbie doll, and Sam, the bear with the patches of bare cloth showing

332

through in the places where, her mother told her, she had sucked the fur away when she was a baby.

Wiping the sleep winkies from her eyes, Zoe thought about her dream, in which she had walked into her father's room and found the bed empty. The sheets were messy and wet, and there was a funny smell, like when she threw her mother's best wool sweater in the fireplace because her brothers told her she would be able to hear the sheep bleat while it burned.

All during the dream, her father kept calling her, but no matter how hard she tried to find him, he remained hidden.

With a sense of urgency, she crawled out of bed and dressed. Relying on the double pack of spearmint gum hidden safely in the secret pocket of her pink parka, she decided she would not take the time to eat breakfast or brush her teeth, so that when her mother called her in the morning, she would be ready to go.

Sneakers and parka in hand, she tiptoed noiselessly out to the landing at the top of the stairs, settling down on the only step that didn't creak, and leaned her head against the banister.

One hour later, Zoe was staring bleary-eyed at the electric pendulum of the fruitwood grandfather clock, when the hospital rang to say they all needed to come in to say goodbye.

Corky lay transfixed in his half-awake, half-asleep dream. In the center of the high school cafeteria, under the spotlight's dazzling glare, a lion cautiously circled the center dining table, aiming a lackadaisical swipe at him each time he cracked the whip over the animal's head. Next to the feline, the beautiful Lucy, attired in a sparkling tutu, effortlessly balanced a five-hundred-pound barbell on her shoulders while Tammy, the exotic snake charmer, sat inside one of the bun steamers coaxing her carving scars to rise up like small snakes and sing old Huey Lewis and The News tunes.

Hovering precariously overhead, a tightrope walker alarmed the students by pretending to lose his balance. Corky could tell by the way the girls screamed and hid their eyes the dude was impressing the hell out of everyone. Even Coach Henny stood mesmerized.

Like an enormous snake, the guide rope wound around Corky, pinning his arms and pulling him steadily up toward the platform, where the figure of the high-wire artist became visible to him in sections: white-stockinged feet tucked into black dance slippers, bright, multicolored balloon pants, red-gloved hands, large red puffball buttons, white ruffled collar, and finally, the red rubber nose set above the repulsive red smile.

333

At the sight, a newer, heavier version of the old panic began in his temples. Why was this happening now? Hadn't he killed the clown in his last circus nightmare?

The red-gloved hand was reaching out to claim him, when Molly Connover flew by on a trapeze and grabbed the back of his shirt. Swiftly the snake released its hold.

He nestled his head on Molly's breasts feeling momentarily saved, until he glanced below and saw Lucy battering the center pole of the platform with her barbell.

The clown teetered. Seizing his chance, Corky swung out on his own trapeze as the band began a thunderous drumroll.

With all his strength, he kicked out and caught the clown in the midsection. The figure fell like a rag doll from a window, its screams almost obscured by the drumroll.

At the clash of the cymbals, Corky exploded with a sense of relief. The finale. Once again he had escaped the worst of all atrocities. Thank God it was over.

"Corky?"

Still swinging, he watched the cafeteria crowd race to where the fallen clown lay crumpled, its arms and legs akimbo. Surrounding the figure, the crowd turned to one another in horror. For a fearful moment, he sensed their confusion, and then heard the whispers that began among them.

What had he done? Why had Corky Benner killed the clown?

The adrenaline rush sent him into another panic. He had to get down and bury the body before anyone guessed what the real story was, or . . . Shit, what if the corpse suddenly revived long enough to tell them everything and ruin his reputation? Clowns were notorious big mouths.

"Corky!"

Molly called to him from her trapeze.

"Pssst. Corky, wake up and help me to the bathroom."

"Can't now, Molly. I've got to bury this jerk before he wakes up."

"What?"

"The clown. I've got to—"

"Corky, you're dreaming. Wake up."

Opening his eyes, he perceived Lucy leaning over him. The beauty of her made him smile, wondering in the murky, preawake state what in the hell he was doing waking up with Lucy. Whatever the reason, it was probably one of the most awesome experiences of his life.

"I can't believe they let you stay in here all night," she said.

"What time is it?"

They both glanced at the bedside clock radio from which faint strains of the tail end of Huey Lewis's "The Power of Love" could barely be heard. It was 6:47 a.m.

Struggling briefly to get out of the overstuffed chair, he dutifully helped her on with her slippers. Together, they shuffled to the bathroom.

At the door, she let go of his arm. "You have to go back to your room now. Get a few hours' sleep, and after breakfast you can come back and we'll have a game of gin and talk some more, okay?"

"Uhn-uh. I'm not leaving you. I have to get you back to bed and besides, I told you I'm—"

"Nope. You've got to. . . . The daytime guard comes on in a few minutes. I can make it back to bed on my own, don't worry." Cross turned him around and gently pushed him toward the door. "I'll be okay. Michael never, ever gets up before ten.

"You need some proper rest. Come back after breakfast—that's only three hours from now." She kissed him on the cheek, felt the peach fuzz, and stepped back into the bathroom. "Go on. I'm going to be in here for a while trying to repair some of the damage, so you might as well go back to your room. I'll talk to you in a few hours."

Reluctantly Corky dragged himself to the door.

"Corky?"

He retraced his steps, wearing a wide grin. "See? I knew you couldn't live without me for very long."

"I know you don't want to hear this, but I've been going over it all night in my head." Cross solemnly scrutinized his face.

"Corky, I really think you should tell the psychiatrist what you told me, and then you need to probably tell the police and your parents, too."

Corky backed away from her, horrified. "No fucking way, Lu. I mean, don't even *say* that."

Using very little force, she grabbed his arm and pulled him back. "Do you want him to do it again to somebody else?"

His mouth grew smaller and hardened. "I don't care about anybody else."

"Oh, I see. So if he decides to try it on your best friend Adam, that's okay with you?"

"I'd take my dad's rifle and kill the fucking son of a bitch."

She stared at the young man before her and felt a flood of pity. "Save yourself a few years in prison—tell somebody who can stop him. This thing is going to keep haunting you. The pressure will

335

build up again. You feel okay right now because I can share part of the burden, but that's not going to be enough later on. You need the right kind of help getting this straightened out in your head."

He did not deny the truth in what she said. Even as he stood there, the last part of the circus dream played over and over again in his mind, and some of the panic crept back into his temples. The dread had resurrected from the rubble of pain.

Fucking A. Not again! No!

In a second he was gone, running out the door and down the hall to his room.

Nora and Cat entered the lobby like one of life's outtakes. The leaking bottle of mountain-fresh seltzer water had weakened the bottom of the recycled-paper grocery bag that contained their completely organic breakfast and lunch. Halfway across the lobby, it broke, spilling three bananas, four carrots, a stoneware bowl full of salad, a half-loaf of sourdough, two ripe avocados, a brick of Monterey Jack cheese of the low-fat, no-salt variety, a box of raspberry almond granola, natural hot mustard, and a half jar of light mayonnaise. The natural papyrus bag of nickel-free silverware fell out last.

Incapacitated by lack of sleep and howling laughter, Nora crossed her legs and leaned against the information booth, while Cat studied the memorial photograph of William Scanlin and took great pains to explain to anyone who so much as glanced in their direction that she most certainly did not know the woman who was in obvious need of psychiatric help.

As they hurried through the lobby a few minutes later, forks and bananas tucked safely into their purses, Cat noticed that Gage's stand was closed—a first in the year since he'd been there. She slowed, waving Nora on.

In front of the locked shutters, the same apprehension she'd felt in the predawn stillness of Nora's bedroom passed over her again.

Unable to get back to sleep, she had found her mind straying from tender and sexually charged thoughts of David Padcula to memories of her childhood. Incredibly vivid visions. Even the smell of the river Charles came up strongly, taking her back to balmy summer evenings when, exhilarated by the sheer energy of simply being alive, she'd run along the Esplanade, dreaming wild dreams that knew no limits or boundaries. Later, she was beset by an unnatural gloom as disturbing images presented themselves to her like a collage of movie clips—men's hands desperately grasping for an oddly shining light;

336

Gage fighting against an invisible vortex of force, his face full of defeat; Walker, pale and calm, standing at the helm of a ship as the wind rushed past him; David, out of breath, worried, his jaw muscles working overtime. . . .

Resting her cheek against the shutters, she closed her eyes and focused on Gage's face. "Please, be okay," she pleaded. "You need to help us here."

She directed her healing power to flow out through the prescribed orange beam of light to the unclouded image of the elfin man shivering by his wood stove. Instinctively she avoided his eyes. Something she did not understand and was not supposed to be privy to—something monumental in the world of spiritual powers—had taken place, and Gage had not come through it unscathed.

A warning that she should not intrude went through her. She struggled to turn her mind away, but failed. As she fused with him, smatterings of his thoughts and visions came to her and caused her to recoil.

"Pull from your source," she whispered urgently. "It's the only thing left to us."

About three quarters of the way through the crowd, Walker realized he was breathing in the slow pattern of Benny's rowing. When he pulled on the oars, Walker took air in; when the oars were above the water, he could let it out. When the oars were at rest, there was no breath at all. After a few seconds of no breathing, he felt as if he were beginning a long fall, but then Benny would let the oars drop into the water and he would breathe again and the fall would stop. A gleaming Mason waited for them a short distance away.

No one in the crowd paid any attention to the rather remarkable fact that they were all standing quite easily on the surface of the water, most of them executing the feat without a trace of any bobbing or weaving. Even the down-and-outers, who frequently bobbed and reeled on solid ground, were steady as poles, blissfully slapping him and each other on the back.

Every so often, when he wasn't reading someone's thoughts, he'd look down and laugh to himself because there didn't seem to be one inch of wet shoe leather among the thousand or so of them who had gathered to love at him.

That's what he decided they were doing—loving at him. What he'd read in every face came out to be pretty much the same: they loved him, or at least liked him a lot. It was, Benny whispered, a

337

result of how much he had loved and how little he had judged. He'd taken people as they were, and he'd been fair.

When the time seemed right, Zoe asked the crowd for quiet and received it. The rowboat stopped. In the ensuing hush, Walker looked around, studying the thoughts of those closest to him.

The boys solemnly sat on the rim of the boat, lamenting the loss of him, not really sure what it meant for them: Petey, ambivalent about his role as man of the house; Garrick, suppressing visions of the new tortures his brother would have the power to subject him to.

Joyce stood to his left, ever devoted, strong, and good-natured. Of course, she would remarry. Joyce had that spark that made a man feel at home right away.

And then there was Zoe. The brightest flame. She'd understood all along what it really was all about. For her, it had always been simply a matter of love. He called out to her and she came to him, pressing her little face next to his. Kissing him, she gripped his hand as if to guide him over treacherous ground.

He felt the falling again, relaxed, and allowed the love to buoy him, gliding gently on the water.

"I love you all," he whispered, though his lips did not move. "I'm Peter Walker and I have loved."

Walker looked at each of his children, then at his wife, then back at Benny, who smiled, his eyes full of compassion.

"I'm ready," Walker said.

Benny nodded, breathed into Walker's heart, and stopped rowing.

Alan was in a snit because during morning rounds Dr. Gillespie had yelled at him for not addressing him properly as "Doctor" in the presence of a patient.

"Gerald," he said, was reserved only for private conversations at the desk or in those rare socially awkward moments when they might be at the same party at the same time. In return, Alan advised Dr. Gillespie to address him as "Nurse Miller" in or out of social situations, period.

But the whole incident had put him in a snit all the same, and as a result, he hated his job, and as a result of hating his job, he treated the patients and his co-workers badly.

And because of this, when Cat asked him to assist her in turning her two-hundred-and-fifty-pound postcholecystectomy patient over onto her side, she got a flat and absolute no.

"What's the matter?" she taunted, smiling down at him. "Got your period or something?"

Alan did not stop writing his nurse's note, though his eyes squinted and his mouth tensed. This, she thought, looking at the whole package, is the embodiment of Ebenezer Scrooge.

"I don't have time."

"Ha! Who does, Alan?" Cat stood gazing for a moment at the top of his partially balding, very greasy head, and decided not to react. She would stop the chain of bad karma that she and this man obviously had together and turn it around. He'd made the initial effort when Professor Dean died; now it was her chance to return it. They might never be best of friends, but she could at least remove some of the stress between them.

Besides, he was the only man other than David Padcula who didn't talk to her with his eyes glued to her chest; and considering Alan had an eye-level view, that was admirable.

Nipping her sucking-sour-lemons attitude in the bud, she separated him from his chair and steered him in the direction of room 517. "Come on, come on, you need the exercise, you little twerp." She smiled, and hugged his arm. "Besides, I don't want to be the only one sitting in a wheelchair on the front porch of the Rest Home for Nurses with Bad Backs."

Not used to having positive attention directed at him by any of the women on the unit, let alone *this* one, Alan allowed himself to be dragged along, wondering if perhaps she had indulged in someone's Demerol.

The patient, fresh from the operating room, was not only gallbladderless but still groggy. The spicy smell of benzoin floated up from the surgical sheets each time she was moved, reminding Cat of her grandma's kitchen. Benzoin was one of those smells people either hated or loved; as with Brussels sprouts, there was never any in-between.

While Alan held the woman, Cat stuffed pillows behind her back in order to keep her propped up on her side.

A familiar impulse, which she had long ago identified as the California-encounter-group urge, prompted a need to interrogate the nurse on the other side of the bed.

"Hey, Al, may I ask you a really personal question?"

"Huh?"

"If you hate this job, and I figure you must, at least as much as I do, why don't you quit?" She began to unpin the layers of the scultetus binder that held the woman's belly together. It was a tedious job, but she needed to make sure the woman wasn't bleeding into her abdomen from some vessel left to pump unrestrained.

"Can't." Alan unfastened the pins from the other side of the binder

339

—twelve in all. "I've got one landlord, four dogs, six cats, and a monkey to support."

"*Six* cats?" She smiled, totally charmed. See, Miss Smarty-Pants, she berated herself, another piece of evidence that it is not wise to jump to conclusions and judge others the way you frequently do.

Alan nodded. "They're all overweight. So are the dogs, but it's really the monkey that's killing me financially. The doctor and vet bills are unbelievable."

"The monkey's sick?"

"Well, not exactly. See, I have friends that stop by once in a while and sometimes, if they forget about the monkey, they laugh and, you know, show their teeth. Primates take a show of teeth and forceful noises like laughter as a sign of aggression, so whenever anyone laughs around him, he attacks and bites."

They both examined the patient's fresh abdominal incision. Cat palpated one side while Alan indifferently poked around the other. Everything seemed tightly packed and secure.

"Sometimes he gets so excited that he'll go into atrial fibrillation, so there's outrageous vet bills. I've been sued twice, and, on top of that"—Alan shrugged—"he's recently discovered how to light matches."

"Has anyone ever suggested getting rid of the monkey?" Cat asked.

Alan looked both horrified and hurt, as if a friend had shot him in the leg on purpose. "My God, of course not! He's like my own flesh and blood! I've raised him from infancy."

"Yeah," she admitted, wanting to bite her tongue off for her show of insensitivity. After all, hadn't she always said she'd run into a burning building to save Saph? "I feel the same way about my cat."

Alan's face brightened, as if he might have some hope for her after all, she thought.

If she squinted, and in just the right light, she imagined the man could almost be considered good-looking.

"You a cat lover?" he asked.

"Fanatic is more accurate."

"Like dogs?"

"Love 'em, but the landlord doesn't."

"Need any more help?" he asked almost eagerly.

"Ah, no, but thanks anyway."

"Well, guess I'll get back to my charting." He backed away, the grin still plastered to his lips.

For one second she caught herself having romantic notions about Alan, and shook her head.

That would be desperation at its peak.

Maybe Nora was right. Maybe she really was waaaaaay overdue for loving.

It wasn't until Tillie stopped rattling the side rail and singing "The Itsy-Bitsy Spider" in her whiny catlike yowl that Stella could be relatively sure the old bat had fallen asleep.

So as not to wake Tillie again, she quietly unfolded the piece of notebook paper and flattened it out in front of her. For the sixth time that morning, she studied the numbers with her magnifying glass even though she had them memorized.

If it was eight in the morning in San Francisco, it would be ten in Arkansas. Her grandson would be at his workplace. An auto repair shop, the detective had said. Owned it himself.

Stella called the operator to tell her she would be making a long-distance call, then laid the handset on the bedside table, looking back and forth from the paper to the lighted numbers, pushing each one carefully—purposefully.

"Otis Gallagher the third?" she'd say. "I am your grandmother."

Her finger stopped in midpush.

What if her daughter-in-law hadn't told him about his father? Maybe she'd told him his father had been killed in the war, a drifter without roots. The girl hadn't liked them much.

And how would it sound, her living in a county-funded nursing home? He'd think she was an old lady moocher looking for a free meal.

She pressed the hook, waited to make sure the connection was broken, and hung up. If only she had something of her own like a house or an apartment, something so he wouldn't think she wanted charity from him.

Well, she could lie. She could tell him she was living in a grand place, and that she was perfectly well-off. Okay. No problem. Family connections were worth a few white lies.

Picking up the phone, she pushed the numbers again with resolve, and waited. On the fourth ring she got scared and started to hang up, when a man answered.

"Gallagher's auto repair. Otis Gallagher."

Stella could not speak, stunned by her husband's voice coming from the grave.

There was a short silence.

"Trip? Is that you again, boy? Where's Mommy?"

Her heart pounded out of her chest, yet she breathed softly into

341

the receiver. She could not bring herself to say "Hello," as if she did not have the strength to form the words.

In the background an automobile horn sounded twice.

"Trip, you little tunahead, does Mommy know you're on the phone again? You know you aren't supposed to call Daddy at work unless Mommy's there." The man laughed faintly, then covered the mouthpiece and shouted a few muffled words of greeting to someone.

Stella blinked. *Tunahead?*

"Trip, hang up now, honey. I'll see you tonight when I get home. Tell Mommy McDonald's for dinner."

Still speechless after the click, Stella held on to the phone in a kind of mild shock.

"Miss Stella?"

She pulled the phone away, looked at it strangely, and put it back to her ear. "Yes?"

"Can I come in and be with you?"

Stella pushed the phone hard against her hearing aid. The muffled little voice seemed to be coming from the dial tone.

"Speak up. Who is this? Are you calling me?"

"It's me, Zoe."

The light touch on her arm startled her.

A stricken Zoe hung her head and shuffled to her side, twisting a jacket of matted pink fur. "My father's dead," she said. Her lower lip trembled uncontrollably.

Stella put the phone aside and pulled the child onto her lap. Immediately Zoe buried her head against her breasts, sobbing.

Stella whispered into the thick hair bunched up at the back of Zoe's small neck, "Cry, child. That's the best thing to do. The pain won't be this hard forever. It has a way of softening over the days that pass."

Zoe cried miserably for a few moments, then lifted her head to search Stella's face for an answer.

The anguish she saw in the child's face reminded her of what her own loss had been like. For the child to feel that? Lord.

But she was young and strong. She would forget.

"I want Daddy back, Stella. I don't want him to die."

"But he's right here, darling. For you, he'll always be right here. He's only moved to a place where there is no pain and he can finally rest."

Stella pulled a Kleenex from the box on the table and wiped the tear hanging from the end of Zoe's nose.

"Do you think he can hear me?"

Stella nodded. "Of course he can."

"Do you think he's sad?"

"Hard to say, but I think he's loving you. Death is a mysterious thing, darling. Nobody really knows what happens when you die. It's one of those things you have to make up your own thoughts about."

Zoe thought for a long time, then relaxed against the old woman. "Do you have a story you could tell me right now?"

As the warmth of the small body radiated into hers, Stella mentally reviewed the tale of the owl and the moon. Of course, it was the perfect yarn. And after that, she would tell her the story about the rabbit and the lion. She stroked Zoe's cool forehead and for a moment, allowed herself to delight in the closeness of her. A perfect winter orange. Bright and sweet, and for the present, all hers.

Stella straightened her shoulders and arranged Zoe's stick limbs in a comfortable position.

She cleared her throat and began.

Gage ran his hand over the shutters of his stand, hesitated briefly above one spot, grunted, and slid them back. He'd felt the woman's energy calling to him earlier, sending him an amazing amount of healing strength—strength she had gained in only a few days.

That she had expanded her awareness so easily pleased and frightened him. Thank God she did not have the desire to tap into the full extent of her power. Without the proper guidance, and if she were ever tempted the way he had been, she could become a mighty and menacing force.

Weak from the events of the night before, he had to rest after carrying out the first two stacks of papers. The battle was the worst he'd had since becoming one of the chosen. His strength had been tested before by the dark side in small, meaningless ways but never like this, never to the point of having it invade him while he was actually in the spirit.

The powerful trap had been cleverly set for him: a sign the evil forces wanted him more than ever. They had made a valiant effort to lure him with a taste of power over life and death. Adding to the bewitching seduction was the promise of his sight if only he would abandon the light and give himself up to the other side.

Killing the man would have been child's play. Of course, the act would have been his initiation—and how clever the darker forces

343

had been, bidding him to slay an evildoer under the guise of a good turn.

The memory of how close he had come to giving in and crushing the man worked painfully through him until he shook it off. Yes, he thought, but he'd triumphed. He'd had just enough strength to fight the evil that had possessed him.

Gage swayed and listlessly passed a hand over his face. It would take time to repair the wound and restore his power to what it had been.

Reluctantly Corky left the two women to themselves and sauntered down the hall. Cat swore the kid's arms were so long they seemed to hang almost to his knees.

Cross was obviously a different woman, and Cat couldn't help wondering how much of her transformation had to do with Corky.

Laurel had confided to her that she'd allowed the boy to spend the night in Cross's room. The door had remained closed until a few minutes before change of shift. According to Trish, he'd appeared tired and pale running back to his room.

"Imagine, that gorgeous young hunk and a woman *my* age!" Trish said wistfully. "Old enough to be his older sister! All I can say is, I hope to hell they had the sense not to rupture anything."

Cat finished listening to Cross's lungs. It didn't matter what anybody thought. The bond between the two was keeping both of them sane, so who cared what the nature of it was?

In clinical terms, Cross was showing what was called the lipstick sign: hair washed and combed, an application of makeup and perfume. She had exchanged the shapeless hospital gown for a pink summer tee under an olive-green flannel work shirt. The black wool slacks were exquisitely made, loose enough to hide the extreme thinness of her hips and thighs, yet flattering to the general outline of her slender waist and buttocks. Even her vital signs and physical assessment were the best they'd been in days.

Cat stood back and took an overall look at the woman's transformation. It was easy to see how the boy would be so taken with her. She was irrefutably attractive, despite her battle wounds, and she gave off a feeling of being truly alive, especially when she smiled.

"You look great," Cat said, meaning it.

"I feel almost . . . normal. First time in . . ."

For a moment the sad, melancholy expression returned. ". . . a hundred years."

"Yeah, well, sometimes it takes a while to get our lives back from those faceless forces."

Cross shyly touched Cat's arm. "Mr. Padcula told me what happened yesterday, and I wanted to thank you. I think Michael would have killed me if you hadn't stopped him. I'm sorry he hurt you. I'm sorry I . . ." She paused, her bruised throat working convulsively.

Cat stooped to hug the woman. "It's okay, Cross. It's all behind us."

"God, I'm scared."

"Don't worry, the police will find him. He won't . . ."

Cross shook her head. "No, I don't mean that. I'm afraid I'm never going to love anybody again. I'm scared that I'll choose another Michael. I don't trust myself. I knew Michael was sick right from the beginning. Even after I saw that my work was being destroyed and I knew how violent he could get, I still couldn't let him go."

"You lost yourself, Cross," Cat said gently. "That happens to women like us. To know the right way of loving is difficult, let alone finding that really solid, good person to share it with.

"Learning how to love and take care of yourself doesn't happen overnight."

"It doesn't matter. I'm too screwed up to learn," Cross said, all dark, intent eyes.

"It matters if you want to heal yourself. Get some counseling, talk to people, join support groups. It's a lot of work, but you do whatever it takes, Cross. And even then, you always have to be on the lookout for bugs in the system. I don't entirely trust myself yet either, and I've been at this for years. I've let my pendulum swing too far in the opposite direction. Now I get defensive and suspicious the minute I start to fall for somebody, so I defeat myself by driving him away. The whole process requires constant fine-tuning—you just have to be willing to keep trying."

They said nothing for a while, staring out into the hallway, watching the nurses rush in and out of patients' rooms. Presently, Cat picked up a stack of sketches and leafed through them until she came to the series of Corky. She was astounded by the lifelike quality of the drawings. Cross had captured every minute detail, right down to the way the light reflected off his hair. She touched one, fully expecting to feel hair under her fingers.

"These are incredible."

"Corky makes it easy," Cross said. "He reads like a book with large print. Everything he thinks and feels shows on his face."

"Well, not everything . . ."

345

Cross looked at her, surprised. "Why do you say that?"

She shrugged noncommittally, observing the changes going on in Cross's face. "Oh, I don't know—everybody has secrets."

Cross appeared to weigh something in her mind and then, against her better judgment, let it go. It was on the strength of the way she set her jaw—in the worried, protective attitude of a mother—and the way the boy clung to her, as if his life depended on her, that Cat realized Cross knew Corky's secret.

Of course. How could Corky have kept it from her, given the amount of time they spent together coupled with the fact that they had both been wounded?

Quietly Cross returned to her sketching. "Well, I suppose everyone has secrets. Some are just more deadly than others."

Cat slipped into the kitchen to heat a blanket in the warmer and found Nora laughing to herself as she prepared the prescribed midmorning snacks for several of her patients.

"Still amused over the red toothbrush, heh?"

"It's not the toothbrush," Nora said. "I was so tired this morning when I got dressed that I put my self-stick panty shield on upside down. I just realized that the sticky part is facing my pubic hair. I knew there was a reason I've put off going to the bathroom."

Cat smiled and removed the warmed blanket without comment.

"What's the matter? I thought you'd appreciate that, especially after the beer phone."

"I stopped in to see the little OD and found out that her parents still haven't contacted her and nobody knows where they are, plus she's not rallying. I don't think she really wants to."

Cat wet a paper towel and worked over a spot of blood on the hem of her scrub dress. It had leaked from Walker's IV site as she wrapped him for the morgue.

"I don't know what the problem is." Cat sighed. "It's Friday. My Monday defenses have been worn away enough so that everything's getting to me. Can't stop thinking about Walker and the fact that I'm as old as he was, and then there's his wife and three kids. What're they going to do now? Corky's all wigged out again and I don't know the right thing to do for him—haven't since he came in. I'm worried about Gage, too. I saw him getting into the elevator, and he looked like death warmed over. Ever since this morning, I've been feeling this heavy doom or something hanging over me." She closed her eyes. "I don't know, Nor, I really think I'm too old for this job."

346

"Oh yeah?" said Nora dryly. "You got something else in mind?"

Cat imagined herself married to David Padcula, living the life of the secure, middle-aged housewife—tennis, sailing, and cooking lessons; trying her hand at human interest stories for the magazines, weekend trips with her husband. Was it selfish to want a normal life? An easier life?

And if she ever convinced herself that it wasn't, would she be able to survive without the stress and the adrenaline fixes? Would she miss her winter oranges?

"Hell, Nora, I suppose even I could find something to do that was considered normal."

Nora stood at attention, quickly hid her spoon behind her back, and mumbled under her breath, "Speaking of normal and its antithesis. . . ."

Cat turned to follow Nora's gaze. Peering through the small round window in the kitchen door, Jo Atwood smiled and crooked her finger.

On impulse, Cat made the sign of the cross and hissed.

Nathan watched as Cross concentrated on the canvas, painting like a house afire. She'd put her hair up in the back the way she always had when she worked, and there was a light in her eyes. No trace of the dull curtain, only a touch of sadness that on another day could well have been called insight.

Stepping back from the canvas, she tilted her head, scowled, filled her brush with cadmium yellow, and made another series of confident strokes.

It was the beginning of an abstract. One of the best he'd ever seen her produce, to say nothing of the speed with which she had attacked the canvas. He'd never seen her so alive or so in love with her art— even before the scum came into her life.

And she'd asked for news. Who was doing what, how had so-and-so's show gone, what about the new gallery, why did so-and-so change styles, and did they miss her—had she waited too long, had she blown it?

No, darling. For your talent they wait.

Then she had hugged him with her uninjured arm and given him a look that said everything: *I love you. Thank you for loving me enough to stay close.* It was when she said what she did in that determined, poised way that he knew she was really back.

"I have been released from hell," she said, placing a thick streak of pearl gray next to the yellow and expertly blending the edges. "And I'm never going to be dead again until I die for good."

Cat knew the small white box in her hand contained some piece of jewelry, and for that reason hesitated in opening it. Gifts of jewelry meant attachment, obligation.

"What's this for?" *As if I didn't know.*

Jo's eyes sparkled. "Open it, Cat. It's a token to tell you how brave I think you were yesterday and to remind you how much I care."

Reluctantly Cat removed the top of the box, and snorted. She had to pinch her nostrils to keep the laughter back.

Resting on its square pillow of jeweler's cotton was a large gold crucifix on a gold chain.

"Oh! It's . . . it's . . . Praise the Lord, Jo, it's perfect." Please, God, why can't someone please code now?

Jo removed the necklace and held it to the light in front of Cat's eyes. "Turn around," she whispered. "Let me see how it looks on that long neck of yours."

Cat made a grab for the chain, missed, and forced a smile. "No, no, that's okay, I have to have the bishop bless it before I can wear it. It's one of the personal commandments of the religion."

"By the way, what *is* your new religion?"

It seemed to Cat there was a hint of mistrust in the question.

"Ah, it's so new you wouldn't recognize it."

"Well, I might, and I might want to look into it . . . to help me understand you better."

There was that shrewd smile, and that mocking tone again. Was it something she had to worry about?

"Well, we call it Severe Catholicism of the Most Holy. It's a new order." Even while it was still coming out of her mouth, Cat thought she might be pushing credibility.

Oh please, why aren't the call bells going off like every other goddamned second of the day? Why are they suddenly silent now? Where are the six or seven people who are constantly asking for help? Or where's Gilly ragging about something I didn't do or did too much of? Oh for Christ's sake!

"Listen, Catalina, I've thought over what you said and I think your religious devotion is lovely. I was wondering if maybe you could come over to my apartment one night this weekend for dinner and tell me about how you got into it and maybe explain some of the philosophy behind it."

348

One of the call bells went off and Cat bolted toward the room. She'd scarcely moved more than a few yards, when Nora, in all her efficient nursely glory, ran into the room. The bell was silenced, her chance of escape destroyed.

I'll kill her, thought Cat. Tonight she gets the red toothbrush shoved down her throat.

And there was that mysterious smile again as Jo moved closer to her. "How about it? Dinner and a little catechism?"

Cat fidgeted. "I have a Severe retreat this weekend, all weekend, won't be back till late late late Sunday night. I'm leaving right after work—one of my spiritual brothers in Christ is picking me up. We're going to pray the whole way up and back."

She lowered her eyes and crossed herself again, mumbling "Lord have mercy" and other similar phrases she had picked up from watching old Civil War movies.

"Oh, that *is* too bad. I thought," Jo looked around and brought her voice down to a whisper, "we might go over your probation reports too. We've only got one week left to respond, and I was hoping we could pick out the ones to be 'misplaced'—together. How about we make it for Monday night?"

Cat opened her mouth to say Monday was prayer night, but Jo pressed a finger firmly over her lips.

"No excuses. It's 2400 Pacific Avenue, apartment 1712. Seven sharp. Be there."

Cat did an about face and quickly headed down the hall.

"Oh, and Cat?"

She stopped but did not turn around.

"We'll be having fish and fresh loaves of bread with homemade wine."

Cross opened the conversation by telling Cat how much she admired her for having so much compassion for the sick. To have power in matters of life and death had to be exhilarating.

Flattered, Cat raved on about the idea of having to answer to no one except the muse. To create what came from the heart, then to be praised and paid well for it, seemed a fantastic sort of dream life that happened only when one sold one's soul to the devil.

Firmly established in each other's graces, the two ingeniously slipped around the subject of men and sex and on to other things of importance in the lives of single women: friends and enemies, family, life war stories, and loneliness.

349

They might have gone on for hours had the sounds of constantly buzzing call bells and the sight of her co-workers rushing through the hall not eroded Cat's ability to concentrate—to say nothing of the guilt.

Cat was halfway to the door when Cross snapped her fingers.

"Hey!"

"What?"

"You live in Mill Valley; could you do me a huge favor and swing by my cabin to pick up something?"

The chance to see the inside of Lucy Cross's cabin in person was not something Cat wanted to pass up. According to the *People* article, not many, including Cross's closest friends, had ever been invited to the spectacular woodsy hideaway.

Trying not to appear too eager, she relaxed her eyebrows and shrugged. "Ummm, well, I guess I could."

"That'd be so great if you could. I want to give Corky one of my paintings. It's a fourteen-by-seventeen watercolor of my garden that's right in the alcove as you come in the front door." Cross quickly drew a map of the canyon and penciled in a dotted line of the coast highway, explaining her cabin was at the end of a little-known fire road.

"Know right where it is," Cat assured her, putting the map in her pocket. If I find this place before next week, it'll be a miracle. "Passed it a thousand times." In my last life, maybe.

"Great, and maybe you could . . . No, never mind."

"No, no, go ahead and ask." But if you ask me to bring you something of Michael's, I'm going to scream.

"Could you go around to the back of the house and take a peek at the garden? It's a mess because I've ignored it, but I want to make sure the storms haven't blown anything major on top of it, like the roof."

"No problem." No problem because I wouldn't know a messy garden from a clean swimming pool, but I can recognize a roof on the ground when I see one.

"Sure it's not too much trouble?"

Cat shook her head. "Nope. I was going home to feed my cat, then come back in the city to spend the weekend with a friend anyway, so one more stop isn't a big deal. I could drop the painting off on my way back to her apartment."

The phone rang. By the way Cross smiled with her whole body when she answered, Cat figured it was Corky. She picked up the keys and had started out the door, when Cross covered the mouthpiece and flagged her.

"One other thing—that's the only set of keys I have, so guard them well."

"You can trust me." Cat waved cheerfully over her shoulder, trying not to think about the seventy-five dollars she'd spent in the last six months replacing locks and keys. In her circle of friends, she was notorious for losing keys—hers and everyone else's. It was long past the point where people had begun collecting her car keys at the door, and hiding them from her until she was ready to leave.

Slipping into the linen closet, she pinned the set to the inside of her bra. Unless she was stripped naked and her clothes burned against her will, they were safe.

Cat came back to a state of semiawareness from a place as profoundly far away as general anesthesia. She focused on the gray metal sheet a few inches above her and yawned until her jaw popped.

She was totally unable to orient herself to where she was or why she was there. It was an interesting feeling, one she was lazily exploring, when the thought hit her that she had been buried alive. She didn't remember dying, but the idea didn't really concern her so much; this place was warm and comfortable.

Her stomach made a long slippery noise that sounded like a puppy whining. She was processing food.

Lunch. Lunch break. Thirty minutes. Job. She was a nurse. The linen closet. Late. How long had she slept? Were her patients in need? Were people searching for her? Was this going to mean another probation?

Cat jumped up, smashed her head on the metal shelf, panicked over her own lack of coordination and inability to orient properly, and dashed for the door. Perhaps she was having a cerebral hemorrhage and she wouldn't make it to the door in time. It could be days before someone found her body.

Bleary-eyed, hair wild, she bounced off the wall two, three times and grappled with the door handle. Frantically swinging the door open, she came face-to-face with the man she had partially decided that she suspected just might possibly be the love of her life.

With no thought for the dark grey eye snot balled in the corners of her eyes, sleep wrinkles slashing her face in half, and deranged expression that would most certainly make him reconsider having anything to do with her, she waved and smiled shyly, wishing her eyes would adjust to the light in a more attractive fashion and that she would stop weaving and fully awaken.

She had almost completely stopped worrying that she was having a stroke, but was convinced someone had slipped a Mickey in her lunchtime tea.

He stared at her, the perpetual smile not wavering even the minutest amount in light of her imaginary imperfections. All he saw was a big, feisty, beautiful redhead with some impressive feet.

"Hi."

"Hi. What are you doing here?" she asked, focusing her eyes on the large clock over the utility room door. Fifteen minutes late. No problem. Sighing with relief, she wiped away her eye gleet and re-braided her hair.

"Lucy Cross called me a little while ago and asked me to come by. She said she'd try to give me some information about our man Mr. Lake."

"Ah, will wonders never cease?"

He stood still, looking at her intently, or at least she thought it was intense from what she could catch behind the glare of his glasses.

"Not in your or my lifetime they won't. The first wonder I'm looking forward to is seven p.m. this evening."

Cat blinked and turned away, blushing furiously.

"Make it seven forty-five instead, would you? I need to run a few errands over in—"

The code bell sounded as the overhead speaker sputtered and filled the air with the words that caused every healthcare professional's adrenaline to surge.

Attention all personnel. Code blue Ward Two acute.

Without hesitation, she joined in with the group of nurses running toward the acute unit. The sight of her so completely focused on her purpose made the hairs on the back of his neck stand up.

"Seven forty-five it is," he said softly, feeling something like pride and admiration filling his gut.

Without warning, for almost no reason at all except that death doesn't have rules or age limits, the eleven-year-old died.

Asystole. Just like that, and no amount of sweat and swearing or a hundred years of combined knowledge and skill could get the young heart to move.

And there was nothing to do but forget her sad child's face and find a way not to care.

Corky put the phone down and turned on his side to stare out at the hallway. He would scrutinize each person entering his room, memorize their faces, then calculate how drastically each of them changed.

Lucy would be with him. That was totally essential. Without her, he'd be history three times over and back the other way.

Fucking A, man, she'd righteously saved his life.

Oh yeah, and the black dude, too. He was really out on some kind of trip into another world. Not like any dude, brother or not, that he'd ever known in his life. Sort of like a Jesus freak guru, totally spaced, but a totally awesome human being too, if that's what he was, in fact.

No way of telling if the dude could actually be one of those *other* beings . . . aliens who come to earth and take over bodies. But man, what a bummer—blind, black, *and* old? Tweaked, man. Somebody should've told him he could've made an easier choice.

Then again, imagine an alien coming down and getting a body like Tammy's.

Corky laughed out loud. So, like maybe it would be okay.

Maybe there wouldn't be a *Cuckoo's Nest* for him after all.

"Hey, Stel! Congratulations, kiddo!" Cat placed the Mailgram in front of the old woman.

Stella stared at the piece of paper with its four lines of large loopy handwriting and looked back at the redhead for some explanation.

"That's your new address, kid. Bresford Place has agreed to take you as a resident strictly on the strength of your being such a sharp cookie. They were impressed with your application papers, especially the part where they asked if you would be apprehensive in discussing your religious beliefs with others, and you answered, 'No. I like to start arguments.' And they're still laughing over the one where it asked your age, and you wrote, 'Old enough for a complete overhaul but young enough to still fool the old goats.'

"They're picking you up Monday first thing."

Stella nodded, only half listening about the new old farts' home. She was thinking that she would not see Zoe again. But she knew that already. She knew there was no holding on to winter oranges indefinitely.

". . . so you'll be working from noon to four on Tuesdays, Wednesdays, and Fridays. If you want, they have a long-distance volunteer program where you'll be bused to other counties for a full day of grandmother duty."

"Grandmother what?" she asked, awakening at the words "working" and "duty."

"Turn up your hearing aid, Stel." Cat sighed. "Okay, this is the last time I'm going to explain this, so listen good. Bresford is a pilot community program where all the residents do volunteer work of some kind, like gardening, or quilting, or grandparenting unfortunate kids. You know, orphans, hospitalized kids, shelters, that kind of thing. On the application, you said kids were your area of interest."

"What am I supposed to do?" Stella was looking at her, trying to make sense of the good news.

"Play with them, give affection, tell stories, help feed the smaller kids."

"Tell stories?"

Cat nodded. "That's a big part of it. Keeping them entertained, and for the sick ones, keeping them calm. If you know a lot of stories, especially the handed-down ones, this is one way of passing them on."

A gentle expression crossed the old woman's face, and for a moment, she became the sapient elder, sensitive yet possessing the strength of the mountain—a piece of soft white cotton with steel threads woven through.

"Hundreds of winter oranges," whispered Cat, "all for you, Stel."

Stella smiled with an understanding of exactly what was being offered to her.

"Okay," she said. "I'll take all you got."

With her hearing aid properly adjusted for maximum reception, Stella counted the number of times the phone rang at her grandson's home.

Two.

She would hang up at six.

She decided honesty was the best policy. That was what Papa always told her. It was just that honesty was sometimes harder to adhere to than the other policies.

Three.

People were more honest when they rode in the catbird seat.

Four.

And she was definitely in the catbird seat.

"Hello?" said the voice of a young person snapping gum.

"Is Mr. Otis Gallagher at home, dear?"

"Who's this?"

Stella hesitated, got nervous, and read from the cheat sheet she'd made for herself. "My name is Stella Gallagher. I'm . . . I'm the grandmother of Otis Gallagher the third, mother of Otis Gallagher junior, and wife of Otis Gallagher senior." Stella waited, her heart skipping beats.

At the other end there was a loud clanking noise, as if the receiver had been allowed to hit the floor, followed by a wail. "Hey, Dad, for you! Some old lady says she's Grandma, but it don't sound like Grandma."

The same voice she'd heard that morning said, "Hello?"

"Otis Gallagher?"

"Yes?" The voice was warm, open, yet careful, like his grandfather's.

"Otis." Oh, it felt strange to say that name. "I'm Stella Gallagher, your grandmother."

Stella waited for an answer, until a man's deep belly laugh caused her heart to thump in her throat.

"Well, I'll be . . ."

He covered the mouthpiece and yelled for someone named Mary to pick up the extension. There was what sounded like an acceleration of excitement with a lot of muffled talk in the background, then a small child's piercing yell that he wanted to go see his grandma with the camels, and someone else shushing him. A moment later, Otis was back on the line.

"Say, Nanmar Tella," he said, still laughing, "where the hell you been, old woman?"

Just as he predicted, the first person to arrive was his mother. She was on the edge of totally freaking out, but acted cool by making jokes about the zit on his neck. She'd said if he was growing a Christmas tree bulb, he was a little late.

Then she started cleaning his room and straightening his clothes, which was what moms did when they were nervous. All of them, even Adam's mom, who was a total punker and part of a heavy metal band, did it. It was a disease of motherhood.

Folding his shirts for the third time, she'd wanted to know, one, why he'd call them in, two, what was so urgent, and three, did he know that he'd scared the living daylights out of them?

His father came in next, and instead of beating around the bush, asked the same three questions immediately, before he even said, "Hello, buddy," or gave him a hug.

For approximately eight minutes, he stalled and they prodded,

355

until Lucy timidly made her entrance. Not a minute too soon either, because he was beginning to have doubts about what he'd done.

The panic that had started up again was held at bay with introductions. Then his mother, who had been practically staring holes into the side of Lucy's head, asked something totally weird about her having been in some issue of *People* magazine, when Dr. Barza entered the room and asked the perfect question that summed up the whole situation.

"Okay, now what seems to be the problem here?"

When everyone had settled, when everything was quiet, Lucy sat next to him and held his hand.

Corky took a deep breath and hung his head as if he were waiting for the hangman's noose. After a few seconds he looked up and studied each one of their faces, settling last on Lucy's.

His mother and father were expectant, slightly fearful. The shrink was neutral. Lucy in the Sky with Diamonds was radiantly confident and proud.

"Here goes," he said.

Lucy tightened her grip on his hand.

"So, like, do you remember the Halloween party we went to all dressed like the Three Stooges?

"Mom? Dad? You with me so far?"

Like a vision from an old "Star Trek" episode, Nora stood next to the bed dressed head to toe in sterile blue paper—shoe covers, head cover, floor-length gown, and mask with eye shield.

"I said I wanted a number eleven blade, not a fifteen!" Dr. Gladstein, usually the most mild-mannered of the brotherhood of physicians at Mercy Hospital, threw the unwanted scalpel to the floor and glared at Nora over the exposed chest of the patient—the rest of the prone body was hidden from view with a large blue paper drape which matched Nora's outfit exactly.

Nora found the correct blade and expertly dropped it onto the sterile surgical tray. "Take it easy, Dr. Gladstein. Don't forget about your high blood pressure. It's only the insertion of a chest tube. I could probably finish up for you, but I'd have to charge you for the service and the A.M.A. wouldn't like that."

Muffled laughter came from under the blue sheet.

"Please," said a man's voice. "Don't make me laugh. It's hard enough trying to breathe under here."

Not to be shaken from his black mood, Dr. Gladstein glowered at her over his sterile eye shield as if to say, "See what you've done?" Nora wondered if Mrs. Gladstein was drinking again.

"Blood pressure check, if you please, Nurse," he growled.

Peeking under the blue sheet, Nora winked at the patient, palpated his brachial artery, and pumped up the cuff.

"Stable at one twelve systolic."

"Dr. Gladstein nodded and, exerting the lightest of pressure, made an incision between two ribs. As the skin split apart, a small trickle of bright red blood spilled out. A hissing sound indicated the expansion of the lung.

"Just like the balloon in freshman physics, eh guys?" Leaning against the door, Cat stood with her jacket and purse slung over her arm in the I'm-going-home position.

Nora dropped a suture pack onto the sterile field. "Hey, where do you think you're going?"

"I gave report early. Thought I'd head over to my house to feed Saph and find a suitable dinner frock. Then I have to stop by Cross's cabin to pick up a painting for her, so after I drop that off at the hospital, I'll be back at your place no later than six forty-five. David is picking me up for dinner around seven forty-five." Afraid Nora might squeal and make Dr. Gladstein nervous, she added quickly, "And how about you? Have a date tonight?"

Nora gave her a sour look. "Honey, after the lecture I got last night, I'm never having sex again! Why, I promise, the next time I get laid, it'll be with my husband on my wedding night."

Cat coughed and nodded toward Dr. Gladstein, who had stopped suturing and was staring at Nora, his face gone pale and sweaty.

"Oops, sorry, Dr. Gladstein, sometimes I forget where I am. I'm so at home here in Turf Tundra that I have a tendency to talk as if we were all one, big, happy fam—"

"Nurse?" Dr. Gladstein was glassy-eyed.

"Jeez, Dr. Gladstein, I didn't mean to send you into shock. You want another blood pressure? How 'bout one on yourself? More suture?"

The physician shook his head. "My foot, please, Nurse."

Cat and Nora both lowered their gaze to the floor. Buried in the middle of Dr. Gladstein's left foot was the number fifteen scalpel. A tiny pool of blood—his—surrounded the foot like a moat.

Cat backed away from the door as Nora bent to examine the injured foot. She knew if she didn't leave at that very moment, she would not get out until it was too late.

As the door to the ward closed behind her, she heard Nora coaxing.

"Come on, Dr. Gladstein, sit down right here on the floor. No. No. Don't pass out on the patient. Here, give me that, I'll finish the suturing. Here, lie down right over . . . Oh God, not on the sterile field, please?"

29 At precisely five p.m., a sharp pain cut through the side of Gage's neck, starting from under his left ear and ending two inches below his right collarbone. It made him pay even closer attention to the spirit moving around inside him like lightning, generating images that caused him to go stone cold. The air was loaded with tension. It would just be a matter of time before the power he drained from the dark side was fully replenished. Good and evil were on their way, traveling their preordained courses to meet and deal with each other. He reminded himself he had only the authority to keep the balance even; to act directly would be too dangerous. Last night had proved that.

The woman needed to pay attention and be open, but she did so only when the power was in her face, spitting at her.

Angrily he snapped at the few lingering customers to leave, then hastily closed the stand, banging its doors and shutters in a flurry of frustration.

Tom Mix pawed at the floor and whined until his master stopped and sat on the floor next to him.

"I know, boy." The black man buried his face against Tom Mix's muscular shoulder. "I gotta take a step back or I ain't gonna be no good to nobody."

Taking a deep breath, Gage let the spirit work.

.   .   .

For the millionth time since she'd purchased the scuffed and dented Volkswagen bug for fifty dollars from a drug dealer in similar condition, Cat thanked the powers that be she had not become a slave to a nice car. Unless one was extremely rich, nice cars had a way of taking the adventure out of life.

And she was certainly having an adventure.

Impatiently she switched the radio dial. She couldn't take more than ten minutes of country music. It all sounded the same to her—the same twanging chords, the same words, and always, the same theme: either, "She don't love me no mo' so now I'm agonna kill her," or "She done left me so now I'm agonna lay me down and die."

Normally the ethereal sounds of New Age music were her favorite, but not for these winding roads. She didn't want to fall asleep, but then again, she didn't want to deepen the purple under her eyes by listening to anything nerve-jangling either.

The two oldies stations played too much Elvis, Beach Boys, and Bob Dylan and not enough Aretha, Shirelles, or Buddy Holly. And the eclectic, in-between station had too much static, although (as always) the Holy Roller station came through with perfect clarity.

For amusement, she listened to the singsong cadence of a southern evangelist proclaiming to his audience that they and their children and their children's children were damned to the eternal agonies of hell if they didn't pay heed to the Almighty. One way of paying heed, the messenger of God assured his radio audience (told to him personally by the voice of Our Lord while he was chopping wood in his backyard one Sunday morning), was to dig deep into their pockets and send what they could—and perhaps even part of what they couldn't—to the Ensure Yourself a Piece of Heaven Fund, P.O. Box blah blah blah.

Cat settled on the classical station and gripped the wheel with both hands as the road narrowed and the turns became more treacherous. But as on many of California's craggy mountain highways, the installation of guardrails had been ignored—a construction faux pas that continually amazed the emergency service personnel who scraped up carload after carload of bodies from the bottoms of two-hundred-foot ridges.

Her headlights pierced the endless void of fog beyond the cliffs as her rear wheels skidded on the rain-slick road. She was relieved she didn't have to deal with other cars. This particular road was in the middle of no-man's-land, and only someone insane would attempt to drive it in the freezing, pouring rain at dusk.

The thought had no sooner become part of her mental monologue than she caught the flicker of a red taillight ahead. Accelerating, she overtook the pea-green Dodge Dart and sighed.

She should have known. New Jersey plates.

It was astounding the number of remote and unbelievable places in which she'd seen cars from New Jersey; in every state and on every back road, New Jerseyites could be counted on to be there as America's professional tourists.

Passing the New Jerseyish–looking grayheaded couple, she wondered, didn't these people have jobs to keep them in New Jersey?

At 17:39 hours, Nora slipped her card into the time clock and waited for the mechanism to give proof that she did not actually live at Mercy Hospital.

She was thinking about the odd way Dr. Gladstein refused her offer to call for help and insisted on lying on the floor chatting with her until she finished suturing in the chest tube. He'd been quite happy and content to wait, even though the scalpel was still embedded in his foot. In the midst of his reminiscences about his med school days, she'd realized the man was simply starved to talk with a woman who actually listened.

Now as she weighed the pros and cons of allowing herself to indulge in an affair of mercy with the older physician, something cold and wet and slimy lifted her skirt and grazed her inner thighs. Instinct caused her to reach down and clamp a firm hand around the probing object.

Tom Mix yelped and pulled his muzzle from her grip.

"Quiet, boy," Gage said sternly.

"Oh, sorry, Tom, I didn't know it was you. How're you doing, Gage? I was—"

"Where Ms. Cat be at?" The question said it wanted an answer without frills or wasted time.

Out of sheer spite, Nora refrained from answering immediately. She had never been able to warm up to the man, resenting his cool irascibleness; the curt way he had of addressing people who came to him for newsprint and gum had always put her off. Certainly Cat's recent affectionate and glowing descriptions of Gage had nothing to do with the uptight little dork standing before her, demanding answers.

Gage briefly laid his fingers on her arm. "You can cogitate on how much you don't like me on your own time, woman. This be a matter

360

of life an' death. Be quick an' tell me where Ms. Cat said she be goin' to."

Nora drew back stiffly and touched the reddening places where his fingers had grazed her arm. The warm, tingling sensation lingered.

"I, ah, I think she was going home to feed her cat and pick up some clothes and then she's going out to dinner with Inspector Padcula. He's picking her up at my place around—"

"Where else she goin' to?" he demanded.

"There was something about doing a favor." Nora strained her memory. "Oh yeah! She's going out to Lucy Cross's cabin in Druid Heights to pick up a painting."

"Druid Heights be in the canyon on Mount Tam?"

Nora nodded, realizing her mistake, and answered him verbally. "Yeah. Her cabin is supposed to be hard to find. It's way back in the woods, and knowing Cat, she'll be driving around forever until she goes nuts."

Gage commanded Tom Mix to go quickly.

"Hey!" she yelled, running after them. She found it hard to believe how fast the pair moved. "Hey, wait a minute. What's wrong? You can't just demand answers, and then walk away. Is Cat in trouble? She's my friend too, you know. What's going on?"

She blocked his way at the entrance of Ward Two acute. "Tell me what's going on!"

Without much effort, he shoved her aside and opened the double doors. "Get out of my way, woman. She be in some bad danger an' there ain't no time."

Tom Mix strained at his harness with Gage running behind him. "The man be here," he whispered hoarsely. "I gotta get to the cop man. He be in this too."

Nora followed closely on his heels, beginning to feel panicky. "You mean Inspector Padcula? What's he got to do with it?"

Without answering, Gage walked past the guard and into Cross's room.

At the intrusion, David Padcula, pen and notepad in hand, turned around and pushed his glasses back up the bridge of his nose to take a better look at the unusual trio.

He immediately thought of how he would describe it to Cat. ("There was no doubt in my mind that it was Dorothy, Toto, and a drastically rusted Tin Man wearing shades.")

From the bed, Cross craned her neck for a glimpse and stared.

" 'Spector?" Gage hitched up his pants. "I hope you got yourself a

361

solid vehicle outside, 'cause you got some fast an' hairy drivin' to do."

Cat glanced at the cheap stick-on digital clock stuck to where the dash would have been if Volkswagen bugs had normal dashboards, and pulled over onto the shoulder of the road. Not that it was necessary to pull off—she hadn't seen another car since she'd passed the New Jersey grayheads twenty minutes ago, and God only knew where they'd gone.

Over the side? She pictured the feature story in *New Jersey Motorist:* "Cliff Diving in Fifty States—A new adventure for the New Jersey driver!"

The radio signals had faded in and out a few times and finally dwindled down to nothing more than a whispery *shwoosh* noise, much like the one she'd heard on her phone message the night before. Gazing into the sea of blackness beyond the car, Cat listened to the rain pelt the windshield and shivered. The uneasy feeling of apprehension that had been lurking beside her all day came up strong and settled itself in her temples. She closed out the noise of the engine and leaned back in her seat to concentrate on the white dot of light in the center of her mind.

Again the images of Gage, David, and another, smaller figure came up. Each of them was tense, distressed, and running. The vision changed and mixed in with cloudy scenes from one of her old recurring dreams, the details of which she found too much work to recall.

She let go of the dark thoughts and was pulled into the more pleasant territory of how she should wear her hair for David. Would he prefer the down and over-one-eye sexy, or the old-fashioned, romantic Gibson girl bun? Then again, it wouldn't matter how she wore her hair if she didn't get moving.

She studied Cross's map, paying close attention to the red X marking the cabin. In Cross's precise hand was written: "Look for green metal post on right side of hwy. Turn onto dirt (probably a sea of mud by now) road. Might be better to leave your car at entrance and walk to cabin. Unless you have four-wheel drive, don't tempt fate! Bring Wellingtons!!"

Cat squinted in the direction of the Pacific. How stupid to have spent all that time giving Saph little lovie kisses on his oversized underbelly.

All right, all right, so that wasn't true. It was the hour and ten minutes she'd spent figuring out what to wear to dinner.

The thought of the three-foot pile of unacceptable outfits stacked on her bed was discouraging. Now that she was going to become part of the social world again, she would have to get some new clothes. Thank God she'd held on to the basic black with the Greek goddess sleeves from Frederick's of Hollywood. Now watch, she thought, he'll show up in jeans and cowboy shirt and suggest The Sizzler.

It was too warm in the car and the windows were beginning to fog from the inside, her defroster having long since given up the ghost. Cat stuck her head out the window, took a huge gulp of cold sea air to stimulate her mind, and looked around.

There was no question she had gone too far. Doing a speedy but cautious U-turn, she hugged the faded divider line and kept her eyes glued to the opposite side of the road, searching for a goddamned green metal post.

At the end of the hallway, Nora and David Padcula huddled close together and listened as Gage spoke in low tones.

"You understand? I know you a man of fact, but you gotta go with me on this, man, an' we gotta get our asses in gear. I keep seein' the shinin' light, an' it . . . it . . . got her in its line, man, sure as you got that picture of your baby brother in the back of your mind."

Gage clenched his jaw and started toward the elevator. "Enough jackjawin', man, we hafta go now, you hear?"

David stood immobile for a moment, thinking of the mutilated body of an eight-year-old boy lying along the banks of the Ohio River. Since then, he'd seen a lot of dead, mangled bodies of people who'd been the victims of desperate, sick maniacs—but they had been anonymous victims, not people he'd recently held in his arms and kissed.

He slipped into his raincoat and, with Nora, ran after the blind man and his dog into the elevator. "I'm going to radio a sheriff's unit to meet us there," he said. "I can give them the directions Cross gave us and they'll be able to—"

Gage rolled his head. "Oh man, they ain't gonna get there faster'n we do if we move. They be draggin' their asses 'round them roads lookin' for a neon sign that say 'Here she be!' Trust me, man, with or without them directions, I can find her quicker'n anybody."

As the four of them hurried out the rear doors of the hospital, David Padcula was stopped dead by something he saw in the emergency room parking lot.

"Hey! Over here!" he yelled.

The other three members of the rescue mission also stopped short and turned.

Inspector Padcula pointed to his left. "That's our ticket, folks."

Think logically, she told herself, not wanting to admit she was lost and was seeing parts of the mountain she'd never known existed. It's ridiculous to keep looking. Even if I find the place right this minute, I'm going to be at least an hour late for my dinner date.

In reaction to this logical thought, the persistent, stubborn streak with which she had been cursed for the entirety of her life, and which caused unaccountable amounts of trouble, pressed her foot to the gas pedal. A normal person would turn back, she knew, but from the time she was dismissed from first grade for refusing to say the Pledge of Allegiance to the day she defaced the door of a Berkeley police station with the words "From the cup of defeat take no draft or else perish in a sea of mediocrity"—and signed her full name—she had not been willing to let go of the intractable willfulness that threatened not only her happiness but at times her very existence.

When she finally spied the green post, the tip of which was sticking up four lousy inches from the top of a thick Scotch broom bush of the same color, the clock on the dash said it was 6:42.

She made up her mind that if she really put on the superhuman rush, she could still make it.

In the morning, policies would change for every ambulance company in the city. No longer would leaving the keys in the ignition of an unattended emergency vehicle be a common practice.

The four of them rode in silence except for the code three sirens and the blue flashing lights.

When Nora dared, she looked at the speedometer needle holding steady at 82 mph, then glanced at the stern and clenched jaw of Inspector Padcula.

She reached over and squeezed his arm. "Good boy," she said. "You're doing great." It was the same kind of encouragement she might have given to Tom Mix after he retrieved a stick.

In response, the inspector nodded and glanced anxiously in the rearview mirror at the trembling blind man strapped into the rear-compartment seat giving directions.

. . .

She'd decided to chance the driveway and turned her mud dream into a reality—except the car wasn't sinking quite as fast.

Gingerly she got out to survey the damage and found the tires sunk to their uppermost lug nuts in thick, black mud.

In an attempt to slam the car door, which was partially rusted on its hinges, she broke the only nail she had that wasn't chipped to the quick, screamed "Fuck!" so loud she coughed, and pounded not just the hood but the "goddamned, fucking" hood until her fists hurt.

Okay, okay, so she was going to have to walk. It couldn't be *that* far.

Retrieving a patchouli-and-mothball-scented shawl (the drug dealer insisted it came with the car) from under the back seat, she slipped it on under her parka, pulled up the nylon hood, and began her journey. She was as determined to ignore the cold, oozy feeling of mud seeping inside her running shoes as she had been to disregard Cross's advice about bringing boots.

As she trudged ungracefully through the thick muck, she listened to the sound her running shoes made as they sank in, then pulled out of the brown silt. *Spock thwuuuck. Spock thwuuuck.*

Now she would have to call a tow truck and God only knew how long it might take someone with half her brains—or eyesight—to spot the four inches of goddamned green pole. And that meant she would have to stand out there in the goddamned drizzling cold waiting to flag them down and she would probably come down with pneumonia and miss work and use up all her sick time and then where was the money going to come from to pay the goddamned rent? And she'd have bags under her eyes and be sickly and ugly for months during her recuperation.

And where did the blame belong? Definitely Cross. Goddamned fucking map. And you'd think with the amount of money the woman must have, she would have paved the goddamned driveway, for Christ's sake.

And goddamned David the Smiley Cop. He *had* to ask her for dinner tonight. Couldn't have been tomorrow night when she was rested and didn't have to work. Noooo. He *had* to see her the same goddamned evening she goddamned volunteered to go out into the boonies on a wild-goose chase. Typical man. Inconsiderate as hell. Only thinking of himself and his own pleasure. Well, he was going to pay for it—he would end up listening to Nora's Mötley Crüe tapes and having to discuss turkey liberation. And too bad if he worried about her being killed in some car wreck. Too goddamned bad if his goddamned ulcer started to ache.

The real culprit though was the goddamned, fucking, miserable lousy job. Scraping by on a pittance after working herself to the bone and being treated like shit by the goddamned prick doctors and the self-serving management. Never having any time to herself. No goddamned fucking time to enjoy anything, ever! Never experiencing life the way normal people did. She might as well have been a goddamned nun.

Not to mention goddamned, freezing cold, Northern California in the winter. Christ! Rain, rain, rain. That's all the hell it ever did, except when they were having a major drought and there wasn't a goddamned drop for five years in a row and they had to conserve water to the point of only flushing once a day. It was total goddamned bullshit.

And when the goddamned hell was the storm going to let up? She was probably suffering from one of those new kinds of yuppie diseases because of the goddamned rainy weather.

The garden spot of the United States? Ha!

Enough was enough, and screw this daylight saving time crap, too. Dark when she went to work, dark when she got off work.

And Gage, damn him. Making her worry all day like that and never once coming to see her. Scaring her to death about bad men coming to get her. Piss on that! She was never going to speak to Gage again. He'd have to do his goddamned spiritual rehab without her.

And where was goddamned Nora? Never there when she really needed her. Always off with one of her goddamned men. Only thinking of herself and who the next lay was going to be. She was never going to speak to her again either. Let Nora live her life out without Cat Richardson's jokes and excellent company. Did she think some man could replace that? Let the clap applaud at her door!

Bitter tears welled up. It had never been so clear before. Nobody *really* cared about her. She would grow old alone and miserable. And then she would die all alone in some disgusting hospital with deadly overhead fluorescent lighting, never having been happy, not *really* happy.

And it was all everybody else's fault.

Angry, depressed, and drowning in self-pity, Cat kicked at a particularly large clump of mud and fell backward on her ass.

Through the windshield wipers of the parked ambulance, Nora and David watched Tom Mix lead Gage across the narrow, two-lane road in the dark. After he sat down cross-legged on the shoulder, the

366

black-hooded figure could have easily been mistaken for a misplaced monk from an Indian ashram.

Gage stood up almost at once and faced into the strong wind. Raising his arms to the endless sky in a gesture of offering, he darted out over the side and disappeared from view.

Nora screamed. David removed the flashlight from the dash and swung open the ambulance door, just as the little man reappeared in the headlights.

Walking at a brisk pace behind Tom Mix, Gage motioned over his shoulder for them to follow: the blind leading the blind.

The hard cry left her feeling better, even a little silly. She stood, scraped off most of the mud, and laughed at herself. Mud baths in January. In the middle of nowhere. In a rainstorm. In the pitch-dark. With David coming to pick her up in the city in less than an hour. What could she do? Turn around and go home?

Never!

Resolutely, she spock-thwuuucked through another half-mile's worth of mud, until it dawned on her that maybe she had the wrong green pole. Maybe she was on an abandoned fire road which would dead-end two miles away in the middle of a bear-and-Big-Foot-infested forest.

When she had gone another fifty yards, her anger provoked her to move at double pace. She was going to find Cross's goddamned cabin if it took all goddamned night.

Cat's Volkswagen had made the road impassable, so they decided to walk, even though Gage said it "be a ways." Hanging on to each other for support, David and Nora followed Gage and Tom Mix through the mud.

"Only Richardson would try to drive through quicksand." Nora giggled, trying to ignore the suggestive sucking noises their feet were making in the mud.

David finished wiping the rain off his glasses and shook his head. "What was going through her mind? Why didn't she wait until morning to pick up the painting? It must have been close to impossible finding this road in the dark, not to mention dangerous as hell."

From over the top of her winter scarf, Nora sent him a withering glance. "Obviously, you don't know Catalina very well, Mr. Padcula."

367

Gage turned and hissed at them, "Stop your jackjawin' an' be listenin'."

Nora was about to ask Gage how he expected them to hear over the noise of the mud, when Tom Mix's hackles went up and he growled, baring his fangs at the stretch of dark road in front of them.

"What is it?" David whispered, moving closer to Gage. Out of habit, he unbuttoned his raincoat and touched the handle of his gun.

"Time be runnin' out an' we still got 'bout two or so miles to her."

Gage gave a soft command to the dog, and the four of them set off at an awkward pace.

Almost three miles from the rusted door of her Volkswagen, she spotted Lucy Cross's "cabin" and stopped to stare, open-mouthed. The fact that she was exhausted, frozen to the bone, and soaked through from head to toe with rain and mud was almost forgotten.

Some cabin, she thought. By any other name, the at-least-six-thousand-square-foot-mostly-glass-stone-and-a-little-wood structure might have been described as a breathtaking three-story blend of neoclassical, Japanese, fairy-hut, and futuristic-spacecraft architecture. Set neatly on what appeared to be a graduated, white marble pedestal, the house was dark within.

Shuffering—a cross between suffering and shivering—Cat cautiously climbed the base of the pedestal to the porch, which ran the entire circumference of the structure. Taped to what she thought might be the front door was a tattered and weather-beaten piece of cardboard flapping against the heavily etched glass.

She strained her eyes to make out the faint inscription. "My little prince—Come in!" It was signed "Isolde, The Guardian of All Colors."

Cat smiled wanly. The small marks and tokens of endearment that developed in relationships had always seemed to her to be special secrets, as individualized as thumbprints. Sadly she removed the note and stuck it in her pocket. One less reminder to Cross. One less thorn to draw blood.

Unpinning the set of keys from her bra, she pulled out the small chain on which were five keys. Two were most definitely house keys, two indisputably belonged to a motor vehicle, and the one short-nosed utility key marked "Secur-Tite" was for the alarm.

In the gray alarm box behind one of the white pillars, Cat found the control panel open and the red alarm switch turned to Off.

Well, no big deal. When Cross left the house, the last thing on her mind would have been alarm systems.

She found what looked most like the key to the house, fit the brass bar into the door, attempted to turn the thing, and got nowhere. When she tried to pull it out, it refused to budge.

She laid her head back.

"Goddamned son of a bitch!" she exploded into the surrounding forest.

". . . bitch, bitch, bitch!" her echo taunted back from the canyon walls.

She struggled with the key again, moving it up, down, from side to side, gently at first, then more forcefully, until her fingers were sore. Resorting for the second time that day to childlike frustration, she kicked and pounded on the door and finally began to cry.

With herculean effort, she pulled at the key once more.

Whatever inanimate-object-fiend had held the key frozen now let it go with ease.

Cat's hand flew back with the force of a heavyweight boxer's and split open her bottom lip.

When she stopped seeing spots, she cried for a few more minutes, sucking the blood from her lip. It tasted strongly of iron and salt. Lacking Kleenex or handkerchief, she leaned over the railing and blew her nose onto the ground the way she had seen cross-country skiers do. Feeling like one of the boys, she spit for good measure.

Okay, the next key had to be it. It slipped easily into the lock, giving her hope, but alas, would not turn. Pulling it out, she tried the alarm key, which proved as useful as trying to turn the lock with a hamster.

She sat down to think.

The night was ruined. Everything was totally, goddamned screwed up.

Give me the absolute worst situation, Miss Richardson.

Dale Carnegie stood in front of the blank blackboard of her imagination tapping his tutor's wand on her imaginary desktop.

Well, basics were, she was not going to trudge all the way back through the mud to the road, so that meant she'd have to break in through a window (although one of *these* windows would cost her a year's salary to replace) and call a towing service.

Then she would call Nora's to tell David she was sorry but they'd have to make it another night. She should also call Cross and—

Cat swallowed hard as Dale Carnegie laughed a horrid, maniacal laugh.

And what if the phone has been disconnected, Miss Richardson?

Sleep here? The house now seemed lonely and forbidding. But then again, what was the alternative? To walk however many miles it was to the nearest house, taking her chances that some motorist from New Jersey might . . .

Nah.

Before he faded out, Dale Carnegie rapped the blackboard with his wand.

Remember, Miss Richardson, exhaust all possibilities before you give up the ship.

Resigned, Cat inserted the obvious car key, the one inscribed "Honda," and the lock released.

Opening the glass door framed by a strip of polished brass, she stepped into the darkness and sighed a clenched-jaw kind of sigh.

Even in the dark, she saw the painting right off, hanging in a stone alcove at the end of the entrance hall. It was exactly as Cross had described it: a watercolor of a garden, extraordinary in its simplicity.

She made a beeline for the table lamp closest to the door and tried the switch.

Of course. The goddamned electricity had been knocked out by the storms.

A brief, blind search yielded a set of glass Art Deco candlesticks and several partially burned candles. Only after she upset an ashtray of half-smoked Players and knocked over a vase of wilted flowers did she find a pack of matches.

Shielding the candle flame, she slipped the dead bolt on the door and walked slowly through the house.

The mixture of complex styles somehow worked together to create a light fluid feeling. The lavish use of glass gave her the sense of being in the open yet protected. In the kitchen, she washed out her lip and made a cold compress from paper towels. She was overjoyed to discover that the gas stove was operational. If she was going to be holed up, at least she'd do it with a hot cup of tea.

While she waited for the water to boil, she found the phone on the floor under the kitchen table, and before lifting the receiver, recited her guardian angel prayer.

The powers that be paid off with a dial tone.

Triple A or Nora and David first?

Her watch said 7:58. David would be innocently sipping champagne while being subtly grilled by Nora, never knowing that every word he uttered would be reported back to her with the accuracy of a tape recording.

Better to get Triple A on their way, then call David and let him know. If it took the road service forty minutes to get to cars stranded right in town, God only knew how long it would take them to get to the Land of Oz.

The phone clicked, there was a pause, then a recording of a man's voice came on the line. "If you'd like to make a call, please hang up and try it again. If you need help—"

Cat cut off the mechanical voice and punched in the number for Triple A. When one owned a twenty-year-old Volkswagen, road service numbers were memorized.

"Triple A road service, Debbie."

Debbie sounded depressed and unfriendly.

"Hi," Cat said softly, slightly intimidated by the officious tone. "I need to have my car pulled out of some mud up on—"

"Card number, please?" Cold patronization laced the voice.

Cat imagined an overweight twenty-five-year-old with deep acne scars sitting in a dingy garage office, forced to smell motor oil and talk to subhuman drivers who constantly smoked and had dirty fingernails.

She suddenly felt pity for the hostile Debbie, sincerely wishing her skin would someday clear up and she would slim down, meet a wonderful accountant, and get married.

"Well, see, Deb, my card is locked in the car, but I've been a member in good standing for almost—"

"You don't have your card with you, ma'am?" The tone was hard and impatient, but Cat noticed she had addressed her as "ma'am" instead of "shithead." It was a start.

"Well, yes, I mean no, I do have it, but it's in the car and the car is about three miles from here down this unbelievable sea of mud. I think the expiration date is next March, and I already paid my dues for—"

There was a disgusted sigh. "Save it for the driver, ma'am. Give me your name and the make and color of your car and its present location. If I send one of my men out there and you don't have a card up front, he won't help you and you'll be charged for the call anyway."

Cat tightened her jaw to stave off the flash of anger. She again pictured the ugly and lonely Debbie, having to refer to the drivers as "her men." Surrounding the doubting Debbie with a stream of healing orange light, she answered as gently as possible.

"My name is Cat Richardson. C-a-t R-i-c-h . . ."

Cat paused. Somewhere in the house there was a creak, like someone creeping on stairs. Listening extra hard, she thought she heard something drop on the floor above her.

The irritable voice interrupted. "Sorry, ma'am, we don't have a membership under the name of Catrich."

"No, no. First name is Catalina, last name is Richardson, and I have a white 1967 Volkswagen bug that's stuck in about a foot and a half of mud. I need a—"

From the other end of the receiver, there was an even, round static, then a noise that sounded like a shorted-out toaster, and finally no sound at all except her own breathing.

She was infuriated. How dare the woman cut her off. Now she hoped the pathetic Debbie really was fat and ugly and had only mechanics to relate to.

She redialed the number. Still nothing. She pressed the hook down slowly, then rapidly.

The goddamned phone was dead.

Goddamn that goddamned Debbie.

Sipping her Relax and Reflect herbal tea, she warily explored the rest of the house. In the English men's club–style library, she found three more candles on the antique desk and two more on either side of the overstuffed leather couch. She lighted them all. Living in such an isolated area, she guessed, Cross was used to being without power during the winter storms. The massive fireplace looked as though it might put out a fair amount of heat. Upon closer inspection, she was relieved to find it had a gas igniter. She took several small logs from a basket and placed them on the grate. The floor of the fireplace was littered with the charred fragments of what had apparently been bedsheets.

Once the fire was going, Cat warmed herself, then walked into the bedroom. The pedestal bed, positioned in the middle of the amazing glass-walled chamber, was inviting even without sheets, but the bathroom was where she finally set the candle down.

The size of the room made her marvel; her entire house would fit into it with square footage to spare. Off to the side, the gleaming brass shower was enclosed in a magnificent floor-to-ceiling glass tube which jutted out from the main structure of the house. She peeled off her wet and muddy clothes and slipped into an oversized terry-cloth robe she found hanging on the marble and brass hatrack next to the sunken whirlpool. Once more appealing to her guardian angel, she tested the shower. To her extreme pleasure, she found the water tepid.

Her image smiled back at her from the mirrored wall. What more

372

could she ask for? Shower by candlelight in a palace of glass, choose a good book, and sleep in the lap of luxury in a pedestal bed.

Now see? Dale Carnegie admonished. *There's something good to be had out of any hard lesson.*

Mud and rain forgotten, Cat picked up one of the brushes from the marble-topped counter and brushed back her hair, trying to imagine what it would be like to live in this splendor every day. Up each morning to the sun flooding over the bed, or watching the rain cascade down the treehouse of glass? Surely that would fulfill her or at least help bring on contentment.

Overhead, she heard muted footsteps, like someone walking on carpet.

Oh, it's just the house settling. But it sounded like—

No! Stop trying to sabotage a few hours of pleasure. Enjoy the beauty of what's been dropped in your lap. Chance of a lifetime, remember?

Cat plucked the red hairs from the brush and dropped them into the wastebasket. God, to make love with David here, in this paradise? No wonder Cross isolated herself, making Michael the center of her world.

A jar of face cream, the most expensive type, the stuff that came from secret caves in the Kwangtung Province of China, tempted her. A smidgen wouldn't be missed. Dabbing a minute amount under her eyes, she spread it over her skin, enjoying its delicate watermelon scent.

A self-satisfied reflection laughed at her. Okay, so she took back all the uncharitable and angry thoughts. She understood Cross's desire for seclusion, and of course David and Nora were probably worried as hell about her, and Gage had probably come down with a cold after getting soaked out on the ledge.

And wasn't she the one who claimed to love the hard rains and pearl-gray mist that covered California each winter? How easily they forget, she thought, shaking her head. After the snow and ice of the eight-month-long East Coast winters, four months of a little wet weather was diddly-squat.

There was movement behind her.

Flickering of the candle. Play of the imagination.

Mechanically she continued to rub the cream into her cheekbone until long after it had disappeared, her gaze fixed on the reflection of the doorway in the mirror.

A prickling sensation waved over her extremities as the air changed, and her heart pounded in her temples. It was like the reverse of when someone died; there was a presence here. Close by. A premonition of disaster, stronger than any dread she had ever known in her life, immobilized her.

Oh God, she thought, wanting to cry, oh God.

Taking a deep breath, she held it and shook her body out to relax.

Of course she was being absurd. She'd seen too many Hitchcock thrillers. She would walk around and make *sure* she was alone. Probably just a family of raccoons living under the bed. Tsk. Of course— that was it. Raccoons or field mice.

But her legs would not move. Her mouth went dry, and she became aware of the cool air moving in and out of her throat. With wooden fingers, she touched another dab of cream to her forehead.

It was silly. She was being silly, that was all.

The floor in the hallway creaked and she saw a definite, purposeful movement of shadow.

Had to be the candlelight.

Yeah, it was just the light creating shadows. That was it. What did she expect? In a strange place, all glass and mirrors and the flame jumping and moving around like that? Sure, it was just the light— had to be the light.

Except the light had nothing to do with the distorted face moving swiftly toward her through the shadows.

30 She didn't struggle at all during the few seconds it took him to drag her to the library. Then again, she wasn't sure if any of what was taking place was real, even though there was solid evidence it was. For instance, there were his shoes. Nike Airs. White and scuffed gray at the toes, laboring to keep their balance. And the Relax and

Reflect herbal tea, which had scalded her leg in the commotion; the shelves of books that had been read and enjoyed and had nothing whatsoever to do with what was happening to her now.

The cold leather of the couch against the back of her legs and the oppressive smell of his dirty hair and cigarette breath brought her to reality. Michael Lake was real. The weight of his body shoving her into the cushions was real.

When forced to it, Cat could be a woman of practical nature. Desperately trying to remember her psych training, she recalled only that it had been one of the most traumatic experiences of her nursing education, since most of the time she couldn't tell the patients from the staff. Understandably, that triggered her own basic fear of losing her mind, especially when she started to recognize psychologically undesirable traits and mannerisms in herself. Soon she began analyzing herself and, even worse, her friends, until, by the end of the second of a six-week rotation, she suffered from a maladjustment known as "paralysis through analysis"—the inability to say or do anything without analyzing it first.

With the next assault of pressure from the man's body, her mind snapped back on and coughed up two pieces of advice for dealing with the severely disturbed or violently psychotic. *Try to diffuse it before it happens, then duck.* And: *Administer psychotropic drugs, use leather restraints, and keep the conversation simple, as with a child who is having a temper tantrum and wielding a loaded carbine with a hair trigger.*

She looked into Michael's eyes, which were wide, the pupils dilated. Their expression said he had vacated the upper chambers of the dream castle in the sky and had moved down into the dungeons and was torturing its inhabitants.

"What's your name?" she asked, feeling as if she were speaking from a deep sleep.

For a moment, Michael was distracted from grinding his knees into her kneecaps in what seemed to be a calculated effort to break her legs.

"Michael," he snarled, flashing her an angry look. "And don't fuck with me 'cause I'm not in the mood to argue with any bitches."

She wasn't sure if talking to him could be interpreted as fucking with him, but she decided to try it; since her left arm was pinned under her and he was crushing her right wrist into her shoulder with a viselike grip, there wasn't much else left to do.

"Hi, Michael." She modulated her voice to the point where she sounded like an instructional recording for the hypersensitive emotionally impaired. "I promise I won't argue with you, Michael. My name is Catalina. Are you going to kill me?"

375

"Probably." The mysterious and sensuous expression he wore in the Blazzie's Secret ads crossed his face. "But not till after."

"After? After what, Michael?"

"You know." He fumbled with the belt of her robe as he tried to yank it out from under her.

The idea that he was going to rape her came as a complete surprise. For a few seconds, she thought maybe he was just trying to frighten her, until she saw that he was stroking himself through his pants.

Once, three years before, she had been required to attend a class on how to protect oneself from rape. She clearly remembered the anger and resentment she saw in each woman's eyes at having to learn something that, in this day and age, was deemed an absolute necessity.

The young, uptight cop stressed to them that rape was a crime of violence. Seldom did the victim matter to the rapist. Rape, he emphasized over and over again (while wearing an expression that came across as "Don't flatter yourselves, girls"), was not an act stemming from uncontrollable sexual desire.

She subtly shifted her weight back, making it harder for him to find the belt, stalling for time.

"But . . . but I'm not your type," she said, sensing this was an unconventional and somehow distantly humorous thing to say.

"You're a fucking whore. That's my type." Michael clawed at the robe until it fell away from her. He stared at her breasts and began to knead them roughly. "You're going to like this so much, whore, that you'll beg me not to stop."

The panic seeped into her. It was real. She screamed and tried to buck him off.

He slapped her hard across the mouth and leaned close to her face.

Cat flinched. My God, she thought, is he going to kiss me?

Michael pulled something from under the throw pillow beneath her head and drew back, making a rapid motion close to her neck. She cried out as a cold shock ran down the left side of her neck to her shoulder and across her chest.

In the candlelight, she saw a hunting knife, the handle of which seemed too thick for his hand to hold comfortably. "Please don't do this," she begged. She thought of all the victims of violence she had seen on the ward. Now she understood the expression they wore— of having seen the other side. The pain in her wrist and elbow was unbearable, and she started to cry.

"I don't want you to do this to me. Please let me go home. Let me leave here and I won't tell anyone I've seen you. You can go on hiding. Just let me—"

"Shut up!" He backhanded her and she saw the glittering shine of the blade still in his hand. She wondered if he had cut her again. Following the knife with her eyes, she watched him set it carefully on the back of the couch where it would wait for a more appropriate time.

"See this face?" he yelled, covering her mouth and forcing her head back into the pillow. The smell of his sour perspiration nauseated her. "No fucking bitch says no to this face. Ever!

"I know that slut told you things about me. I know all about her. She's no good. She's a lying whore. You're all whores!"

Michael rocked back and hesitated for a moment, as if unsure of what to do next. For a heartbeat, the pressure on her legs eased. Instinctively, she drew her knee up to cover her pubic area.

Something sticky dripped under the arm that was pinned. She dared to move her head an inch or so and saw that the sleeve and shoulder of the robe and a section of the couch were saturated with blood. Her arm was completely without feeling and she wasn't sure how deep the laceration in her neck and chest went.

She licked her lips because they were dry and because the feel of her tongue helped keep back the pins-and-needles sensation trying to cloud her mind. If he'd cut any major vessels, she would not be able to keep her thoughts clear, let alone fight him off.

Michael pushed between her thighs and on her throat at the same time. She strained at keeping her legs together, but she was weakening and it was becoming increasingly more difficult to breathe.

"No, please, no," she gasped.

Moving his hand from her neck to her mouth, he released her wrist and unzipped his pants.

His breath came faster and she could feel him trembling. "Just relax, you'll love it," he murmured, prying her legs farther apart. He stroked his penis a few times and then touched her belly with the tip of it. She started to struggle, but thought better of it and stopped.

"If you give me a hard time, I'll have to kill you now instead of later. Makes no difference to me one way or the other. Understand?"

Don't fight with them, the young cop had said. *Women who put up a fuss or fight, get killed.*

Fuss. She thought at the time it was a condescending word to use, and meant to mention it to the cop after the class. "Fuss" was a word one usually associated with unstable, hysterical women.

Then she thought about Michael forcing his way into her body, defiling her, leaving her his touch and the sound of his grunting as her last sensations. It was a given he would kill her anyway, so why not put up a fuss? She was a big, strong girl.

377

Amazon. Isn't that what everybody, husbands and boyfriends included, had called her—at least once each?

Pure indignation caused her to squeeze her legs closed like a steel trap. The son of a bitch was not going to do this and kill her too.

She felt his rage start up over her resistance. Quickly reaching over his shoulder, she groped until her fingers touched the cold steel of the blade. She grasped the weapon, surprised to find it so light.

What was it again that the policeman had told them? If the situation ever came up, and of course, if they just happened to have a gun or a knife pulled and ready to go (there was some strained, halfhearted laughter over that), then they had better mean to use it, or take the chance of having it used on them.

Michael was punching her thighs and ribs, pulling back, searching for something on the back of the couch.

She felt the knife in her hand and thought of the hundreds of times she had assisted in surgery, watching the use of blades to repair and restore life.

Her absence of emotion over the prospect of deliberately taking a life seemed strange: calmly calculating where to make the . . . incision? No, uhn-uh. Incision was a misnomer. Stab wound was the correct term.

Next to slitting his throat, aiming for the heart would be the quickest, surest way of stopping him.

Flip to Dr. Ryno's anatomy class, 1964. The heart, Five inches in length, three inches in width, and two inches thick. Placed behind the lower two thirds of the sternum and lying more to the left side of the chest cavity than the right. The apex of the heart lies between the cartilages of the fifth and sixth ribs. . . .

She brought the blade to what she calculated to be his left midchest and, squeezing her eyes shut, hesitated until the instant she sensed him discover the knife missing.

His eyes alone had time to shift back to her hand before she thrust in the blade, felt it graze a rib, then slide in easily until it hit something hard and unmovable, like hitting bone with a needle. It made a sound like a muffled *kunkchink*.

When she forced herself to look, she saw the handle jutting from his lower left chest, angled upward, between maybe the seventh and eighth ribs. Already a dark red liquid, like fake Halloween blood, oozed out around the knife in a single, thick dribble.

Michael stared at the knife handle in shock, the way a little kid would stare at a leech he'd found on his belly after swimming. Flicking her hand away, he grabbed the handle and before she could stop him, pulled it out.

378

The very worst thing to do with an impaled object, said Mrs. Coleville's instructorial voice, *is to remove it. Wrap the protruding part of the object in sterile towels and do not disturb. Let the surgeon do that, once the patient is in surgery where the bleeding can be controlled.*

No control here, Cat thought, as his blood came faster, gushing over his bare abdomen and the exposed penis and testicles, now hanging limp from his fly.

He rolled off her and tried to stand, but sank to his knees at the side of the couch, still staring at his blood in disbelief.

Torn between wanting to stop his bleeding and running away, she rose unsteadily, and with weaving, slow-motion steps, backed toward the door.

Michael fell. With some effort, he lifted himself up on his elbow. "I'll kill you," he said with such venomous hatred, it obliterated all thought of assisting him. She stumbled into the hall and on to the living room, where she tripped over an iron statue of some kind of animal, caught herself from falling, and vomited.

Not stopping to clean herself, she continued to stumble toward the front door. In the entrance hall she swayed, grabbed onto the wall for support, and found herself staring at the watercolor. For an instant, she thought of David Padcula's face and the harmony of sounds in his voice. She started to cry again.

She would not let life be taken from her. Not its color, not its pain or its simple pleasures. Acting out of blind duty and stubbornness, she reached up and pulled the garden painting from the wall of the alcove.

She made it to the door and hugged the painting; its cold surface rubbed her skin, reminding her she was naked. Not that it mattered —she was numb, and even if she ran fifteen miles in freezing rain, she would remain numb but alive. To her way of thinking, a chill beat death by a long shot.

From the hall came a soft thud, like someone bouncing off the wall. Blood from her neck and shoulder ran down her arm in rivulets, and her fingers slipped off the knob of the dead bolt as she worked frantically to pull it back.

Through the dark spots that dotted her vision, she saw a glint of silver light as the man weaved toward her. Unable to breathe, she half growled, half screamed and gripped the knob of the bolt with her teeth.

It was the ultimate realization of all her chase dreams when he kicked her legs out from under her and snapped her arm back. The pain triggered a last, overwhelming surge of rage.

She shrieked like a wounded animal and tried to bite his arm, but he had her pinned by the neck. For a brief second, she caught a glimpse of the watercolor leaning against the door.

This is it. Oh shit. Oh God help me. Nora? Gage. Oh, David.

To be a covered-body photo in the newspapers captioned "The victim" was not the way it was supposed to end for her. She wasn't supposed to be murdered. She was in line for one more try at living. To do it the right way. To love and be happy. To grow old and complain of arthritis and edematous feet.

Michael held her head in a vise-like grip between his knees and raised the knife unsteadily above her. At the sight of the blade, she at once felt herself urinating, and passed into a long-forgotten dream that had regularly haunted her childhood.

It is after dark, and the Saturday movie where she has spent the day to escape her parents' quarreling is closing. She has just stepped into the night air and has gone no more than a few yards from the front door of the movie house, when Mr. Fisk, the theater owner, calls out after her to hurry home and closes the last of the double doors.

As she passes the dark space between the theater and the ice cream shop next door, a man steps out and begins to follow her. She hears the irregular pattern of his footsteps and turns to see if she recognizes him, but he is wearing a hat that shields his face from her view.

His steps match hers until he is on her heels and she can hear him breathing. Without a word, he swiftly grabs her head in the crook of his arm and she sees the glint of the razor, then feels a dull, throbbing pain in the left side of her throat.

The man eases her gently, almost lovingly to the ground and she watches him run away. He has a limp, and she tries to think of a reason why someone would want to hurt her. Under her head there is a slippery warmth, and her arms and legs feel tingly. She wants to yell for help, praying that Mr. Fisk will hear her and stop her from dying, except she has no breath left.

There is a fleeting glimpse of the crowd forming over her, silently staring, no one moving to help. Standing behind an old woman holding a bag of groceries is the man with the hat, and she sees the gloating smile as she tries to tell the others.

"It's him," she thinks so hard it must translate as a scream, but she is paralyzed and cannot speak or move. She wishes she could point at him.

Before she slips into her deathlike sleep, someone—she imagines it is the old woman with the groceries—leans over and lightly touches the open wound in her neck.

She emerged from the dream to a high pitched, continuous buzz filling her ears. Beyond the incessant sound, she barely heard shouts and a dog barking.

Incredibly, the knife was still above her, a few inches from her eyes, sawing the air back and forth. A lot of hands were grasping for the handle—like kids' hands climbing the handle of a baseball bat, choosing up. The brilliance of the blade mesmerized her. It was a streak of shining silver moving down, seeking her throat.

Drifting above the confusion around her, she waited for her life to pass before her and kept a close watch for the tunnel of white light.

Monday

31 San Francisco weather. There was never any way of figuring it. The smudge-gray storm clouds had disappeared as quickly as they came, leaving one harmless cumulus puff to drift lazily around the blue sky like a slow-moving filter in a swimming pool.

Walking toward the hospital, Cat savored the warmth of the morning sun penetrating her windbreaker. The earth had been hung out to dry and the melancholy of winter was passing into the season of promise. Love, like impending death, had made her acutely aware of everything occupying her world, as if all five senses had gone into overdrive.

Trish and the night supervisor passed by and nodded, their stares bordering on downright ogles. Not bothering to lower their voices, they immediately commenced discussing her.

"Is that *her*?"

"Shhh. Yeah. Did you read the article in the *Chronicle*? God, I always knew she was . . . but with a . . . can't believe sh . . ."

Cat sighed. It had made the second-section cover story. With headlines.

The celebrity photos of Cross and the quarter-page Blazzie's Secret ad featuring the "Divinely Devastating Model Michael Lake" were tastelessly overdone. That Gilly had given out her employee identification photo was unforgivable. How they got hold of her college graduation picture was beyond her, although she suspected it was Nora who told them her shoe size.

David warned she would have to get used to the attention. She was considered public property until people forgot—assuming they ever did.

By Sunday night, she had received sixty-five messages on her answering machine: twenty-eight well-wishers, five Jesus freaks offering to help her to salvation, four heavy breathers, one editor for a national men's magazine wanting to do a photo spread of her wearing nothing but a nurse's cap and combat boots, three specialty-shoe-company reps, seven calls from Jo Atwood, five newspaper reporters, three radio station producers, three national-talk-show producers, two women wanting to start a Cat Richardson fan club, and four telemarketers.

Accidentally on purpose, she erased them all.

She regarded her sudden notoriety as mildly amusing until she and David were mobbed by a group of camera-wielding reporters during the soup phase of their dinner at a downtown restaurant. Most of the questions were simply too bizarre to answer, but when they got to asking her about her measurements and her sexual history, and if they could photograph her bare feet, David flashed his badge and threatened arrest.

It was David who finally allayed her mounting fears of never again being able to go out in public. He pointed out that she could take comfort in the knowledge that there were probably small towns in Oklahoma or Nebraska where there was still an outside chance she wouldn't be recognized—provided she dyed her hair, bound her feet, and wore dark glasses.

Every once in a while she'd forget about it, as if it were something that happened way back when. But it had taken place; she knew that for sure because there were a million newspapers and fifty-eight sutures in existence to prove it.

The ambulance ride stuck out clearly in her memory, probably since she'd never ridden in one lying down before. Nora had tended to her wounds and monitored her blood pressure while David held her hand and narrated the events from Gage's crying the alarm to Michael kneeling over her.

"You were so pale," he said, "and there was so much blood everywhere, I thought I was too late. When I went for the knife, he didn't have any strength left, anybody could see that. We struggled for a minute or so, but it was like fighting with a ghost. He just fell over and that was it."

Nora cut in to change the pressure bandage on her laceration. "Anyway, right about that time, Gage runs over, grabs your head,

386

and starts chanting and doing all this weird shit that looked like he was picking fleas from your hair and hurling them across the room." She shrugged. "Who knows, except you did seem to come out of it right after that.

"Our marathon mud runner here"—Nora smiled at David in a way that Cat thought unnecessarily sensuous—"raced back to the ambulance and retrieved a stretcher. By that time, the backup men our hero had radioed from the ambulance had arrived, and they all helped carry you out."

Cat winced now, remembering that she had been incontinent. What a sight she must have been: smeared with blood, mud and vomit still caked in her hair, naked feet with the toes as long as a man's fingers, sagging breasts exposed to the world.

But David had seen her at her worst and still wanted her. She supposed that put her one step ahead of the game. Even on her rottenest days, she would never be able to match that look again.

Dr. Gladstein limped past, glanced up, and did a double take. He smiled nervously and hurried on. She could almost hear the word that crossed his mind.

Murderess.

Nora and David had been careful not to mention Michael, and it hadn't dawned on her to ask about him until they were halfway to the hospital.

She stared at David, David looked at the floor, and Nora tried to change the subject.

Finally David told her, using phrases like "self-defense" and "justifiable homicide."

From the hospital, he'd taken her directly to his house and cared for her in a way no man ever had. He fed her, read to her from Dorothy Parker, Malraux, and Wodehouse, massaged her back, changed her dressings, listened to her, held her while she cried, told her jokes and secret things about himself. He even fetched Saph and gave him a flea bath in his kitchen sink.

Saturday night he put down the Gary Larson book they were in hysterics over and said, "I want to make you happy. I've got a storehouse of love and other great things inside me and I want to share them with you."

By Sunday morning, they felt like best friends camping out in the backyard together: wise about each other, comfortable with each other's souls, as if they had been together for a hundred supreme years. Sunday afternoon he made chicken soup from scratch and served it with hot French bread dipping garlic butter. She ate

387

ravenously, convincing herself that the food he brought to her had no calories.

Sunday night she remembered that going to bed had another meaning besides sleep.

They were at the kitchen table playing blackjack, when she startled them both by placing her bare feet in his lap. Not looking at her feet directly, he tentatively rested his hands on the cold flesh of her toes. She closed her eyes and moaned a little, letting her head fall back. Intently studying the contour of her neck and breasts, he began light, teasing caresses down her long and narrow instep.

"I think we should . . ." His voice was tremulous. He cleared his throat and the teasing caresses turned into a deeper massage. "I think we should go to bed." He paused, then added, "Together."

Her stomach flipped onto its side and perched there while her throat went dry. He was kneading her feet—hard.

Shaking off the subtle pins-and-needles feeling creeping into her temples, she pulled her feet from his hands and leaned forward. Far away she heard a voice similar to hers say, "What a good idea. I'm not tired at all."

Neither of them had any recollection of how they got to the bed or who or what had removed their clothes.

Unable to wait, they offered their mouths to each other in a kiss that did not, would not stop. When he felt her body involuntarily pressing against him in rhythm, he pulled her legs around him and the passion she had neglected for so long, awakened.

Their lovemaking began with the wild motions familiar to younger lovers, but the urgency gave way to a sort of wise, sexual composure that allowed them to savor, then linger over each sensation.

By morning, they had proved the old adage "It's never as good as the first time" wrong—three times over. . . .

Feeling weak in the knees, Cat stopped at the top of the hill to catch her breath.

David was probably right about her staying in bed another day. She didn't need to be superwoman at her own expense anymore. She could finally afford to be gentle with herself.

The two women looked at each other. Virtual strangers, Cat thought, as she placed the painting carefully on Cross's bed, forced to share the intimate pieces of their souls like the survivors of a plane crash waiting in close quarters for rescue.

On the bedside table, the *Chronicle* lay unfolded to the middle section. Cat's eyes immediately went to the top of the page to read what she'd read a hundred times already: NURSE SLAYS ARTIST'S LOVER. Then, in bold type, "In a bizarre series of events which began Friday afternoon . . ."

"Pure melodrama," Cat said with a feeble laugh, folding the paper and placing it out of sight.

"I'm sorry," Cross began carefully. "I don't know what to say. It was the last place I would have thought he'd be. I didn't think. Even the police said it was unusual for him to have—"

"It's okay," Cat interrupted. "It wasn't your fault."

Cross laid down her brush and wept.

"Listen, Cross, I wish none of this had ever happened, but it did and I'm . . ."

What could she say? That she was sorry she had killed Michael trying to save herself? She handed Cross a Kleenex. "You'll heal. You need to move on—we both do."

Cat looked about her and studied the room littered with new sketches of various nurses and hospital hallway scenes. She recognized Mathilde in one and Nora with Gage and Tom Mix in another. At last she rose and picked up the watercolor of the garden.

"When are you going to give this to Corky?"

The artist blew her nose in a way that was anything but dainty and wiped her eyes. "Today. He's coming by after school."

The boy and the woman would remain friends for a long time, Cat thought. It was a healthy alliance and would help them both through the hard times ahead.

"I took a look at his discharge chart. I suspect you had something to do with the meeting on Friday with Dr. Barza and the parents."

"I only made the suggestion. Corky made the final decision to tell them what happened. He's got a lot of guts. I don't know if I could have done that at his age. It seems to have worked out pretty well, though. The man was arrested and charged, and Corky's going to therapy with someone Dr. Barza recommended who specializes in . . ." Cross paused and looked away. ". . . that sort of thing."

Cat took a long last look at the garden painting and committed it to memory. "Well . . ."

"I'm going home tomorrow," Cross said quickly. "Would you want to come up to the cabin on Thursday for dinner?"

"Our chances of meeting on a Siberian tundra are better," Cat said, making a face. "I mean, don't get me wrong, I'd really like to become friends, but I'm not sure I want to see the inside of your place again for a long time. How about if you slum it for a while? Come to my house in town, meet the cat, see how the rest of the world lives. Might not be bad for a change of scenery. Heck, you might even get some ideas for poverty paintings."

Both women smiled and Cross took note of Cat's glow. On the redhead, love was a highly visible emotion.

"Well . . ."

"Well . . ."

"I'd like to do a painting for you," Cross said shyly. "Something special. Something big and vivid and"—she looked at Cat's hair and laughed—"red. Like you."

"Do me a favor," Cat said. "Don't use red. Make it orange. The same shade as those winter oranges you can sometimes find in roadside stands if you're lucky? You know the kind—they're the ones you always remember as tasting so sweet."

Gage felt her presence but continued to unpack the newly arrived boxes of Juicy Fruit gum before acknowledging her.

The face of her spirit was changed: kinder yet stronger and more potent in an easy, floating-down-the-river sort of way. She was not yet aware of the subtleties behind what she sensed merely as new freedom and a spiritual journey, but with time, well, with time he could only guess at what she would do with the path she chose.

Of course, all that would be, provided she worked out the stubbornness that kept her imprisoned, limited to meager portions of what could be hers.

"Hey." She tapped him lightly on the shoulder and knelt to give Tom Mix a hug.

Gage murmured softly and turned to her. "How you be, girl?"

"Alive, thanks to you."

He scowled and shook his head. "None of it didn't have to go that far, girl. You know that."

"I know," Cat said quietly and continued rubbing Tom Mix behind the ears. "The dreams. I should have paid more attention to the dreams and all those weird feelings. I knew I should have turned around, but I was so determined to do what I said I would do, that I felt I had to go through with it, no matter what."

Gage made a face. "Aw, don't be handin' me no shit, girl. You ain't gotta do nothin' except listen to what your gut says. That mule head of yours be the best thing the bad powers got to keep you in line."

She walked away and stood with her back to him for several moments'. When she faced him again, she took his hands. "Gage, I want to learn a different way of living. I think it's time for me to learn what you have to teach."

He turned her hands over in his, running his fingers gently over the backs and palms. "I don't know, Ms. Cat. I can tell 'bout what you gotta do to make the power feel invited, an' maybe how to keep it from turnin' on you, but you gotta learn peace first—on your own —an' *that* ain't easy." He thought for a moment then sighed. "But, I don't suppose it gonna hurt nothin' for me to walk with you for a ways."

He left her and disappeared through the rear door of the stand. When he reappeared, he was carrying several medium-sized cardboard boxes which he set at her feet. From his sweatshirt, he pulled a handkerchief and wiped the sweat from the back of his neck.

"What you gonna do now, girl?"

She shrugged. "I don't exactly know. I've got four weeks medical leave; that'll be enough time to decide if I want to come back or do something else.

"Twenty years is a long time to be giving yourself to the nurturing of other people, especially when my so-called superiors constantly remind me that I'll always be 'just' a nurse no matter how much I care."

She knelt down to stroke Tom Mix again and waited until she could speak around the lump of sadness that had formed in her throat.

"But you know what, Gage? The truth is that all those years of being 'just' a nurse has made me an extraordinary human being. I've left a gentle mark on a lot of lives." She stood. "It's almost enough."

Leaning slightly, Gage let his arm barely touch her. "An' what else you think gonna make it enough?"

"When they were carrying me to the ambulance from Cross's house, I had an idea. I must have been delirious or something because I saw myself clear as day kneeling on the ground listening to a woman's heart. We. . . ." She changed her mind. "Forget it. It's a crazy idea."

"No it ain't," Gage said calmly.

Cat smiled, wondering if they might ever get to the point of not having to talk at all.

"So, was that the power talking to me?"

"Wasn't exactly the power. More like the power just helpin' you hear what your heart been sayin' to your head. 'Bout time you started listenin', girl. Visions comin' from your heart don't lead you down no wrong paths."

391

He opened the top box which contained a dozen or so packages of Good & Plenty. Bringing one of the cellophane wrapped boxes to his nose, Gage sniffed then ripped off the wrapping.

He found her hand and shook out five or six of the pink and white candies into it. Shaking out another batch for himself, he placed the entire handful into his mouth.

To guide the woman wasn't going to be easy, although, like her, the easy way had never been his to choose. It would take time, but she would learn . . . they would learn.

Cat listened to the building's heartbeat. The cycle of suffering and healing would go on as always. The insignificant gap her absence created would be momentary, filled in and covered over as if it never existed.

She felt no regret or longing. Opening the door, she stepped outside into the light.

It was time to begin.

About the Author

Echo Heron received her nursing degree in 1977 and has practiced as a registered nurse in coronary care since that time. Ms. Heron is the author of *Intensive Care: The Story of a Nurse* and is currently working on her third book. At present, Ms. Heron lives in San Francisco's North Bay with her lunatic cat, Mooshie.